Clouded Judgement

...Trust is fragile

NICHOLA HARVEY

ISBN: 978-1-7638328-1-7

DEDICATION

To my husband, for the constant encouragement and support regardless of the countless hours I spent paying attention to my books and not him. Without his nagging over my procrastination, this would never have become a reality. I love you.

Another shout out of support to my children and their partners, their love and faith in me also gave me the encouragement to keep writing and to never give up. I love you all to the moon and back.

Most importantly, to my supporters who seem to be just as dedicated with their nagging for the next instalment. I just hope I don't disappoint.

Love you xx

TRIGGER WARNING

Contains themes of sexual assault, suicide, domestic violence and drug use.

Recommended for Mature Audiences 18+

∞ **Denotes change of POV**

DISCLAIMER

Most places visited in this book are mostly fictional.

1

Ari

Melbourne had an extraordinary ability to irritate me in ways both subtle and profound. From the thirtieth floor, the city looked deceptively composed — glass façades catching the light, streets arranged in neat geometric lines, a sky so relentlessly blue it bordered on smug. Yet beneath that polished veneer churned the usual pandemonium: horns blaring in futile protest, trams clattering with theatrical self-importance, cyclists weaving through traffic as though the road were their personal fiefdom.

It all felt uncomfortably aligned with my mood.

I rested a hand against the cool windowpane, watching Collins Street heave under the weight of its own population. Pedestrians spilled across the pavements in frantic clusters, each propelled by some private urgency. I envied them — their direction, their purpose, their uncomplicated ability to simply move. I, meanwhile, was anchored to an office, a desk, and a contract that stubbornly refused to sign itself, no matter how long I glared at it.

The damned thing lay before me, pristine and accusatory. I'd read it repeatedly, yet retained none of it. My thoughts drifted, unbidden, to Teddy — to the brittleness in her voice, the volatility simmering beneath her skin, the emotional landmines I seemed destined to trigger no matter how carefully I tread.

Duty, I reminded myself. She needed me. That should have been enough.

But when I glanced at the clock and realised I'd be working late yet again, a familiar heaviness settled in my chest. Teddy would not take the news well. She hadn't taken much well lately.

I retrieved my phone, tapping its edge against my fingertips — a nervous habit masquerading as contemplation. Her name illuminated the screen. She answered immediately, dispensing with pleasantries.

"Don't tell me you're working late again." Irritation, sharp and unfiltered.

I exhaled slowly. "I'm afraid so. I can't leave until this is finished."

A clipped huff. "Maybe it's for the best. I'm going to bed early anyway." Her tone was strained, thin around the edges. She'd been crying.

"Do you want me to stay at my place tonight?" I asked, though the answer was already a foregone conclusion.

"Actually, yes."

My spine straightened. "Is something wrong?"

"It's been a long day. I'm tired. I'm not in the mood for any more bullshit."

The words landed with unnecessary force. I swallowed the instinct to defend myself. Arguing with her these days was like attempting diplomacy with a storm — noble in theory, catastrophic in practice. "Fine."

"So I'll see you whenever then."

My jaw tightened. "I'll see you at dinner tomorrow night." A deliberate pause. "I love you."

Silence. Only the faint tinkering of piano keys in the background. Then, flat and obligatory: "I love you too. Bye."

The line went dead.

My temper snapped. The phone left my hand before I could stop it, shattering against the wall in a spray of plastic and regret. I crouched to gather the pieces, muttering at my own idiocy. Losing my composure never achieved anything; it merely confirmed how tightly wound I'd become.

Pocketing the SIM card, I rose and returned to the window. The city sprawled beneath me — indifferent, relentless, utterly unmoved by the chaos consuming my life.

Ever since Teddy's past had clawed its way into our present, everything had become precarious. I'd foolishly believed that honesty would bring calm. Instead, it had ushered in volatility — hers, mine, all of it tangled until I could no longer distinguish where one ended and the other began.

Asher's voice echoed in my mind. *Perhaps a break would do you both good.*

The suggestion lodged itself in my chest like a splinter. Sensible, perhaps. But logic had never stood a chance against the way I felt about her.

I dragged a hand through my hair, returned to my desk, and forced my attention back to the work awaiting me. Bourbon would follow. Reflection, whether I wanted it or not, would follow that.

And beneath it all, the quiet, unyielding truth: something had to give.

One of the more pressing matters occupying my thoughts was the revelation that my uncle had been the culprit — a confession so unexpected it rendered my entire family momentarily speechless. Something inside me fractured at the admission. In truth, I went ballistic. A statue and another priceless relic bore the brunt of my temper, both reduced to shards across the floor. The repercussions — and the repair bill — were, unsurprisingly, not well received.

My outburst had stunned everyone present. Teddy and my mother were beside themselves, pleading with me to stop as though their voices alone might anchor me. My father attempted the more practical approach of physically restraining me. Neither effort was particularly successful. My behaviour, regrettable as it was, sent Teddy spiralling into self-recrimination, culminating in her confession about Emmett's recent conduct at Bricks and Mortar.

"It was my fault! By not running from him, I allowed that animal to hurt me — allowed him to act out whatever sick fantasy he had planned in his disgusting mind!" she had cried, her entire body wracked with sobs.

Her distress pushed me to confront my father about Emmett's assertion that he'd known her whereabouts.

My father's indignation was immediate and absolute. *"I did no such thing! And how dare that lying sack of filth slander my name in pursuit of his own twisted agenda!"*

As if matters weren't already strained, Teddy then admitted she had caught Emmett weeks earlier in the underground garage at Bricks and Mortar — lurking behind a concrete pillar, watching her. It took every ounce of restraint I possessed not to react in the moment. It wasn't that I doubted her; I simply needed to see it for myself. Spencer provided the CCTV footage without hesitation or intrusive questions. The footage confirmed everything: the stalking, the persistence, the months of calculated observation. It also explained Teddy's increasingly erratic behaviour in the weeks that followed.

Right alongside Therese, the depraved bastard had secured his place at the top of my list. He was a dead man.

Despite the turbulence in our relationship, my love for Teddy remained absolute. Moving forward was inevitable — but only if we found a way to resolve our issues and learn to compromise. With any luck, our therapist might offer the clarity we so desperately needed in our upcoming appointment.

Until then, I had a promise to uphold. And if I failed, I suspected World War Three would seem like a mild inconvenience by comparison.

2

Judging by the delightful aromas drifting through the air as I arrived at Teddy's, my timing was impeccable. Even so, as I walked up the path and onto the front porch, my stomach gave an undignified lurch. Nerves — ridiculous, unnecessary, and entirely unwelcome — surged as my imagination conjured every possible scenario of the greeting I might, or might not, receive.

I lowered myself onto one of the antique metal chairs beneath the verandah, the cushions soft beneath me. The delicate petals of the two dozen pink tea roses brushed my chin as I sat — flowers I'd purchased on the way over in the hope of igniting forgiveness, in both directions. That was the plan, at least.

A shuddering breath escaped me. I stood, steeling myself for whatever awaited. But the moment I stepped inside and closed the door behind me, the sound of piano from Teddy's playlist drifted through the foyer, mingling with high-spirited laughter. My fears, it seemed, were unfounded. Confidence bloomed, widening my smile as I strode towards the kitchen.

It didn't last.

The instant I heard Dominique utter the name Damien Rivers in her typically rapid-fire manner, my smile collapsed into a hard line and my steps slowed. Of all people, why was she giving that little charmer any oxygen? Hadn't he learned his lesson the last time I belted him? Memories I was more than willing to recreate if he ventured anywhere near her again. Clearly, my idiotic sister needed a reminder as well.

But when I marched into the kitchen, my aggrieved steps faltered. I absorbed the sight before me, the impact sharp enough to halt my steps.

Tears pricked my eyes as I took in the image of an emaciated Teddy moving between the gas cooker and the island bench, passing trays of homemade gourmet pizzas to Poppy.

Poppy spotted me first, offering a small, polite smile. "Hey, Ari." She worked the pizza cutter with meticulous precision, each slice perfectly measured.

"Um... hi, Poppy." The words stumbled out as I scrambled to collect my thoughts.

Our awkward greeting silenced the room. Every gaze turned towards me, waiting — almost expectantly — for the tension between Teddy and me to ignite.

When she finally looked up, her expression was cool, her voice clipped. "It seems I'm not worthy of a hello."

Shame burned through me. I dipped my head, avoiding the judgement radiating from every corner of the room. My jaw ticked. My thoughts spiralled. How had I not noticed her pain? Her weight loss? Her sleeplessness? How had I convinced myself my feelings took precedence over hers? The truth was simple and damning: I had failed her. If I'd spent less time wallowing and more time paying attention, she wouldn't look so fragile.

"Ari, are you all right? You look pale." Her soft voice and the sound of her bare feet padding across the timber floor snapped me back to the present.

I was about to offer a similar observation when I wisely thought better of it. I was here to make amends, not provoke another argument. Instead, I set the bouquet on the bench and swept Teddy into my arms, kissing her with a hunger that surprised even me. Her scent, her warmth — God, how I had missed this. Missed us.

Underappreciating what we had had cost us dearly. These past few days apart had taught me to value the warmth of our love all the more. And as she kissed me back with equal fervour, her hands roaming greedily over my torso, the message was unmistakable: she felt the same.

Unfortunately, our audience did not share our enthusiasm.

"All right, you two, enough with the CPR. We'd enjoy our food a whole lot more without the porn show," Dominique drawled, snapping her fingers.

I peered over Teddy's shoulder and scowled, flipping my treasured sister the bird.

She tutted. "You're such a charmer, brother."

Smirking, I retrieved the bouquet and handed it to Teddy. "These are my apology," I murmured, suddenly shy.

A sincere smile softened her swollen lips. "Apology accepted." She buried her nose in the petals, inhaling their fragrance before looking up at me. "We need to talk, but it can wait until after dinner — and away from ears." She flicked her chin towards our gossiping sisters.

A lump lodged in my throat. I nodded stiffly.

She squeezed my hand gently — cold, tense, nothing like her usual warmth. “Don’t stress; it’s nothing bad, I promise.”

Relief sagged through me. “Thank God.”

She laughed softly at my expression. “Come on. Let’s eat. I’m starving.”

I noticed — but if one valued their manhood, that was the sort of observation best kept to oneself.

Dinner with Teddy’s roommates seemed like old times – before that ominously dark cloud had descended upon us. For the first time in days, I relaxed, cherishing the moment before it evaporated. And as Teddy’s excessive giggling intensified thanks to the crude and sometimes inappropriate jokes frequently rolling off my sister’s tongue, my heart warmed. I paid no mind to them as I sat back, enjoying Teddy’s tasteful playlist whilst sipping on the glass of bourbon clutched in my hand. Occasionally a subtle chuckle slipped when the odd joke diverted my attention and away from my dubious thoughts. Although, not for long.

To others, Teddy appeared happier, yet I knew differently. Hidden beneath that steely armour was a sense of sadness and uncertainty over us, and our future. Likewise, her concern and fears were unfounded; I was here, wasn’t I?

Though at this stage as I peered down at her plate, feelings were the least of my worries. For someone who earlier admitted she was starving had barely taken a bite. I frowned, surreptitiously shaking my head as she played with her food.

Rather than eating her dinner, she spent most of it dissecting the tiniest sliver of pizza, chewing individual fragments of topping with painstaking slowness. Even then, she lifted the back of her hand to her mouth, attempting to hide the gag that followed as she forced herself to swallow. Her worried gaze flicked towards me soon after — checking, no doubt, whether I'd noticed.

Unfortunately, I had.

When our eyes met, my dismay was evident. A guilty flush crept up her throat and across her cheeks as she toyed nervously with the white-gold locket at her neck. Her mouth parted as if to speak, but nothing emerged beyond a strangled little sound. She tore her gaze away, and I — coward that I was — hid my disheartened sigh behind a long, unnecessary sip of bourbon.

Teddy was wasting away in front of me, and unless I spoke up, she'd continue to wither. Perhaps her lacklustre eating habits were a matter best raised in Doctor Montgomery's office — safer, too, if I valued the head on my shoulders, which I was admittedly quite attached to.

I'd just drained the last of my drink and reached for the bottle, fingers curling around its square-shaped base, when Teddy's fingertips brushed my thigh beneath the table — discreet, deliberate, unmistakable. She was ready for that dreaded talk.

My chest constricted as I set my glass down with reluctant finality. And, of course, the moment we pushed our chairs back and rose in unison, our sudden departure was immediately clocked by our eagle-eyed sisters.

Dominique's eyes narrowed first, Scarlett's smirk following a beat later. Poppy attempted diplomacy by pretending not to notice, though the slight lift of her brow betrayed her curiosity. Teddy shot me a warning glance — don't engage — and for once, I obeyed. Whatever she needed to tell me — whatever had been gnawing at her for days — was finally coming to the surface.

And I wasn't ready. Not remotely.

Without argument, they promptly began cleaning up. After the past few hellish weeks, they'd learnt not to disagree with me — particularly after Teddy's flat refusal to disclose Emmett as the culprit to her roommates. Given he'd been the catalyst for everyone unravelling, I believed honesty kept people safe. My ideology wasn't met with the same belief – not by a long shot.

Blindsided by Teddy's rebuttal, a truly appalling bout of gumption seized me with his name 'accidentally' slipping off my tongue. That single lapse irrefutably sparked a colossal row – tempers flared and voices raising, Dominique and Scarlett leapt to my defence with all the grace of a pub brawl. Before I knew it, the three of us were storming out, leaving a fuming Teddy in the doorway.

Dom and Scarlett promptly followed me home, where they made themselves far too comfortable in the spare rooms for my liking. They settled in as though they'd been planning a long weekend, offering sympathetic looks that only made me feel more like the idiot who'd lit the fuse.

The stalemate lasted for days – the three of us holed up in my place, the silence between Teddy and me stretching into something brittle and unpleasant. Then she appeared: unannounced, breathless, and visibly frayed, standing on my doorstep as though she'd sprinted the entire way. Her apology was nothing short of epic. A rare, unguarded moment from Teddy – all contrition and cracked pride – and I'd forgiven her twice over for it, a sentiment she later reciprocated with... admirable dedication.

The memory loosened its grip slowly, the edges of it blurring as the present came back into focus — Teddy in front of me, her silence taut enough to snap. Whatever she needed to tell me was still there, waiting, unchanged by the detour through everything we'd survived to get here.

Still, I held her gaze, bracing myself for whatever storm waited on the other side of her silence.

We slipped out of the kitchen and into the quieter stretch of the hallway, the noise of clattering dishes fading into a distant hum. The air cooled around us, tension thickening with every step.

She reached her bedroom first, slipping inside without a word. I followed a beat later.

Stepping through the open doorway, my gaze drifted to the wingbacked chairs — and to the tension etched across her drawn face. Her anxiety about the conversation ahead betrayed her; she crossed and uncrossed her legs in quick succession, her hands performing a restless choreography in her lap.

I closed the door behind me, shooting her a furtive glance. "Are you nervous about our conversation?"

The wavy curls draped over her slim shoulders swayed as she shook her head. "No," she readily admitted, following me with a jaded gaze as I strolled across her room. "I'm just on edge and have been ever since I revealed my secret to your parents."

"Yeah, it's been a pretty shitty time all round, I'd say," I uttered despondently, raking my hands through my hair as I settled into the chair beside her. Sitting askew, I casually rested an ankle over my knee and leaned against the backrest, motioning with a wave of my hand for Teddy to begin. "So, what did you want to talk about?"

"Everything."

I frowned. "That's rather ambiguous."

"Don't be difficult," she tutted disapprovingly.

"I apologise. But what exactly do you want to talk about?"

"Us, this dark cloud, and... Emmett," she informed me hesitantly — and with good reason. Just hearing my depraved uncle's name made my skin crawl and the rage boil away inside. Had I known we were venturing down such a difficult road, I would have swiped the bottle of bourbon off the table, forgetting the glass intentionally. I tugged at my collar and loosened my tie. "What about—Emmett?" Christ, even speaking his name burned like acid on my tongue.

"We've not discussed the aftermath. Not civilly, anyway — and that's mostly due to your anger management issues," she reminded me reproachfully.

"Yeah," I scoffed, dropping my elbows to my knees and leaning into the palms of my hands. My head hung in shame as I judiciously recalled my latest outburst. "Not my proudest moment, admittedly. But in saying that, there were several reasons behind my abysmal behaviour — not that I'm trying to justify my actions either," I clarified as Teddy opened her mouth to argue. I held up a hand. "Just hear me out, okay?" Once she nodded, I continued, "Firstly, learning my uncle was the culprit was quite the shock. Then the realisation that he, along with your bloody mother, were behind us remaining apart all these years. And compounded by everything else they'd put you through recently, I simply couldn't take any more and just... lost it."

As I uneasily purged my feelings, Teddy remained quiet, my heart quaking at the flow of tears streaming down her pale, hollowed cheeks. "Ignorance, selfishness — whatever you want to call it — I wasn't thinking. I simply reacted every time, never giving a thought to your feelings." Her tightened sob was enough to break me. I reached out and slipped our hands together, my voice trembling as I expressed my remorse. "If it's any consolation, I sincerely regret every aspect of how I've acted and responded; from that initial day at the island up until now."

Her voice, a croaky whisper, shared her own sorrows. "Carys blames me for the discord in the family and still refuses to speak to me whenever I try to make amends. Bryson mercifully still picks up when I call."

Peeved by my oldest sister's indifference, my lips thinned. "Don't worry about Carys; she'll come around eventually."

She snorted, wiping away her tears with the pads of her fingertips. "I'm glad you're the optimist. Currently, I feel anything but."

"Carys was always close to Em... *he* and his family. He doted on her, being the first-born and all. I suspect it's just the shock causing her odious behaviour. Give her time, okay?"

She stiffly nodded before casting her saddened gaze downward.

"What else is bothering you?" I quietly asked, my head cocking as her trembling lips clammed up. As per usual, she compelled me to impatiently ask again. "Teddy, what else?"

"There's another reason I look awful."

I eyed her quizzically; she cocked an eyebrow. The penny eventually dropped. "Ah — your weight loss."

"Yeah, that. I saw the condemnation on your face when you first came in, not to mention over dinner."

"Condemnation is a tad harsh, wouldn't you say?" I argued defensively, earning a deathly glare. "I was merely shocked by your appearance, is all."

"I've been sick — and not just from stress either!" Teddy snapped before tentatively adding, "...I'm pregnant."

My jaw dropped open. What the—? Pregnant? I licked my drying lips before swallowing the shock. "How? I mean, I know how, but... how? I thought we were careful?"

"Not careful enough, apparently," she stated flatly. "The doctor explained it only took one time without the use of a condom. I have a feeling it was the night I instigated our lovemaking, remember?"

How could I forget? That lovemaking was beautiful in every sense of the word. That aside, I wanted to kick myself for my carelessness — more so after not heeding Doctor Montgomery's advice, sternly given to me only weeks before.

"Aren't you happy about the news?"

"Y... yes, yes, I'm thrilled, actually." As I pathetically stumbled over my words, she snatched her hand away.

"You could have fooled me!"

I inhaled sharply and ran my clenching hand through my already dishevelled hair. Why was it that no matter which way I responded, it was seemingly the wrong way?

"I'm just worried about the impeccable timing — you know, with all that's going on currently." I held Teddy's misty-eyed gaze and swallowed. The tension between us grew palpable, and not in a sexual nature for a change.

"You're right, the timing isn't great," she replied despondently, sagging against the backrest and rubbing her flexing fingers across her forehead. "I'm only a few weeks along, so I guess having a termination isn't entirely out of the question."

Teddy's abhorrent answer to the ill-timed nature of the pregnancy sent me flying out of my chair. "No! No abortion! We shall work through this. I know we can.... unless that's what you want?" I knelt in front of her, searching her troubled face with pleading eyes. "Please, tell me that isn't so?"

A feeble smile formed as she sifted her fingers through my hair. "No, the thought never crossed my mind. I guess we just got our wires crossed."

I sagged as the relief washed over me. "You have no idea how pleased I am to hear you say those words." I brushed a lock of hair behind her ear and clasped her sweet face, locking our lips together in a gentle embrace. Our foreheads touched as we parted; Teddy's voice trembled, reciting her fears.

"What if I can't be a parent, Ari? What if I'm far too damaged? I'd hate myself if I inflicted –"

I immediately tilted her chin, my gaze intent as I quietly assured her, "Hey, hey, stop, right there; you shall be an incredible mother to our child, and I shall make certain our child never doubts your love for them. So, no more of this self-doubt, okay?" Her head reluctantly bobbed, causing my brow to furrow at the untold worry, but as she was already fragile enough, I remained silent. I urged her towards my embrace, my voice shuddering regardless of the optimism I attempted to convey, "*Everything shall be fine*."

After further discussion regarding the rest of our future, we crawled into bed and made sweet, sweet love – an all-consuming feeling that radiated through every responsive touch and languorous kiss, leaving me yearning for more. Likewise, as we snuggled tightly, and my fingertips lightly caressed along her sticklike torso, I had another erection. As part of my conscious effort not to overdo the sex, I, however, raised a subject guaranteed to leave me limp.

"I'm buying earmuffs – and not just for our ears, your belly too. I refuse for our child to be subjected to or deafened by Mother's high-pitched squeals."

Teddy snorted derisively. "Your poor mum, she thinks none of her children appreciates her enthusiasm."

My lips twitched in suppressed amusement. "We do. Well, sort of." I scoffed. "I just wish Mother wouldn't hurt our ears with all that blasted excitement." I peered down at Teddy just as her beaming smile faded and she rolled away from me, flopping an arm across her creasing forehead. "What's wrong?"

"We need to tell Doctor Montgomery sooner rather than later about the baby – mostly because of the medications I've been on."

Concerned by the worry etched in her voice, I rolled towards her, coaxing gently as I cupped her cheek. "Hey, look at me, please?" With a languid sigh, Teddy slowly met my tender gaze. "It'll be fine. He's a doctor, and astutely aware accidents tend to happen from time to time."

She grimaced, unconvinced by my optimism. "Doctor Montgomery's already warned me that getting pregnant wasn't the best option for me – right now anyway. His prime reason being that he's also extremely aware I'm still not in the best place mentally to have a child anytime soon."

Drawing Teddy closer and encompassing her within my arms, I pressed a lingering kiss to her forehead. "Let's wait and see what he has to say before we jump to any conclusions. You never know – he might actually be thrilled for us."

My optimism could not have been any farther from the truth.

Doctor Montgomery's jaw hit the floor the second we shared our joyful news with him. "Well, I'm delighted to see you took my advice," he eventually uttered caustically. "But how could you both be so bloody reckless?"

"It wasn't intentional, Doc..." I countered calmly. "It just happened."

"Unintentional or not, adding a defensive child to the mix while these unpleasant issues remain in your lives – it's just damned irresponsible!"

At that point, I believed his comments were unwarranted and seriously thought about putting him back in his place. But as if the good doctor sensed my irritation, he glowered, raising a pointed finger directly at me.

"Don't bother, Ari! You *both* need to hear what I have to say! So, I suggest you sit there quietly until then!" he growled. "Am I clear?"

"Crystal," we replied in unison, shrinking back into our seats.

Other than that little reprimanding, life had changed — at home and at work.

My staff, in particular, were thrilled. You'd think they'd survived a natural disaster the way they spoke about my "improved temperament." One even admitted she no longer did a silent prayer before knocking on my office door. Charming.

Discovering I was about to become a father was the principal reason behind my chuffed mood, I suppose. Something Asher kindly noticed, his rare praise catching me off guard during one of our regular lunches at Rockpool Bar and Grill, Southbank beside the Yarra River – or as we Melburnians quaintly called it, the upside-down river.

"Wow, look at you, one minute you're all dark and gloomy, now you're all sunshine and roses. What's gotten you so sappy lately?"

Shoving a piece of the deliciously juicy scotch fillet on my plate into my mouth, I glanced up and grinned. "Just life. Ultimately, Teddy and I are on the same page and in a beautiful place, and that's all you need to know – for now," I simpered, chewing away happily.

Asher twisted the fork in his hand and chuckled. "You normally tell me everything. Anyone would think Teddy was pregnant the way you were acting."

Unwittingly, I began choking on my food.

His eyes widened. "Teddy's preggers?"

"Keep your voice down," I whispered hoarsely, lifting the water glass to my lips and taking a few tentative sips. "The answer to your ever-enquiring mind is yes – Teddy *is* pregnant. Nevertheless, we are only in the first trimester, meaning we aren't telling anyone just yet. So, Asher, I implore you, please be a mate and keep it to yourself because if I receive an angry phone call from my mother, then I'll know you shall have told yours."

"My lips are unequivocally sealed," he wisely replied, closing an imaginary zip across his lips.

I gave a satisfied nod. "Good."

Asher eyed me speculatively over the lip of the wine glass in his hand. "Well as your mate, I'm curious – particularly when only days ago you were contemplating taking a break. Care to fill me in?"

I shrugged apathetically. "All it took was one night of carelessness, my friend. And just so you know, Teddy *isn't* aware that's what I was thinking, so for the love of God, please don't tell her."

He picked up his knife and fork, resuming his meal of Asian-style pork belly as he scoffed. "No, I'd hate to upset a pregnant woman – specifically yours."

"Thank you. I appreciate your discretion."

"I've always got your back, Ari; you know that. Anyway, let's discuss finding you a new engineer. When do you want to start headhunting?"

And just like that, the discussion regarding my private life was over.

"The sooner, the better." I smiled widely sawing off another chunk of steak. "And whilst we're on the subject, can you ask HR to advertise further afield for both the engineer as well as a grad student. Stipulate that the grad student needs to be either fresh out of university or about to graduate. But as long as they're more than happy to work whilst learning beneath our new employee, I don't mind either way."

"Like an understudy?"

I concurred with a brief nod. "Something along those lines, I suppose."

"Fresh meat. I like your thinking." Asher grinned and dug into his pork. "This little search is going to be fun."

I lifted my fork to my lips, murmuring in agreeance, "Indeed, it shall."

.

3

Teddy

"Pack an overnight bag – enough for two days," Ari sultrily requested, gliding the tip of his tongue along my sweat laced spine whilst skimming his fingers between my parted thighs through my swollen cleft as I lay sated on my stomach.

I tutted mockingly, "Manners, Mr Jaeger. Whatever happened to please?"

"Ms McGovern, it would please me greatly if you packed an overnight bag," he poshly murmured against my dampened skin.

"Ooh, so formal. I like," I playfully breathed. "Now, *fuck me*."

Tutting disapprovingly, he unexpectedly and firmly spanked my arse, making me groan loudly before swiftly flipping me over and pinning my wrists either side of my head. Burning, darkened eyes stared as Ari hovered above me, his warm breath whispering across my face as he scolded me, "Whatever happened to please, Ms McGovern?"

"Fuck me, *please,* Mr Jaeger."

His intense gaze seared. "Much more appropriate."

From there on in, he left me far too incoherent to bother asking him how he'd convinced Spencer to let me take yet another day off work. I didn't care; I was too busy riding high.

The sun blazed through the tinted windows of Ari's sleek BMW as we cruised along the freeway, leaving the outskirts of the city nothing more than a multicoloured blur.

Raising a dubious brow, I looked over at a whistling Ari. "So, where are we going?"

His mouth curled into a rather devilish smile as he tapped the side of his nose. "It's a secret. But I shall tell you this: I thought the two of us escaping the rat race for a few days wouldn't hurt – and trust me, you won't be complaining about our mini getaway for long...cause every damned minute shall be extraordinarily pleasant."

My brows furrowed. "Why do you have to be so damned cryptic?"

He chuckled. "Makes life less dull, wouldn't you say?"

Accepting he wasn't about to tell me willingly, I sank against the soft leather seat and reached across the centre console, stroking the inside of his thigh over his tan chino shorts. "Not even a little hint?"

"No, I told you, it's a secret. Just sit back and enjoy the ride," Ari simpered as my fingertips tantalisingly grazed over the swell bulging at his crotch.

Made cranky by his impervious attitude, I snatched my hand away and began trolling through the music selection on the dash. "Well, Mr Jaeger, you keep your secret, but as punishment, it means you have to put up with my singing for however long we're on the road," I singsonged.

Ari groaned humorously as Tim McGraw's, *I Like It, I Love It* began blaring through the car's speakers. "It's a sacrifice I'm willing to make." He chuckled loudly before finally giving in and joining in with me.

After what seemed like hours, we eventually stopped.

"We're here," Ari announced, forcing me to drag my head out of the dreary gossip magazine I'd purchased during a short stop along the way.

"Thank fuck for that," I uttered tossing it aside, making him laugh.

"I honestly don't know why you bother with that trash; good for firelighters, and that's about it in my book."

"It's amusing, that's why." Both of us released our seatbelts and climbed from the car. But the second I stepped out and realised where we were, my doldrum mood disappeared. I squealed excitedly. "Oh my god, Ari – The Sorrento Hotel?" I ran and jumped into his arms, wrapping my arms and legs around him as I peppered his face with chaste kisses, making him chuckle. "This place is gorgeous! Thank you!"

"I was desperate for some alone time with my girl. No distractions, no family, and most importantly, no work," he murmured, skating his lips along my throat. "Now, let's simmer down and hurry inside before we give anyone else more than they bargained for."

"Good idea."

He grinned before slanting his lips over mine in an enticing kiss as he slowly guided me along the length of his well-defined body until the sole of my strappy wedges touched the bitumen. My gaze glued to his beautifully shaped backside, I followed him as he strolled to the boot. Popping it, he bent to grab my small suitcase first, eliciting a groan upon lifting it. Whoops, my bad.

"What in the devil did you pack in this thing?" he complained, dropping my case beside him with a thud. "I said *two nights*, not a bloody week."

I struggled to subdue a smile. "Oh...I may have bought a few extras for you know...a little fun."

Darkening eyes perceptively glinted as the air around us profoundly shifted. "Oh, did you just?" The huskiness of his voice alone did enough to send that all-knowing flutter directly to my groin.

My throat bobbed in anticipation. "I figured it would have been remiss of me *to* forget."

"That it would." Ari's searing stare rested solely on me as he ventured past, a chuckle eliciting as he caught sight of my broadening grin. "I'll deal with your glee shortly, but first, we have to check-in."

Inwardly patting myself on the back for my foresight, I trailed behind Ari up the limestone steps. We casually strolled along a widened hallway, coming to stop inside the newly renovated foyer. The luxurious reception embodied its rich history with a desk shaped from the limestone on which the original hotel was initially built back in 1872. Light poured in from the glass ceiling overhead, showcasing the matching limestone wall behind the receptionist serving Ari. I hovered against the wall separating the reception from the formal dining wall. But upon surveying my surrounds, my thoughts quickly detracted from the nuances of the perfectly blended architecture. With an unmistakable air of desire burning around us, it wasn't surprising.

I pivoted on the heels of my wedges and met the darkened eyes viewing me. Hmm, Ari appeared to be just as distracted as I was.

With one ankle crossed over the other and one elbow propped on the dark timber countertop with his chin resting in his palm, his head tilted marginally – paying more attention to me than the receptionist. Even passing her his credit card, he barely glanced her way. Not that she seemed to notice; her professionalism continued as she handed the card back, along with the key to our room.

"Thank you, Mr Jaeger," she exclaimed, smiling brightly. "I hope you and your wife enjoy your time here at The Sorrento Hotel, and please don't hesitate to let us know if there's anything else you need during your stay."

Again, he briefly looked her way, if only to politely thank her. Sliding his card back into its slot in his wallet, he shoved it into his back pocket, all the while approaching me in smooth, leisurely steps. "I'll be the gentleman my parents raised me to be and devotedly carry our bags…" Ari encircled my waist effortlessly and tugged me towards him. Our bodies gently collided as I closed my eyes and leaned into his broad shoulder, inhaling his divine scent. His lips grazed my cheek as he potently whispered, "…While you run along and find our room."

The moment my lids flew open, and our heated gazes met, I knew I was in for quite the stimulating afternoon—more reason to push the boundaries with him. Just thinking about the possibilities was enough to set the heat aflame between my thighs.

Ari, typically reading my mind, caught my chin between the soft pads of his fingers. "Wait for me – and don't undress," he huskily instructed, staring so salaciously my knees turned to jelly. "I want the pleasure of divesting you of your clothes bit by bit for myself." His kiss, firm and ardent, stole the breath from my lungs. "Now, walk ahead of me. I won't be far behind, I promise."

Swiftly shoving my wicked thoughts aside, I scurried towards the bank of lifts and stabbed the button inset in the wall. I fidgeted on the spot, just wishing the damned elevator would just arrive already.

Ari rapidly caught up and stood behind me, brazenly pushing the entire length of his body flush with mine. "Antsy, are we?"

I sagged against his torso, rolling the back of my head along his broad shoulder. "For you, always."

Determined to keep me on edge, he whispered decadently in my ear, articulating every word – "Feel how much I want you. Feel how hard I am for you."

My quickened breath altered to a soft pant as he relinquished his grip on the suitcase handle and grasped my hips, yanking me closer. I quietly moaned and gyrated against him, not caring for the other guests making their way towards us.

As timing would have it, the doors on the lift soundlessly slid open, and again he sternly ordered me to go ahead.

Miserably, I obliged and marched inside the car, my frustration only increasing as I spun and saw the smug expression written all over Ari's face. I made my dissatisfaction known by grunting at him as I stabbed at the button for the second floor, leaving him chuckling at my expense. I loved him dearly, but dammit, he could be such an arse at the most inconvenient times.

By the time I'd reached the second floor, the ache between my thighs had amplified. So, when Ari said he wouldn't be far behind, I sincerely hoped he wasn't lying. It was torturous enough waiting for him as it was.

Strolling out into an airy hallway, I discovered I only had to walk a few steps before finding our room. But as I swiped the electronic key on the lock and swung the door open, the view outside our private balcony caught my wandering gaze.

Excitement surged as I bounced towards the slim French doors and dramatically pulled them open. Hanging onto the antique chrome handles, I allowed myself a wondrous minute to take in the Peninsulas shimmering waters, calmly and quietly rippling from the vast seas beyond. Phillip Island was beautiful, yes, but in comparison, it was nowhere near as breathtaking as the natural splendour before me.

The room itself was equally stunning – limestone walls carried the outside in, adding an entirely new dimension to the light-filled space. Plush linens and pillows covered the king-sized bed facing the wide-open windows, with a sitting room to my right housing a corner chaise cushioned in soft, supple leather, and a small two-seater dining table to my left. As I ran my hands over the differing textures blending luxury with old-world charm, I silently applauded the designer. My tactile delight then led me to a walk-in robe and the connecting ensuite bathroom – another room just as beautiful as the rest. I grinned salaciously at the size of the walk-in shower; oh, the possibilities had now increased tenfold.

I peered over my shoulder and called out to Ari. “Ari, come and take a look at the shower, it’s huge!” When he failed to reply, I frowned. Odd considering I’d heard him trailing in only seconds ago. “Ari?”

Long fingers skated down my bare arms and curled around my wrists, subduing me as warm, sensual lips trailed along my neck. The heady scent of citrus and spice flooded my lungs –

intoxicating, wicked – leaving me entirely at the mercy of Ari Jaeger. I bowed back against him.

"Keep still," he firmly purred, my breath catching as he caught my earlobe between his teeth. Ari's soft skin radiated a burning heat as his forearm brushed over my midriff and gravitated towards my infamously short denim shorts. His gifted fingers unfastened each button with quiet patience, only to send my shorts to the floor with a single, gentle shove. My underwear, a delicate lace, suffered an entirely different fate as he tore at the thin waistband before flagrantly tossing them aside.

Entranced by my dominating lover, my mind and body drifted to a place of bliss. More so as his fingers glided through my ultrasensitive flesh. With each stroke of my aching clitoris and teasing circles around my trembling rim, my desire grew. And instinctively, my hips began to undulate, prompting a growl from Ari.

"Mmm, you're very wet..." God, that warm timbre voice: it was raspy and indulgent like the man himself. "But keep still."

A strangled whimper escaped my throat. "Ari, please..."

His darkened eyes glittered sensuously as his stubbled chin jerked towards the mirror on the bathroom wall above the sink. "Just watch... and don't come...not yet, as I want to savour this – *and* you."

My head swivelled slowly and met his fiery gaze in the reflection. I stared fascinated by the hedonistic sight playing out before me. The vision of his fingers moving with deliberate, devastating precision – each slow, controlled motion – was exquisite. I was riveted. Not just by Ari's beautiful lovemaking, but by the person he had become with this sudden need for control. I was aroused far more than I ever imagined.

I had always loved his dominant side, but this… this was something else. Something more. A version of him I wanted to explore, to coax further, to meet with equal intensity. As a Dominant in the making, Ari was devastatingly magnificent.

“Remove your blouse – slowly,” he whispered, his words, absolute and unyielding. “Keep watching.”

A perceptible blush rose over my dampened skin. My delight visibly shared in the way of a fulfilled smile as I nimbly undid each tiny button by moving my fingers provocatively slow until I reached the last one, parting and pushing the blouse off my shoulders.

“Now your bra.”

“Then will you fuck me?” I coyly asked, freeing my breasts in the same unhurried manner.

“All in good time, my love.” He slid an arm around my waist and pressed his well-defined torso along the curve of my spine. “Just enjoy…this.” Motioning to the mirror with his free hand, he gyrated, pushing his hardened and pulsing length between my cheeks. “You’re soaking. Watching me finger fuck you turns you on, doesn’t it?”

“How could it not?” I croaked out.

A victorious smile flittered as he continued his pleasurable torture. “Touch your breasts for me.” Ari’s command was firm, yet soft, and without hesitation, I obeyed. “Pleasure yourself for me.”

Palming each swollen breast, I mewled, tweaking, and rolling my hardened nipples between the pads of my fingertips. My core, along with my will to obey fought against one another as Ari’s circling fingers slid inside me. With each methodical stroke of my inner wall striking every nerve throughout my trembling body, I was losing the battle, and Ari knew it too. The wicked gleam flashing over his handsome face told me so. Mostly as he abruptly stopped and swung me around, lifting me with ease onto the vanity. His chocolate orbs gazed intently as he gruffly ordered me to lock my hands behind my back and not to move.

Digging my fingernails into my palms, I gritted out my displeasure, “Let me fucking come!”

“No,” he abruptly replied, dropping to his knees and spreading my thighs to eat at my swollen cleft in the same savage manner.

I laboured against the ferocity of his lovemaking, every nerve alight. Sweat beaded my forehead, forming warm rivulets over my heated skin. My feet arched instinctively, bracing against his broad shoulders as my body strained to meet his. His muscular arms – slicked with perspiration – wrapped around my writhing form, and his robust fingers curled around my wrists, holding me utterly still, utterly his.

Unable to deal with the painful throbbing coursing between my legs any longer, I let out a wrenching sob. “Ari…p…please.”

Beautiful eyes framed by raven eyelashes peered up at me. “Soon, my love, very soon.”

“In the very least, kiss me then. Gimme a taste.” My tone was husky yet demanding.

Within seconds, he’d relinquished his grip on my thighs and rose silently from his knees only to fist my hair with a rough, possessive certainty. Our moans mingled as he yanked my head back and pressed his mouth to mine in a red-hot kiss – one that escalated the instant I tasted the salt of my arousal, coating his lips and tongue.

My fingers tangled through the silky strands of his hair while my other hand slid over his shoulder blades. He flinched as I dragged my sharpened nails into the soft flesh of his back.

"Ah – and here I thought I was in charge," he grunted against my lips.

"Oh, you still are. *Now, fuck me. Hard*."

A sexy chuckle rumbled as Ari scooped me off the vanity beneath the thighs. "Be careful what you wish for, my love." His mouth landed on mine before my back hit the cold tiles in the shower stall with a muted thud. And through our cacophony of pleasured moans, he fumbled beside me flicking the tap to release an invigorating rush of temperate water from the rain-head shower rose above us. Droplets cascaded over our heated skin, steam curling around us in a hazy veil. And without any warning – he thrust into me, drawing a sharp gasp from my lips and forcing my back to arch instinctively.

With every smooth and powerful lunge, he made me feel every pulsing inch until gradually, his raw fucking built up to something much harder. Eventually, he stilled, his entire body tensing as his climax rushed out of him in long hot spurts inside me. His groans were muffled against the slope of my shoulder as he sank his teeth into me.

I tensed as the sharp pinch pierced my skin, a hiss tearing from my throat.

Ari swiftly lifted his head and winced at the sight of the broken skin. "Sorry – my intention wasn't to bite you," he breathlessly apologised, running his fingertips across the deep indentation. "That's probably going to scar."

A wry smile appeared on my lips. "Think of it as payback for the sex wounds I gave you."

“Fair trade I feel,” he murmured between each lazy pleasurable kiss.

The back of my sopping head flopped against the tiles. “You’re incredibly sneaky undressing without me noticing, aren’t you?” I coaxed, smiling up at him.

Jet-black brows shot up above mischievously sparkling dark eyes. “I know,” Ari crooned, his body shifting with a confidence that made my breath catch. Our mouths curved salaciously in unison as we instinctively flexed, the air between us thickening with promise.

“More?”

“More.”

Silently, slowly, Ari’s mouth lowered over mine. His languid kiss so skilful, so consuming, it left me breathless – slipping into that space where surrender felt not only possible, but inevitable. Finally.

4

Ari

I had undoubtedly made the right choice spiriting Teddy away to Sorrento – that much was clear as I peered out from beneath my sunglasses at the vastness before me, the last biting rays of sunshine gradually sinking beyond the horizon. No blaring of horns or sirens and no phones shrilling with staff chattering in my ear. It was just Teddy, this picture-perfect environment, and me. My gaze roamed, appreciating the diamond-bright reflections bouncing off the peninsula's tranquil aqua water, each glint a silent echo of the sun's farewell. The breeze carried a salty stillness, and for a moment, time itself seemed to pause at the edge of the horizon.

Sheltered by the lush curve of Port Phillip Bay, the calm, shallow stretch of water was serene — gentle waves lapping at the soft, sandy shoreline. The crystal-clear shallows offered a perfect haven for families with young children, often seen frolicking in the warm sunshine, splashing through the shallows or exploring the nearby rockpools. In stark contrast, just across the peninsula, the back beach faced the vast Southern Ocean, where nature unleashed her raw, untamed power. There, rugged, undulating cliffs rose above wild seas, and the thunder of crashing waves echoed against weathered rock formations—a coastline shaped by time and tide.

A broad smile grew. The day, thus far, had turned out to be beautiful in every sense of the word. Well, perhaps if Teddy learnt the importance of time, it might even end up perfect. I let out a small chuckle; that alone would be a miracle in itself.

I strolled back through the open French doors of our hotel room and glanced at my watch, calling out, "We need to get a move on, or we'll miss our reservation." Naturally, she was running behind thanks to a bout of vomiting – our afternoon of rough sex partially the blame. We needed to learn the importance of restraint, but the probability of that ever happening would be zero on both parts.

"Couldn't we just stay here and order in?" Teddy proposed, emerging from the bathroom, her hazel eyes glistening with hopeful mischief as she slid a lip-gloss into the white clutch clasped in her hand. "Staying in bed sounds so much more enticing...not to mention delicious..."

My case in point about restraint made. Now, it was up to me to show some.

I buried my hands in the silken tresses tumbling around her shoulders and dipped my head. The distinct flavour of strawberries coating her parted lips as my mouth brushed over hers evoked memories of that infamous lollypop. "No, we need to get out. That's why we came away if you recall?"

"I suppose so," she hummed, trudging behind me for the short stroll to the rooftop restaurant and bar.

I severely underestimated the meaning of *short stroll* where Teddy was concerned. Besides reciting the history on the hotel's grand architecture, she insisted we stop and admire every intricate detail along the way. We ought to have taken the lift. Nonetheless, she was in her element and denying her was virtually impossible – once again, displaying my ineptitude for restraint.

But no longer could I deny my growling stomach, or the call of an icy cold beer, and had to drag Teddy up the last few steps. A wide smile formed as we finally strolled into the crowded but jovial rooftop space, where locals and tourists alike lined the bars and filled the restaurant's tables patiently awaiting service. Raised voices filled the voids, competing with the clatter of dishes and the live band currently playing a Cold Chisel rendition in the background – Water into Wine, if I wasn't mistaken. By the time we manoeuvred through the crowds and stepped outside through a set of widely opened bi-fold doors overlooking the peninsula, I was practically drooling from the scent of food alone.

Paving the way for us was our bubbly waitress, Joey, her brightened smile beaming as she attentively gestured to the sturdy round timber bar tables with white metals stools, their seats padded with grey cushions and neatly piped edging. "Can I get you both a drink to start?"

I swiftly ordered two – a Peroni for me and a ginger beer spritzer for Teddy.

"Will there be anything else, sir?"

"Just our drinks for now, please; we'll order shortly thank you," I replied, dismissing her with polite firmness.

With a dazzling smile, she spun on the soles of her black Vans and returned a few minutes later with our drinks, setting them down with brisk, efficient ease beside the menus.

I glanced upwards, politely thanking her.

"No worries. Enjoy." Clutching the tray to her side, she bounced around the rest of the tables collecting several empty glasses before heading back inside.

Lifting the Peroni to my lips, my gaze drifted across the table to Teddy as she sipped her ginger beer – the only remedy that seemed to ease the constant bouts of morning sickness. She'd be far happier once that stage passed. As it stood, she was far too thin and needed to regain a few kilos – a concern I'd stressed during our most recent therapy session. According to Teddy, though, my worry was unwarranted. A flippant response I found somewhat alarming.

"Look at the sky, Ari," she suddenly voiced, pulling me from my musings. "That sunset's glorious." Her excited gaze homed in on the colourfully warm hues of oranges and reds streaking across the evening sky. "It's a pity you don't see them like that in the city."

My lips quirked. "They're the same sunsets, you know."

With a roll of the eyes, she huffed, "I know... What I meant was, smart arse, we don't usually experience them the same because of the city skyline poking well above its measure."

Another adjustment: the caustic attitude courtesy of her ever-changing moods. During our last session – teary, irritable – she'd informed me, "*It's not my fault! It's these damned hormones making me cranky!"* To a certain degree, yes, they were at fault, but my rebuttal had only sent me back to the doghouse yet again – as in my house for the night.

"I knew that's what you meant; I was just checking."

"Don't be an arse."

"And the list grows – from a caveman to an arse." I chuckled, lifting the beer to my lips. "I'm moving up in the world."

∞

Teddy

I began to stir as another glorious sunrise slowly crept out from behind the parting of white, fluffy clouds, signalling yet another resplendent day. A pity we weren't sticking around to enjoy it. Still, as I snuggled into my pillow and gazed out with a sleepy smile, my thoughts drifted to what had been a rather enjoyable weekend away anyway.

From the rejuvenating couple's massages at the spa, easing every knot from our bodies, to the locally caught fish with crunchy deep-fried chips on the beach – every moment had been a delight. The local galleries had piqued our interest too, with Ari indulging me in one of my favourite pastimes: shopping.

He'd taken me to Cote Salt, a boutique store selling exclusively bespoke and ethical interior pieces, and indulged me by spending a pretty penny on whatever I fancied. Our beautiful day drifted into the evening with a late, romantic dinner at one of Sorrento's best-kept secrets, The Three Palms, where we indulged in the pleasure of feeding one another from our shared tapas plate. At some point, Ari had led me to the dancefloor, our limbs fluidly moving together in a sensuous display to the guitarist's acoustic take on Enrique Iglesias' *Only a Woman*, attracting the attention of the staff and patrons alike. It was a dance that seamlessly flowed well into the deep of night.

Overall, my favourite part had been our lovemaking – mostly due to the shift in sexual dynamics. I let out a gratified sigh. Ari had shown me repeatedly over the weekend just how naturally dominance came to him, and he'd been nothing short of exceptional. Not once had he left me disappointed.

But that was last night, and a little more pleasure before heading home wouldn't go astray. Someone else appeared equally eager as Ari shuffled across the mattress, fitting his well-shaped physique along the length of my body. The corners of my lips quirked the moment his warm hand curled over my waist and he pressed closer, his intent unmistakable.

I hummed appreciatively. "Well, good morning to you too, big boy."

"Good morning, gorgeous," he rasped pleasantly, gliding his hand up my torso to cup my breast, his tweaking of my nipple enough to draw a soft gasp. "Up for a little more fun?"

A thin, croaked "yes" was all I could muster as he suddenly thrust his hand between my thighs, parting them widely for his probing fingers. "Remain on your stomach and put that pretty arse high in the air for me," he softly instructed, "but leave your head on the pillow."

A tremor of anticipation rippled through me as I hurried into position, clutching the pillow's edges while he pushed up from the mattress and knelt behind me. My hips writhed as Ari's fingers deftly and shamelessly explored, trailing along my aching cleft. A resounding slap to both butt cheeks promptly followed, triggering another scolding as I squirmed.

"*Stay still,*" Ari enunciated, his voice dropping into a low growl. My mouth curled into a satisfied smile; my dominant lover had surfaced, and in that moment the stars felt truly – and positively – aligned.

Then as the broad head of his lubricated cock slowly and gently nudged inside of my tight rosebud, I buried my face into my pillow and groaned. The intensity and the nirvana I experienced as Ari sank deeper was unbelievable. I deliberately pushed back knowing it would earn me another spanking, only it was harsher, rapidly reminding me who was in charge.

I smiled; perfect.

"I know you don't want to go either, but we must. I have work to complete, as do you."

Ari had sensed my gloomy mood the moment we vacated the bed. It hadn't improved by the time we started packing our bags either; if anything, it had worsened. He tried whatever he could to appease me – including a promise of more... attention... when we arrived home.

"Besides Miss Pouty, we shall soon have an entire month off to enjoy each other over the Christmas break."

"Hmm, yeah you're right, as always," I conceded, sighing as I watched Ari neatly place the last item from the bed into his leather overnight bag and zip it up. "This weekend has just been so good... and I hate the thought that we have to leave our little bubble." In all honesty, I sounded more like a whiny brat than a grown woman in her mid-twenties, but I was far too busy crawling up the bed and snaking my arms around Ari's waist to care.

"We can revisit this magical place another time, okay?" He bent down and pressed a chaste kiss to my pouty mouth. "I had a lot of fun also. Come on – let's go."

5

Ari

With an unexpected pregnancy sprung upon us, a decisive chat with Teddy about our living situation had grown necessary. Living between two houses was no longer practical, nor was sharing a home with our impetuous sisters. An arrangement that was hellish enough without adding an innocent child to the equation. And with Poppy also sharing, there was barely enough room for a nursery, let alone any semblance of space.

During my search for something suitable, I discovered two properties that might meet our needs: a block of nearly six acres at Mickleham, and a five-bedroom house directly opposite the beach in the lovely suburb of Hampton. Each naturally had their pros and cons. One required an entirely new build; the other was outdated and in dire need of renovating – top to bottom, judging by the photos. My intuition told me Teddy would take one look at the amount of work required to reach her standards and simply suggest we demolish it. On the upside, both were only a twenty-minute drive to the city on a good day.

I had barely finished my enquiry email to the real estate agent in a brief email when, as usual, Asher barged into my office, unannounced, munching on an apple as if he were a Highland cow chewing on a patch of grass in the green fields of the English countryside.

"Hey boss, whatcha looking at?"

Raising a brow sharply, I jerked my chin towards the door. "Do you know Thomas, my assistant?"

Amid the strange look I received, Asher scoffed. "Is that a rhetorical question?"

"Surely you're aware he's there for a reason, and not merely to answer calls?" I growled, rolling my fingers fluidly over the keyboard as I replied to another email – ironically forwarded to me by my faithful assistant.

He shrugged nonchalantly. "Yeah, and? I thought I had carte blanche to your office like always. Surely that hasn't changed – has it?"

Hitting send, I ran both hands through my hair and snorted. "No, it hasn't changed, but what if I was otherwise preoccupied?" A lazy smile formed and broadened as I watched the penny drop – slowly, and only halfway.

"Oh, you mean in case Teddy's here?" He gestured around my office with a pointed finger.

I met his obvious statement with an impatient roll of my eyes. "Yes, numbnuts, that's precisely why."

"That's an occupational hazard with you these days." Another nonchalant shrug rolled over his well-built shoulders. "Just put a sock on the door handle like we did in our uni days."

"How professional of you." I grimaced, shuffling completed contracts from my in-tray to my out-tray. "Now, besides annoying the absolute shit out of me, why the intrusion?"

"Well, since you asked so nicely..." Asher's amused gaze glanced across the desk as he flopped into a chair. "... I'll tell you. I come bearing gifts: possible candidates for filling James' position and postgrad students' applications." He took another loud bite of his apple as slid the iPad – gripped in one of his sticky hands – across the desk. "Some look rather promising, particularly the chicks from Perth, Alexandra Kiddell and Karsten Shaw; both have rather appealing credentials."

My eyebrows shot up as I read between the lines. Would there ever be a time my manwhore friend rose his head above his waistline? I sighed. "You looked them up, didn't you?"

His excited nod unequivocally confirmed my question. I stared reproachfully and shook my head. Unbelievable.

"I base my judgement on their talent alone, Asher, not their looks. And as my lawyer, you ought to understand discriminatory law better than anyone."

"Oh, I do. You just misunderstood me, is all." His sphinx-like smile was somewhat disconcerting. "Anyway, back on track, my man. Considering we have several options based in the sunny state of WA, I had a thought."

"A dangerous task, I'm sure."

"Ha fucking ha! Anyway, smart arse, I was thinking – instead of flying them here, we go over there. Whatcha think, bossman?"

"I've always liked Perth...." I languidly murmured, giving a bob of the head, indicative of my approval. ".... Sure, why not. You organise the interviews and pass on the finer details to Thomas to organise – flights, accommodation etc."

A scarily eager Asher leapt from the chair and rubbed his hands together. "I'm considering taking up ornithology as a hobby during our visit. They have a particularly rare breed of bird I'm interested in researching – I hear they're rather alluring, and the best part is, they mostly reside at Perth's most prestigious beaches."

"I wasn't aware your fetish extended to seagulls," I drawled.

He waltzed towards the door, laughing. "Nah, I prefer a bird who has the gift for deep throating; a pelican, for example..."

As mortifying, and crude as the visual picture was, it failed to prevent an eruption of roaring laughter. "Get out gigolo! Your damned pheromones are stinking up my office!"

Unable to help himself, Asher stuck his head back around the door and squawked.

I roared in stifled amusement. "Out!"

Life was never dull with that clown. That said, I had a mountain of work to scrape through before the day was over, and his antics certainly weren't helping my concentration. Still shaking with laughter, I scanned over my schedule. To my surprise, I discovered I had a few spare minutes before my next appointment and made use of my time by checking my emails. Again, to my surprise, Drew Griffyn, the Managing Director of Griffyn Real Estate, had promptly replied to my request, informing me that both properties were available to view that very afternoon if it suited me.

Before committing, I picked up the phone and called Teddy. "Hey gorgeous, are you busy?"

"No, not really. I've been staring at the same set of damned plans for the last ten minutes if that's any indication. So, what's up, handsome?"

Her endearment prompted a warm smile. "Do you think you could leave work a little earlier today? There's something I would dearly love to put past you before making a life-altering decision."

"Am I allowed to know?"

I chuckled upon hearing the amusement in her voice. "No, it's a surprise."

She tutted disapprovingly. "Party pooper. Aha…well, I'll wait for you to pick me up in say, an hour?"

Pleased, my smile broadened. "You know me – always punctual."

Teddy's sweet laugh echoed down the phone. "Don't I know it? I had better get some work done then, hadn't I? I would hate to be late or fired. Love you."

"Love you, too."

At least I kept my promise. Unlike Teddy, who left me waiting at the kerb for another ten minutes, and like the patient man I'm not, I called her. "Where in the devil are you?" I gruffly asked.

"I'm coming now, as we speak. Be there in two," she breathlessly answered before hanging up on me.

Unimpressed by the lack of punctuality, my lips flattened into a hard line. Without question, her rushing was due to a distraction – a frequent occurrence of late. I frowned. Perhaps there *was* such a thing as baby brain after all. I might simply have to delve into some research after dinner. Who doesn't love a little homework after a gruelling day at the office?

Just as I tucked my phone into my trouser pocket, a flash of copper hair caught my eye. Surprise, surprise – Teddy was indeed rushing. She barrelled through the glass doors directly into my arms, kissing me as though we hadn't seen each other in months.

She pulled back nervously, eyeing my disgruntled expression, "Sorry, time slipped away from me."

"I thought as much," I dryly murmured tucking a loose curl that had slipped from her ponytail behind her ear. "Now, get into the car, or we'll be late. Traffic's hell as it is."

Her nose scrunched guiltily as she lowered into the passenger seat. "I said I was sorry."

"I know you did, doesn't mean you can't make it up to me later," I growled before closing the door – only to chuckle as her audacious smile radiated through the tinted glass.

Rounding the bonnet, I slid into the driver's seat and buckled up before turning the key and chucking the car into gear. A horn blared behind me as I swerved into the busy traffic. "Fuck off and get in line!"

"Ooh, someone's grouchy!" Teddy quipped.

"And whose fault might that be, I wonder?" I asked pointedly, settling into the flow of painfully slow-moving vehicles.

Hazel eyes mockingly rolled, challenging me. "Our impending child's, that's who."

I tutted. "Poor little mite's not even here yet, and already you're using our son as an excuse for slowing you down. Shame on you."

"A *he*, huh?" Teddy scoffed, lightly patting her still-flat belly. "This little tot might be a *she* for all we know."

"Hence why we're running late then," I wryly countered motioning to the chaotic traffic surrounding us.

"Ouch, you're so sexist, Mr Jaeger. And here I thought you were all about equality..." she argued through a yawn.

"Oh, I am," I assured her as she yawned again. "A bit tired, love?"

"Yeah, I'm drained. I might close my eyes for a minute. You don't mind, do you?"

Curling a hand over her shapely thigh, I shook my head. “No, it’s fine. I’ll wake you once we’ve arrived at our destination, okay?”

Her head tipped into her palm as she closed her eyes, humming a weary reply that made me chuckle. My poor petal. Yet another unpleasant side effect of early pregnancy.

I hit the freeway and pushed my foot down on the accelerator, though the journey still took the better part of an hour thanks to suffocating peak hour traffic. Relief hit the moment we veered off the bustling Nepean Highway and onto St Kilda Street – much quieter, thankfully. Quiet enough to appreciate the rumble hiding under the bonnet at least.

Finally parked at the kerb of our first stop, I failed to resist the enticing sight of Teddy’s parted pink lips and leaned over the console, pressing mine to hers in a slow, coaxing kiss. The persuasion of my sedate kiss was rousing enough as glazed, sleepy eyes fluttered open and peered up at me. I smiled warmly – she looked adorable.

“We’re here,” I murmured, brushing my knuckles along her cheek. “Do you want a hand?”

She nodded amidst another yawn. “Yes, please.”

“Well, allow me,” I offered, slipping out of the car and circling around to open her door.

Her hand slid into mine as she unfolded her lithe body from the seat. A gust of wind caught the hem of her short peplum skirt – and predictably, the attention of a passing jogger. His eyes widened, practically bulging from their sockets as he paused to ogle at the enticing view of her long, shapely legs and the soft curve of her pert behind. I hastily pushed the skirt back down and lifted my sunglasses, fixing him with a dark glare. He wisely heeded my silent warning and promptly hot-footed it out of there. My hand lingered protectively in place as an oblivious Teddy shielded her eyes and looked around.

"Ari, where are we?"

I grinned. "We're in the lovely suburb of Hampton." I stiffly swivelled and swept a free hand towards the ranch-style house. "And this is the surprise I wanted to show you – a house, obviously. One that unfortunately needs work. A lot by the looks of the rather dated and austere façade."

"You're not wrong there," she agreed, screwing up her nose at me. "You *are* aware Mid-century isn't exactly my favourite genre, aren't you? Well, you should, considering our many discussions!" she added with a scornful flick.

Ignoring the snippy attitude, I inhaled sharply and turned as a silver Audi SUV pulled up alongside us. The engine cut out, and a stout, middle-aged man in an expensively tailored suit stepped out. His thick, slicked-back hair gleamed in the sun as he closed the door and strode towards us with confidence.

"Mr Jaeger, I presume?" He beamed, thrusting out a hand. "Drew Griffyn, owner and Manager of Griffyn Real Estate."

"It's a pleasure," I responded, reciprocating with a firm shake before politely introducing Teddy. "And this lovely lady beside me is my girlfriend, Teddy McGovern."

"Lovely to make your acquaintance, Ms McGovern," he articulated, slipping her hand into his and shaking it far more demurely – before lifting it to his lips.

Teddy blushed. I sighed. What was with the men around her today? They were behaving as if they'd never seen an attractive woman before. Call it jealousy, but I'd had enough. I tugged

Teddy to my side, forcing Drew to release her hand. His brows shot up – surprised or put out, I couldn't tell. Well, fuck him. Either way, he was lucky I opted for the gentlemanly approach instead of punching him.

"We are here to view a house, are we not?" I queried icily through clenched teeth.

He smoothed a hand over his jacket and flashed a well-rehearsed smile. "Of course."

Not about to let him perv on my girlfriend's behind, I gestured curtly. "After you, Mr Griffyn."

He took the hint and prudently walked ahead. He wasn't the only one to pick up on my ill-tempered mood.

"Was that caveman behaviour necessary, Ari?" Teddy hissed, folding her arms across her chest. She checked to ensure that Drew was out of earshot before continuing, "Drew was only being friendly."

I scoffed sarcastically. "Oh, I noticed."

"Just because he held onto my hand –"

"And kissed it! Although, you might want to sanitise. Who knows where those lips have been!"

"You're never this bent out of shape when your father's kisses me!"

"My father's a gentleman, that's why!" Her mouth tightened before she huffed. "Can we go view this house now, please, instead of arguing?"

"Fine! But no more caveman bullshit! And get out of your bad mood – you've been cranky ever since you picked me up."

I scrubbed my hair and sighed. My foul mood had been uncalled for, that's for sure. Teddy's upset expression sobered me instantly. "I'm sorry."

Her passionate kiss said all was forgiven, and with both of us smiling, we made the ascent up the curved, cracked concrete driveway. The front door, painted in a grotesquely bright blue, loomed ahead with Drew eagerly awaiting us in the foyer – which was just as outlandish.

“I’ll wait here, and feel free to ask me any questions once you’ve completed your tour.” He swiftly stepped aside into another room and answered a phone call, his exuberant voice booming throughout the empty house whilst we freely wandered.

An eager Teddy launched with her suggested changes. The colour was merely the beginning. Upstairs, the layout and bedroom sizes were another issue entirely. I endeavoured to keep up with her – barely.

“It doesn’t work—any of it,” she categorically stated. “If we knock out a wall here in the main bedroom and take away space from the bedroom next door, we could rebuild the entire ensuite, making it substantially bigger and add a decently sized walk-in-robe to suit both our needs. We’d need to ensure the walls weren’t load-bearing beforehand though.” She sighed sadly. “Even better yet…”

“Knock it down and start again?”

“Yeah, that’s what I was thinking.” She gave me a wry, conceding look – the type that said I’d read her perfectly. “The entire layout of this house is such a mishmash. For it to make any sense, it would require ripping out and rebuilding every single wall – upstairs and downstairs. Not ideal, is it?”

“Not particularly no. But we have the advantage of remaining in either of our houses whilst we rebuild at least,” I remarked as Teddy’s nose scrunched at the distasteful musty smell seeping from inside one of the small wardrobes. “Unlike the unlucky few, who unfortunately have no other choice but to live amongst the rubble and the constant dust until completion.”

“That’s true, too,” she murmured thoughtfully, looking out over the busy road at the gentle surf. “It’s not aesthetically pleasing either; it needs to fit in with its surrounding environment.”

“That we can both agree on,” I replied, slipping my hands inside my trouser pockets. I observed her as she listlessly wandered. Eventually, she paused in the doorway of the ensuite. Decorated with garishly bright blue tiles, the current size of the bathroom was barely big enough for one person, let alone two.

“Yeah, that’s true...”

“I sense a ‘but’ coming on?”

Pivoting on one of the spikes of her heels, she propped a slim shoulder against the mud-coloured doorframe and stared apologetically. “I’m not sure I could be bothered with the headaches renovating brings either, particularly now we have a baby on the way.”

“Whatever you want. You’re the architect – you know what works or what doesn’t.”

Teddy’s dim mood rapidly evaporated as she strolled in long strides towards the large windows. “Imagine,” she breathed, enthusiasm blooming as her designer’s eye took over, her arms spreading wide to showcase her vision, “Clearing the entire block and building a house that actually embraces the stunning view outside?”

Standing alongside her, I envisioned the picturesque view instantly. “With our bedroom taking front and centre stage, blessing us with that splendid sight every morning.”

"Precisely," she chimed, looping her arms around my shoulders. "How perfect – or enticing – does…." Her mouth ghosted over mine in slow, suggestive kisses, each one drawing out her next word. "…. Lazing about. In bed. Eating breakfast. Making love. Every. Single. Morning. Sound?"

A pointed throat-clear reminded us we weren't alone. We turned to find our overzealous agent smiling broadly at us.

"Mr Jaeger, Ms McGovern, I take it you're both pleased with the house?"

"The house, no, but the location, yes," I conveyed respectfully. "Do you mind if I email you tonight once Ms McGovern and I have discussed this further?"

"Of course. But please be aware this house has other interested parties who are considering placing a substantial offer."

My eyes rolled. Clearly, Mr Griffyn was ignorantly unaware of my reputation. "Mr Griffyn, *please*, I researched the property market *thoroughly* prior to our contact, and this anaemic residence…" I gave a vague wave of my hand. "Has been listed for quite some time, correct?" I fought the smile threatening to grace my face as he reluctantly nodded. Slipping my hands back into my pockets, I stared him down. "So, knowing that's not the case, I shall inform you sometime later this evening with an offer. How's that for you?"

Caught out, he rapidly cleared the lump of bullshit choking his throat. "Of course, Mr Jaeger."

I smiled triumphantly. "Right, now that's sorted, we ought to get going so we can view another property."

Teddy raised a questionable brow, sandwiching one of my hands between hers. "Where's this one, may I ask?"

"Mickleham." I smirked. "So, either way, Mr Griffyn, there shall be a sale by the day's end."

"Thank you, Mr Jaeger."

With that, we left our grinning agent behind – his eyes lighting up like a pokie machine about to pay out. With the commission from the new property and the sale of my Beaumaris house, he might be able to retire.

Well, almost.

Whilst I quietly stood aside, Teddy quietly inspected everything the empty block in Mountainview Lane had to offer – or, more accurately, everything it currently lacked. Aside from the cows lowing in a distant paddock and the occasional crow cawing above the screeching cockatoos perched in the gum trees overhead, there wasn't a sound for miles. Not even the faint hum of the bustling freeway. To my mind, a cul-de-sac this far from the city meant tranquillity: the perfect place to recharge one's batteries after a long day at the office.

"What's the land size again, Ari?" she asked, carefully tiptoeing through a blend of long grass and weeds in strappy four-inch heels.

"Just under six acres. Plenty of space for a big house with a growing family." Linking our fingers, I led Teddy by the hand, steering her towards the fence line. We stopped before a sagging, rust-flecked wire fence held up by antiquated, rotting boxwood posts. "Well, which one would you prefer: the beach house or the rural property? The choice is yours. Or I could painfully continue my search if neither suit you."

She contemplated, chewing the corner of a glossed, plump bottom lip. "Living close to the beach would be lovely. However, the location along that main road was horrid; all that bustling traffic would eventually drive me bonkers, even with double-glazed windows. And unless my mother takes the Cowes house as part of the divorce settlement, we'll still have that as our beachside residence."

"If that occurs, we'll buy a house there, too."

Teddy's lips curved into a radiant smile. Pushing up onto her toes, she pressed her lips softly to mine. "Thank you."

"You're welcome," I murmured, gliding an arm around her narrow waist. "So, which one?"

"Let's buy this property. Albeit it's quite the mess, it doesn't mean we can't make this place beautiful. It also has another advantage," she added sassily.

I cocked my head and waggled my eyebrows. "Besides the wide-open spaces without having to worry about pesky neighbours catching us naked outside, what other reason is there?"

Teddy shrieked with laughter. "No!" Her tune changed rather quickly after giving my idea some thought. "Hmm, that is an advantage I suppose..."

I chuckled.

"But it also means there's enough room to build a set of stables for that temperamental horse of yours." She giggled as I lifted her off the ground and spun us around – only to stop abruptly when she clapped a hand to her mouth. Even the threat of vomiting didn't stop her from mocking my prized thoroughbred stallion. "Bear's just like his owner; cantankerous and whines a lot."

Laughter rumbled in my chest. "What do you expect? We're both British."

I was barely off the phone from our overeager agent when I made the mistake of walking directly into a room full of incessantly nattering women. My exuberant sister was the first to pounce.

"Ari!" Dominique squealed, throwing slim arms around my waist. "That's so exciting – you and Teddy building a house together. A fresh and untainted start for you both."

I smiled perceptively; she understood all too well. "The prospect is exciting, yes, but what I'm most enthused about is the fact Teddy's designing our home. It shall be one of a kind," I stated proudly. "How about we go out for dinner to celebrate?"

"Yes, please!" she replied gleefully, clapping her hands with far too much enthusiasm. There had to be a catch. "But you're paying, bro!"

A restrained breath escaped; I knew it.

"Um, I'm broke." I tugged at my empty pockets. "See? Moths... Perhaps you could kindly pay instead. Surely you've dipped into that trust fund of yours by now?"

A well-shaped eyebrow raised sharply. "Don't give me that crap, brother! You just doled out a cool half a mil purchasing five acres –"

"It was closer to a million for nearly six, actually," I smugly corrected.

"Whatever," Dom scoffed, waving a dismissive hand. "The point is you just parted with a shitload of cash buying a property in an upcoming suburb – without a frigging house!"

"Precisely why I'm now broke," I countered dryly. Dom's hand smacked my chest with impressive force. "Ow! I'm telling Mum."

Sardonic eyes rolled at me again. "Oh, grow up!"

I watched my sarky sister with merriment marshal her roommates, gleefully informing them, I was indeed paying. The ensuing whoops of delight made my head shake as I remained rooted to the spot, arms crossed, following the wild trio up the stairs. A riotous snort drew my attention to a mirthless Teddy, and immediately, the seductive sway of her narrow hips had me undone.

“I take it Dom didn’t believe you?” she asked, snaking her arms around my neck and toying with the shortened hair at my nape with her fingertips, making me purr like a contented cat.

I let out a humourless laugh. “What do you think?”

Pointedly, she answered, “Have you seen your car, or where you live for that matter?”

“Fair point. I wasn’t very convincing, was I?”

“No, you weren’t,” she murmured, rubbing the length of her slender figure against me. Perhaps we were both cats in another life. “Shower before we go out?”

The corners of my mouth quirked into a lascivious grin as I wound my arms around Teddy’s torso and yanked her closer. “Only if you join me…” I immodestly invited, between soft, chaste kisses.

“Only if we shower.” The scorching fire in her eyes told me otherwise.

“Oh, my darling Teddy, you wound me so.”

∞

Teddy

My head rolled on the pillow and lifted just enough to peer at the clock on my bedside table. An exasperated sigh escaped as I thumped back down. Two in the frigging morning – I was still wide awake! Lovely. I closed my eyes and tapped the edge of the white sheet gripped between my fingers as I attempted to count sheep. Another pointless exercise. Ari, unconscious beside me, began snoring. A low groan slipped out. How in the hell was I meant to sleep with that racket? But as quickly as the thought formed, he stopped, mumbled something incoherent and lurched onto his stomach. I sighed. Peace at last.

Settled again, I rolled onto my side – only for the willy-wagtail camped in the crepe myrtle outside my bedroom window to erupt into a shrill, indignant tirade, as if personally offended by my attempt as sleep.

My eyes snapped open. Apparently, I wasn't entitled to a good night's sleep like Sleeping Beauty beside me. Not that Ari's deadened state surprised me after he'd downed several glasses of champagne at dinner. Unbelievable.

I rolled my eyes and flopped onto my other side, hoping a change of position might help. Nope. Nada. Not gonna do the trick. My brain chose this exact moment to shift into overdrive, spiralling through thoughts of us living together full-time in our new house. The prospect thrilled me – and terrified me in equal measure.

Since deciding on the block in Mountainview Lane, Mickleham, design ideas kept flourishing, *really* exciting me. Then, in typical

Ari fashion, he casually announced over dinner that he'd bought the Hampton property anyway – purely as an investment, he'd explained. He intended to flatten the original house, rebuild a new home based on my design, and resell for a substantial profit. All in a day's work for Ari.

So, given I was wide-awake, I might as well make use of the time and jot down my concepts *before* they slipped away. Forgetting even the simplest of tasks had become a regular occurrence thanks to my little invader turning my brain into mush – frustrating me to no end, and not just because of the forgetfulness. It was a feeling of being ... overtaken. Of my own body doing things without my permission again, and I hated that I couldn't quite explain why.

A nagging need to write in my diary tugged at me too – the negative thoughts had been relentless lately. One, of course, was my unexpected pregnancy. Doubts still lingered. Was I ready for a child? A child meant responsibility, nurturing. Some days I struggled to take care of myself – how was I meant to care for someone else – especially an innocent infant who never asked to exist in a world as cruel as this one? Worse still, I couldn't shake the unsettling feeling that I was *meant* to feel something than this vague, hovering uncertainty.

I understood these doubts weren't unusual, and I wasn't alone. Ari was thrilled about impending fatherhood and would support me in every way possible. He always did. Well... most of the time. I snorted quietly. I could name a few exceptions. Still, writing everything down and speaking with Doctor Montgomery might help me untangle the mess in my head – or at least help me understand why this whole thing felt heavier, more complicated, than I could admit aloud.

I frowned as I slipped out of bed. Just once, I wanted to wake up and face my life without fearing a past that insisted on reminding me there was no future with Ari.

One could hope.

Amidst planning our ensuite bathroom, Ari's warm hands glided over my bare shoulders. "Hi there."

"Why are you awake?" I quizzed, sketching a nib shelf along the main wall of the spacious shower stall.

"I could ask you the same thing," he retorted, raising a questionable brow. "I'm sure whatever you're doing at four o'clock in the morning could have waited until tomorrow..." He yawned, glancing at the clock on the wall above his head. "Or today, for that matter."

Beaming, I swivelled on the stool and thrust out my arm, handing him several rough sketches. "This is the reason."

Flopping into the oxford blue aniline leather highbacked chair beside my desk, Ari took the drawings, his bleary eyes widening as he studied my modern yet French-Provence-inspired designs. "You drew these up in a couple of hours? Teddy, these are remarkable. I knew you'd design us a beautiful home, but these exceed all expectations."

"I couldn't sleep," I admitted, omitting the part about my journal and my spiralling thoughts. "So, I made a start. I sketched a few concepts for the inside as well." I nervously passed him the rest.

"These are impressive. Six bedrooms? Planning on filling them all up, are you?"

"No. Two, maybe three at most." The answer rolled off my tongue far too easily — the one he wanted, not the one I meant.

The unfairness of choosing comfort over honesty caught beneath my ribs.

"I'd have a football team if that's what you desired," Ari whispered, "but two or three is fine," he added quickly, laughing at the horror on my face. He wanted more — I knew he did — but he'd never ask. Not if it meant risking me. And that knowledge pressed heavily against my chest.

"I would certainly hope so or having sex with me would be like throwing a hotdog down a hallway." The laughter came easily enough, but underneath it a sharp, guilty panic flared — because joking was simpler than admitting how much this whole conversation terrified me.

Ari chuckled heartily. "I think that's a slight exaggeration, but may we please go back to bed so I can lovingly roll my sausage between your buns?"

"Oh, my god, you're so damned crude!" I giggled, swatting his arm and switching off the lamp clamped to the desktop. "Do you speak to your mother with that mouth?"

He cheekily grinned. "You know, I do."

My eyes rolled; why'd I bother asking?

6

"Here you go, this should wake you up," I murmured, passing Ari his usual morning coffee in a stainless steel travel mug as he wandered into the kitchen.

He noticed the way I held it out to him – overextended arms, the nose wrinkle – and smiled gently before taking the steaming mug from my hands and setting it on the island behind him. "Morning sickness?"

"Yeah. But whoever coined that term clearly never suffered morning, noon, and night." The aroma hit me and I inhaled sharply, exhaling in a shudder before braving it and stepping into him. Snaking a hand around his neck, I toyed with the short strands at his nape while pressing my other palm against his firm chest, feeling the steady thrum of his heartbeat beneath my fingers. "Anyway, handsome, where's my kiss?"

"Demanding little thing, aren't you?" He smirked and bent his head to meet my puckered lips with a soft, lingering kiss. "Mmm, good morning, gorgeous."

I brushed my thumb along his cheekbone, guilt pricking as I caught the faint shadows beneath his eyes. "I'm sorry I disturbed you last night."

"I didn't mind one bit – especially when we ventured back to bed."

Heat flamed my cheeks. "I'm sure you didn't."

"You look lovely today, by the way." Ari's splayed hands stroked my backside over the top of my white Capri pants. "The blouse, especially."

"Thank you. Your shirts not bad either," I purred, trailing both palms down the front of his slim-fit navy shirt. "It hugs your gorgeous body perfectly."

"It's one of the shirts you bought me, if I recall," he breathed, giving me a look so searing my knees nearly buckled.

"So it was." I nuzzled into his chest, breathing in the heady scent that was Ari Jaeger — citrus and woodsy. Tilting my head, I skimmed the tip of my tongue over his bottom lip, savouring him. "Mmm. Yummy. All my favourite flavours rolled into one."

Ari's eyes glinted. "You make me sound like an ice cream."

I chuckled. "No, you're more like my favourite chocolate — sweet and rich on the outside with a creamy, decadent surprise on the inside."

"So, so bad." He tutted, gripping the back of my neck as he dipped his head to claim my mouth savagely, stealing the breath from my lungs. His skill, his certainty — it always undid me.

I threaded my fingers through his hair and tugged him closer, a soft mewl escaping as the roughness of his beard grazed my jaw. "Just sayin', but we're home... alone."

Hips pressed suggestively. Breathing shifted. The air thickened.

"If only I didn't have to attend a meeting across town..." Ari caged me between his body and the island, the edge digging into my lower back. "I'd have you bent over this bench right – about – now," he illuminated between hard, chaste kisses.

I moaned, softly. “Such a pity we’re out of time then.”

Ari elicited a hoarse growl and withdrew – reluctantly. “Tonight?” One word, and undeniably full of promise.

“Tonight then,” I hummed, waving as he headed out the door — a flutter of guilt catching in my chest as it closed behind him.

∞

Ari

Summer had indeed made its presence known. The heat had settled over the city like a thick blanket, punctuated by short, teasing showers that only served to make the air rancid.

Opting for a short-sleeved shirt and tan chinos was undoubtedly the right call – Teddy’s reaction alone had confirmed that – but the stares from my staff as I crossed the foyer were equally telling. Accustomed to the well-tailored suit version of me, my casual attire was clearly an anomaly to them. Their hushed whispers amused me, so I greeted them with a bright smile and a cheerful hello as I made my way towards the elevators. My chuckle echoed softly as I pressed the button.

While I waited, my gaze drifted around the airy foyer and a warm swell of pride rose in my chest. I’d achieved what others thought impossible, and all within a year of completing my MBA. Planning and due diligence had played their part, sure, but JPD only ran like a well-oiled machine because of my wonderful employees. Without them, the entire company would collapse faster than any sceptic could say I told you so. Anyone who dared to believe that owning a business was a mere pipedream could go kiss my arse.

The same applied to the sceptics who doubted the expansion. Yet here I was – the proud owner of two more colossal towers, both standing proudly in Sydney's central business district, with sweeping views overlooking Circular Quay, Darling Harbour and its surrounding areas. Whenever inquisitive minds queried as to who they belonged to, I took momentous pride in telling them every square inch was mine. Incredulous looks typically followed. The design input was mine too, but the credit for the build belonged to my retiring architect and engineer, James Newman – a man whose steady hand had shaped more of my success than he'd ever admit.

Losing him was a blow, but circumstances were beyond our control. His wife of forty years, Helena, an MS sufferer, was declining rapidly, and home was where he needed to be. He'd spent more time there than in the office these past months, and begrudging him for putting family first would have made me a hypocrite. Instead of making him wait until March, I granted him an early retirement — which he accepted gratefully — along with a financial contribution to help him through the difficult period. His early departure simply meant bringing forward our search for a replacement.

Still, nothing could dampen my buoyant mood. Even Thomas noticed as I stepped off the elevator and crossed the small foyer, reaching for the stack of messages in his hand.

"Good morning, Mr Jaeger."

His mirroring smile amused me. Perhaps something was in the water?

"Good morning, Thomas," I cheerily replied, dropping the latest addition to my newest look at my feet – a green khaki messenger bag courtesy of Teddy. Compared to my stuffy briefcase, it was far more hip, giving me a younger appearance, apparently. I suspected my father and uncle were next on her hit list. "What's my schedule for today?"

He passed me the open iPad over the counter. "You have one cancellation: Mr Chandler. He's rescheduled for tomorrow morning, citing personal reasons, and sends his apologies."

"Thank you. I'm assuming you've organised the staff Christmas party invites?"

"Done. Sent out last week with RSVP's flying back already. Most are a yes, of course."

Pleased, I smiled. "The Dome? Is it –"

"Already booked," Thomas pre-empted, pushing his round, black spectacles up the ridge of his crooked nose.

Impressed by his efficiency, I beamed. "Thomas, you are a gem! Without you, I'd be lost and tearing my hair out by now."

"You are most welcome, sir." He blushed, clearly tickled pink, which made me laugh. I was full of surprises today.

"I'll leave you to it then," I joyfully murmured, picking up my messenger bag. With a satisfied smile, I strode into my office and closed the door, hanging my bag on the hook on the wall beside it.

Settled into my chair, I leaned back and traced my bottom lip with my forefinger, my eyes drifting to the framed picture beside my computer. My favourite. A rare moment captured minutes after Teddy and I had made love for only the second time – both of us smiling up at the camera clasped in my hand, dishevelled and content, blissfully unaware of the imminent dramas that lay ahead.

A disheartened sigh escaped as ran a hand through my hair.

Despite the long discussions Teddy and I had had about our future, something in me still clung to the past. With a baby on the way, the topic surfaced more often now, hovering between us like a question neither of us knew how to answer. Marriage, however, remained largely untouched — not because I didn't want it, but because Teddy's uncertainty made it feel almost taboo. And Mother didn't help matters. She'd been the loudest instigator the first time around, and once the family learned about the baby, the pressure to marry would only intensify — old-fashioned expectations wrapped in well-meaning interference. The thought of Teddy being cornered by the family's relentless expectations made my stomach twist. Whenever either of us edged towards the subject, her doubt rose first, tangled with insecurities she never meant to weaponise, and the conversation inevitably unravelled into a disagreement.

Thomas buzzed interrupting my thoughts. "Sir, Mr Bradford is here to see you."

I chuckled, amused by both the hilarity in Thomas's voice and the mere fact my wayward friend had adhered to my request. I pressed the keypad. "Thank you, Thomas. Send him in, please."

Asher entered quietly. "Hey bossman, how's it hangin'?" Well, almost quietly.

"Where it's always been – between my legs," I retorted blandly, watching my longtime friend stride towards me with his usual swagger.

"What can I do you for?"

Sliding into the chair adjacent to my desk, he leaned casually, slinging an arm over the low backrest. "Thanks to your wonderfully efficient PA organising the necessary arrangements, we're all set to head to Perth for these interviews: business class of course."

Not surprised, I scoffed sardonically. "A suggestion you orchestrated, no doubt."

"Naturally."

Eyeing him suspiciously, I cocked a brow sharply. "I sense a hidden agenda."

It was Asher's turn to scoff. "You know me..." That I did.

With a resigned wave, I motioned for him to continue. "Enlighten me."

Asher straightened in his chair, practically vibrating with barely contained delight — a habitual signal I recognised far too well. Whatever was about to come out of his mouth would be fuelled entirely by his libido.

"Firstly, the booze. Secondly, the gorgeous, leggy airline hostesses. With any luck, one might join me in the Mile-High Club."

I couldn't help the amused huff that escaped me; trust Asher to turn a business trip into a sexual expedition before we'd even booked the seats.

"Righto." He glanced down at the iPad balanced in his lap. "Monday, next week – that suit you?"

I acknowledged with a curt nod. "Fine. I'm assuming we'll be there for a few days, yes?"

"We arrive Monday afternoon, so I figured we relax, have dinner, start fresh Tuesday. Space interviews until Wednesday afternoon, fly home Thursday morning. Sound good?"

I voiced my approval. "Sounds good. So, where are we staying? Leaving the details with Teddy's imperative."

A ghost of a smile danced on Asher's lips. ".... Whittemore's on Adelaide Terrace." His choice of accommodation hadn't surprised me either.

What began as a small luxury hotel in South Kensington in the late nineteenth century — all polished mahogany counters, gaslight glow, and the soft clatter of hansom cabs over the cobblestone streets — had been founded by my cousin's great-great-great-grandfather. What started as a modest family venture had grown into Whittemore's Hotels, one of the fastest-expanding chains in the world. Damon, his wild and womanising great-great-great-grandson, managed the Perth branch with his quirky parents, Sebastian and Catherine. Philandering aside, he was a visionary. His recent purchase of fifty-six hectares on Phillip Island for four million proved it. He'd also contracted my company to build the one-hundred-room resort — though we were stalled until Port Phillip Council approved the plans.

I scribbled a reminder to call them later.

"I'll flick Damon a text, informing him of our visit," I stated happily. "I haven't seen the old boy in ages, so a catch up is well overdue."

"Hence my reasoning behind us staying a few days." I chuckled as Asher continued, "Damo's quite the character, so it'll be good to let our hair down."

My brows shot up. "Where he's concerned, we'll be doing a lot more than that, I can assure you."

A dirty laugh escaped Asher's quirking lips. "Demon Damon has always been a hoot to hang out with."

I snorted derisively; Eve hadn't called us the troublesome trio without reason.

"Is that all?" I queried, shifting the subject. "I've got a few tasks to finish before day's end. Otherwise, Teddy shall kick my arse if I spend another late night at the office."

Asher's azure gaze twinkled. "I swear your brain's visible man, 'cause that thumbprint...has grown to a cavernous size."

I hurled my pen directly at his head. "Haven't you got someone else to annoy?"

"Only the lovely lady at the coffee shop downstairs." He grinned, ducking. "But she's not free for another hour."

∞

Teddy

Having spent the morning running around in the scorching heat, I thumped down into the chair and leaned back, grateful for the cooling vent above as it fanned my overheated face. "It's bloody boiling out there."

"I feel sorry for anyone who doesn't have the luxury of air-conditioning," Emily rambled, slouching in her seat and propping her Roman-sandal-clad feet up on the desk.

"I'm glad I have it – and the pool, which I'll be jumping into the second I get home." I sighed and took a long sip of the bottled water I'd grabbed from the café downstairs. "Do you mind if we have lunch downstairs in the café today? This weather is making me nauseous, and I don't feel up to walking far." Strangely enough, I was starving. Pregnancy was weird that way.

"Sure."

Considering how hungry I was, I barely touched my food. Instead of eating my choice of salad – quinoa, brown rice and grilled salmon, I just stared at it, letting my thoughts drift. The café noise blurred into a low hum: chatter, clattering dishes, scraping chairs... all of it fading into the background.

Emily faded too.

Honestly, I think I'd switched off before she even started eating her Thai beef salad and talking about the guy she'd been seeing for a few weeks. She might have told me about him before. I couldn't remember. My mind had been too full — past, present, future all tangled together. Even though time had passed since telling Ari everything, the fallout clung to me. And the tension brewing in his family — tension I'd caused — ran alongside my morning sickness: persistent, draining, impossible to ignore.

Apparently, Ari's family weren't the only ones feeling things.

Emily's sudden frustration snapped through the haze, her fork slamming onto the boho-patterned ceramic plate.

I jolted. "Was that necessary, Emily?"

"Have you heard anything I've said? At all?"

My brows pulled together as I met her blazing stare. "Honestly? No. I must've zoned out for a minute."

"Oh, it's great to see you're interested in whatever I have to say," she shot back, hurt sharpening her voice.

"I wasn't doing it intentionally." I dropped my cutlery with a tight breath.

She scoffed. "What, just because my life isn't as exciting as yours, it's not worth listening to?"

"I've always shown an interest in your life," I argued, lowering my voice as I realised people were staring. "And please keep it down. People are watching." The second it left my mouth, I winced. I sounded like my mother.

Emily's aggrieved gaze flicked around the café. "Yeah, so? They should mind their own business."

"Don't be childish, Ems." The words came out low, tight with warning. "I do listen to you. I'm sorry I wasn't earlier. I've just got a lot going on right now — no excuse, I know."

"You've been distracted for months. I thought we talked about everything, and lately you've shut me out."

I sighed and twisted the napkin in my lap, trying to find the right words. Emily's patience had clearly run thin; her huff made that obvious.

"Well?" she pressed. "Are you going to tell me what's going on, or keep acting like my feelings don't matter?"

I closed my eyes and inhaled deeply. *Count, Teddy. Just breathe.*

In the end, the briefest explanation was better than nothing. "Something terrible happened to me when I was fifteen, and now..." I swallowed hard. "...the pain of my past has resurfaced. I don't want to go into detail — it's not pretty. But can you trust that when I'm ready, I'll tell you more?"

A defeated Emily lifted both hands. "Fine. I'll accept that for now. Just remember I'm here for you too, okay?"

I nodded stiffly and picked up my fork again, quietly returning to my salad.

7

The day had grown long, and it was about to stretch even further. When the last two staff members strolled past my cubicle, I remained anchored to my chair, offering a vague bye to their exuberant waving and overly cheerful goodbyes. I waited for the soft clink of the glass door opening — and only when it shut behind them, did I release a long breath.

Quiet at last.

Or so I naïvely thought.

I was about to reconfigure the laundry and add a mudroom off the three-car garage when the soft, deliberate click of heels tapped across the timber floorboards. My stomach plummeted.

“Hello? Who’s there?”

Silence.

I tried again — still nothing. The silence pressed in, triggering a sharp, rising panic.

God, please... don’t let it be Emmett.

The fear alone should’ve kept me rooted to my chair. But I forced myself to stand, my steps tentative as I moved into the hallway and into the common area — just as the lone figure strolled towards me.

She shifted direction, cutting me off with calculated ease. My footsteps halted.

Entrapped, I glared. “What in the hell are you doing here?”

“Now that’s a terrible way to greet your mother, Theodora,” she replied tartly, dropping her expensive designer purse onto the coffee table. The midi-length camel-coloured linen dress — contrast stitching and all — swayed as she slipped her slender hands into the front pockets, regarding me with that cold, emotionless stare she’d perfected.

Honestly, she looked more like gingerbread than a woman of supposedly high stature.

“I’ll ask again, Mother — what in the hell are you doing here?” I demanded, crossing my arms rigidly over my chest.

Her green eyes swept the room. “Are you alone, dear?” she asked, the mockery unmistakable as she ignored my question entirely.

“That’s the only reason you’re here, isn’t it, Mother? Because I’m alone?” I motioned to the empty cubicles. “No witnesses means no need for pretence, doesn’t it?”

Her expression confirmed everything I feared.

I shook my head and snorted, earning another scornful look. “Yeah, that’s what I thought. So no need to fret, Mother Dearest — you’ll be able to swan out of here with your virtue completely unscathed by scandal.”

She skimmed a slim finger over the back of the club lounge, eliciting a humourless laugh. “Still full of dramatics, I see. And where are your manners? Not offering a drink in this blistering heat — such poor etiquette, Theodora.”

“We aren’t in the habit of serving witches’ brew here.”

Her eyes narrowed. "Hmph. Such a childish remark — but one can't expect anything less from you, I suppose."

My impatience spiked, along with the darker thoughts I tried to swallow. "What do you want?"

She tapped her scarlet-painted finger against her chin as a malicious smile spread. "A little birdy told me some rather disturbing news, so I thought I'd come by to see how you were faring. But judging by your current demeanour, I'd say... not very well."

I paled, a bitter laugh escaping. "How altruistic of you, Mother."

She gasped. "Trying to take your own life, Theodora, is no laughing matter. It's offensive, and a sin in the eyes of God," she tutted, lifting her eyes and hands heavenward. "And what about poor Ari? What must his family think of you dating their beloved son now? They must be urging him to run." A derisive sigh escaped my mother's tightened lips. "I know I would..." Her words sliced deeper than any knife she'd ever used on my heart.

My face dropped and my shoulders sank under the weight of her words.

She smirked. "I've hit a nerve, haven't I?"

Instinctively, I shielded my stomach — as if my unborn child needed protection from Satan herself.

A grave mistake.

Her horrified gasp filled the room.

Mother approached in slow, measured steps, driving the blade deeper. "You're pregnant, too?"

Heat flooded my cheeks, giving my precious secret away.

"How dare you contemplate something so selfish!" she scoffed. "Particularly when you're barely stable enough to take care of yourself!"

My eyes misted as doubt clawed its way in.

She was right... wasn't she? What was I thinking? I wasn't in the right place or mind to be having a child — not now, maybe not ever.

And she knew it. She revelled in the knowledge of my suffering. The heat in my cheeks blurred into something indistinct — shame, fury, I couldn't tell. Everything she touched became indistinguishable pain.

"I'm not dignifying your inquisitive mind with an answer. Presume all you want — you aren't worthy of my time or the energy I waste trying to talk to you."

"Oh, come now, Theodora — that's an admission if I've ever heard one. You're pregnant when clearly, you shouldn't be. Have you forgotten what happened to your last child? She died because your body was incapable of taking care of something so precious. Do you want that to happen again?"

By now, my betraying tears streamed freely. How could a mother be so callous? She knew exactly what she was doing — excavating the most painful memories she could find, just to watch me bleed.

My anger boiled over, venom spilling as toxic as the woman standing before me. "You condescending bitch! How dare you come here — to the one place not tainted by your malice and lies — under false pretence? Then you add salt to the wound by self-righteously mocking me. Is this how you get off, Mother? Hurting me? Just get the hell out of my life and stay out of it. I don't need you. I hate you!"

In the blink of an eye, my head snapped sideways. The imprint of her hand burned across my cheek, igniting a wave of corrupted anger I unleashed on the woman who was supposed to be my mother.

She no longer deserved the title.

I cupped my burning cheek and met her hardened expression with a glacial stare. “Get. The. Fuck. Out.”

She didn’t move. “Are you quite done, Theodora?”

My teeth clenched. “I said — get the fuck out.”

A malicious smirk curled her lips as she seized my wrists, her grip cruel and unyielding.

I struggled against her hold. “Let me go — or else.”

Unfazed, her cold stare dropped to the faded scars. “Hmm. You do realise you cut in the wrong direction, don’t you?”

Suddenly, whatever bravery I’d scraped together collapsed in on itself.

My hands shook so violently they barely felt like mine, sweat slicking my palms. My breath hitched, sharp and uneven, my throat tightening as my heart slammed against my ribs — too fast, too loud, too much. Each inhale scraped like it had to fight its way in. “You... bitch. Leave me... the hell alone.”

She rolled her eyes and dropped my arms as if they bored her.

Her lips kept moving — sharp, clipped, cruel — but it reached me through a thickening fog. The words drifted in fragments, catching on the edges of my awareness without fully landing. *Embarrassing... neurotic... needs someone better than you...*

I watched her bend for her purse, straighten, speak again — but the movements lagged, as though the room had slowed while my pulse raced ahead. My vision tunnelled, the edges of the common area blurring into nothing.

Her smirk blurred. Her heels clicked — too loud, too far away, too unreal.

The door opened. Closed. And I stood frozen, staring at the distorted reflection she'd left behind... the one I'd always dreaded facing, and feared was true.

"Teddy...wake up."

A lilted, timbred male voice drifted, first, threading through the staticky fog. Then came the soft brush of knuckles against my cheek – too gentle, too familiar, too much. A raw groan tore from me as I swatted the hand away. "Don't touch me!"

"Teddy! Wake up!" The voice sharpened, louder, urgent. The sound ricocheted painfully inside my head.

My eyelids fluttered open, and my vision swam as I tried to decipher the figure looming above me. "What the f...?" I rasped, sitting upright far too quickly. The room spun in a nauseating spiral, forcing me to drop back down as queasiness surged, thick and merciless. Ari's presence, although grounding, felt suffocating. Even the cologne I usually adored turned cloying.

"You're as white as a sheet, what's wrong?"

I was about to respond when the nausea surged past the point of no return. I jolted upright, clapping a hand to my mouth and shoving Ari aside with the other. The bathroom door slammed open under my weight, then the stall door, just as my trembling knees buckled and I collapsed towards the bowl.

Ari rushed in behind me, crouching awkwardly to hold my hair back in a makeshift ponytail while I clung to the porcelain, heaving. For how little I expelled, it drained me entirely. When the retching finally subsided, I slumped against the cubicle barrier, sweat cooling on my lathered skin. The tiles looked blissfully cold, and I began lowering myself toward them when Ari caught my shoulders.

"You want to lie across the floor? In here, Teddy?" he sputtered haughtily. "It's a dreadfully unhygienic place for a rest!" I understood his concern, but his prim and proper attitude was the last thing I needed.

I glared. "Either help me lie down before I pass out, or leave. Your choice."

He opened his mouth — I raised a finger, warning him.

"Don't!"

With a clipped exhale, he begrudgingly guided me downwards. "Careful, watch your head."

Relief exhaled in the form of a satisfied sigh as my cheek met the cold tiles. Ari knelt beside me, brushing damp strands from my face with the tips of his fingers — a gentle, almost reverent touch that coaxed a fleeting moment of peace. My eyelids drooped.

"What's brought this on?"

Well, that peace lasted all of five seconds.

Swirling emotions, along with a killer headache had put me in a choleric mood, and at best, I managed to reply with a vague wave of the hand, displeasing him immensely.

"Could you be a little more specific?"

My eyes flicked open. "No," I growled, barely mollifying Ari with a verbal response. "Help me up..."

He produced a heavy sigh and folded taut arms across his puffing chest.

With a roll of the eyes, I huffed. "...Please." That solitary word was apparently sufficient. But just as he helped me to my feet, I was ambushed by another wave of nausea. I lunged for the toilet bowl, retching despite having nothing left. When the nausea passed, I sagged against the cubicle wall, utterly depleted.

"Your bout of illness hasn't anything to do with the pregnancy, has it?"

I managed a shallow shrug, my shoulders sinking under a heaviness that didn't feel entirely mine.

Ari shot to his feet. "Stop with the nebulous responses, Teddy; they're damned exasperating!"

I snapped my head up, regretting it instantly. I winced. "Then help me up off this damned floor and I'll tell you!" I quavered, grinding my palm against my throbbing forehead.

"Christ, you're frustrating tonight!" He hooked his hands beneath my arms and eased me up from the tiled floor with a gentleness that belied his impatience. One strong arm remained wrapped around my waist as he escorted me towards the common area.

"How'd you know I was still here?" I queried, gradually lowering onto the sofa with his assistance. I shuffled backwards and sank against the cushions, welcoming the reprieve.

"I rang Spencer after several unsuccessful attempts to reach you. Fortunately for me," he informed me gruffly, "he knew you were still here!" He stormed into the kitchen where the cabinetry wore the wrath of his foul mood. Cupboard doors crashed, a glass scraped loudly, and the fridge door slammed shut. Twice. With a drink in hand, his heavy footsteps marched towards me soon after.

"Here, drink this," he grunted, thrusting the tall water-filled glass into my hand.

I took the glass with shaky gratitude, the icy-cold water offering a fleeting reprieve to my parched throat.

"Better?" he asked, settling beside me and slipping an arm around my back.

I nodded. "Much, thank you."

"Good," he uttered, sharply exhaling a cleansing breath. He took the empty glass from my hand and set it on the small occasional table beside him before slumping back against the cushions. His fingers found my waist and tugged gently, prompting me to shuffle closer. I obliged, drawing my feet up and curling into his side. A content sigh escaped me as he pressed a soft kiss to the crown of my head before continuing. "Spencer mentioned you were working on a unique project..."

"Our house," I whispered hoarsely. "I was drawing up our house." Fresh tears pooled, spilling over my cheeks.

"Teddy, talk to me." He cupped my cheek and guided my face toward his, worry etched into every line of his expression. "Did something happen? Was it Emmett? Did he come here again?"

"No, it wasn't him."

Ari's shoulders eased by a fraction — a fleeting relief — before tension reclaimed them. "Well, what's upset you then? You were content this morning, what's changed?"

My lower lip began trembling uncontrollably. ".... My mother."

A vicious growl erupted from Ari's chest. "*What did she do*?"

"She came here just to purposely berate me."

His strong jaw clenched, the muscle ticking as he forced out the words. "What did she say to you?"

My cries collapsed into full-blown sobs as I miserably repeated each horrid word. With every one, Ari's anger darkened. When a sudden, sharpened pain lanced my bicep, I winced. "Ari — you're hurting me."

His gaze snapped downward to where his fingertips dug into my arm. "My apologies. I didn't realise..."

His hands slipped away as he sat forward, and the moment his touch left me, a hollow loneliness opened in my chest.

"I'm lost for words, Teddy. Truly. And I'm tired — tired of this never-ending drama with your fucking mother and Emmett. It's sucking the life out of us. When will it ever let up?"

He scrubbed both hands over his face, then turned toward me. The thunder in his gaze made my stomach drop; fear fluttered through me as I tried to read between the lines.

"But before you go flying off the handle at me, I'm well aware you're exhausted by their reprehensible conduct too. I know none of this..." He waved a dismissive hand. "...bullshit is your doing. But will we ever have any semblance of normality? At all?"

"I'm beyond tired, Ari — I'm exhausted!" I cried. "Their mental games are exhausting. But what can I do right now? Until there's enough evidence to lock them away, I'm powerless to stop them. I just wish I understood what drives my mother to treat me so abhorrently. And Emmett's insidious obsession — I'll never understand that either. But I'm done torturing myself trying to."

I pulled my knees up and hugged them tightly as more tears spilled. Even the crying felt exhausting. "Can we just go home, please?"

Ari dragged a hand down his face, brooding. "Yeah. Fine. After today, I need a stiff drink."

I sensed the indifference the moment he hauled me off the sofa — not in the action itself, but in the way his body moved. His hold, usually warm and protective, felt wooden. The space between us widened, not physically but unmistakably, as though he were present only in the most superficial sense. The emotional absence broke something small and fragile inside me.

Shutting me out when things got difficult had become an irritatingly familiar habit of his, and it was seriously beginning to piss me off — especially after his recent apology and that unequivocal promise that there would be no more outbursts or selfish brooding.

Everyone let me down in the end.

Why should Ari be any different.

8

Ari

Therese's dastardly visit – along with the cruel words that had spewed from her venomous mouth – churned on repeat, needling at my already frayed patience. My futile attempt to analyse her intellect only worsened the headache I'd acquired as a result, as if my patience needed any further encouragement to unravel. Perhaps a timely visit to her house was in order. As a reasonable man, I naturally sought to reason with an unreasonable person – though even that felt generous. And as I peered down at a peacefully sleeping Teddy, convincing her mother to shut her poisonous mouth by any means necessary was worth the imposition.

I craned my neck and pressed a gentle kiss to Teddy's furrowed temple before easing my arm out from beneath her head. To my surprise, she didn't stir, even as I slipped out of bed and strolled into her walk-in robe – all soft lighting and boutique elegance – where the few clothes I'd left behind after her suicide attempt still hung neatly beside hers. A quiet, sobering reminder of those weeks. I switched on the light and opened the drawer containing my workout clothes, throwing them on quickly. The surging angst demanded a punishing workout at the twenty-four-hour gym up the road.

The Gym, I was pleased to discover, that aside from the few hardcore fanatics, was moderately empty. A scattering of bodies moved through their routines — the hum of machinery, the faint scent of rubber and disinfectant, and the occasional grunt or strained exhale punctuating the otherwise cavernous quiet. At one in the morning, you wouldn't expect anything less. It suited me. I needed space, movement, and the freedom to burn through this agitation without interruption.

I shoved my bag into a spare locker, grabbing my AirPods and slotting them into my ears as I marched across the carpeted floor towards the row of treadmills. The thought of running until the muscles in my thighs burned, my lungs clawed for air, and my chest heaved sounded like bliss. I stabbed at the control panel, selecting a sprinting program in the hope a brutal run might alleviate the lingering angst. The belt began rotating. The momentum built beneath my feet, the incline rising, forcing me to run harder, faster, longer. But with every pounding step, something held me back — as though invisible hands gripped my shoulders, dragging at my resolve. In the end, the run felt pointless. My palm slammed against the emergency button.

Damn it to hell! I'd come seeking bloody catharsis – a clean burn, a release – not this simmering, stubborn discontent.

Snatching up my towel from the handrail, I jumped off the base, my feet hitting the ground before it fully lowered. As I scrubbed sweat from my face and neck, my disgruntled gaze swept the warehouse conversion. My mood lifted marginally when I spotted the boxing bags hanging in a neat row along the rear wall. Perfect – or as close to perfect as I was likely to get tonight.

I thumped onto a black leather bench set against the faded brick and had scarcely donned a pair of boxing gloves when a deep Welsh-lilted voice came out of nowhere.

I ripped the AirPods from my ears and tilted my head, directing my gaze upwards at the tall, burly stranger sidestepping around the bag. “Excuse me?”

Smiling broadly, he graciously repeated himself, “Do you want me to hold the bag for you?”

Rolling my shoulders as I rose to my feet, I warned him sternly, “Thank you, but you may want to hold on tight.”

Unperturbed, the beefy stranger gripped the sides. “Ready when you are.”

“All right – it’s your funeral,” I firmly stated, bouncing lightly on the spot and throwing a few air punches.

For months, an indescribable rage had manifested and gradually eaten away at me. Each deliberate jab represented every ounce of anguish forced upon me, my family and Teddy’s by the same, despicable person.

Now it was a pain I shared, viscerally and unashamedly. Catharism, finally.

“That was some hitting you were doing back there. Something has clearly gotten you wired up for you to be out this late,” the stranger noted, running fingers the size of thick sausages through the top of short, dampened spikes. The rest of his hair was shaved into what Teddy called a classic skin fade — similar to my own semi-pompadour, apparently. A style she insisted suited me. Versatile, polished, appropriate for any occasion. And she wasn't wrong. Even now, damp and dishevelled, it held its shaped – mostly.

A reluctant grin tugged at my mouth as I ripped off the gloves and offered a sweaty hand. "Ari Jaeger – angry businessman."

Sea-green eyes twinkled as Logan warmly reciprocated, his shake firm. "Logan Ayres – security guard and bag holder."

My gaze drifted over his bulging muscles. "I assumed professional bodybuilder. Seems I was wrong on that score, wasn't I?"

Logan chuckled, settling his bulky frame at the opposite end of the bench. "Nah, I'm not that narcissistic. Besides, bodybuilding's usually a sign you're overcompensating for what you lack in the appendage department."

I huffed a laugh, lifting my water bottle to my lips. "My girlfriend would love you then. She's not a fan of narcissists."

"Lucky me."

"Indeed," I returned, amused. "What field of security are you in?"

"I work for a small outfit called Mass Security. We manage crowd control, private events, the odd VIP job when someone decides to get rowdy. Keeps me busy and out of trouble, mostly. Why, you in the market for a guard?"

"Quite possibly. My girlfriend more than me."

Logan raised a pierced right brow. "What, from you?"

"No!" I laughed heartily. "Teddy's whom I need protection from; she can be rather feisty. I blame the red hair." My smile swiftly faded. "Jokes aside… would you consider working for me full-time?"

"For you?" he asked, slugging back a mouthful of the red concoction from the clear plastic shaker clutched in his hand. "Or contractual through my current employers?"

"My lawyer would need to sort out the legalities, but after thorough vetting, you'd be contracted primarily through me."

Without hesitation, he nodded. "Sure, why not. I'm after a change of scenery anyway."

I stared in utter astonishment. "Just like that? Are you not concerned with hearing what the job entails first, or the inducements I typically offer?"

Logan shook his head. "No need. You seem trustworthy enough, and I'm only assuming, but I can't imagine you're in the habit of steering anyone up the garden path."

"My word is my bond."

"That's good enough for me then."

I gaped. "Wow, I wish all business deals were conducted as smoothly as this one. May I at least grab your number to contact you to finalise our deal?"

"Yeah, sure." Logan pushed to his feet and walked over to the lockers in long strides. I promptly followed. He pulled out a worn leather wallet and extracted a business card, passing it to me. "Call me anytime."

"Thanks," I expressed, exchanging cards. "My work and mobile number are both there, just in case you need to get in touch."

Logan studied the card and let out a riotous snort. "Your company I take it?"

Smiling proudly, I stiffly nodded. "From the ground up."

"That explains the angry businessman part then." His green eyes sparkled mirthfully, making me laugh.

"It does, doesn't it? Anyway, I had best be making a move – or Teddy shall wonder where I've disappeared to." Slinging my bag over my shoulder, I extended a hand. "I look forward to hearing from you."

"How does tomorrow sound?"

"Perfect."

After a quick shower, I silently slipped back into bed. Teddy had shifted to the other side of the mattress, sleeping soundly – or so I thought.

Sensing the dip, she rolled towards me, flinging an arm around my waist. "Where'd you go?" she mumbled, curling the length of her slender frame against me.

"The Gym," I whispered, exhaustion pulling at my eyelids. "Go back to sleep."

"'Kay." She let out a contented sigh. "You smell good."

Smiling lazily, I wrapped an arm around her shoulders and drifted off with Teddy's fingers linked through mine.

∞

Teddy

"Asher and I are flying to Perth first thing Monday morning," Ari respectfully informed me the next morning over what was already a quietly tension-filled breakfast.

My dissatisfied, sleep-starved gaze lifted over the rim of the cup nursed between my hands. "What's in Perth?"

"I'm recruiting a new architectural engineer for JPD as well as a graduate – preferably a postgraduate," he replied with a maddening calm, navigating the scrambled eggs from the glazed off-white porcelain plate onto his toast. "Candidate interviews begin Tuesday –"

My cup abruptly clashed with the saucer.

His darkening gaze flicked up. "Was that necessary?" he acknowledged coolly, lifting the fork to his mouth and chewing with deliberate, unbroken eye contact.

"Wouldn't it make more sense to fly them here?" My blazing gaze dropped to the cutlery nestled in his hands, observing the curl of his long fingers tightening around the handles.

"No, not at all, as most of our candidates live there," he reasoned, resolute and immovable.

"Why do *you* need to go, Ari? I need you here – at home – with me!" My fingers impatiently drummed the table, awaiting a response as he steadily set the knife and fork down and wiped his shapely mouth with the linen serviette. But my hot-headed nature refused to wait. I pushed. "At least give me the courtesy of a response!"

I was met with an oppressive silence and thinning lips – both subtle warnings for me to quit while I was ahead.

He shoved the chair back without a word, not bothering to tuck it beneath the table before storming past me and making his way towards the hallway.

"Yeah, great, walk away!" I shot to my feet, ignoring the crash of my chair hitting the floor as I stomped after him. "Quit ignoring me!"

Again, he stonewalled me, keeping his back turned as he reefed his messenger bag off one of the newly installed wall hooks and marched out the front door – which surprisingly, remained upright considering the force he used to open it.

The stubborn part of me refused to heed Ari's warnings. "What's your damned problem?" But as a visibly aggrieved Ari spun to face me, provoking him wasn't the best idea after all.

"For fuck's sake, Teddy, will you quit your belligerent badgering!" he roared – not loudly, but with a depth that rattled something inside me. The ticking jaw, the stony gaze... they left me too stunned to argue back. "I *need* the week away as a chance to gather my thoughts – *away* from all this constant fucking drama surrounding our life!"

The bluntness of his words stung – sharp, humiliating, and unbelievably true.

Tears welled as I confronted him, "Why are you still here then? Why haven't you just left?"

He inhaled sharply. "Because, Teddy, unlike you, I at least have the decency to inform you of my plans in advance! Running away from problems is more your style than mine!" He snarled the last part with earnest frustration before spinning back to his car and ripping the door open on his beloved BMW.

For once, I had no comeback.

The reality – along with the damaging anguish of truth – stunned me to the core. And while my lead-like feet remained riveted to the grass, Ari angrily reversed out of the driveway and sped off. Squealing tyres and the roar of the V8 engine were the last I heard from him for the rest of the day.

First, it was my mother and her unwelcome visit.

Then Ari – with an attitude so raw and unfiltered, my brain felt addled, and my concentration shot to hell. Part of my issue was my job. I felt disengaged – disconnected – and had for some time. Case in point: the floor plans for the Hawthorn office rebuild sitting in front of me. I'd failed to make any sort of progress, or changes for that matter. For the last fifteen minutes, I'd simply stared at the screen, twirling a pen between my fingers, the lines blurring into meaningless geometry.

My blank stare drifted to the clock above the cubicle doorway. I watched the second-hand tick, tick, tick until the minute hand finally shifted. Time felt painfully slow — heavy, dragging, mirroring the weight in my chest. Ari's unexpected, short-notice announcement had dramatically darkened an already foul mood. Albeit it was a business trip – but why wasn't Human Resources handling the interviews. That was their job, was it not? And the crux of my issue wasn't the trip itself.

It was the playboy accompanying him. That was just asking for trouble.

Speaking of which, I was in desperate need of time away myself. So I contrived feeling ill – not entirely a lie – and inwardly made plans to head to Phillip Island as I switched off my computer and packed up my desk.

Ari's acidic tongue lashing earlier had a hit a nerve. A deep one. The problem was... he was right. I always opted for the easy way out. I always ran. Therefore, I set about proving him wrong and decided to phone him once I reached the car. Except each time I tried, the calls diverted straight to his message bank – once again filling me with self-doubt. Tugging the seatbelt across my torso and ramming the buckle in, I let out a despairing sigh; perhaps he was still upset with me.

"*Or just maybe, Teddy, he was too busy to talk?*" I singsonged sarcastically before blowing out a frustrated sigh and stabbing the dial button for the umpteenth time. I drove up the ramp of the subterranean garage listening to Ari's raspy voice instructing callers to leave their details in that typically formal manner of his. "Just like you, I need a break before I break, so…I'm off to Cowes. I'll see you when I come home," I paused, swallowing my pride, "…and I'm sorry about this morning. I love you."

∞

Ari

Frustrated with the initial start to my day, I thrust a hand through my hair and shared my displeasure with Asher, "Bloody unions. They're so damned pig-headed – and these negotiations, they were a bloody joke. The settlement ought to have taken days, not weeks."

Adding to my irritation throughout the long, high-tense meeting was the constant buzzing of my phone. Annoyingly, it vibrated again. I yanked it from the inside of my jacket pocket and frowned at the unusual cluster of missed calls — five of which were from Teddy.

Across the table, Asher lifted his brows, clearly having noticed my expression.

"I agree." He strolled over to the coffee station to top up his empty mug — his third in the space of two hours. Holding up the cup, he offered, "Do you want another?"

"Unless there's bourbon in that cup, no thank you," I droned, leaning back in the chair, and throwing my feet up onto the desk, crossing them at the ankle.

Asher scoffed derisively, propping his backside against the dark timber cabinet. "You have a severe drinking problem, my friend."

"Blame my mother; she fed me booze instead of formula."

Blowing on his coffee, he chuckled. "Audrina wouldn't deny such an allegation either."

"Nor would she own up to it. 'Plausible deniability' she calls it," I remarked dryly, grimacing as I listened to Teddy's one and only voice message.

Since her mother's previous visit, Teddy and I were back at loggerheads, and it wasn't boding well with me at all. She at least had the decency to let me know where she was heading this time, easing my mind a fraction. My harsh truths had glaringly hit quite a nerve.

A knowing finger wagged at me as Asher settled back into the chair opposite, bringing his size twelve feet down with a thump on the tabletop. "Ah, yes, your mother – the only person I know who has bullshitting perfected into an art form." His blonde brows lifted as his nosy gaze peered over at me. "Everything all right?"

I briefly glanced up from my phone. "Yeah."

"Teddy?"

"Yeah."

He snorted. "Am I going to get anything other than the one-syllable answers you're giving me?"

I chuckled and tossed my phone onto the table in front of me. "No."

Asher took a sip of his coffee and shook his head. "You're such an arsehole."

I smirked. "Yeah."

∞

Teddy

Considering the hectic traffic along the way, I arrived at the island within record time. I even managed a quick stop at the supermarket for groceries, buying just enough supplies to see me through until the weekend. Unfortunately, the bottle of Pinot Grigio I longed for had to stay behind on the bottle-shop shelf. Another inconvenient side of pregnancy — enforced sobriety when all I wanted was escape. After the past twenty-four hours, the thought of drinking myself into a merciful stupor carried a dangerous sort of comfort. Anything to hush the old wound my mother never stops reopening, that familiar sting of a woman who can't — or won't — love me.

Once unpacked, I set about opening both sets of French doors off the living room and kitchen, ridding the place of its stale air. A mild, balmy breeze wafted in its place, lifting the sheer white voile curtains in a delicately dancing sway. It was a perfect summer's day. For a moment, I toyed with the idea of staying inside and playing the newest addition to the house – a shiny black grand piano my father had recently purchased. But in the end, I decided I craved the sunshine more, especially as I checked out my arms and legs. After one of Melbourne's typically long, cold winters, they were looking a little pale.

Okay, outside it was.

Having finally quit my procrastinating, I decided I also needed music. I wandered over to the tall Bluetooth speaker in the corner of the living room, opening Spotify. Immediately, Zayn's,

Fool for You – a song Ari found and added to my playlist – began playing. Maybe he was trying to tell me something? But, like always, I was overthinking things. An annoying habit that frustrated Ari to no end. My burdening thoughts continued to torment me as I meandered through the wide-open doors and out onto the balcony. The temperature noticeably and rapidly dropped as the balmy breeze shifted direction the moment I settled into an outdoor recliner.

I grimaced; so much for getting a tan.

A shiver curled around me as my wistful gaze drifted across the darkening horizon. What had started out as a warm, sunny day, had suddenly turned stormy. The gentle wind of earlier had become a strong gale, rolling ominously blackened clouds across the sky and shadowing the sapphire blue seas of the peninsula. Thunder rumbled above me, followed by numerous cracks of lightning, illuminating the heavens as the air thickened with the refreshing scent of forthcoming rain.

Breathing in deeply, I closed my eyes and skimmed a hand over the soft curve of my belly. Not that I looked pregnant. It was early days yet – giving me ample time to decide, whether rash or not. Right now, though, that was irrelevant. My life was spiralling; *I was* spiralling. No child, especially mine, should ever have to suffer because of their parents' choices, right or wrong.

Substantial sheets of rain suddenly began to fall, disrupting my thoughts as I listened to the pelting drops hammering the colorbond roof in a deafening roar. It was a blessing in disguise.

As a child raised in a dysfunctional family, the rain had been my saviour – an ideal tool for drowning out arguing parents, granting my siblings and me a momentary lapse of peace. It was having the same effect now, lulling me enough to contact Ari once more. I ran back inside and grabbed my phone. Dialling his number, I anxiously waited for him to answer.

9

Ari

Teddy's recent flight response to our issues had tipped me over the edge, and there was only one person to blame. But when wasn't she at fault? My resentment towards Therese radiated as I stabbed at the brass button embedded in the brick wall. I scoffed, slipping my hand inside my trouser pocket. What a charming tune. Although, the occupant inside was decidedly distant from any sort of harmony. Perhaps I ought to suggest an alternative as dark as the front door. That, at least, corresponded with the colour of her heart.

The ghost of a smile that flitted over my lips swiftly vanished as the door opened. For a mere moment, I found myself caught off guard by Therese's rather youthful appearance. For someone in her mid-fifties, she had barely aged a day and appeared beguiling. Be that as it may, as her perfected mask slipped into place, I was reminded that she was merely a blade wrapped in red satin.

Visibly unperturbed by my presence on her doorstep, she smoothed the coiffed auburn hair resting over flawlessly creamy shoulders and offered a pleasant greeting. "Ari, what a lovely but unexpected surprise."

"No doubt."

My contemptuous tone dulled her brightened expression. Beneath cold, unblinking green eyes, a tight smile formed over red-stained lips – her signature colour, according to Teddy.

"Well, are you going to invite me in?" My brusqueness clearly took her aback; her head jerked.

She promptly regained her composure, opening the antique door wider and stepping aside. "Of course. Where are my manners?" With a gracious sweep of the hand, she invited me inside.

"Thank you," I replied forcefully, stepping over the threshold into the foyer as Therese's suspicious gaze shot sharpened daggers into my back.

Her black leather loafers tapped quietly on the contrasting diamond-shaped tiles as she sidestepped past me and gestured towards the living room. "Come through. May I offer you a cup of tea, or perhaps a cup of freshly brewed coffee? Katrina can make you either...."

I halted on the edge of the doorway between the sunlit foyer and the living room and stared darkly. "Neither, thank you," I snapped. "In contrast to you, I'm not here for idle chit-chat, nor am I visiting under false pretences."

My offhand response sent her veneer mask slipping to the floor, revealing a notoriously icy expression. "Ah. I see Theodora told you about my recent visit?" she bitterly deduced.

"You aren't completely obtuse then, I see?" I ignored the offending demeanour as I fixated my narrowed gaze on her. I cut straight to the chase. "You insist on calling your daughter by a name she detests. Why?"

"Always the drama queen, isn't she?" Tutting, her soulless green eyes rolled as long, skinny fingers toyed with the double-stranded pearl necklace at the base of her slender neck. "It was the name I gifted her with, and besides, she ought to be grateful I hadn't named her anything worse. However, I'm sure you aren't here to discuss name choices for one's child, are you? Unless, of course, you want my advice on names for –" she paused, lips curling, *"– the said child?"*

The said child? Seriously, where did this woman get off?

I frowned.

Teddy wouldn't have willingly told her about our baby, so how the hell did she know? I exhaled sharply – yet another piece of information she had failed to mention. That then begged the question: what else hadn't she told me? Regardless, I bristled at the derogatory contempt she aimed at my unborn child.

"I neither want your advice nor am I here to discuss our unborn child, as your opinion isn't worth shit to me," I expressed dispassionately, slowly edging closer. "But whilst we're on the subject of one's children – why do you loathe your daughter so?"

She choked out a humourless laugh. "My husband asked precisely the same question, defending her as always the night he packed up and left our family home." The bitterness in her tone was distasteful – as was the deflection, a well-versed trait she excelled at.

My expression hardened, conveying my discontent. "Answer the bloody question." My raised voice barely affected her. I was starting to believe Teddy's mother was fashioned from stone. She wasn't that unfeeling... surely?

"I never uttered such ludicrous words." Focusing her detached gaze on me, she spoke earnestly for the first time in her miserable life, “I merely tolerate my daughter – I just don’t love her.”

Astounded by the coldness, I gaped. “Your cruelty knows no bounds.” Again, not a flinch.

“I wanted another son.” She brushed my opinion away with a flagrant wave of the hand. “They’re less...” She paused, searching for a suitable description. Therese and ‘appropriate’ were two words never meant to be synonymous. “Trouble,” she finally stated. “Daughters are such vulnerable creatures, and they only ever bring you heartache and shame. Surely even you, a man as worldly as yourself, would have to agree. Theodora has proven this thus far, has she not?”

“With you constantly nipping at Teddy’s heels, it’s no wonder she’s so vulnerable,” I countered sharply. My beratement didn’t end there. “As opposed to showering her with a mother’s love, you cast her aside and continually shunned her, causing an infinite number of issues. But your lack of humility no longer surprises me – particularly after her disclosure.”

My revelation struck home. Her infamous steely mask slipped, revealing a flicker of recognition.

I stroked my chin thoughtfully. “Humour me: was it plain old ignorance, or just your maladjusted mind, that prevented you from recognising the enormous implications of your denial over your daughter’s rape?”

“Is that what your precious *Teddy* told you... that she was *‘raped’*?” she spluttered indignantly, raising her chin defiantly. “My god, she’s truly sucked you in, hasn’t she?”

Astounded by her pugnacious attitude, my angst rose. I stepped closer until the stench of her putrid perfume burned my nostrils. “Unlike you, I do believe her. And unlike you, I’m not conceited, and I'm most certainly not worried about self-preservation."

She flinched – making me smile – but it vanished as she set about spinning more lies.

"Theodora distastefully had an affair with a much older, married man. He didn't want his wife finding out, so I took care of certain matters myself. Discreetly, of course."

I scoffed. "By certain matters, you mean the baby Teddy bore?"

She smirked perceptively. With a leisurely spin, she sauntered towards an antique sideboard and poured two bourbons into crystal tumblers. "She was always such a flirt, running around in highly inappropriate shorts and low-cut tops. She's our very own version of a *Lolita,* wouldn't you say?"

Outwardly, I remained indifferent. Internally, my instincts fought to break free. Any more filth out of Therese's mouth, and they just might.

"She left you, a virile young man, lusting after her for years in the same manner. She is beautiful, no? So, it's no wonder you're unable to resist her advances."

I took the tumbler because if I didn't, I might have wrapped my hands around something far less breakable than crystal. Her self-righteous smile only sharpened the urge.

"But then," she continued, "she makes it impossible for any man to resist her. Even now..."

I hurled the glass at her pristinely wallpapered wall. Her insinuations had finally tipped me over the precipice.

Therese's head snapped sideways, her cold gaze glaring reproachfully at the dripping amber liquid and shattered glass before turning her acidic tongue on me. "I'll be sure to send you the bill for the repairs."

I shook with rage and roared, "Are you that devoid of emotion, that all you care about is fucking wallpaper? You're nothing but a monster! Stay the fuck away from Teddy, or you'll regret ever knowing me – and my family! Are we clear?"

"Oh, very."

Her casual reply only fuelled my hostility. I turned my back on Therese before I truly lost it, my quickening footsteps marching me towards the front door. I had to leave. No wonder Teddy despised the place; this house was suffocating.

"Oh, and Ari – one more thing."

My grip tensed around the brass knob. "*What?*"

Her shoes clicked in slow, measured steps on the tiles behind me. "Leave her before it's too late. She'll only tear you apart with her fabrications – which, clearly, she's already doing."

My jaw ticked. Never before had I wanted to hit someone simply to silence them. But my parents had instilled morals in their children – violence against women was abhorrent.

I ignored her provocations and reefed the door open, unnervingly aware of her eyes pinned on me as I stormed towards the car. But as I slid into the seat and turned the key, I looked back.

Why, I didn't know.

All I saw was Therese standing in the open doorway, her malicious expression staring back at me.

A shudder crawled down my spine.

Her true mask had finally revealed itself. She was evil—pure malevolent evil.

∞

Teddy

An entire day had nearly passed before Ari decided to call me back. Deliberate or not, his delay got my back up, and I told him so – which predictably spiralled into yet another argument. I hung up on him like a petulant teenager. Days later, nothing had changed. We still hadn't spoken.

Oddly enough, the silence hadn't destroyed us. If anything, it proved we needed the breathing space.

I tried distracting myself with endless walks along the beach, streaming movies until the early hours, and playing the piano my father had graciously bought for me. But each distraction only made me miss Ari more. They were all things we'd done together — here and at home — which made my decision to leave by the end of the week a helluva lot easier.

I sped out of Cowes toward Beaumaris, the intention clear: surprise Ari with a candlelit dinner, sexy lingerie, and the kind of make-up intimacy that usually solved everything between us. That was the plan, anyway.

Then the self-criticism set in.

As the roadworks ahead forced me to slow, I leaned my elbow against the window and pressed my curled hand to my cheek, releasing a heavy sigh. Anything was possible with the tension simmering between us. Anything.

A horn incessantly honked behind me, startling me. "All right, I'm going! Arsehole!" I yelled, glaring into the rear-view mirror. I inched forward, only to brake again. For the next two kilometres, I rode the brakes like a learner driver until the road finally opened into dual lanes. The impatient driver behind me swerved past the moment the speed limit changed.

I pressed down on the accelerator, setting the cruise control once I reached the appropriate speed. All I could hope for was the reunion I'd planned — not the one I'd dreamed about the last few nights.

Only time would tell.

As it turned out, forewarning my hot-headed lover that I was leaving the island a day earlier than expected hadn't been my brightest idea. I'd given him the opportunity — and the means — to turn the tables on me.

Something I discovered the second I stepped into his bedroom.

His hand slid down my arm, slow and deliberate, until his fingers wrapped around my wrist. The gentleness lasted all of a heartbeat before he turned me, pinning me to the wall with a force that stole the air from my lungs. My bags hit the floor with a dull thud.

If not for the familiar scent of Ari's intoxicating cologne, or the scrape of his beard against the back of my neck, I might have screamed.

Music curled through the room — something slow, soulful, deceptively gentle — before shifting into a darker rhythm that matched the tension coiled inside him. This wasn't the Ari who held me tenderly. This was the Ari shaped by the past week: distant, simmering, unreadable. A version of him I'd helped create.

"Did you miss me?" he murmured, his voice low and rough, his breath brushing my neck. His free hand slid into my hair, tugging sharply, tilting my head to the side. "I know I did..."

His stubble grazed my cheek, my ear, sending a shiver spiralling down my spine. When his teeth caught my earlobe, an untamed sound escaped me before I could stop it.

"Oh, God, yes..."

"Your arms stay where they are," he instructed, his tone clipped, controlled. "Palms flat against the wall." His hands moved with deliberate slowness, gathering the hem of my fitted jersey dress and pushing it upward. The cool air of the room met warm skin, and his breath hitched — barely, but enough for me to feel it.

"Such a gorgeous derriere..." he praised, his touch firm, appreciative, claiming. "I've thought about this more than I should."

The tension between us — the arguments, the silence, the longing — condensed into something electric, something that pulled me taut against him. Every inch of his physicality radiated heat and restraint, as though he was holding back a week's worth of emotion with nothing but sheer will.

And I knew, with absolute clarity, that whatever happened next would be the collision we'd both been hurtling toward.

I relaxed into the soothing caress of his palm — right up until the sharp snap of elastic made me jolt. "Ow!"

"Hush..." Ari warned, his voice low and uncompromising. His hand connected with my backside in quick, deliberate succession. Each strike sent a sting blooming across my skin, heat spreading in its wake. I sucked in a breath, half-shock, half-need, and he gave me more — measured, controlled, devastating. His touch shifted, his fingers teasingly tracing the curve of my hip, the inside of my thigh before slipping into my wet heat. I moaned. I craved more. I pushed back instinctively, my body seeking relief, seeking him. My hips gyrated against the rigid length pulsating between my cheeks.

"Don't move," he growled against my ear, the command vibrating through me. He stepped back just enough to let his hands roam, slow and possessive, over the heated skin he'd marked. The contrast made me shiver. When he struck again — harder, sharper — I bucked, a cry tearing from my throat before I could stop it.

"You like that?" he rasped, breath unsteady, fingers gliding up the length of my spine. He paused at the small of my back, lingering there, letting the anticipation coil tight and hot between us.

Instinctively, I pushed back again — a silent plea, a surrender, a challenge.

"I said don't move." Another resounding slap followed, firm enough to steal my breath, controlled enough to remind me exactly who held the reins.

The room pulsed with heat, with tension, with the unspoken promise of what came next — a promise neither of us was in any state to resist.

"Much better. Now, shall I fuck you here," he murmured, circling my puckered rosebud. "Or here, where you're so wet and so needy with desire already?"

I rolled my head in the dip of his shoulder as he inserted two fingers and began thrusting. The tips methodically grazed my inner wall, pushing me closer and faster to the edge. Added to my fight was his stubborn refusal to let me come.

My insides quivered, fighting for release. Out of desperation, I begged for mercy, "Ari...please."

"I'm well aware of your desperation," he taunted, his voice a decadent whisper as his stubbled chin brushed my neck. "But you're not entitled to one. Not yet anyway."

Ari yanked out both fingers, exacerbating my frustration.

"*I need to come*!"

A wicked smile curled over delectable lips. "I told you, not yet, my love," he purred, burying his nose in my hair and skating teasing hands along the curves of my torso.

Much to his delight, I huffed.

"Huffing won't earn you that orgasm any quicker either," he sternly reprimanded. "Drop your arms – they must be tired by now..."

His sarcasm wanted to make me scream as they dropped to my sides like dead weights. The relief was short-lived. Ari reefed my dress over my head in one swift motion and tossed it to the floor beside what remained of my tattered underwear.

"Come over here...." He patted the top of the occasional chair. "Now bend over."

Still clinging to my sullen mood, I wandered towards the chair with all the defiance I could muster. It didn't last. The moment I bent forward, Ari corrected my attitude with ruthless efficiency. His hand came down in quick succession – sharp, deliberate, unrelenting. Each strike sent a jolt through me, heat blooming across my skin, the sting settling deep and insistent. My breath hitched, my fingers curling against the fabric beneath me as he continued, repeatedly, until the last of my resistance dissolved into something far more dangerous.

The room seemed to narrow around us, the air thick with everything we hadn't said, everything we'd avoided, everything we'd been aching for.

A sound tore out of me before I could stop it. “Oh—God!”

The force of everything — the week apart, the arguments, the longing, the sting still blooming across my skin — crashed through me all at once. Exhaustion and exhilaration tangled together until my limbs gave way, and I sagged over the backrest like a ragdoll, breathless and trembling.

The moment hung suspended, heat pooling in the air, thought dissolving until there was nothing left but sensation. Nothing but him. Nothing but the sharp, undeniable truth of how much I’d missed this — missed him — even when I’d sworn I didn’t.

Ari’s presence loomed behind me, steady and silent, his breath a slow, controlled rhythm that made the space between us feel charged. His hand hovered at the small of my back — not touching, but close enough that my body leaned toward the promise of his intention, dark, focused, unmistakable.

“Good,” he murmured, voice low, roughened by something darker — something he’d been holding in since the moment my mother spat her poison at him, at me, at us.

The words settled over me like a shiver, anchoring me in place, every muscle taut with anticipation.

“Don’t get too relaxed.”

His tone cut through the haze — firm, unyielding, threaded with the frustration he’d swallowed during every second of that confrontation, every hour of our silence, every moment he’d been forced to sit with the fear that I’d run again.

The warmth of him, the weight of his focus, the deliberate stillness he held — it all pressed against my skin more effectively than any hand could.

I swallowed hard, my breath catching as he let the silence stretch, purposeful and punishing. He wanted me to feel it — the control, the restraint, the simmering edge of everything we hadn't said. Everything he hadn't been able to say.

A single fingertip traced the curve of my hip, slow enough to make my subordination weaken.

"That's better," he murmured, the approval dark and quiet as he lubricated me with slickened fingers, readying me. "Don't move an inch."

Stillness claimed me, not out of obedience, but because resisting him felt as impossible as resisting gravity.

What pressed against me wasn't confidence or experience — it was something raw, unsteady, volatile. A man pushed past his limits, stripped down to the truth he never let anyone see. I could feel it in the tension of his breath, in the way his restraint shook at the edges, in the storm he was trying not to unleash.

Awareness prickled — the realisation that beneath the dominance, beneath the command, beneath the tension that had nearly broken us, was love.

Fierce, frustrated, terrified love. And this flash of dominance wasn't desire so much as the only honest way his feelings could break the surface without destroying him.

"No more climaxes either until I say so."

I inhaled deeply as the tip of his cock nudged at the entrance of my rosebud, pausing briefly before proceeding to fill me entirely. The air ruptured, torn from our lungs by the force of emotion and pleasure colliding simultaneously — snapping the tightly coiled tension clean through.

Ari's hands seized my waist, rougher than anything I had ever experienced from him — a frantic, volatile culmination shaped by every argument, every silence, every fear of the past week. His grunt, low and rasping as his thrusts grew into a punishing rhythm. He fisted my tresses and tugged my head back. With each frantic thrust, his cock plunged harder, deeper, and staving off an orgasm impossible. I let go.

Fulfilled cries filled the air as shattering orgasms erupted.

Ultimately spent, I sagged further into the chair. A similarly exhausted Ari folded against me, his sticky chest pressing to my equally sticky back.

“Let’s take a bath,” he heaved, his lips brushing my shoulder blade.

“Aha.” At best, that’s the most I could manage.

He chuckled and peeled himself away. I winced. Then to add insult to injury, he slapped my tender backside. “Come on. Bath.”

Yeah. That had been a punishment fuck. If only Ari understood the significance.

When the water finally stilled, a heavy, breath-thick quiet settled over us — the kind of quiet that felt warm, weighted, and worryingly fragile. Ari’s forehead rested against my shoulder, his breathing uneven, his body loose but his emotions still taut, tangled, trembling beneath the surface.

“You cheated,” I grumbled, relaxing into Ari’s chest as I sank a little deeper into the warm water. It soothed every inch of my aching, satiated body, even as my mind churned beneath the surface.

He raked his fingers through his damp hair and grunted, feigning innocence. “I did nothing of the sort.”

“You were naked when I came home, how’s that fair?”

He shrugged nonchalantly, brushing his lips along my shoulder in a slow, languid sweep meant to distract. “It made my job easier,” he confessed, gliding his palms over my breasts in a familiar, coaxing pattern – used whenever he wanted to avoid talking. “I only had to undress you then.”

“Fair...” My breath hitched as he continued his deliberate teasing. “...Enough. Although, you seem to have a bad habit of doing that to me. A lot.”

“I know I do,” he mumbled against my neck, trailing soft, lingering kisses along my damp skin — kisses that were tender, distracting, and very clearly meant to derail the conversation he sensed coming.

“Ari...”

“Mmm....”

I skated a finger up and down my raised thigh as I hesitantly broached the elephant in the room. “We need to talk.... about what’s going on with us.”

The mere mention of talking about our issues sent him ramrod stiff. His tender kisses ground to a halt. I had hoped we could discuss our issues with civility; without ending up in another fight. But the splash behind me and the thud of Ari hitting the far end of the bath made it painfully cleat my expectations didn’t match reality. Still, I forced myself to stay calm – for both our sakes.

I inhaled deeply. “Why are we at each other’s throats so much lately?”

“Honestly...” His voice wavered, thin and unsteady. “I haven’t a clue, other than we’re both frustrated and keep projecting our aggravation onto each other.”

I winced as I spun around to face him. "Fair point." Drawing my knees up, I hugged them tightly. "But this arguing isn't good for either of us – let alone the baby. Don't you agree?"

A penetrative gaze regarded me intently as he shoved a hand through his wet hair, the movement sharp, restless, revealing. He stretched his arm along the lip of the stone tub. "We just need to act a little more conscientious than we have been." He studied the pads of his pruning fingers as he gingerly walked them along the narrow edge.

"How about this," he continued, "Before an argument erupts, we take a walk – separately – or find refuge in another part of the house. And only once we've calmed down..." His dark eyes lifted slowly. "...do we continue discussing whatever the issue is in a more civilised manner. Agreed?"

My head bobbed. "Agreed. I hate fighting with you. I also hated being away from you. But the trip gave me clarity – time to reflect – and I'm sure it offered the same opportunity for you?"

"It did. Next week shall offer the same result."

"With Asher tagging along I don't doubt it," I muttered, instantly aware I'd added to Ari's irritation.

He lifted my chin, his tone calm, yet firm. "I'm aware you aren't Asher's biggest fan. Nonetheless, he's my best friend, and he'll always be a part of my life, *no matter what*." The muscle in his jaw ticked – a small, sharp betrayal of the frustration he was trying to mask. The unspoken meaning behind those last three words landed heavily: he wouldn't ever choose me over his friendship with Asher, regardless of my feelings or our long history.

Unable to face that reality, I relented unhappily, "Yeah, I know. I'll try and make more of an effort. I promise."

"Good." Leaning in, he tenderly pressed his lips to mine before tapping my nose with playful affection. "Don't forget I'll also be catching up with Damon during my trip, so my visit to Perth won't be completely terrible," he murmured – reminding me about the other bad influence in his life. The only difference was, I liked this one.

Skimming my fingertips along his torso and happy trail, I paused at the edge of his pubic line and smiled coyly. "How could I forget the little charmer?" I had only ever met Damon a handful of times, and with his deep, calming lilted accent similar to Ari's, his square jaw, ginger hair, and startling blue eyes, he was just as dreamy. He and I had hit it off like a house on fire, which in turn had made Ari jealous.

A splash of water hit my face, snapping me out of my musings. I jerked back. "Hey, what was that for?"

"Daydreaming about my cousin."

"Are you still jealous?"

Ari pouted, adorably jutting his bottom lip like a sulky child. "No. Why would I be when I won the grand prize."

Hope bloomed inside my chest. I crawled into his lap, straddling his thighs, and wrapped my arms around his shoulders. Resting my head against his chest, I listened to the even rise and fall of his breathing and the smooth, rhythmic beat of his heart — both soothing my tortured soul as I thought about our life, before and after revealing my past.

Mostly it had been blissful – albeit rocky at times – but somehow, we always found a way to overcome the hurdles we faced. Now, we struggled. A civil conversation without arguing was a rarity, and even then, we had to fight to claw our way back to each other, bruising both our pride and egos in the process.

I also loved and hated that I depended on Ari. I was fiercely independent until we became a couple. I had to be.

To survive, we had to learn to fight the evil surrounding our life, and not each other. Easier said than done when we seemed to argue non-stop. We were slowly imploding, and it was only a matter of time before that explosion erupted, causing more untold damage.

10

Ari

A new day heralded abruptly, and indeed well before dawn as an anxious Teddy pawed at me, desperate to make love. I too, endured the same affliction, so I happily obliged her. What threw me, however, was the inconsolable crying during and after. Her clinginess lingered even as I departed for the airport. For the first time in our relationship, I truly felt smothered.

Teddy consumed my daily thoughts – and rightfully so – but lately, it seemed to be for all the wrong reasons. Yes, we had spent the weekend talking productively, and yes, the sex was incredible, but shaking this unabating conflict was damned near impossible. Even as I sat back in the business lounge, observing the plane taxi along the tarmac through the oversized window beside me, my entire disposition grew inflamed.

Tossing back my third bourbon in a matter of minutes, I caught Asher eyeing me from the adjacent chair with worrying speculation. His gaze narrowed as I lifted my glass and signalled for another. The bartender waltzed over immediately, with a fresh drink on a tray, placing it atop a new napkin on the low-lying table in front of me – a pointless exercise considering I'd down it in a flash. I ought to have just requested the bottle. Not that they would hand it over – responsible service of alcohol and all that. I would've paid handsomely, too.

"What's eating you, my friend?" Asher probed, polishing off his macchiato – his third, judging by the jitter in his knee.

"Nothing." Teddy's revolving moods and our non-stop problems weren't up for discussion – not with him, not with anyone.

"You sure?"

"Yes!" I barked, sharper than intended.

Asher held up both hands defensively and flopped into the ruby-red club chair. "All right, all right. We'll just sit here quietly then."

I glowered and threw my drink down just as a voice blared over the loudspeaker, politely announcing we could finally board.

"About fucking time," I muttered, snatching up my bags and marching back downstairs. My footsteps barely slowed as we made our way along the terminal walkway with Asher's amused gaze still irritatingly glued to me. "What?" I snapped as we queued in the priority line.

"We're on our way to sun-drenched Perth, man. Be happy about it – and quit ya frowning while you're at it!"

"I wasn't frowning; I was simply thinking." I handed my boarding pass to the smiling attendant.

"Well, whatever you're thinking about is creating crevices bigger than Kings Canyon into your forehead. Not even Botox could fill 'em!"

I huffed and marched up the gangway. "If you must know, I've just got a lot going on at home. So do me a favour and quit badgering me!"

Asher's mulish reminder about my unabating mood only worsened my attitude. Or was it the bourbon? In all likelihood, both were to blame. Keeping that in mind, I made a conscious effort to rein in my ornery attitude and plastered a smile to my face as another flight attendant – an attractive brunette – warmly greeted us at the plane's open door.

"Welcome to Elite Airlines, Mr Jaeger."

"Thank you," I replied politely, handing over my boarding pass.

"You're in Row Three, Seat F on your left towards the back dividing wall," she explained, gesturing towards my seat in Business Class with a perfectly manicured finger. "Have an enjoyable flight."

Thanking her again, I shuffled along the narrow aisle, reading the seat numbers until I found my allocated seat. I tossed my small luggage case into the overhead locker, shrugged out of my charcoal jacket, and neatly placed it beside the suitcase before slumping into the spacious black leather recliner. Undoing my matching vest, I sighed as my blurred gaze drifted around the cabin. *Whatever this was* – this tension, this heaviness – would have to wait until I returned.

Asher's disarming smile blazed down at me as he shrugged out of his navy pinstriped jacket, carelessly tossing his jacket into the overhead locker beside mine. "Don't stress, mate. We'll have those blues drowned out in no time once we're airborne."

Briefly looking askance, I snorted derisively. "Yeah, where your heads always been – in the clouds!"

Thumping into the seat alongside mine, he grinned. "I don't deny it. But hey, sometimes it feels good to be high." His sanguinity raised a genuine chuckle – as did the subliminal message.

"And as always, you are so right."

"And that's why you pay me the big bucks, my friend, 'cause I'm always full of good advice."

"More like full of shit, my friend."

Amused azure eyes sparkled. "Hey, I'm not gonna *ever* deny I enjoy having a good time."

"Gentlemen, would you like me to place your briefcases in the overhead locker?" A soft, cultured voice swiftly diverted Asher's short attention span.

He looked up at the attractive stewardess hovering above him and flashed one of his famously dazzling smiles. "Yes please, love. *I would gladly* let you put my briefcase away."

My eyes rolled at the shameless flirting.

Although at some stage during our four-hour flight, I happily joined in. Both the alcohol and the antics proved to be an enjoyable – if temporary – distraction from my current woes. It also meant my drunken gaze wandered, raking over the leggy brunette consistently topping up our drinks.

Before we knew it, our non-eventful flight – if that's what you'd call it – had landed in Perth by mid-morning. Thankfully, our tickled driver Louis, another British ex-pat, was waiting inside the terminal to greet us. Proving he was quite the multitasker, he managed to collect our luggage all the while simultaneously directing us to the right car without raising a sweat—what a bloody champion. Once we'd stumbled and flopped into the backseat, he thrust tall, steel travel mugs into our hands.

I removed the lid and sniffed the strong black coffee inside. Ah, delightful. "Lemme guess – Mr Whittemore provided these?" I lazily slurred.

Louis tipped his black chauffeurs cap, his entertained expression visible in the rear-view mirror. "Yes, sir."

I hiccupped, causing a drunken chuckle. "Good ole Damo. He knows us far too well." Raising my mug, I instructed, "Go forth, driver – weary travellers aboard."

"We also need music. Something upbeat, please, Louis," Asher crowed beside me.

"Yes, sir. Will Maroon Five do?"

"Perfect!" Moves like Jagger blasted from the speakers directly behind us, and Asher launched into wiggling about in his seat like a caffeinated toddler at a disco. "Come on, man, dance with me!"

I shook my head and laughed. "No, I'll leave that to you, my friend. You're doing such a superb job all on your own!" As if to torture me further, he started singing along. I'd heard alley cats sound better. I waved my mug in the air. "Hurry, please, Louis – I believe Asher's dying."

By the time we reached the hotel, the coffee had eased my intoxication somewhat. Asher's singing, on the other hand, hadn't improved the slightest. Although, coherently speaking seemed to be an issue for the both of us, as was our less-than-civilised behaviour. Both ostensibly upset the resentful, stuffy concierge who had the misfortune of checking us in.

Entering the lift with our porter, I smiled brightly and wiggled my twinkling fingers – or was it spirit fingers? Whatever. I waved at the pompous arse.

His lips thinned, a perfect picture of disdain.

"Tootles…" The doors slid closed. "How rude, not even the decency of a goodbye."

"Speakin' of rude, dude, don't forget ya need ta message the ball and chain," Asher snickered, stumbling against the elevator wall.

A menacing growl erupted as I fished my phone from my jackets inside pocket. Yet somehow, through my drunken haze, I miraculously typed out a message informing Teddy of our safe arrival. I just prayed she could read it, because I damned well couldn't.

Instantly, my phone beeped. Swaying and squinting, I attempted to scan what I assumed was her immediate reply – alas, no. It was only my ever-faithful PA, Thomas, emailing me with a follow-up itinerary for the ensuing days' interviews.

A disheartened sigh escaped me.

She probably took one look at my disjointed sentences and realised I'd written them whilst drunk. Without a doubt, that doghouse would be my new bed once I got home. Perhaps contemplating a kennel out the back wasn't a bad idea...with all the mod cons of course. A man had to be comfortable. The thought drew a riotous snigger.

Our equally solemn middle-aged porter, Simon, silently gestured to the open doors, signalling we'd reached the twentieth floor. My eyes rolled – couldn't he have just told us? Ushering us from the lift, we shadowed him, our incoherent state giving us no real clue where we were headed. Admittedly, we were dragging the chain a little – acting the fools, as my mother would say – until we finally reached our suite.

As a glaring Simon opened the double doors, I appeased his sour arse by shoving a more than generous tip into his hand. Almost immediately, he tried to give it back.

"There's no requirement for tipping here at Whittemore's, Mr Jaeger."

I tetchily waved him off. "Just accept it and take it with you."

"Thank you, Mr Jaeger," he meekly replied, sliding the wad of cash into the front pocket of his black vest before spinning on his heel and marching from the room.

A stern chat with Damon was clearly in order – specifically about his miserable staff. I'd suggest he replaced them with others that were a damned sight more cheerful. If not, I'd recommend a strict talking-to, ordering that they pick up their bottom lips at least. Otherwise, consider themselves fired. Knowing my cousin though, he'd merely pull them aside and sugar-coat the conversation. That's where he and I differed in the business world; he was the marshmallow, and I was the hot-headed hard arse. According to him anyway.

But as my blurry gaze swept over our suite, I smiled. Damon had done me proud. Two spacious bedrooms, both well-appointed with plush king-sized beds and ensuite bathrooms; a central living room filled with luxurious modern furnishings; and a ridiculously overstocked wet bar. Judging by the used glass on the coffee table, I'd say Asher had already taken the liberty.

Not that he needed another drink — he was drunker than I was. And it showed. I winced as I listened to his singing drifting from the bathroom; he still sounded worse than a back-alley cat, if that's possible.

Laughing to myself, I staggered toward my bedroom, stripping as I wandered into the ensuite.

Apart from the occasional romp under the water, a shower had never felt so good. Nor had the needling warmth over my head, as though it might somehow clear my drunken haze. In retrospect, I was merely steeling myself for the evening's onslaught with my cousin and Asher. Speaking of which, the little troublemaker ought to have arrived by now.

Flicking off the tap, I stepped out and grabbed one of the fluffy navy-blue bath sheets hanging neatly from the railing, drying myself as I strolled back to the bedroom. I opted for a casual approach: faded blue denim jeans, a slate-grey V-neck sweater, and suede lace-up desert boots. Once I'd quickly styled my hair, I made my way into the living room, a sly smile forming as I spotted my troublesome cousin.

With one Italian-leather-clad foot casually draped over a pair of pristinely pressed English wool dress pants, and a blue floral bone-china cup and saucer balanced between perfectly manicured fingers, he'd waited for me. But he'd also made it far too easy for me to needle him.

"What, too early for your usual bourbon, was it, Damo?"

His broad smile beamed, and his steely blue eyes brightened as I approached. "Never in my life has it been too early!" With an excited rattle, he set the near-empty cup on its saucer, practically dropping both onto the coffee table in his haste to rise to his feet. "Hey, old boy, it's been too long," he exulted, grasping me tightly and squeezing the life out of me.

"I agree, it has, old son," I replied, flinching at the jolting slap he delivered between my shoulder blades.

Having released me, he stepped back and eyed me, a mischievous glint forming. "About time you joined us, too, sunshine. Asher and I were beginning to worry you'd slithered down the plughole." I snorted — if only. "And how's the infamous Teddy? I hear you two finally— you know..."

Shaking my head, I couldn't help but laugh at the zeal in his voice or the flexing hips. "Let me guess — Eve?" His salacious expression said it all. "Yes, we are indeed a couple," I proclaimed, earning another painful slap between the shoulder blades as Damon smiled proudly.

"Well done, old boy, well done. She's quite the beauty — not that she wasn't when we were kids. Asher showed me a recent photo..." Damon whistled, gesturing crudely. "You're a lucky man; those legs... and those breasts, absolutely divine."

I peered over at an unusually quiet Asher, my brow lifting instinctively. "The two of you are worse than those high-society gossips we utterly despise." He dared to smirk. "Can we please quit the salacious subject of my girlfriend's body and talk about something less crude? Such as what dastardly plans you've made for us, Damon?"

Ginger brows jiggled, and the broadened grin that followed was... worrying.

I was a sucker for punishment. Why hadn't someone reminded me that partying on a weeknight was an incredibly horrible idea before venturing out with two of the worst influences I had ever known? As a rule, I generally refused for that very reason. What made me regret our little outing even more was the knowledge that we had interviews to conduct, with the first candidate arriving precisely at eight-thirty. And ringing your pregnant girlfriend whilst drunk — then discovering you'd missed two of her calls — was a fate worse than death.

Her teary abuse was more than I could bear. Making it worse were the two larrikins jeering and giggling in the background. My high-spirited laughter at their behaviour only added to my woes, and in the end, she hung up on me — not without sullenly advising me, and the two buffoons accompanying me, to grow the fuck up first.

Asher and Damon's torment continued well into the early hours of the morning, until I eventually and crudely told them where to go as I walked away, leaving them to drink their way through the bar's entire contents.

Attempting to navigate the journey up to my room — well, wasn't that an adventure. I stumbled through the hotel and eventually made it to my bed completely unscathed, crashing the moment I hit the mattress.

The following morning, I was undoubtedly suffering from quite the vicious hangover. Other than that, I had slept relatively peacefully.

Asher, on the other hand, looked rather haggard.

He strolled through the arched doorway of the downstairs restaurant and thumped into the adjacent chair, ordering a full English breakfast with a black coffee in the process. "Make that extra strong, please," he grumbled to the amused waitress, clutching his aching head between his hands.

I mockingly gaped. "What, no flirting? I'm shocked."

His middle finger extended, giving me the bird. I laughed. "And no witty comeback — well, there's a first."

"My chances of trying to get it up right now would be zero. What's worse, I hate myself for even admitting to that."

I chuckled. "I'm certain you'll make up for it later, my woeful friend."

"Gimme a couple of days. Then I'll be raring to go like a prized stallion on a stud farm."

Lifting the cup in my hand to my lips, I smiled. “I knew the old Asher was hiding in that dishevelled body of yours somewhere.”

Already on my second cup of black coffee, I watched as the waitress noisily dropped Asher’s breakfast in front of him. I winced alongside him. The next time we partied that hard, I was ordering room service instead. With the constant clatter of plates and cutlery, along with the loud, incessant chatter of the other patrons, nothing in that dining room was helping either of our aching heads — nor was the reminder of how much alcohol we’d consumed.

“That copious amount of bourbon we drank — or sculled, rather — last night has given me the shakes,” he whispered, eyeing his plate with disdain.

I groaned empathetically. “Let’s not forget the cocktails Damo poured down our throats. If he doesn’t look as green as we feel, I’ll be seriously pissed.”

Asher nursed his hanging head over his food. “I don’t know what shade of green you’re thinking, but when I looked at myself in the mirror this morning, the resemblance was pretty fucking close to the Grinch.”

I laughed. “Now you mention it, you do have the appearance of what I threw up after trying a few too many apple martinis.”

He gagged. “Please don’t...”

“Eat your breakfast. Trust me, it helps. We both need to be somewhat respectable for these interviews. And the sooner we get through them, the sooner we can head back to our rooms and rest our weary heads.”

Asher nodded enthusiastically; we were both optimistic about finding our new employees over the ensuing days. But by the second day, my optimism had well and truly exited the building. I was about ready to quit when our final interview swanned into the small conference room Damon had kindly lent us, wearing towering black stilettos on a pair of the cutest feet I'd ever seen. Something in my chest gave a faint, traitorous jolt — inconvenient, to say the least.

Asher hadn't exaggerated when he'd said Alexandra Kiddell was gorgeous.

With thick, shining mahogany hair and flawlessly smooth olive skin, she was indeed strikingly beautiful. She also possessed a warm smile — the kind that lit up a room — undeniably highlighting the depth of her beauty. I found myself noticing far too much for a professional setting and promptly straightened in my chair, as though posture alone could restore my sense.

"Alexandra Kiddell." Holding out a petite, slender hand for us to shake, she fixed us with almond-shaped eyes the colour of deep, rich bourbon. Too blindsided to notice, Asher and I just stood there, riveted. Fantastic. Asher's idiocy was clearly contagious.

Her forehead furrowed, puzzled as to why we'd left her hanging, no doubt.

Clearing my throat, I took the extended hand and shook it firmly. Her skin was warm — warmer than it had any right to be — and I released her hand a fraction too quickly.

"Ari Jaeger, CEO of JPD, and beside me here is my lawyer, Asher Bradford." I discreetly tapped the drooling idiot, snapping him out of it.

"Yes, what he said."

My eyes rolled in exasperation. Well, weren't we off to a great start? Thankfully, Alexandra saw the funny side and bit down on a plump bottom lip, subduing her bubbling laughter. The sight nearly made me choke on my own attempt at composure. The merriment in her eyes was... distracting.

With a shake of my head, I gestured to the upholstered leather chair opposite ours. "Ms Kiddell, please, take a seat and we'll get started."

Asher continued to stare, forcing me to reach up and smack him on the back of the head.

"Asher, sit!" Like a compliant dog, he obeyed — once he'd picked his jaw up off the floor and clamped it shut, that was. In this instance, I couldn't fault him; she was lovely. Confident, too, by the way she carried herself, settling into the seat and crossing one shapely leg over the other beneath a stylish asymmetrical dress. Something low in my chest tightened at the sight — inconvenient, unnecessary — and I forced my gaze to the résumé in front of me as though it held the secrets of the universe.

I sat back in my chair and crossed my legs, hoping to appear as I had with previous applicants: indifferent and aloof. I failed miserably. My body leaned forward of its own accord, betraying me before I caught myself and eased back again.

"Now, Ms Kiddell, tell me about yourself and what you have to offer JPD other than your amazing credentials?"

Fuck. I closed my eyes, shielding my obvious embarrassment as Asher snorted riotously. I couldn't believe I'd just unwittingly mirrored his words and wanted to strangle him with my bare hands for implanting his libidinous thoughts into my brain. I opened my eyes and shot him a threatening glare before turning my attention back to the lovely Ms Kiddell, clearing my throat. "Please, continue."

Thankfully, Alexandra — or Lexie, as she preferred — remained undeterred, exhibiting her professionalism. Someone had to. "Well, as you know, I currently work for..."

Her voice glided over me like smooth silk, effortlessly answering every question we threw at her. Too smooth. Too easy to listen to. I caught myself following the cadence of her words rather than the content and forced my focus back into line.

Not only was Ms Kiddell intelligent, but she took her career seriously. Not overly so, I'd say, judging by the thickly lashed eyes that twinkled as she made a joke about her short stature, making us all laugh. I stroked my chin thoughtfully. It appeared Ms Kiddell had quite the underlying streak of mischief. She was humble, too — another redeeming quality I admired. Never once during the interview did she mention the architectural awards she'd received for sustainability and new housing, just to name a few.

Enchanted by the beauty seated in front of me, the interview was sadly over before I could blink. A faint, unwelcome disappointment flickered through me — absurd, considering I barely knew her.

"We thank you for attending, Ms Kiddell. You've answered the relevant questions, so I'd say this meeting is now concluded."

Alexandra replied with the same poise and grace she carried herself with. "Thank you for giving me the opportunity."

"Do you not have any questions for us?" I queried, my eyes on her as I gently closed the folder in my lap. Her gaze held mine a fraction longer than necessary, and something warm curled low in my stomach. I ignored it.

"I only have one."

I glanced at her curiously. "Well, ask away."

"When do I start?"

If she hadn't succeeded in flooring me before, she had now. And Alexandra wasn't kidding around. Her determined gaze met mine, challenging me. The air between us tightened — or maybe that was just me being ridiculous again.

Tenacity and balls — two other qualities I admired.

My brows shot up as her steadfast gaze held mine. "As you are well aware, Ms Kiddell, the position isn't available until February next year, meaning subsequent interviews aren't until mid-January."

She pressed on with the same steely determination. "How long shall I have to wait, then? Before I know that I've successfully made that subsequent interview?"

I chuckled. Ms Kiddell's confidence knew no bounds. And damn if that confidence didn't land somewhere it shouldn't.

"The lucky candidates shall receive an email from my PA within the next couple of weeks. Don't get your hopes up, though; a second interview doesn't always guarantee the job's yours either," I clarified, mustering up my sternest voice. "That's the most I can give you, for now, Ms Kiddell."

An undeterred Alexandra steadily pushed to her feet and held out her hand once more, which I eagerly took. Her hand was warm again — too warm — and I released it a heartbeat later than I should have.

"Well, I look forward to hearing from your PA then, Mr Jaeger." With that, she dropped my hand and pivoted with ease on five-inch heels, strolling self-assured from the room.

I watched her go for a second too long before catching myself.

I slipped my hands into my pockets and spun to face a broadly grinning Asher. "Ms Kiddell is one helluva spitfire."

Asher cocked his head in appreciation. "You're not wrong. Beauty and brains — the perfect package. So was Karsten Shaw..."

Laughter rumbled out of me. "You need sex addicts anonymous. If — and that's a big if — we employ either of them, sexual relations are out of the question, my horny-toad friend." I began shutting my laptop down and shoving résumés back into a folder. "And don't pout. Workplace relations don't work, remember?"

Asher's shoulders sagged. "How could I forget that little debacle."

I jolted his memory. "Stella, wasn't it, if I rightly recall?"

"Sexy Stella; she was one gorgeous gal."

"Yes, she was — but she was also extremely good at her job."

He sighed regretfully. "Kara in HR has never forgiven me for Stella's rather sudden departure."

I wonder why, I thought quietly.

Sleeping with a married woman was a mistake I paid for dearly on Asher's behalf. At the time of their little indiscretion, Stella's husband, Hunter Patterson, happened to be an investor with JPD. As one might imagine, when Hunter found out, all hell broke loose. First, he cancelled our contract, which consequently resulted in litigation with our lawyers — I was forced to hire someone else for the duration of negotiations due to the conflict of interest. Naturally, the judge ruled in Hunter's favour, costing my company a rather hefty sum in restitution.

From then on, I enforced a strict no-fraternisation policy, hoping to prevent another costly mess in the future. Whether Asher learned from that experience remained to be seen. He ought to have, considering the dressing-down he received from me after I signed the cheque for Hunter.

Still, even as I lectured myself on professionalism, my mind flicked back — annoyingly — to the way Lexie had held my gaze. A steady, unflinching challenge. I pushed the thought aside before it could settle.

That wasn't the only time I'd interfered with his love life. The other was upon discovering the dalliance between him and Florence — Ren, as I affectionately called her — a younger cousin on my dad's side. Ren, unfortunately, hadn't appreciated my interference in their 'friends with benefits' scheme and refused to accept my apologies. Eventually, her initial frustrations with me gave way when she met and fell in love with Rylen Astor, a wealthy lawyer employed with my father's firm, to whom she was now happily married. Upon reflection, she appreciated I was only looking out for her best interests due to Asher's notorious reputation. He was my best friend, and I loved him dearly; however, I was all too aware of his 'bed them and leave them' attitude. Again, which Ren realised due to the slew of girls Asher bedded afterwards.

I slapped him on the shoulder. "Come on, misery guts, let's get out of here so we can find the other bad influence in my life and go out again. Who knows — you may find someone silly enough who isn't related to me or doesn't work for me to sleep with you!"

"Oh God, I hope so!"

I laughed heartily. "Let's go shower and change, 'cause man, those pheromones would repel anyone from getting too close!"

And yet, as we walked out, a faint, unwelcome warmth lingered in my chest — the echo of a smile that wasn't Asher's. Irritating.

Neatly tucked in a small laneway, The Jazz Bar was a hidden gem and one of Perth's nicest little surprises. With a theme inspired by nineteen-forties New Orleans, the décor, the patrons, and the live jazz band were mercifully far more sophisticated than the lads' original choice of a heavy-metal pub with wall-to-wall crowds.

I was excited — though no more than Asher and Damon. Almost immediately, they began perusing the room in that extensive search for "the one," and by that, they meant the next notch on their bedposts. For the next half hour, they charmed their way around the bar and main floor, offering to buy drinks in the hope it would appeal to whichever lucky lady caught their eye.

I left them to it and sat back, relaxing in my chair, sipping my tumbler of bourbon and enjoying the tapas selection we'd ordered while listening to the band perform the great classics. Perhaps it was a place worth revisiting with Teddy in the near future.

Unlike our previously tense chats, our earlier call was an improvement — if only slightly. We'd used video link this time, at my insistence; my safety net, if you will. There was nothing wrong with ensuring Teddy saw a sober me, not the train wreck she'd witnessed previously.

Regardless of my effort, her demeanour struck a worrying chord. Distracted and fidgety, she barely made an effort to make eye contact. As for our conversation — what conversation? I probed and pushed, asking questions, only to receive short, curt responses. Trying to pry any sort of answer out of her was comparable to a tooth extraction; downright painful. It was unlike her, especially when I enquired about the pregnancy.

Instead of the delight she usually displayed, she became evasive and abrupt, leaving me confused and lost for words.

I let it go; it wasn't worth the pain of another argument.

Shortly after, she bid me goodnight and a safe flight, hanging up before I'd even had the chance to tell her I'd extended our stay until Friday — or to say I loved her. The call had scarcely lasted ten minutes.

Something was up, and that pit of fear returned. Hopefully, I was merely acting paranoid.

As I polished off my drink, a small group of friends entered the bar, their girlish giggles distracting me from my moment of self-pity.

That wasn't all that caught my attention.

Dressed in a strapless, fitted knee-length white lace dress over a nude underlay, paired with six-inch blush-pink heels tied with wide ribbons around her tiny ankles, was a familiar face. Her long, shiny mahogany waves flowed over her shoulders, the ends curling over small but perfectly proportioned breasts. She was prettier than any picture I'd ever seen.

A pang of guilt washed over me, forcing my wandering gaze away. Thoughts such as these weren't right. Nevertheless, as I began to question my lapse in judgement, a confidently sweet voice pulled me from my musings.

"Mr Jaeger, what a pleasure."

Ridiculously, I acquired a sudden inability to articulate, and my confidence evaporated. I eventually found my voice and cleared my throat as I pushed politely to my feet. The linen napkin in my hand dropped inconspicuously to hang over my crotch before I extended my other hand to the vision before me. "Ms Kiddell, what a lovely surprise."

She produced a beaming smile in return. “Lexie, please.”

“Lexie it is, then.” Chuffed, I offered her a seat and a drink. My night had just improved dramatically. And as she settled gracefully into the chair beside me, a breath caught somewhere between my lungs and logic — ridiculous, and swiftly dismissed.

11

I was right to be paranoid. Teddy was a mess, and according to the girls, had been since the day I left for my business trip. An indescribable pain gripped my chest as prolific tears streamed down her cheeks while she choked out the word miscarriage. Three days ago. The day after I flew out.

The revelation made me regret staying on an extra day to attend a fundraiser dinner at Sebastian and Catherine's home in Peppermint Grove — a night spent drinking and schmoozing with Perth's socialites. All of it now seemed frivolous, meaningless, because our child was gone. Gone while I was away, acting and behaving as if I were a single man.

Reality set in as a consuming guilt weighed me down. But as a broken Teddy lay sobbing on the bed, it was enough to recentre my world in an instant. I slumped onto the mattress beside her, cocooning her within the warmth of my arms.

"I'm... so... sorry, Ari... it... just... happened."

Pressing my lips to her forehead, I drew her shaking body closer.

"Shh, I know. I'm just so sorry you had to endure this without me." Swallowing the lump that was my heart lodged in my throat,

I cupped the back of her head with my palm. "I just wish you'd told me sooner."

Her head shook heatedly against my chest. "It wouldn't have made any difference... and you wouldn't have gotten here on time." She tilted her head back, searching my aggrieved face with her watery gaze. "There was nothing you could do."

Her expression broke my heart. "At least I would've been here to hold your hand, console you sooner, grieve together." Regret engulfed me the moment the words left my mouth. "Forgive me — that was insensitive."

Thankfully, she understood my turmoil. She lifted a trembling hand to my face, gently caressing my stubbled cheek. Then, joining our lips, she gave me the sweetest of kisses. "You're here now, grieving with me, and that's all that matters."

I buried my head in the crook of her neck, my throat thickening as unbearable grief surfaced — our sorrow for our lost child leaving us utterly shattered.

The weekend passed in a blur as we spent the entire time immersed in one another, curled up either on the sofa or in bed. Facing the outside world was inconceivable. Only on the odd occasion did Teddy retreat, mostly to play the piano. Bach, Chopin, or some other familiar melodist — each composition soon became a constant reminder of her overwhelming sadness and grief.

That was short-lived.

Come Monday, Teddy ventured off to work as if nothing had happened — a move that astounded me, almost as much as her decision to quit her job. A decision she nonchalantly informed me of while flouncing about the kitchen amid dinner preparations.

"I've taken far too much time off as it is, and that's not fair to Spencer," she reasoned, dipping a flour-coated chicken breast into a bowl of beaten egg.

"Neither was quitting," I argued, my disbelieving gaze following her as she moved on to the next bowl.

Rolling the chicken breast in a mix of panko crumbs and fresh herbs, she glowered. "How isn't it? Explain it to me, Ari, seeing as you're the expert!"

I bristled and returned the glare. "Where would you like me to start?"

As I foully began explaining why one shouldn't give up so easily, I threw in my discoveries about her duplicity — and the figurative shit hit the proverbial fan. Our argument escalated from there, ending with Teddy rushing off to her bedroom in a flurry of tears, leaving Dominique to finish dinner. I stormed out and licked my wounds by the pool.

What a mess we'd become.

Drawing deeply on the cigar nestled between my fingers while downing more glasses of bourbon than intended, a hand came down on my shoulder, startling me. I glanced up at my surprise visitor. "Jesus! Evan? What the fuck are you doing here?"

Evan regarded me compassionately. "Scarlett called."

"Of course she did," I muttered, leaning forward to grab the bottle of bourbon and liberally topping up my near-empty glass.

He slid onto the soft cushion of the rattan chair beside me and poured himself an equally liberal measure, making it abundantly clear there was a long chat ahead. "Don't shoot the messenger, Ari; she's quite concerned about both you and Teddy."

"The lack of confidence in me is positively heart-warming," I murmured with a derisive roll of my eyes.

"No one doubts your ability to care, Ari. From what she's told me, you and Teddy have been at loggerheads — quite a lot lately, too, by the sounds of things." Cocking his head, his silvery brows lifted in question.

Looking out over the garden, I dragged on the cigar. Plumes of smoke billowed as my sloshed gaze drifted. "Yeah, we have. I'd be lying if I said things had been easy."

"I can imagine; Teddy can make you work for it, that's for sure." Evan let out a nervous chuckle.

I scowled. "You know that's not what I meant."

He sagely and uneasily conceded, "I know... I was just trying to make light of the situation..."

"Well, there's nothing light about this current situation!" I barked, making Evan blanch. "Everything has changed, since—"

"Since Teddy told you about her rape..."

I scoffed. "Oh, not since we informed my family, disclosing her attacker in the process. But let's not forget your fucking bitch of a wife with her latest and greatest verbal tirade — topped off with a miscarriage." I knew I sounded reactive and bitter, but present circumstances warranted my odious feelings. "I'm fucking exhausted, and honestly, Evan, I don't know how much more of this perpetual drama I can handle."

"What are you saying, Ari?" Evan's perplexed expression hardened. "Because from where I sit, it sounds as if you're giving up on my daughter... now it's gotten all too hard!" His throat bobbed as his face reddened. “I thought you loved her enough to never give up on her! You promised me!”

Enraged by the hypocrisy, I pushed off the chair and loomed over him. “Do I need to remind you about the last time we had a differing opinion over Teddy? Don’t you dare sit there and lecture me about giving up when you gave up on her ten years ago!” I roared, wagging an accusatory finger at him. “A pattern you clearly repeated when you decided she was ‘well enough’ just so you could return to your cushy little life with your mistress. So since then, Evan, it’s been me...” My voice shook as I stabbed a finger at my chest. “...picking up the remaining pieces of her shattered heart — not you!”

Unperturbed, Evan calmly set his glass down on the table between the chairs and rose to his feet. “You’re drunk and don’t know what you’re saying. Maybe go take a shower while I make some coffee. Once you’ve sobered up enough, we’ll talk.”

“Don’t patronise me, Evan!” Quivering with indignation, I lashed out, striking him squarely in the mouth. I watched as he stumbled backwards into the pool and disappeared beneath the surface, only to resurface moments later.

“What the fuck, Ari!” he raged, baring bloody teeth.

“Well don’t piss me off and I won’t hit you!”

Hauling his sopping body from the pool, he glared. “It seems Teddy’s not the only one who needs therapy!”

My response to that ludicrous suggestion was another smack to the face.

“What I need, Evan,” I growled as he spluttered and swam back to the pool’s edge, “is for all this bullshit to end!”

I was about to walk away but stopped and crouched before him. He’d left me no choice but to make him aware of his daughter's deceit. "Are you even remotely aware Teddy has skipped her therapy, and only attended the first half-dozen sessions because I practically held her hand? Oh, and her medication — she's stopped taking that too, by the way."

By now, my anger had turned glacial, biting back at the wool she'd pulled over her father's eyes. Hanging onto the pool's coping, he remained sheepishly silent.

"You and Therese are truly moulded from the same stone when it comes to hiding behind your fucking blinkers..." I tutted. "And at this moment, the level of disgust I feel for you, Evan, is equally parallel."

I straightened and spun away, leaving him and his bloody state behind — he'd more than likely have black eyes tomorrow. Too bad; it was his fault for aggravating me in the first place. I stormed inside and paused near the family room.

"Scarlett, I suggest you attend to your father; he's in the pool and may need medical attention after I belted him. Twice!"

She shot out of her chair and outside at lightning speed. I'd never seen her move so fast.

I grouchily turned to my sister, who was finishing off dinner in the kitchen. "Dom, can you drive me to my place, please? Being here is a bad idea right now, and I'm far too drunk to be behind the wheel."

She shot me a muddy look and huffed. "Fine, but you ought to make Teddy aware of your intentions; she's upset enough thanks to your tyranny."

I gaped. How was I suddenly the villain when Teddy had lied to everyone — including herself?

Vexed with everyone and everything, I threw my arms up and slapped them back to my sides. "Fine! I'm a masochist anyway, it seems, and it's the only reason why I love enduring the pleasure of Teddy yelling at me!"

Yes, I was drunk — and being drunk made one feel a little sorry for oneself. With all the presently annoying goings-on, I felt entitled to act mortally wounded, even if no one else thought so. Eh, fuck 'em all.

I staggered toward the bedroom, immediately sobering when I found a distressed Teddy curled in the foetal position on her side of the bed. One look at her blotchy face and red-rimmed eyes told me leaving would be a mistake. She was far too fragile, and if anything happened to her, living with my choice would be unforgivable.

So, rather than wallowing further, I jumped beneath a cold shower before crawling under the covers beside her, sleeping off my drunken stupor before anyone else categorically upset me.

"Good to see you came to your senses, brother, by staying instead of leaving," Dom asserted as I breezed into the kitchen the next morning. She passed me a mug of freshly brewed coffee, which I gratefully took. "It would've broken Teddy's heart."

As if I needed reminding. I glowered. "Teddy's not the only one with a broken heart, Dom; mine is too." My tone was harsher than intended. "The degree of everyone's empathy isn't helping Teddy; it's hindering her, and as of now, it has to stop."

My sister's jaw dropped. "You can't be serious? Teddy's been through hell and back, and turning our backs on her when she needs our help would be reprehensible—"

Slamming my mug down on the island bench, I let out a frustrated sigh. "Dom, calm down. I wasn't suggesting anything so heinous, nor can I believe you deduced I'd be so cruel." Hurt edged my voice, and she winced.

"Sorry," she mouthed.

"My feelings aside, I'm deadly serious when I say we can't continue like this. Walking on eggshells for fear of upsetting Teddy doesn't solve a bloody thing. She's skipped therapy, stopped her medication — shall I continue?" I sounded like a broken record, always having to justify my feelings.

Dominique blanched at my stern expression. "I'm so sorry, Ari. I honestly had no idea, and I bet my bottom dollar Scarlett and Poppy aren't aware either. I thought Teddy was still attending her sessions — she's been out an awful lot lately. No wonder you're frustrated."

"Well, it shows I'm not the villain you three make me out to be."

She slid both hands into the back pockets of her jeans, awkwardly swallowing her guilt. "No, I guess you aren't. Sorry, bro."

I pressed my lips to her temple before sliding onto a barstool. "All good, sis. Nevertheless, just do as I've asked and start pushing Teddy; she needs it. And if she's leaving her job, I'm employing a full-time personal trainer to get her exercising four days a week, as well as a minder. Which I was going to do anyway thanks to bloody Emmett and Therese's harassing ways."

"Wow, you really are coming down on her, aren't you?"

"It's either that, or I give up and walk away. But as you know, I'm not one to give up that easily."

Dominique's nose scrunched as she smiled knowingly. "No, you're not. But that's because you're rather tenacious when it comes to the people you love." Cocking her head, she paused, skimming her palm over the marble counter. The overly cautious silence was trying my patience.

"Spit it out, Dom."

"Perhaps take a leaf out of your own book and go back to the gym a little more often? And maybe think about slowing down on the drinking?" She was right; how was Teddy expected to make changes if I wasn't — or hadn't?

"Relationships are about compromise, right?"

My gleeful sister threw an arm around my shoulders. "Now I understand how our mother feels when she's right."

Twisting in my seat to face the island counter, I opened the newspaper to the business section and chuckled. "Stop your gloating, little sister."

"I would never dream of doing such a thing, big brother."

Dominique was starting to sound more like me every day. Her brows creased as her concerned gaze settled on me. "Where is Teddy, by the way? Is she still sleeping?"

"No, she must have left early."

"Well, where'd she disappear to? It's far too early to start work."

I pursed my lips and shrugged. "That's what I'd love to know too."

∞

Teddy

Ari's reaction to my resignation was nothing like I'd expected — at all. To be honest, I'd hoped for something a little less angry than the tirade I received. Rather than supporting me or taking the time to hear me out, he chucked a tantrum — over my life, of all things. Apparently, my decision was rash and thoughtless. Then I dared to ask how my departure would affect others — the wrong question, evidently.

What about my clients, and where did that leave them? They had counted on me to see their projects through to the end, and without extending them the courtesy of my notice to quit, I was breaking a judiciously built trust... blah, blah, blah.

He was furious. We'd reached a critical point in our relationship, especially since his return from the business trip — and argue? Christ, we hadn't stopped. Most of the arguments were my fault, I'll admit. The unopened packet of antidepressants he found. The therapy sessions I'd skipped — courtesy of the good doctor ratting me out. And quitting my job had simply topped off an already shitty day.

Facing Ari this morning would've been like facing a firing squad. After drinking excessively last night, he'd have woken like a bear with a sore head anyway. The truth was, I didn't have the strength to argue anymore. I'd set my alarm earlier than usual and escaped before anyone in the house could corner me long enough to cast their judgemental stares.

I spent the morning at the pier in Port Melbourne, eating an extremely unhealthy breakfast while watching the sunrise over the ocean. Not that it mattered — I needed to regain some of the weight I'd lost, and a greasy egg-and-bacon burger with a hash brown, washed down with a milky vanilla latte, would undoubtedly help. My arteries might protest later, but for now, the junk food soothed my wounded soul.

For all intents and purposes, I was pushing Ari away. Ten years of baggage was a hefty weight to carry, and worse still, the burden I'd placed on his shoulders — that alone was killing us.

The once calm, rational man I'd known my entire life had grown tetchy, frustrated by anything and everything. He'd slowly disintegrated into a shadow of his former self. Even the sex was different.

Throwing my rubbish onto the floor of my car, I wiped my hands with a paper serviette and tossed it aside as I turned the key. My thoughts drifted to his dominant side as I reversed out of the parking space.

Exerted several times, the sex had been liberating and freeing. Not new to me — but to Ari, it was. Perhaps there was a silver lining after all. Maybe, if I discussed the BDSM lifestyle with him and he agreed, we could make it a permanent fixture in our lives. It might give us the cathartic release we both desperately needed, and with any luck, draw us closer.

Persuading him shouldn't be too difficult… surely.

Nonetheless, before making such a risky suggestion, fixing our relationship through communication — not sex — was paramount. My mouth quirked. What a turn for the books, considering that had always been my preferred method. Perhaps I ought to warn Ari to sit first, so he doesn't fall over from the shock.

I laughed to myself as I pulled into my allocated car park in the underground garage and switched off the engine. Checking my makeup in the mirror and satisfied the dark pits beneath my eyes were covered, I climbed out of the driver's side and shut the door.

Strolling over to the bank of lifts, I pressed the button on the wall. The doors glided open immediately, and I stepped inside, absently pushing for the fifth floor. My idle thoughts crashed to a halt as a hand shot between the closing doors, forcing them apart. Tears spurted as I sagged in relief, staring misty-eyed at the impatient occupant in the threshold, devilishly grinning at me.

"Hello there, love."

I threw myself into Ari's arms and began sobbing. So much for my meticulously applied makeup. His arms — warm, steady, wrapped in navy pinstripes — closed around me, anchoring me.

"Hey, what's all this about?" he murmured, stroking my back with a tenderness that only made me cry harder.

I nuzzled into his chest, inhaling his familiar citrus scent. "Sorry... I was worried it was someone else for a minute. I'm just so grateful it was you and not—"

Ari's hands came up to cradle my face. "Just stop talking."

His mouth found mine in a fierce, hungry kiss that sent us stumbling across the tiled floor, my back thudding softly against the wall.

The intensity of him — the relief, the frustration, the need — poured into me. I tugged at his shirt, desperate for more, while his hand skimmed the length of my torso, leaving a trail of heat in its wake. I melted into him, breathless, wanting him with a sharpness that bordered on painful.

Then the elevator dinged.

Dammit.

We broke apart, panting, taking a moment to absorb each other's dishevelled state as I pressed the inset button to keep the doors open. Ari's dark eyes were molten, his breath unsteady, his expression a mix of desire and restraint. My own reflection in the mirrored walls betrayed me — flushed cheeks, shining eyes, lips swollen from his kiss.

He adjusted himself subtly, catching my gaze with a knowing smirk.

"Later — *after* we've talked."

I scrunched my nose. "If I last that long."

He shook his head, holding the doors open. "You'll have to. Or else."

A shiver ran through me at the warning threaded beneath his tone — not unkind, but firm. A reminder that this wasn't the moment to lose ourselves again.

Exhaling a frustrated sigh, I relented. "Okay. I'll wait."

"Good." He nodded, satisfied, and stepped back as the doors finally closed.

I bit my lip, unable to stop the smile tugging at my mouth. If anything, the moment had only strengthened my resolve. Raising the idea of exploring further — sooner rather than later — suddenly didn't seem so far-fetched.

Pivoting on the spike of my heel, I pushed open the etched glass door and strolled into Spencer's office.

"Spencer, may I speak with you, please?"

He glanced up and smiled warmly. "Please tell me you're here to rescind your resignation?"

I smiled widely. His shoulders sagged in relief.

"Oh, thank God. But you know, I never really accepted it anyway."

I laughed softly. "I thought as much.

12

Ari

Upon entering my office, Asher's perceptive gaze immediately clocked my jovial demeanour.

"What's got you licking your lips like the cat that got the cream?"

I wordlessly waggled my brows.

He flopped into the adjacent chair with all the grace of a dying swan and speculated, "I reckon you had your breakfast between your girlfriend's thighs before coming to work... It's the only reasonable explanation, 'cause yesterday, man, you were so damned uptight."

I remained tight-lipped and diverted the subject to more critical matters, hoping to capture his short attention span. "Have you gone over the interviews conducted in Perth?"

Asher narrowed his gaze, wounded. "You aren't going to tell me, are you?"

Perhaps I was wrong — there's a first for everything.

Skimming my finger over the mouse pad, I kept my eyes glued to the computer screen. "No. Interviews, please."

"Spoilsport."

"You'll get over it. Now, who are the lucky candidates?"

He rolled his chair closer with a dramatic pout and slapped the compiled list on the desk between us.

We spent the rest of the morning poring over résumés and comparing notes. Many disagreements later — and with much deliberation — we'd narrowed the potential candidates for Head Engineer down to three, including the elusive Ms Kiddell. Sorting our grad students was far easier; we both took a shine to the three hopefuls we'd interviewed Tuesday morning.

I pressed the button on my phone and called Thomas into my office. As usual, he arrived well prepared, handing me a stack of new messages before perching on the empty chair beside Asher.

"Are these the compiled lists of rejections and subsequent interviews?" he asked, pointing to the neatly stacked folders on the right-hand corner of my desk. Astute as always — I thanked the man upstairs daily for the day Thomas Garcia walked through my office door.

I nodded. "Correct. The blue folder is the list of unsuccessful candidates — send them an email thanking them for their applications. The six in the pink folder are to attend interviews in January; I've listed the dates in the notes. They'll require flights booked — premium seats. Accommodation: the usual hotel. Use the company card. The itinerary and secondary interview details must be a separate attachment, and attach a receipt as confirmation. Make my conditions abundantly clear: if they fail to respond by the date I've set, they forfeit their interview."

Thomas took notes on his iPad, nodding. "Certainly, sir. I'll have these emails sent out by day's end."

Asher watched the exchange with open admiration. "Can I steal him? Please?"

"No, you most certainly may not," I countered.

Thomas rose, collecting the folders.

"Will that be all, Mr Jaeger?"

"Yes, that's all. Thank you, Thomas."

As he strode out and closed the door, Asher slung his feet onto my desk, singing Thomas's praises.

"He's good. I knew there was a reason I liked him."

Slightly distracted by my messages, I snorted. "Indeed, he is. He's also far better than my last assistant. She spent more time vying for my attention by flashing her pathetic cleavage than doing the work I paid her to do."

"I banged her; she was a dud in bed," Asher blurted.

The thought of those two tangled together made me shudder. "Why does that not surprise me? Please tell me you at least had the sense to use a dinger?"

"My name's Billy Hunt, not silly c—"

I held up a hand, laughing. "That, my friend, I could never accuse you of being. Crude, yes — but not that."

"On that less-than-appealing note," he replied, pushing to his feet, "I'm going to slink back to my office to eat my lunch. Unless you want to join me at a restaurant instead?"

I shook my head. "No, thanks. I have another matter requiring my undivided attention — one that doesn't require your sticky nose."

"Me?" Asher pressed a hand to his chest, feigning mortal injury. "I never! But I might later!" His eyebrows jiggled above glistening eyes. "With any luck."

"Get out!" I yelled, shaking with laughter.

He was a shocker — but in tough times, as Poppy was to Teddy, he was my rock. Without him, life would be awfully lonesome. Although, come to think of it, my office might be a lot quieter too.

Chuckling to myself, I rolled my chair backwards, grabbed my wallet from the locked drawer in my desk, and pushed to my feet. Sliding it into my trouser pocket, I strolled to the door and reefed it open, startling Thomas.

Fumbling to close the magazine in front of him, he clumsily rose to greet me. "Mr Jaeger… I… I—"

I held up a hand to reassure him. "Sorry, Thomas, I didn't mean to frighten you."

"I was just catching up on a hobby of mine," he stuttered self-consciously, flashing the front cover of a chess publication.

Hoping to ease his embarrassment, I offered him a lifeline. "I'm an avid player myself. The strategy keeps the mind active — and it's a great stress reliever, don't you agree?"

Chuffed, he smiled proudly. "Of course, sir."

"Well, how about a game sometime?"

Nonplussed, he stared at me like a deer caught in headlights. I eased his flustered state. "A gentleman's game only, of course — over a glass of bourbon, or wine, whichever you prefer."

His mortification subsided, replaced by a broad smile. "I'd be delighted, sir."

I reciprocated. "Great. I'll set aside a day. My place all right with you?"

"As long as it's no bother to you, sir?"

I shook my head. "Not at all. It'll be a pleasure to play a worthy opponent — someone who actually understands the game." A wry smile tugged at my lips as I recalled my numerous attempts to teach Teddy; it had been fruitless and frustrating for both of us. The only lesson she ever truly mastered was how to drink bourbon properly — which somehow devolved into a catastrophic game of Naked Twister that ended with us laughing ourselves senseless and... well, let's just say my grand piano has never quite sounded the same since.

Not that Dominique ever recovered from walking in unannounced and catching us bare-arsed in the middle of it either.

"Anyway," I continued, clearing my throat and dragging myself back to the present, "I'm heading out to run an errand and shall be back shortly. Do you need anything whilst I'm out? What about some lunch?"

"That would be lovely, Mr Jaeger, thank you."

"Anything in particular?" I asked, tapping the top of his desk.

Thomas shook his head. "I'm not fussed."

"No worries. See you soon."

Leaning an elbow on the glass counter of my preferred jeweller, Diamante Jewellers, my foot tapped over the glossy Carrara marble tiles beneath the soles of my leather shoes in the hope of gaining the attention of the store's owner. Dion eventually acknowledged my presence, his agonised expression peering at me from beyond the sheer voile curtains behind the counter.

"Oh, merde! Jaeger, vous êtes là!" His explicit gasp, paired with the widening eyes, piqued my curiosity — especially as he muttered under his breath in rapid-fire French, rudely turning his back on me to scramble about before ducking through an adjoining door. More expletives followed.

"I can see and hear you, Dion," I called out irritably in French, bringing his flapping about to an abrupt halt.

He looked up at me in wonder. "I'll be right with you, Mr Jaeger," he finally replied in English.

Straightening the collar of his pale pink shirt and smoothing the front, he cleared his throat before dramatically parting the white voile curtains and strolling his willowy frame toward me. His expression was apologetic. "Mr Jaeger, I'm truly sorry for my atrocious manners in making you wait, but it seems your order was merely completed — as in barely a minute ago."

My lips thinned. "One of your staff left a message informing me it was ready before I arrived at work this morning."

Dion squirmed, shifting his pointy-toed shoes beneath my bristling gaze. "Again, my apologies, Mr Jaeger. I assure you it wasn't ready when they called. I'll reprimand them for the mistake." He lifted his hands placatingly. "However, it is ready now. If you'll follow me, please?"

"Certainly," I growled, following him to a private room behind the service counter. He motioned toward a Danish-designed royal blue velvet chair with a tufted finish in the corner. I sank against the high back, my gaze immediately drawn to the cherry-red box with its piano-gloss finish and bevelled edges sitting in the centre of the polished table.

"Ah, here it is, Mr Jaeger — your masterpiece," Dion gushed, presenting the box with a flourish. "Has it been made to your specifications?"

A bespoke eighteen-karat white gold eternity band, its circumference pavé-set with forty-eight micro-diamonds, cradled a flawless princess-cut centre stone that glittered between my fingertips. I slid it over my pinkie; it fitted perfectly. "It's exactly as I requested." At least they'd managed to get that right.

Pleased, Dion clapped his hands together like an excited seal. "Excellente. Now, as we discussed, the matching wedding band shall be made when it is required, yes?"

My impassive mask slipped into place, making him gulp. "As long as today's debacle doesn't happen again."

He nodded vigorously. "I'll oversee the order myself if that's what it takes."

Setting the ring back into its velvet bed and snapping the lid shut, a ghost of a smile flickered. "Then, of course, you'll retain my business."

Satisfied, I handed over my credit card.

By the time I strolled back to the car, I had 'the when' part of my proposal thoroughly established. But it was figuring out 'the how' that was proving to be more challenging than I initially thought. I considered asking my father for advice but decided against it as he'd only spill the news to my mother. I loved her dearly, but her exuberance at times was a little overwhelming, and that was putting it mildly. So, for now, my plans simply had to remain under my hat until such time arose. I kept that in mind as I wandered into Bento, a Japanese restaurant close to the office, purchasing sushi as well as an orange juice for both myself, and Thomas.

I set the plastic sushi container, chopsticks, and a drink on Thomas's desk. "I hope you love sushi," I tossed out cheerily — the question purely rhetorical

He looked up and smiled appreciatively. "I love Japanese food. How much do I owe you?"

"Nothing."

"I have the cash here—"

I glanced at the small wad of notes pinched between his skinny fingers and waved dismissively. “Keep it for a rainy day. You work hard; lunch was the least I could do.”

Realising it was pointless to argue, a red-faced Thomas quickly slid the money back into the front pocket of his black dress pants. His charcoal vest and neatly knotted tie framed a crisp button-up shirt, and the black-rimmed glasses perched on his nose completed his usual understated, professional look — competent, reliable, and just shy of polished, which suited him perfectly. “Thank you, sir.”

“All good.” Spinning leisurely, I wandered into my office, dropping the second sushi container and my iPhone onto the desk. I had barely settled into my chair when my phone vibrated.

Exultation surged as Teddy’s name flashed across the screen. “Well, hello there, gorgeous.” A wide grin formed as she giggled. “What can I do for you on this fine afternoon?”

“Someone’s in a rather buoyant mood,” she remarked, chirpy and amused.

My grin turned embarrassingly goofy. “Talking to you always puts me in a good mood, even on the worst days.”

“I’m glad I can be of service. Be careful, though,” she teased, laughter bubbling in her voice. “I charge hourly, you know.”

“Lucky I can afford you, then.” I chuckled, swivelling my chair to face the rare cloudless blue sky beyond my floor-to-ceiling windows.

She giggled. “We’re so off track here, as usual.”

“And whose fault is that?” I simpered, feigning indignance. “It’s certainly not mine.”

“Yeah, it was mine,” she admitted through a breathy laugh. “Anyway, back on track, Mr Jaeger — I was calling to see if you’d made any dinner plans. I know you wanted to talk, but my father called asking us to join him at the Rare Steakhouse on Little Collins Street. I'd say he's trying to smooth things over between you."

As he ought to. Apologising in a public place was a strategic move if ever I saw one. "Sounds good. Will it be just us, or is Scarlett joining?"

"Scarlett won't be, no. She has a date apparently — some guy she met at the gym around the corner from my place."

My brows shot up. Since when was Scarlett interested in exercising?

"Did she mention who the unlucky fellow was?" I teased, sliding the ring box from my jacket pocket and flicking the lid open. The princess-cut diamond caught the light, and for a moment my pulse stumbled. I wasn't a man easily rattled, yet the idea of offering her forever — of her accepting it — sent a strange, exhilarating tightness stealing the steadiness from my breath. A smile tugged at my lips as I imagined Teddy's reaction.

"She did, surprisingly — Logan something. I can't recall his last name. I wasn't paying close attention; I was too preoccupied with a little project for you," she added coyly.

My interest sharpened, and the lid snapped shut. "This project... any chance I'm allowed a hint?"

"No, you aren't!" she declared, her wicked laughter spilling through the line. "It'll ruin the surprise, so you'll just have to wait. And don't pout — it won't work."

I threw my head back and laughed. "I'm starting to believe I'm dating my mother. The similarity is uncanny. And for the record, I wasn't pouting — though I can't believe you thought I would."

"Well, normally you use it as a tactic to get me to cave," Teddy scoffed. "You forget how well I know you."

"That you do," I agreed, leaning back in my chair, "and I'm incredibly thankful you do."

"Hmm, you'd be stuffed without me otherwise."

"Getting dressed in the morning without you just wouldn't be the same."

"Or undressed..." she purred, her tone dipping into something that made my pulse spike. "Anyway, I need to go — some of us actually have to work for a living."

"What are you implying, Missy?"

She giggled. "Oh, nothing at all. Anyway, see you tonight. Love you. Bye."

Her chortle echoed through the speaker before the line abruptly went dead.

Gaping, I stared at the phone. "She hung up! I can't believe she hung up — the little wench!"

"Who hung up, sir?" Thomas asked, stepping into my office with a curious glance.

"Teddy! That's who!" I tossed the phone aside and swiftly rolled my chair under the desk, concealing the inconvenient evidence of Teddy's effect on me. "Don't ask."

"I wasn't about to." Thomas smirked, handing over the mail and the hard copies of the interview emails for the new year.

"Good." I nodded, shifting in my seat and cursing Teddy under my breath for leaving me hanging. Literally. She'd pay for that little stunt later. Hopefully sooner — as in immediately after work.

Except time, as usual, had other plans, ruining my fun.

Once I left work, I sped to Teddy's to shower and change, with the two of us rushing back out the door shortly afterwards. If the weather hadn't been so damned hot and muggy, staying in my suit might have remained an option — sans the jacket and tie. Thankfully, my loyal housekeeper had been accommodating enough to deliver a packed overnight bag directly to my office.

Dinner, at least, didn't threaten to raise a sweat.

The Rare Steakhouse, uptown on Little Collins Street, was an absolute delight with its faded red brick walls, timber columns, and scrolled metal screens dividing the bustling restaurant into six defined seating areas. Evan had cleverly booked a semi-private section — secluded enough for comfort, yet still technically public. I suspected he'd chosen it to hide the atrocious sight of his blackened eyes, and only once the three of us were tucked out of view, did he remove his sunglasses.

He needn't have worried. We shook hands, apologised like gentlemen, and moved on, settling into light, comfortable chatter while feasting on roasted garlic-butter field mushrooms. That was merely the entrée. My main — a two-hundred-gram prime Angus steak smothered in black pepper sauce, cooked medium-rare, just the way I liked it — followed shortly after.

Determined to keep a cool head, and remembering my sister's nagging about slowing down, I kept my drinking to a minimum: two mid-strength beers for the entire evening. Teddy, shocked beyond measure, took immense pleasure in teasing me relentlessly about my rare restraint. Her amusement only grew when her father ordered yet another beer on top of the half-dozen he'd already downed.

"Are you ill? Do I need to take you to the hospital just to be sure?"

"No, I only felt like a couple. What's wrong with that?" I argued spiritedly.

She shrugged impishly. "Nothing, I suppose. Normally when we dine out, you have more than your fair share."

"Admittedly, yes, I do. But tonight I decided it was in my best interest to restrain myself."

"I didn't realise restraint was part of your vocabulary." She giggled.

I leaned into her ear and whispered, "I'll show you the meaning of the word restraint once we've closed the bedroom door."

"Bringing the dictionary to bed isn't very romantic." Her witty reply made me chuckle as our smouldering gazes locked.

"You know that's not what I meant," I murmured, skating my fingertips along the length of her semi-naked back.

Goosebumps rose over her cooled skin — and the cause had nothing to do with the chilled air streaming from the large vent above us. Adding to the charged atmosphere was the sound of Duffy begging for mercy from the ceiling speakers.

"Oh, I understood perfectly well what you were implying. But if you must know—" She leaned closer, her voice dipping into a husky, salacious whisper. "I look forward to your... lack of restraint."

My eyes glistened. "Indeed, as do I."

Evan cleared his throat, a timely reminder of the company surrounding us, snapping our attention back to the table.

I swallowed tightly and had to stifle my laughter at his rankled expression. "Who's up for dessert?"

During the drive home, I deviated from the usual route and headed towards St Kilda, the beach drawing us in. After such a putrid day, the darkening sky and the balmy breeze flowing through the open windows were a welcome relief.

Teddy's quizzical gaze drifted outward as she tucked a delicate strand of unruly copper hair behind her ear. "Where are we going?" she asked, glancing sideways at me. "I thought we were heading home and learning the meaning of the word restraint from the dictionary?"

I smiled broadly. "I thought we could grab an ice cream from the kiosk at St Kilda Beach and eat it while strolling along the pier. The night's warm — why not."

She snorted loudly, shaking her head. "Have you got worms? Surely you can't be hungry after that massive dinner and the flourless chocolate cake you inhaled for dessert."

"Worms are most definitely not the culprit," I chuckled. "You can blame my increased appetite on the excessive energy I burned at the gym this afternoon between meetings."

"I'll say," she murmured, swivelling in her seat. Her gaze warmed, openly appreciative. "I hope you conserved enough energy for later. You have a promise to uphold, remember?"

"How could I possibly forget?" I released my grip on the gearstick and reached across the centre console, curling my hand over Teddy's thigh. We shared a slow smile as my fingertips traced lightly along her skin, raising goosebumps and deepening the charged awareness humming between us.

For once, she ignored my distracted state and unashamedly widened her legs – an invite I couldn't possibly refuse. Teddy gasped as my fingertip brushed her engorged nub through the skimpy lace thong barely covering her derriere.

Granted, she looked gorgeous in her chosen outfit; however, my issue lay with the back of the short beige jumpsuit. Besides the thin spaghetti-crisscross straps, there was barely anything there — meaning she'd gone without a bra, capturing the attention of every other hot-blooded male in the restaurant, much to my chagrin.

She whimpered as I pulled my hand away. "Why'd you stop?"

My lips quirked at the sound of her breathless complaint. I grasped the gearstick and pushed down on the clutch, slowing the car enough to turn into the St Kilda Beach car park. Once I'd eased into a bay beneath a streetlamp, I switched off the engine and leaned over the centre console, gently capturing her chin between my thumb and forefinger. "Don't fret. There's plenty of fuel left in my tank for you when we get home, my love."

Her breath exhaled in an excited shudder. "Good to know."

Tugging her forward, I slanted my mouth over Teddy's parted lips. Pleasured, honied moans swiftly suffused the air as one of her fingers weaved, clutching the roots of my hair, deepening what was already a heated kiss. I broke away before either of us forgot why we'd come here.

Teddy huffed in frustration. "You're such a tease tonight!"

My unrepentant gaze stared as I caressed the soft skin of her cheek. "Sorry to burst your sex hazed bubble, but we still need to have that chat."

With a flare of annoyance, she threw her strung out body against the seat. "Fine. Let's get this over with."

I stepped out of the car and rounded the bonnet, opening her door.

"Thank you." Taking my outstretched hand, she lifted her lean body from the low-lying vehicle and slid upwards, brushing her noticeably erect nipples against the length of my torso.

Chuckling, I shook my head. "You're most welcome. Now, how about that ice cream?" I flashed a wicked grin hoping to mask the nervousness welling inside. "With any luck, the kiosk shall have rum and raisin."

Teddy playfully smacked my arm and laughed. "You're hopeless." Her cheerful giggle persisted as I expressed my delight when I saw they indeed had my preferred flavour.

"Two of life's delicious delights for the price of one – rum and ice cream. A perfect pairing, if I say so myself."

Teddy, amused, opted for a scoop of mint choc chip.

Carrying our small buckets, we silently began our stroll along the newly rebuilt pier, its wide timber decking stretching cleanly ahead beneath the soft glow of the lamps lining one side. To our right, the curved breakwater arced out into the bay, its sculpted stonework guiding the water into gentle folds. Ahead, the old kiosk stood untouched — the lone remnant of the pier's former life.

Strangely enough, neither of us knew where to start – or so I thought.

"You mentioned earlier that you wanted to talk?"

I dug the bamboo spoon into the ice cream and took a mouthful, slowly chewing on the rum-infused raisins whilst searching for the right words. So much for discarding the eggshells. I inhaled sharply. "Things must change, not just you...but for me also," I articulated. "Retaking your medication would be the first step; it helps you immensely. The same applies to your therapy." She opened her mouth to protest, but I held firm. "No arguments. You said yourself this constant arguing is hurting us, and with this blasé approach to your recovery, we're one argument away from ending."

Teddy paused, leaning over the smooth white railing, muddling her spoon through the melting ice cream in her palm as her troubled gaze drifted down to the turquoise waves rolling calmly below. "I know...that's because it's been deliberate on my part."

My spine stiffened. "But why? Why would you?" Tossing my half-eaten dessert into the bin beside me, I tugged gently at her shoulder, urging her to face me. "Answer me, please."

She wiped her tears away with the back of her hand before lifting her haunted expression. "Because I thought it was best. We don't belong together, Ari – not in the eyes of everyone else. Even your family. They look differently at me now. I see the pity... but I also see the contempt for what my baggage is doing to their beloved son."

I gaped. "Are you pulling the piss? My parents adore you. And yes, naturally, they're worried about me – I'd be worried if they didn't care." I gripped the railing, my fingers furling tightly around the cool metal, the clean finish grounding me. "Dammit Teddy, why must we keep rehashing this? My feelings haven't changed. Yes, I'm pissed off most of the time, but who wouldn't be when drama after drama keeps unfolding and throwing itself into our laps?"

The conversation I originally planned was not going well. I was angry – again. Teddy was crying – again. But why should this day be different from the others?

I closed my eyes and turned towards the ocean, letting the sounds around us settle into something steadying. Waves washed against the shoreline in a rhythmic hush; a dog barked at the seagulls squawking overhead; children played in the nearby park, their squeals of laughter drifting on the evening breeze as their parents pushed them on the swings. I inhaled sharply, the salt-laden breeze cooling my skin and calming me enough to gather my thoughts.

When I spoke again, my tone was quieter, softer. “Look... rather than rehashing everything, can we please get back on track to what I initially intended to say?”

Teddy nodded silently and stepped into my open arms, looping hers firmly around my waist. I cupped her face in my hands and lowered my mouth to hers, kissing her gently.

“Please don’t cry, Teddy. It’s tearing me up,” I implored, tasting the salt of her tears over our grazing lips.

She crumbled against my chest. “I’m sorry...”

Resting my cheek against the crown of her head, I exhaled slowly. “All I wanted to say tonight was...is that I’m hiring you a personal trainer to encourage you to exercise three, maybe four times a week. Someone who might keep you motivated more than I have – it served you well last time. Furthermore, I’m employing a personal minder, a bodyguard if you will, to stay by your side.”

Teddy let out a flare of exasperation as she pulled away and tossed her melted ice cream bucket into the bin. “I don’t have any choice in the matter, do I?”

I remained adamant. “No, you don’t. Not with Emmett lurking about – or your mother, for that matter. When I swore I’d never give up, I meant every word.” I paused, tipping her chin. I gazed studiously. “That’s not to say I haven’t had reservations lately.”

Her brows furrowed at my honesty. “Yet you’re still here.”

“Surely that speaks volumes?”

Affection glowed through her watery eyes. “You’re the balm to my wounded soul, Ari Jaeger.”

A sharp breath exhaled in a rush. “So you’ll agree to my terms? No going back on them?”

“I promise,” she capitulated earnestly, stepping back into my arms. I enclosed my hold around her tightly as she continued, “I was just too damned stubborn to realise how much I needed you. You always go above and beyond for me – more than anyone else has.”

The next subject made my stomach tighten. I speculated it was probably too soon, but I reminded myself: no more eggshells. “One more thing… we need to get you back on contraception. You and I both know neither of us is ready for a child. There are too many obstacles to face before we even dream of venturing down that road.”

“I agree wholeheartedly. As much as the miscarriage hurt… maybe it was for the best.”

Eyes pooled with grief. Just speaking about our baby's loss dredged up feelings still painfully raw. As we held each other, we silently wept for a child that was never meant to be.

13

Teddy

As promised, Ari kept true to his word: one burly bodyguard and one super-duper delicious personal trainer, both effective immediately.

At an intimidating size of six feet, three inches with an infinite amount of well-defined muscles, Austin Mackenzie was pure, prime Aussie male. In short, he was damned hot – from head to toe. Short, spiked dirty blonde hair, piercing blue eyes, and a wide, beaming smile that disarmed every person who passed him. Including me.

Needless to say, Ari caught me perving multiple times. Austin didn't seem to mind in the slightest. With an ego as big as his appendage, why would he? Ari, on the other hand, had a *very* different opinion – one that stirred a level of jealousy I'd never encountered with him before.

Barely had we finished our joint workout when Ari acted on it. One moment I was catching my breath, the next I was hoisted over his shoulder and carried straight into the bedroom. Protesting would have been pointless; he was a man on a mission. Nor was I protesting either. What followed was intensely possessive, dominating sex, and the two rounds left no room for doubt about how he felt. My smart mouth didn't help matters either. In between each toe-curling spanking, I fearlessly reminded my green-eyed lover, *'If you don't sample the product, then flicking through the pages was perfectly acceptable.'* A comment that left me sore for hours long after he'd screwed me into oblivion.

Little did Ari realise, he was unwittingly being nudged towards a lifestyle I both missed and craved. By highlighting the positives, I hoped he might begin to understand the part BDSM had once played in my life – *long before* we started dating. It helped me through a dark period once; why couldn't it offer the same grounding now?

The proof was in the pudding.

My mental wellbeing had improved dramatically, as had my sleeping and eating habits. Well… except for two other luxuries: chocolate and wine. Outside of debauchery, a girl needed her coping mechanisms. There were worse vices in life, so surely it wasn't a problem. Right?

In addition to the gruelling workouts, attending regular therapy sessions had also contributed to my new outlook on life. Having the right therapist helped there too – one who refused to put up with my nonsense. Doctor Montgomery never minced his words, and didn't I know it.

Take our first session, for example. I'd barely walked through the door and said hello when he abruptly ordered me to sit. I wasn't permitted to speak or interrupt – under any circumstances. Talk about tough love. But once we'd moved past the awkward scolding over my wrongdoings, he softened. He's kept me on my toes ever since.

He wasn't the only one.

Each night in the bathroom, Ari and I followed the same ritual — except now it included both my antidepressant and birth-control pills, with him intently watching as I swallowed them. When he said he was coming down hard, he meant every word. His motivation was purely love and concern. I finally saw that now, and it made me love him even more, if that was possible.

With Logan as my bodyguard, however, Ari hadn't shown an inkling of jealousy. The two had met one night — or morning, technically — at The Gym and hit it off immediately. As it turned out, Logan was the Logan Scarlett had gone on a date with, and unbelievably, still was. What a small world. He was sweet, in a marshmallow-wrapped-in-an-oversized-tank sort of way, harbouring an immense amount of strength. Without it, how would he put up with me, let alone my diva-like sister? "Unlucky fellow," as Ari once teasingly put it.

Part of Logan's daily instructions were to ferry me to and from work and to my appointments. No matter the reason, he was to remain glued to my side — except for the toilet. Even then, he was expected to wait outside the door, which I initially found humiliating. Now, I barely noticed he was there.

And as he drove me to work, I could honestly say that having a former SAS soldier shadowing me whenever Ari wasn't around offered a sense of security. At a towering six-foot-four with the build of a rugby player, not even I dared to mess with him. Unfortunately, his lingering presence had a downside: the curious stares he attracted from my colleagues at Bricks and Mortar. Not everyone, though. Spencer, in particular, was impartial — as he was with most people. But then again, he didn't have much choice after Ari had been in his ear. But when wasn't he?

If anyone, it was Emily who appeared more suspicious than curious. In fact, her weird behaviour had increased lately, making me question everything about her. Insidious remarks about my relationship with Logan — or Ari, depending on her mood — were incessant. Whether she meant them or not, I had no idea. I just hoped she'd be in a better mood when I arrived, or I was bound to snap.

I was wrong. Emily started the second I walked in.

"Why aren't we taking on the Stark project?"

My brows shot up as I set my bag on my desk. "Our current undertaking is enough already, Ems."

"I don't understand the issue. The process wouldn't begin until after Christmas anyway, and our diary will be clear enough to fit them in by mid-January. They're Ari's family, so why on earth would you turn down such a lucrative project?"

I flopped into my chair and buried my face in my hands. Emily sounded like one of those annoying wind-up toys with the never-ending batteries I had as a child. That explained why my mother removed them the moment we ripped open our gifts.

Dropping my hands, I stared at her head-on. "Just because it's Ari's uncle doesn't mean I'm obligated."

"Well, I think that's a bullshit reason, and we should take it on." Clearly itching for a fight, her combative persistence grated on my last nerve.

My clenched fists slammed onto the desktop. "We aren't, and that's final!"

Then she fired the first shot.

"Is it because Emmett's your secret lover and you don't want his wife finding out?" Emily accused smugly, folding her bony arms across her small chest. "You don't think the flirtatious gazes between you that day went unnoticed? Or the touches you thought were inconspicuous?"

"How dare you make such a hideous suggestion!" I hissed. "Our families go way back — that's all there is to it!" It took everything in me not to reach across the desk and snot her one.

She smirked just as Logan stepped into the cubicle. I twisted at the waist and held up a hand, silently telling him to back off. Not that he listened; he continued hovering in the doorway like a storm cloud.

Mirroring my movement, Emily pushed off her chair and pushed my buttons further as she leered across our adjacent workspaces. "Well, if you're supposedly family friends, then why was he fondling you and whispering sweet nothings in your ear as they said goodbye?"

Was Emily for real? She damn well knew how I felt about Ari, and yet here she was, stupidly goading me – completely oblivious to the real truth behind Emmett's 'fondling'.

"You know what, I'm done," I growled, throwing my hands up as I straightened and spun toward the door. "I'm going to speak with Spencer about having you moved to another desk!"

"Yeah, go shake your arse at him. I'm sure he'll give you whatever you want — he always does. It's obvious Ari's not enough for you," she sneered, pausing just long enough to twist the knife. "And that's why you aborted your baby."

I stiffened. The blow landed squarely in the centre of my chest. Downright low and dirty. Rage swept through me in a hot, blinding wave. How Emily knew about our baby wasn't even the issue — it was the fact she mocked my loss that sent something inside me snapping clean in half.

"Fuck you, bitch!" I lunged, grabbing hold of her scrawny neck with one hand. Pinning her against the desk, I repeatedly rammed her face with the other. A distinct sound of cracking echoed as my knuckles connected with her nose.

She clawed at my hand, desperate to free herself from my tightened grip, her manicured fingernails digging and scraping at my skin. Not that I felt it; I blocked the pain.

"No... fuck ... you ... bitch!" she garbled through a mouthful of blood. "I...can't...breathe..."

"Why can you still talk then?" I spat just as two sets of sturdy arms ripped me away. Logan and Spencer: a combined strength I had no chance of fighting against. Nonetheless, it was worth a try. I lunged again. "Lemme kill the bitch!"

Spencer's grip around my bicep tightened. "Settle down!"

"She provoked me!"

"I don't care! Just stop!"

"You're so unstable," Emily spluttered, pushing herself upright and dragging in breath that I seriously wanted to drain from her. "Be grateful your lost child won't have to suffer the chaos of a suicidal parent." Her voice carried across the office, sharp and deliberate, as she dabbed at her face with trembling tissues. The smirk she flashed — triumphant, poisonous — drew horrified gasps from every corner of the room.

The rage resurfaced. Witnesses be damned, she was a dead woman. Logan pre-empted the murder I was about to commit and flung his burly arm around my waist. I hissed as my slender frame bounced against the brick wall of his torso.

"Let. Me. Go!" I screeched.

"No! She's purposely antagonising you," he firmly whispered in my ear, "and you'll only make the situation worse if you keep going."

"My office. NOW. Both of you." Spencer's voice cracked through the air like a whip, slicing straight through the horrified silence that had settled over the floor. He didn't wait to see if we followed — he simply turned and strode toward his office, expecting obedience.

Logan's hand hovered near my elbow, ready to intervene if I so much as twitched. Emily trailed behind us, muttering under her breath, still wearing that smug, self-satisfied curl of a smile that made my blood simmer.

We reached Spencer's doorway, but he stopped short, blocking the entrance with his arm.

"Emily — inside. Sit."

She scoffed. "I'm not a child, Spencer."

"Then stop behaving like one," he replied, his voice clipped. "Sit. Now."

With a dramatic roll of her eyes, she slumped into the nearest chair, limbs flopping like a sulking teenager.

Spencer turned to Logan. "Stay with her. Don't let her leave this room."

Logan stepped inside without hesitation, positioning himself between Emily and the exit.

Then Spencer angled his body toward me.

"Teddy," he directed, leaving no room for argument, "a word."

The corridor suddenly felt too narrow, too bright. I followed him a few steps away from the doorway, my pulse thudding in my ears. He didn't look at me the way he usually did — no warmth, no subtle patience, none of the quiet fondness he'd always shown me. Just a tight, controlled expression that made my stomach drop. Beneath it, I could see the strain — the awareness that whatever he said next mattered to Ari as much as it did to me.

His jaw flexed, disappointment settling into the lines of his face. “I expected better from you, Teddy,” he delivered quietly — not harsh, not loud, just devastatingly sincere.

The words hit harder than any reprimand. A stone dropping straight through my chest. And for the first time since working here, I felt the distance between us like a physical thing — the shift from friend to employer, from indulgence to consequence.

Spencer inhaled sharply, then stepped back toward the doorway. “Logan, stay here with them while I call Mr Jaeger. I expect my office to be in pristine condition when I return.”

His reproachful gaze flicked between us before he strode down the hallway, tugging his phone from his back pocket with a weary exhale.

I sank onto the sofa, rubbing my forehead as his voice carried faintly from the corridor.

“Ari, mate… sorry to be the bearer of bad news, but it appears we have an issue here…”

My stomach knotted. Ari was going to be furious. Then again, maybe there was one tiny silver lining — a wry smile formed.

Emily’s voice sliced through my thoughts like a blade. “Thinking about Emmett again, are we?”

Fuck Spencer and his rules. This bitch had it coming. I flew out of my seat, and not even Logan was capable of holding me back.

“Teddy! Stop!”

∞

Ari

"Thomas, cancel the rest of my appointments, please. I have a dire emergency that requires my immediate and full attention, and I won't be returning."

I didn't wait for a reply — I was already striding from my office, fingers drumming a frantic rhythm along his desk as I passed.

"See you tomorrow!" I called over my shoulder.

"Yes, sir. Good luck."

The grim look we exchanged said everything. Either he'd heard Spencer's call, or he'd simply heard me shouting. In all likelihood, half of Melbourne had.

The moment I stepped outside, the stifling humidity slapped me across the face. I broke into a three-block sprint toward 101 Collins — a feat Teddy had once managed in five-inch heels, no less. Though I doubted she'd been anywhere near this drenched by the time she reached me.

By the time the lift deposited me on the fifth floor, my shirt clung to me like a second skin. I wished I had another to change into, but pressing matters awaited — and they were far more important than my appearance.

My footfalls thundered over the timber boards as I strode out of the lift, drawing the attention of Spencer's staff. Heads popped up from behind monitors; faces pressed to the glass of the common area. Their curiosity was understandable, but this wasn't a bloody circus.

"Don't worry about what's going on here," I barked, silencing them instantly.

But the shrill screaming echoing down the corridor — punctuated by Spencer's deep roar — told me the urgency had escalated. Then Logan's Welsh lilt cut through the chaos, sharp and panicked.

"Teddy! Calm the fuck down!"

I ran.

The moment I burst into Spencer's office, I was thrust straight into the middle of Teddy and Emily's catfight. Their shrieking collided in the air like shrapnel. Instinct took over — I surged between them, arms outstretched, forcing them apart with every ounce of strength I had.

"Enough! Both of you!"

Teddy froze immediately, her clenched fist dropping. Emily, however, made the idiotic decision to reach around me.

"I said, enough!" I roared, shoving her back — straight into Spencer's waiting hands.

"Of course you're here!" Emily spat, twisting against his grip. "The great white knight, Ari Jaeger, had to come and save poor whittle Teddy!"

"You—" I growled, stabbing a finger toward her, "I don't want to hear another word out of your malicious mouth. Now be a good girl and sit."

She huffed, defiant to the last. "Fuck you and the white horse you rode in on! I don't work for you — I work for Spencer! So quit barking orders like I'm one of your obedient little minions."

Spencer's glare dropped the temperature in the room by ten degrees. "That's right, you do." His voice dropped to something cool and razor-edged. "And now I'm ordering you to sit your arse back down. Don't move, and don't speak. You're skating on thin ice as it is."

She obeyed — but not without flicking a murderous glare in our direction first.

A seething Teddy moved toward the opposite sofa and flopped against the cushions, and only then was I given a proper look at her — the bloodied knuckles, the torn shirt, her hair in complete disarray. My mouth tightened. Christ. She'd clearly had quite the crack at Emily, too. One glance at Emily's battered face confirmed it.

Doctor Montgomery was going to have a conniption — and not just over the injuries. Logan had taken a hit as well. A nasty gash sat just below his right eye, no doubt earned while trying to do his job. No wonder he'd yelled at her.

The urge for a stiff drink rose hard and fast, but as tempting as it was to raid Spencer's stash on the sideboard, I refrained. Instead, I perched on the edge of his desk, flexing my fingers over my forehead before exhaling through my teeth.

"Can someone please explain *what in the hell* happened here today?"

Teddy shrank back into the cushions. "Emily just kept goading me."

"About what?" My exasperation made her blanch.

"Over why I refused to take on the Stark project."

My brow lifted. That was a no-brainer. But that wasn't the reason — not the real one. There was more, and as usual, I had to drag it out of her. I wound my hand impatiently, urging her to continue. "And?"

She stared down at her fidgeting hands, flicking a piece of imaginary lint from her black capri pants.

"I know there's more..." I pressed, watching her swallow tightly as tears welled.

"...And then Emily brought up my miscarriage — something she knew nothing about — so I snapped."

A cold, sharp fury sliced through me. Teddy hadn't broadcast our loss. She wouldn't. So how in the hell had Emily found out?

Raking my fingers through my hair, I inhaled deeply. Something was off. Emily's fixation wasn't random — it was deliberate. And it required digging.

I turned my daggered stare on her. "You're aware Teddy hasn't been well. And the extra workload would've been detrimental to her wellbeing."

Emily's dark eyes rolled with theatrical disdain. "Who fucking cares. If Miss Prissy can't handle the heat, then she shouldn't be in the fucking kitchen."

Breathe, Ari. Breathe.

"And what's with bringing up her miscarriage?" I asked, my voice low, controlled, and meant to intimidate. "That's of no consequence to you or anyone else but Teddy and me."

She didn't even flinch.

Her brows snapped together. "No consequence, huh? Every time she's had any sort of breakdown, I'm the sucker left behind to pick up the slack. And then she just waltzes back in without a care in the world."

My jaw clenched as I stared her down. Did Emily not know Teddy at all? For someone so brilliant, she was remarkably obtuse.

"Wow. Some friend you turned out to be. Unlike you, Teddy would bend over backwards to help a colleague."

She ignored me entirely and kept ranting. "Do you want to know what else is pissing me off? The fact she flaunts your relationship — not just the sex, but the house. Then she was pregnant. What's next, an engagement?"

My mouth twisted. If the situation weren't so serious, I'd laugh.

Teddy, however, was far from amused. "Oh my God. You're jealous?" She scoffed. "So all this bullshit today was over my supposedly charmed life?"

Emily shrugged. "Well, everything just seems to come so easy to you, including your Prince. Between him and Spencer, they fawn over you, handing everything to you on a polished platter. I don't have that, Teddy. I've had to fight for everything in my life."

Letting out a humourless laugh at the feeble excuses, Teddy inched forward in her seat. Logan immediately shifted closer, bracing for the next round of catfighting.

"You think my life has been roses, Emily? Let me tell you a little story that might enlighten your pea-sized brain."

And somehow — miraculously — we had a breakthrough. Teddy faced her demons head-on, baring her damaged soul and exposing Emmett as the culprit. She had come a long way to be able to speak those words aloud.

When she finished, the room fell into an eerie, suffocating silence.

Emily, of course, showed no empathy. Her catlike features hardened, and her thin lips curled into a malevolent smirk that made the hairs on the back of my neck stand.

"What's to say he's even finished with you yet?"

Fury blinded me. I leapt off the desk, fully intent on strangling her myself, when Spencer stepped in front of me, his darkened eyes silently warning me to back down.

Reluctantly, I held up my hands and backed off. "Okay, she'll live — for now."

He nodded and sidestepped, giving me enough space to move past.

I sat beside a profusely shaking Teddy, a deep frown carving into my brow as I wrapped an arm around her shoulders. Something was terribly wrong. “Are you all right, Teddy.”

“Aw, can’t the little princess cope?” Emily jeered.

“Emily, I suggest you stop,” Spencer warned, his voice cold with restraint.

My head swivelled toward her. “You’re a nasty piece of work, aren’t you, Emily.” I forced her to meet my hostile gaze. “I suggest you leave now — or things won’t end very well for you.”

Emily almost choked on her words as her soulless gaze narrowed. “Are you threatening me.”

“I don’t make threats, Ms Smith.” My upper lip curled in a snarl. “Take it however you please. But mark my words — cross me again, and you’ll know about it.”

“Go your hardest.”

Emily just didn’t know when to shut her mouth. And I thought Teddy was stubborn. That smug smirk needed wiping off her face, and quick smart.

“Spencer, I’ll leave the decision on whether you want to fire Ms Smith or not up to you.”

Emily’s bottom lip trembled as she fearfully glanced up at her boss. “What? No! You can’t fire me. I need my job. Please, Mr Hughes.”

Spencer rocked on the balls of his feet, contemplating heavily. “Your behaviour today was uncalled for, and everyone agrees you antagonised Teddy until she snapped. That’s not to say I’m condoning your behaviour either, Teddy. I’m putting both of you on suspension, effective immediately. We'll revisit this when we resume in the New Year."

A glum Emily dragged her limp but relieved figure toward the door. "Yes, Mr Hughes. I'll collect my belongings and leave now."

"You're still welcome at the staff party, Emily — only if you want to come."

I frowned at his impartial tone.

She tapped the doorframe with her fingers and glanced over her shoulder, her eyes blackened with something chilling. "Oh, don't worry. I'll be there with bells on."

That expression — that darkness — was familiar. Too familiar.

A cold shiver ran down my spine as the connection snapped into place.

Fuck...

14

Upon our return home, Teddy had spent most of the evening either broodingly silent or crying when she wasn't lashing out. I wasn't sure whether to steer clear or try to comfort her; she wanted neither. Dinner was equally stagnant.

Case in point: as I reached for the bottle of Shiraz, her arm shot out, snatching it from my grasp.

"Surely I'm entitled to more than one glass, or are you planning to consume the entire bottle yourself?" I protested.

She glowered and silently poured a generous amount into her glass.

"I guess it's the latter then."

"There's another bottle in your pantry, so quit your whining," she muttered petulantly.

I snorted and picked up my measly filled glass, taking a small sip. "You sound like my mother."

Teddy scowled. "We're two completely different people, thank you very much."

"Don't take it so personally. I was only joking."

"I wasn't. You're just taking my response out of context, is all."

"I think it's best I keep my opinions to myself," I uttered, sawing into the marinated chicken breast on my plate.

"That's the smartest thing you've said all night," she hurled back before swallowing the last of her food and pushing her plate away.

Caught off guard by the offhand comment, I could only stare in disbelief.

"Don't," she warned sharply, pressing her fingers against my lips. "Just so you know, I've made plans to head out with some of the girls from work for a few hours — and for the record, Logan's *not accompanying me*."

"He's your bodyguard for a reason," I argued.

"Precisely why I don't want to take him. He's a reminder of why I need one, and after today's fiasco, I'm in desperate need of some space."

I opened my mouth to object, only to slam it shut as Teddy defiantly held up a mildly bruised hand.

"Can't you just respect what I want for a change?"

"I do, but I'll worry if he's not with you," I refuted — and quickly relented when she rolled her eyes. My lips thinned. "Fine. But keep your wits about you, please. For me."

"Fine," she huffed. "Whatever pleases you... *sir.*"

With that, she pushed away from the table and headed upstairs, leaving me dumbfounded, my gaze trailing after her. Most intriguing was the news she'd chosen to spend time with someone other than her roommates. She was full of surprises lately. But on the contrary, I'd always pushed her to let others into her life.

Shrugging, I shoved a blend of chicken, broccolini, and balsamic-glazed Dutch carrots into my mouth and chewed, feeling moderately satisfied she'd enjoy herself. I wasn't thrilled about her refusal to let Logan accompany her, but Teddy was adamant.

I tapped the fork prongs against my lips. Unless...

No. I couldn't do that to her.

Having Logan follow discreetly was a terrible idea — especially if she spotted him. I'd end up in the doghouse for breaching her trust.

Just leave her be, Ari, I told myself.

In the meantime, I sincerely hoped nothing untoward happened to her.

An hour later, freshly showered and dressed in an elegantly slim-fitting pale-pink dress with a plunging neckline that showcased her assets beautifully, Teddy sauntered down the stairs. Her mouth curved into a heart-stopping smile when she caught sight of me waiting at the bottom.

"Well, what do you think?" she asked, reaching the last step and carefully stepping onto the timber boards. She twirled, revealing a bare back beneath a mass of bouncing curls, then turned to the foyer mirror to apply a rose-pink gloss to her plump lips.

"I approve."

In slow, measured steps, I inched closer, taking my time to enjoy the delectable view standing before me in sky-high heels. A sensual smile tugged at my lips as my gaze lingered on the skinny straps wrapped around her slender ankles. I hummed in appreciation. I wished she'd agree to drape those bad boys around my neck instead of ruining them on the dancefloor.

I attempted to persuade her anyway — my prowess usually worked. “Is there any chance I could sway you into, say... swapping your dancing for some untamed sex instead?” I murmured, grasping her waist and burying my nose in her thick tresses.

A riotous snort erupted. “Not a chance, big boy.”

My head jerked back, arms dropping to my sides. “Well, isn’t this a turn for the books...”

Dropping her lip gloss into her silver clutch, Teddy frowned at my stunned reflection before spinning on the spikes of those sexy heels to face me. “Don’t act so hard done by. And I did warn you earlier — after today’s BS with Emily, I need some time out, and dancing is the perfect medicine.”

Skimming a flattened palm down my sternum, she tartly changed tack. “You look like you could do with some stress relief yourself. Why don’t you call the boys? Invite them over for a workout and have a few drinks afterwards. I doubt any of them will say no.”

I thought I’d push my luck one more time.

Snaking my arms around her waist, I lightly trailed my fingertips along her half-naked spine, triggering a delightful shiver. “Not a bad idea,” I purred, dipping my head to pepper soft kisses along her perfumed clavicle. “But I’d prefer a workout with you. The two of us getting all hot and sweaty in the bedroom with a few toys... perhaps some bondage thrown in. Sounds much more enticing, don’t you agree, my love?”

Hanging onto my biceps, she threw her head back, exposing her slender neck for my slow-moving mouth and tongue as I skated both along smooth, fragrant skin. “Depends...”

“On what?”

"On how much I've had to drink, or how much dancing I do. I might be too tired."

My head lifted, brows furrowing. Once again, she'd left me lost for words. What in the devil was going on with her?

A loud rapping on the door prevented me from asking. I released her from my hold. "Car service, I take it."

"Yeah... didn't feel up to driving. Safer, you know..." The vague reply was concerning.

"Yeah, I suppose it is..."

Exchanging a chaste kiss with me, Teddy checked her clutch and waved a hand, her heels clicking on the timber boards as she skipped out the door, reminding me not to wait up.

Standing in the middle of the foyer, I watched as she elegantly lowered herself into the car. The vacant driver closed the door behind her, then moved to the front seat with the same wooden precision before slowly pulling away.

By the time I stepped back and closed the front door, I'd convinced myself stress was the cause behind her peculiar behaviour. It couldn't be anything else... surely.

With a shrug, I strolled into my study. But one look at the pile of paperwork beside my computer made me scrub at my forehead and rapidly change my mind. Why was I thinking of work when hanging out with the boys sounded far more appealing?

So, instead of trudging away for hours, I took Teddy's advice and picked up the phone — calling Asher first, then Bryson and Michael, neither of whom needed much convincing.

Rubbing my hands together, I marched into the kitchen. "Rosa, could you be a darling and whip up a tray of tasty treats, please? The boys are coming over! Look out!"

Her face dropped as she wandered into the pantry, muttering in her native tongue under her breath.

"You're the best, Rosa!"

Like always between us boys, our competitive streak took over — starting in my home gym. That, in turn, moved to the pool for the roughest game of water polo we'd ever played. Mother, had she been present, would've scolded us for our buffoon behaviour. Thankfully, and much to our relief, she wasn't. Instead, poor Rosa had the misfortune of traipsing after us.

From there, the cheerful chaos shifted to the rumpus room, where we played snooker and laid ridiculous bets before each game.

Rosa made her loathing abundantly clear. Her hands wafted through the plumes of cigar smoke as she crossed the floor. Amidst flinging the French doors open, she reprimanded us, "You boys are terrible! Stinking up the house with your cigars and bourbon! And your music—" She slapped her hands over her ears. "Too loud!"

During which Asher made the grave mistake of sneaking up behind her and enveloping my feisty housekeeper in a bear hug. She immediately swatted him away, scolding him in her native language. I refused to interpret the names she'd called him, prolonging his suffering and sending the rest of us into hysterics.

Rosa marched off, curtly informing me she was going home.

Now, as we sat around my poker table playing yet another round, we downed more bourbon than any of us cared to admit while chuffing away on another cigar. None of us knew when to quit. I certainly hadn't — not with the worrying.

"Stop looking at your watch," Asher scolded, flicking another card onto the pile and nodding at Michael for another. "Teddy's letting her hair down with a group of friends; she'll be fine."

I drunkenly chuckled. "Yeah, I know. But with him out there, I can't help but fret."

"Bro, your hand," Bryson growled, dragging me from my troubled thoughts. "You ready to fold yet."

Smirking, I threw a stack of fifty dollars onto the table. "Not a chance, little bro. Can you match me."

"You're on," he retorted smugly, tossing a matching wad of cash on top of mine.

Somewhere around two, I rolled into bed. Teddy crawled in beside me sometime later, sliding an arm over my waist. I rolled over and forced an eye open, peeking at her as damp curls slid over a slender shoulder. She smelt intoxicating, and regardless of my drunken state, I was as horny as a three-peckered goat. But as my hand drifted over her panty-clad behind, she whimpered and thwarted my dreams of seduction by pushing my hand away.

"No, Ari. I'm too tired, and my period started while I was out," she grouched, rolling over and shuffling away. "You also stink of those damned cigars. You know I don't like kissing an ashtray."

Talk about harsh.

"Have you taken your medication — including your birth control — tonight?" I bit back.

She huffed, threw the blankets aside, and stormed into the bathroom. Obviously not.

Making quite the ruckus, she slammed the shaving cabinet door and crashed the glass onto the vanity. "Well, are you watching?" she snapped from the threshold.

Rubbing my eyes, I sighed heavily and rolled over, thrusting the sheet down to my waist. "Yes..."

Glaring at me through bloodshot eyes, Teddy threw her tablets back and opened her mouth wide, lifting her tongue from side to side.

"Was mocking the situation necessary, Teddy?"

"Yes, it was!"

She marched back into the bathroom, slammed the cup onto the counter, flicked the lights off, and stormed back to bed.

"There. Done. Are you happy now?"

"Was that a rhetorical question?"

"Fuck off!"

Thumping about, she yanked the sheet over her shoulders and shifted toward the edge of the mattress, leaving me frustrated and confused.

I rolled away and stared into the darkness. "Whatever," I muttered, closing my eyes in the hope the next day would herald a better mood.

"Did you have a delightful evening with your colleagues last night?" I questioned cautiously, steam from the bathroom swirling around me as I wandered into the wardrobe for my clothes.

Teddy glanced up as she tied her sneaker laces. "I had a marvellous time, thank you. It was just what I needed to loosen up."

"Did you loosen up a little too much, perhaps," I suggested quietly, opening the drawer of boxer briefs. Dropping my towel, I stepped into the first pair I grabbed.

She eyed me curiously as I tugged them up. "What do you mean by that?"

"Well, you refused to let me touch you. Anywhere. Care to explain that little oddity to me?" I probed, shrugging into a sky-blue shirt.

Her brows furrowed.

"You whimpered when I touched your arse. Why?"

"Oh, that. I just got a little carried away and tripped over my own feet."

She jumped to her feet and planted a chaste kiss on my cheek. "You know me after a few too many..."

"Yeah... I guess I do."

"Anyway, I'm off to meet Austin on the beach. Why aren't you?" she asked as I slipped on a pair of light grey trousers.

"I need to go to the office early and get a few things in order before the Christmas break."

"Oh. I'll see you later, then, I guess," she murmured, spinning on her heel and disappearing with my perplexed gaze trailing after her.

At times, she was quite the enigma, and it forced me to question whether I knew her at all, irrespective of our history. Possibly, I was reading too much into things — unsurprising, considering recent events. Perhaps she'd feel more grounded if I moved ahead with my plans. Anything to make her feel less insecure.

Teddy was undoubtedly worth the risk.

A few days later, Teddy's ornery mood had seemingly dissipated. For a moment, I worried the tension between us would overshadow my well-organised plans. I had a vital part of those plans tucked safely inside my jacket pocket — and at present, those plans were sliding downhill thanks to a troublesome bow tie. No matter what I tried, the damned thing refused to cooperate. Where was my mother when I needed her?

But judging by the resplendent sight of Teddy in a knee-length crimson satin cocktail dress, I'd say it was a sign — possibly an omen — that I needn't worry.

"Ooh, don't you look good enough to ravage."

"Don't get any ideas, Jaeger!"

A bright red talon matching her dress wagged sternly in my direction. "I need to stay looking somewhat dignified, thank you very much." She winked, hooking diamond drops through her ears. "Making an impression on the big boss is kinda on my to-do list tonight."

Sliding in behind her, I skimmed my hands over her soft curves, her floral fragrance arousing me as my lips brushed the back of her neck. "Oh, he's extremely impressed already."

She squirmed out of my hold and passed me the matching diamond necklace over her bare shoulder. "Can you please leave the gutter for a second and help me with this?"

"With pleasure." I smirked, letting my fingertips graze her skin as I slid the chain around her neck, and was rewarded with a delicious shiver. "God help me... I shall be the envy of every person there."

She scoffed. "Despised, more like it."

"Why on earth would I want any other woman when I have the sexiest woman alive in the whole of Australia?" I countered, gesturing to the enticing vision before me.

"You seriously need your eyes tested."

Her head shook firmly. "Other women are way hotter than me."

Since her fight with Emily, her self-esteem had taken a nosedive.

"You are resplendent, Teddy," I murmured. "And if I had my way, you'd be covered head to toe in a hessian sack to stop any other man from ogling you. But I'm not that controlling — and I wouldn't get the pleasure of showing you off either."

"I was so right in what I said to you."

Teddy chuckled, spinning on the spikes of her white Louboutin's to face me. Hooded hazel eyes glinted as she stroked my rarely clean-shaven chin.

"Which was?"

"You could charm the habit off a nun."

"I only enjoy taking the pants off you," I purred, before capturing her mouth with mine.

∞

Teddy

"Are you ladies ready?" Ari bellowed from the bottom of the stairs. "We're leaving in five minutes — with or without you!"

He checked his watch for the second time, and I couldn't help but laugh at the state of his obvious fluster.

"We've plenty of time, so quit your nagging."

He glowered. “What in the devil is taking the little hellions so long? We’re ready; why aren’t they?”

Blowing out his cheeks, Ari stalked back into the kitchen. I watched in wry amusement as his hands flexed and hovered above his head, fighting the urge to run his fingers through his hair. Not wanting to ruin his lovingly crafted ‘do, he fidgeted with his bow tie instead.

The side-slicked style was a nice change from his usual tousled spikes or pompadour — and only added to his dashing allure. A soft, involuntary sigh escaped me as I eyed the heavenly sight pacing in front of the kitchen island. Especially in that black dinner suit… he was simply edible.

“Don’t forget your sister kindly did our hair for us — including herself — so be patient. The party won’t start without us,” I reminded gently, pouring a champagne flute and handing it to him over the marble countertop. “Are you nervous about tonight?”

“No. I’ve done this several times now,” Ari assured, swiping a bead of sweat from his brow.

“True, but you didn’t have me by your side until tonight. It’ll be fine. Stop stressing.”

Setting my glass down, I rounded the bench and straightened his crooked tie. “The evening will be beautiful — one we’ll all remember for many years to come, no doubt.”

“You have no idea,” Ari muttered quietly, lifting the bubbling champagne to his lips and taking a generous sip.

“What was that, Ari?”

“Nothing.”

15

"Don't you ladies look lovely?" Audrina beamed, embracing each of us at the bottom of the steps leading to The Dome's entrance.

"Thanks, Mum," Dominique replied, twirling to give her a full view of her floor-length blush-pink strapless gown.

Scarlett rushed past everyone — me included — before pausing far too closely at Ari's side. I watched their intimate interaction intently, seething at the exchanged whispers. But it was the clasped hands and warm smiles that truly enraged me.

Having had enough of their secrecy, I hurried closer. "What are you two whispering about."

"Nothing. Absolutely nothing," Scarlett retorted, lifting the hem of her black floor-length cocktail dress as the side split parted to reveal one long limb. Carefully, she made her way up the steps with Logan's splayed hand pressed to her naked back as he trailed behind her.

I glowered. Boyfriend or not, wasn't he meant to be my bodyguard, not hers.

My suspicious gaze narrowed. "Hmm. There seems to be a whole lot of nothing going on tonight."

"No, there's not. It must be your vivid imagination," Ari remarked haughtily, tugging at his bow tie as if it were strangling him. He'd been antsy the entire day — he was up to something; I was sure of it. "Are you ready to go inside."

I huffed indignantly. "Yes. Are you."

Noticing my wary gaze tracking his fidgety demeanour, he quickly dropped his hand and cleared his throat. His eyes darted before he pressed a hard, chaste kiss to my lips.

"Then shall we," he murmured, offering his arm like the perfect gentleman as we made our way up the incline of steps.

But the moment we stepped through the doors of The Dome, Ari's strange behaviour became the furthest thing from my mind.

My head swivelled in wondrous delight, my jaw falling open as the space unfolded around me. The octagonal-shaped room rose into a barrel-vaulted ceiling, its height amplified by the majestic Baroque and Italianate granite columns flanking each archway. Soft light spilled from the clerestory windows above, catching on the ornate wrought-iron gates that guarded the grand entrance. The painstaking restoration was nothing short of breathtaking — every surface gleamed with history.

"*Le morceau de résistance* — the piece of resistance in an intricate puzzle," I whispered, awestruck. "Ari, this place... it's stunning."

Dark eyes filled with fiery warmth gleamed under the muted glow. "That's why I specifically chose this setting for tonight. For you, my love."

I pressed a hand to my heart. His thoughtfulness — for my passions, for me — knew no bounds. "Oh, Ari, thank you."

His smile was just as breathtaking. "You're most welcome." Sliding an arm around my waist, he offered a brief insight into its antiquity. "They began building The Dome in eighteen ninety during the land boom, but it wasn't fully completed until sometime later. That's only a snippet of its remarkable history, but I'm sure with your epic skills of retaining information, you'll uncover the nitty-gritty in no time."

"I love that you know me so well," I murmured, skating a finger along the smooth skin of his cheek.

He bent his head and slanted his mouth over mine, tenderly pressing our lips together. His dark eyes seared as he lifted his head. "Come. Our table's this way."

My white heels clicked over the brilliantly tiled mosaic floor as he guided me toward a single row of rectangular tables positioned ahead of dozens of circular ones filling the expansive space. Each table was lavishly decorated with black table runners, white linen napkins, and hurricane candles whose flames cast a shadowy, flickering glow across the dimly lit room. Posies of fresh red and white roses sat beside them, their sweet fragrance weaving through the air like a delicate thread.

Thomas, Ari's assistant, followed a few steps behind us, silent and unobtrusive, blending so seamlessly into the grandeur of the room that he might as well have been part of the restoration.

Our stroll was cut short as a larger-than-life Asher sauntered toward us in long strides. His broad smile beamed — while mine faded — as he approached, waving one of the two tumblers he'd just snatched from a passing waiter's tray in Ari's face.

"Ari, mate, it's about time you arrived! And here I thought you were gonna miss your own party."

Ari scoffed and took the glass from Asher's outstretched hand. "What, and leave you miserable lot to drink all my booze? Not a chance in hell, my friend." Then he finally remembered his manners. "You remember Teddy, Asher."

Dazzling azure eyes lit with recognition. "How could I forget this ravishing redhead."

Politely smiling, I offered a handshake. Even in five-inch heels, he towered over me. "Hello, Asher. It's been a while."

"What's with this handshaking nonsense? Gimme a hug!" He hauled me against his muscular frame, crushing me under firm biceps. "If you ever get tired of the other clown, gimme a call."

Ari grinned and tugged me back to his side. "Enough of fondling my girl. Go find your own."

"Is there anyone here worth fondling?" Asher drawled, raising a perfectly shaped blonde brow as he scanned the rapidly filling room. I cringed at the sleazy behaviour. "Who's the beautiful...?"

"Anyone here but my sister," Ari growled protectively.

"Whoa, whoa, big fella." Asher lifted both hands in surrender. "Before you get those tightly wad knickers in a twist, hear me out first."

"Make it fast..." Ari grunted, swilling back the bourbon.

The smug smile on Asher's lips widened. "I was actually going to ask who's the beautiful honey in the green strapless dress. She looks mighty fine."

I instinctively jumped into protection mode. "That would be my roommate Poppy Fleming — who also happens to be my best friend." Somewhere in that thick skull of his, surely he understood the subliminal message.

"Oh, I see." He peered over the crowd to check her out — not that he needed to. "Is she a nice person? You know, like... nice, nice."

I sighed. Evidently not.

"Speak English, Asher," Ari muttered, one brow lifting.

"I figured I was speaking your language, my friend."

Ari waved his empty glass toward Poppy. "And in what fantasy land are you living? Poppy's far too sweet and innocent for the likes of you." She wasn't that naïve either.

Asher pressed a hand to his chest. "Are you implying I'm a manwhore?"

Well, if the shoe fit.

"I never realised you were so slow, Asher," Ari retorted dryly.

I rolled my eyes. I never realised you were either, hanging out with this idiot.

"I'm dreadfully wounded." He laughed, mocking Ari's cultured accent.

Ari scowled and grabbed another bourbon from a passing waiter's tray, along with a champagne flute for me. "Besides, Poppy isn't the type of girl you typically go for."

"Oh, you mean skanky and easy, like you?" I interjected before clamping a hand over my mouth and feigning innocence. "Oh no! Did I just say what I truly thought out loud? How careless of me."

"Ooh, you're right — she does have a smart mouth!" Asher chortled.

I watched with wry amusement as Ari's clenched fist connected with his friend's shoulder. Rubbing his arm, Asher grimaced. "Ow! What was that for?"

"That was for repeating what I told you in confidence! It wasn't meant to leave your big fat mouth!" Ari snapped.

It was my turn to smack the pair of them.

"Ow! What was that for?" they yelped in unison.

"That was for you repeating whatever bullshit Ari fed you about me!" I growled at Asher. "And you—" I glared at my stunned lover.

"That was for gossiping behind my back to your mate with the big fat mouth!"

Storming off, I made my way toward a curiously staring Audrina, elegantly seated at the bar. I hopped onto the barstool beside her.

"May I ask what that was about, Teddy?" Audrina ventured, amusement dancing in her eyes.

I grinned, lifting the champagne flute to my lips. "Oh, like always, they were misbehaving — so I simply and effectively put them back in their place."

"I wouldn't expect anything less from them, to be honest. Never have."

Audrina giggled. "So the reprimanding, I believe, was undoubtedly well deserved."

Apart from Asher and Ari's insensitive indiscretions, the evening was going relatively smoothly. Ari had at least learnt not to act so impolite and spent the time prolifically introducing me to high-flying executives and a handful of notable politicians. Their talk of business, economics, and policy bored the hell out of me, but I smiled politely and nodded in all the right places.

The real highlight came when I was introduced to two renowned football players and their equally famous wives. I'll admit, I was starstruck at first — who wouldn't be — but the longer we spoke, the faster the novelty wore off. They were warm, grounded, and surprisingly easy to talk to.

But it didn't take long for their curious minds to steer toward the topic everyone seemed hungry for: my relationship with Ari. And the more we delved into the enigma that was Ari Jaeger, the more I realised how little I actually knew about him.

Not the intimate parts — those I knew well. But the rest of him.

The parts that existed outside our bubble.

His world. His reach. His influence.

I'd always assumed our history meant I knew everything that mattered. Yet here were people — strangers — who knew facets of him I'd never even heard of. They spoke of him with a familiarity that made something inside me twist. Envy, perhaps. Or the uncomfortable awareness that I'd been so wrapped up in us that I'd never bothered to look outward.

They told me about his outreach in the sporting community, how he'd quietly supported countless athletes and clubs. How he'd hosted fundraisers that raised millions for causes he championed. How his generosity had earned him the affectionate nickname Saint Ari.

Saint Ari.

A name spoken with genuine affection — and not by one person, but by all of them.

I was floored.

And the more they shared, the more I wanted to know. I questioned the wives extensively, and they happily indulged me. I learnt he was an avid supporter of both Collingwood and Melbourne Storm, attending every game without fail. He followed them interstate. He had corporate suites in all three major Melbourne stadiums, plus the SCG, and others across neighbouring states.

Yet since we'd become a couple, he hadn't attended a single game. Not one.

Not even Chelsea in England — a pilgrimage he'd made yearly until recently. He'd given all of that up.

For me.

And suddenly, I wasn't sure how to feel about that. Guilty? Flattered? Overwhelmed?

Perhaps all three.

As the conversations around me shifted to deals being brokered and friendships being cultivated, I found myself watching the waiters instead — their trays balanced expertly as they weaved through the crowd, topping up glasses and offering appetisers with flawless precision.

At exactly seven-thirty, the music softened and the emcee's voice boomed over the microphone, announcing dinner. The floor cleared as guests hurried to their seats, and staff disappeared into the kitchen to prepare the next round of service.

Prepared by three-time Michelin-star chef Neil Perry, the premium three-course meal was outstanding — another testament to Ari's connections, influence, and the quiet power he wielded without ever flaunting it.

And as I sat there, absorbing everything I'd learnt, one truth settled heavily in my chest: Ari Jaeger was far more than the man I thought I knew. And I wasn't entirely sure what to do with that.

I had barely polished off the crème brûlée on our mini dessert plates and was licking the spoon when Ari pushed his chair back and buttoned his dinner jacket. He bent down, brushed a chaste kiss across my lips, and confidently strode toward the lectern positioned nearby. The room descended into silence as he adjusted the microphone.

"Is Ari making a speech?" Dad whispered, leaning across my grandmother, Violet — an invitation I still didn't understand.

"It's all part of the formalities, I suppose."

Ari began eloquently, thanking the staff for their hard and often challenging work throughout the year. I glanced around the room, taking in the candescent expressions. He welcomed new employees, farewelled retiring ones, and presented each with a generous gift — a reminder of their dedication and loyalty to JPD. He even coaxed Neil Perry from the kitchen, the amiable chef taking a bow before Ari pulled him into a firm handshake and friendly hug, lifting the entire room to its feet in applause.

Believing the formalities were over, I began to retake my seat.

“I wouldn’t just yet, sis,” Scarlett simpered, clapping enthusiastically.

I shot her a questioning look. Her chin jerked toward Ari, who was stepping back to the lectern. He raised a hand, quietening the room once more.

“Thank you. But before you all run back to the bar and take full advantage of my overly generous tab, there’s one more item on my agenda tonight — something I’ve been dying to share for quite some time.”

I gulped. What was Ari up to?

“As you’re all painfully aware, I’ve been rather distracted these last few months. Pleasantly so, if you must know.”

Excited nods and chuckles rippled through the room.

“Well, this distraction has been well worth my time. And let me tell you — she’s one special lady. One I’ve had the privilege of knowing my entire life.” He paused, swallowed, emotion tightening his voice. “And I waited what felt like a lifetime for her to remove me from what is painfully known as the friend zone. Much to my delight, on one sunny Sunday in September, she finally agreed.”

Heat the colour of my dress crept up my cheeks as the blinding spotlight Ari had requested swung onto me. Thousands of eyes bored into my skull. If the floor could swallow me whole, now would be ideal.

"Teddy, will you please do me the honour of joining me up here, so I can finally show you off to my wonderful staff?"

When I refused to budge, Ari masked his nerves with humour, twisting at the waist to grin at me. "Don't leave me standing here by myself — my staff might begin to question my sanity otherwise."

The room erupted with laughter.

"Not helping, Ari," I muttered under my breath.

"Oh my god, Teddy! Don't leave the man waiting!" Scarlett hissed, smacking my bicep. "Just go already!"

"All right, I'm going!" I snapped through clenched teeth.

My cheeks ached from the forced smile as I unsteadily rounded the table. Ari met me halfway — and before I could protest, he snaked an arm around my waist and dipped me. I yelped, clinging to his shoulders, mortified. "Ari, what are you doing?"

He beamed above me. "Just go with the flow, my love."

I opened my mouth to object — but his lips met mine in a passionate kiss. The crowd erupted into applause and wolf whistles, making us laugh breathlessly as we came up for air.

"PDA, Mr Jaeger? Or was it the bourbon that made you lose your inhibitions?"

Still hovering above me, he brushed his nose against mine and grinned. "Alcohol had nothing to do with it. And what's wrong with wanting to show you off? I love you."

He pulled us upright with effortless strength. "Now, look up."

He swung us around to face the large screen bolted to the wall. My nose scrunched as the camera zoomed in.

"Oh my god, you can see my wrinkles up that close!"

Ari chuckled and pivoted back to me, entwining our hands just as Ruelle's soft, husky voice filled the room with I Get to Love You. My heart melted.

"Teddy," he quivered, "from the moment I laid eyes on you, you had me smitten. As that smitten four-year-old, I wasn't old enough to grasp the meaning of the word love. It was just something my mother said each night as she tucked me in — a gentle word, wrapped in warmth, though I never imagined it would one day define my entire world."

Warmth flooded my chest. I choked back a sob. "What about now?"

"Now, it means everything. Whenever I look at you — or even think about you — my heart aches and my stomach flutters. Or was it the other way around?"

Laughter rumbled through the room as Ari, usually so composed, stood before me in a complete lather.

"Faux pas or not... for however long we're blessed to remain on this earth, I want to feel the impact of our love every day and every damned night."

"As do I," I whispered.

He smiled shakily. "I would've waited an eternity for you. But as you know, I'm not that patient."

"I do — better than you do."

That was when Ari dropped to one knee, an open cherry-red box balanced between his fingers.

A sob tore from my throat.

"Teddy Vivienne McGovern, will you please do me the greatest honour by becoming my wife?"

"Yes! Yes, I will!"

I dropped to the floor and threw my arms around his neck. "I love you infinity, Ari Jaeger," I whispered, crushing my lips to his.

"And I love you," he murmured, pressing his forehead to mine. "Hold out your left hand."

I gasped as he slipped the divine infinity band onto my finger. "Oh, Ari… it's beautiful."

He lifted my hand to his lips, the photographer capturing the moment perfectly. "No — it's exquisite. Just like you."

He wiped my tears with his thumbs and helped me to my feet.

Unbeknownst to him, they were tears of guilt.

"Oh, Ari… this certainly explains the nothing's going on tonight."

"Yeah, you got me."

He exhaled and pulled me closer, nuzzling into my cheek as I nestled into the crook of his neck. Citrus and mint drifted around me, making my heart flutter.

"But it was worth the nerves."

I tilted my head back, meeting Ari's searing gaze as his fingertips caressed my face. Oblivious to the taunts and the dark eyes watching from the shadows, we drifted across the dance floor, our lips locked in an all-consuming kiss.

∞

Audrina

"Look at them, Jaxson," I murmured, watching our beloved son dancing cheek-to-cheek with his new fiancée. "Ari and Teddy are completely besotted with one another."

"Indeed, they are."

His beatific gaze followed mine, softening as he took in the sight. "I was considering raising an issue that's come up with Teddy's legal case — but perhaps it's better left for tomorrow. Let them enjoy this moment."

Jaxson's smile warmed. "We ought to do the same and savour this blessed union."

Before I could reply, he grinned like a man half his age and swept me into a playful spin, pulling me back into his arms with an exhilarating rush.

"Yes, let's," I breathed, resting my cheek against his shoulder. My eyes fluttered closed as a wistful sigh escaped me — a mother's wish that joy could remain untouched, unshadowed, and that we didn't have to be the bearers of unwelcome news at such a beautiful time.

16

Ari

"I can't believe we're engaged," Teddy marvelled, propped against the disarray of pillows, her gaze fixed on the ring glittering on her finger. "It feels so..."

"Surreal?" I offered, grinning as the same wonder rippled through me. Flicking the crumpled sheet aside, I rolled out of bed and wandered toward the bathroom. "I know what you mean. I think I've pinched myself a dozen times just to make sure it's real."

I paused in the doorway, unable to stop myself from looking back at her. The morning light softened every curve, every line of her body, and the sight of her — flushed, tousled, radiant — made something warm and possessive unfurl in my chest.

"Shower with me?"

Her brows lifted, curiosity flickering.

"Just a shower?"

A slow smile tugged at my mouth. "Let's see where it leads," I murmured, my tone giving away exactly where my mind had already gone. A breeze drifted through the open balcony door, carrying the sweet scent of star jasmine into the room.

Teddy rose with that effortless, feline grace that always undid me. The faint trace of her perfume mingled with the warmth of her skin as she crossed the room, and the way she moved — confident, unhurried, entirely aware of the effect she had on me — sent a familiar pull low in my stomach.

"Coming?" I asked softly, though the answer was already written in her eyes.

"By the feel of this," she breathed, her lips brushing mine as her fingertips skated along the length of my growing cock, "it won't only be a shower." Her teeth sank into my bottom lip, indicating her deepest desire – unfettered play. An attractive request I found impossible to deny and began to oblige her by seizing her hips, gruffly yanking her against me.

Her fingers weaved and tugged my hair at the roots, crushing our lips together. Our intended shower temporarily abandoned as we fervently stumbled backwards, thudding back onto the mattress.

My arm flung outwards, hitting the bedside table. "Roll over and kneel," I softly demanded, clutching my bow tie.

Without question, Teddy crawled to the centre of the bed and circled her arms behind her, resting them at the base of her shapely back. A sublime position that pushed her pert breasts upwards as I shuffled on my knees beyond her, binding both wrists together.

I inched closer and glided my splayed hands over her soft skin: up her arms, over her shoulders, and each perfect mound. Pleasing me were her deep pleasured moans as I tweaked each raspberry peak in my fingers. My fingers skimmed along the soft curve of her belly and paused at the swollen parting between her spread thighs.

"I want to blindfold you..." I grasped her thick tresses and swept them over her left shoulder with my free hand whilst trailing my lips along her tilting throat. All the while, brushing continually over her highly sensitised bud. "...Is that okay?"

Gasping breathlessly, she flinched beneath my touch. "Yes..."

A small smile graced my face as I slipped off the bed and ducked into my wardrobe, snatching up the first necktie I set my hands on. But in my haste to rush back to the bedroom, my footsteps faltered in the doorway as I observed Teddy's tranquil pose. The similarity to that of a practising submissive was uncanny, and honestly, it caused some worrying speculation.

I sighed. Bloody BDSM – a lifestyle I had shown very little interest in actively pursuing, predominately through my own misgivings. That all changed when I encountered Seth Cooper, an employee of JPD, Sydney branch and his stunning wife, Davina Cooper. A couple who practised religiously, and neither were shy about sharing the fact either as they happily cleared up any misconceptions I had when asked to share my thoughts—an in-depth conversation which inadvertently led to Teddy and her desire to experiment in the bedroom.

Although warned of her traumatic past without revealing details, they advised me to consider her wishes rather than fighting them. Baby steps, they'd counselled, as asserting my dominance too early on may frighten her off, ruining what was meant to be an extraordinary and pleasant experience for both of us. But many unanswered questions remained, ones they promised to answer in good time. For now, though, I simply decided it was in Teddy's best interest to table my uneasiness.

But as I clambered onto the bed and slid the tie around her head, covering her eyes, I questioned her certainty anyway, "Are you sure you're completely comfortable with this type of play?"

"Yes, sir." Her controlled reply stunned me into silence.

Both hands tying the firm bow at the back of her head dropped to the mattress. I hadn't ever classed myself as a Dominant in any sense of the word, and excluding the office, no one ever called me sir. Teddy had on the odd occasion, but I always assumed she was having a bit of a lark. In hindsight, perhaps it wasn't fortuitous like I first thought. Again, as my gaze travelled over her serene figure, with her head bowed and positioned on her knees patiently awaiting instruction, I had to admit she looked beautiful. Nevertheless, if this was what Teddy fantasised, far be it for me not to oblige.

The joke was on me as I suddenly found myself unable to perform – which never happened. Ever.

Panicked, I loosened both ties and yanked them away from her head and wrists, leading Teddy to question me as her perplexed and blinking gaze whipped around. "What's wrong?"

I silently and self-consciously gestured to my lap.

Slowly spinning on her knees to face me, she bit down on her bottom lip, stifling her rising laughter. "Oh. That's never..."

I scoffed. "Happened? Yeah, I know."

Teddy's suppressed laughter was short-lived as she began to giggle, adding to my embarrassment. "Maybe we overdid it?"

My head shook. "No, that's not it," I refuted, scrubbing a hand through my untidy hair. "Why, exactly, did you call me, sir?"

"Oh—that. It just... slipped out." Her answer came too quickly, the flush rising along her neck giving her away.

Astounded, I stared. "How? We've never discussed the BDSM lifestyle in any real sense, so why does it seem like you're suddenly familiar with it?"

"I've read up on it...a lot...lately," she stammered, eyeing me tentatively. "It's a lifestyle I believe I need... Besides, it's not as if we haven't tried aspects of bondage before, have we?"

I opened my mouth to argue but she lifted her hand sharply, stopping me. My mouth clamped shut.

"No, hear me out. You've restrained me before, and let's not forget the spankings you've dished out on more than one occasion. Some of which, has been rather rough."

"I thought that's all there would be," I demurred, scrubbing my hands over my face. "Just...play. Nothing more."

"The idea of you leaning into your dominant side with me turns me on," Teddy insisted, her unwavering gaze staring head-on. "Surely, you worked that out during our trip to Sorrento. Or since then? Or before then as a matter of fact?"

"Call me stupid, but no. I simply assumed we were just experimenting, you know, to keep the sex from becoming routine and dull."

Straddling my lap, she locked her ankles at the curve of my spine and began rocking her wet cleft against my twitching cock. "You're not stupid, just a tad obtuse maybe."

"Obtuse, am I? Charming," I growled smacking her backside. Fire reignited in her eyes. Maybe I was obtuse. I decided to placate her curiosity. "How about before we venture any further down this road, we research it – together. As in speaking to a couple, I know who live and breathe the BDSM lifestyle. Doctor Montgomery's another worth speaking to, only as a precaution...." I swiftly added through a moan as glazed eyes locked with mine.

I swept my hands over her dampened back, encouraging her to rock harder. Her panting increased as her need to release her imminent orgasm rose. “Don’t come yet,” I quietly ordered, cupping her sweet behind. “Now, lift…”

Teddy raised her hips and sedately sank back down, taking the fullness of my hardened length inside her tight little rosebud. We groaned pleasurably. The emphasised tightness was unlike anything I’d ever experienced.

Her head thrown back in ecstasy, her mouth gaped, soaking in every bit of pleasure of my cock inside her. Her pert breasts bounced softly, rubbing tightened nipples against my chest.

Damn, that felt tantalising.

The second she clung to my neck with one hand and began circling her clit with the other, my cock swelled. I was in ecstasy heaven. I clamped onto a nipple, sucking harder than I ever had, and Teddy cried out, her hips undulating faster, harder.

She lifted her hips and slammed back down as she climaxed spectacularly. I roared as her inner muscles gripped my cock tightly, climaxing equally hard.

In our dazed post-coital bliss, our heaving bodies rocked together and searched out one another’s mouths. Our breathless pants mingling as we sensuously kissed whilst trailing fingers roamed over sweat-laden torsos.

“That was amazing,” I murmured, against Teddy’s swollen lips.

“It was, wasn’t it?”

“Shower or bath?”

She winced, easing off me. “Bath.”

I laughed mercilessly, earning me a slap to the chest.

“Not funny, Jaeger!”

∞

Teddy

Perching gingerly on a modern blonde-timber chair inside the Hoodwink Café—just around the corner from Ari's—was no easy feat when every part of me ached. Naturally, he found my discomfort endlessly amusing.

"Don't laugh."

His mouth and eyes twitched with barely contained mirth. "I'm not laughing."

"You are so. It's written all over your face."

"Aw, my poor petal." He jutted out his bottom lip in exaggerated sympathy. "To be fair, I'm a little sore myself. We may have to abstain for a while."

Appalled, I grimaced. "Abstain?"

"You say it as if it's a filthy word." His chuckle was anything but innocent.

"It might as well be," I shot back. "If we keep having sex as often as we do, your penis may whittle down to nothing more than a toothpick."

Ari lifted the menu and scrunched his face. "What a dreadful thought."

"We'd better stop then," I muttered, scanning the single-page menu.

"Hah. You wouldn't last five minutes. You'd be too lost without my..." He leaned forward, dropping his voice to a wicked whisper. "...cock."

I shrugged, feigning indifference. "Admittedly, I would be left dreadfully unsatisfied... but all is not lost. I have my vibrators."

"It's not the same," he declared smugly. "A B.O.B. can't get you off the way I can."

Keeping my eyes on the menu, I let a ghost of a smile tug at my lips. "Not entirely true. How do you think I got off before we started dating?"

His hand splayed over his eyes as his shoulders shook with laughter. "You're unbelievable."

"Can't whatever it is wait?" I whined as he made that dreaded beeline for his office the moment we returned home from what had been an enjoyable lunch. Yes, he'd warned me in the car, and yes, he reminded me again as he paused in the doorway of his study—but still.

"I told you, it's just a few emails." With an impatient sigh, he strode back toward me. "I won't be long, I promise." One of his dashing smiles, then a soft, chaste kiss—far too chaste—left me even more dissatisfied.

I caught him by the hair, holding him hostage. He chuckled against my mouth before gently prying himself free. "How am I meant to get any work done if you've ensnared me?"

"That's the idea. You can't."

"Generally, your powers of persuasion work a treat, but the sooner I deal with these emails, the sooner I can give you my undivided attention."

"Fine," I muttered, arms dropping in a sulky huff. "While you attend to your *work*, I'll go entertain myself by practising some new pieces on your piano."

"Love you!"

"Yeah, yeah, love you too," I mumbled, waving him off as we drifted in opposite directions.

A gentle breath of wind brushed my skin as I stepped into the living room. The balcony doors stood wide open—Rosa must have thrown them open while we were out—letting the temperate sea breeze drift through the house.

I smoothed the back of my dress and perched on the piano stool. What to play? Or rather, what suited my mood? I tapped my chin, thinking.

Big My Secret surfaced, and as my fingers began to float over the keys, the melody unfurled through the room, confirming I'd chosen well. I closed my eyes and slipped into a place where there were no secrets. No lies. No fear.

But reality returned the moment I opened my eyes and glanced down at the engagement ring Ari had given me so unequivocally. He'd poured every ounce of passion into its design—an infinite pattern meant to symbolise us. Our love was unique, yes, but so much of it was fuelled by the intensity of our sex life. It begged the question: were we truly compatible enough for the utopian future Ari dreamed of?

And then there was the heartache we'd already endured in such a short time. That alone gave me cold feet, made me fearful for what lay ahead. Still, I had to try. I had to trust that we would work. Otherwise, these past few months would have accounted for nothing. Hurting Ari was the last thing I wanted. The last thing I could allow. Even if it meant hiding my duplicities. If he discovered any of them, he would end us for good.

"Scusa, Miss Teddy..."

Annoyed by the interruption, my fingers crashed against the keys. "Yes, Rosa?" I replied sharply, keeping my back to her and tinkering in hopes of drowning her out.

"Mr and Mrs Jaeger have arrived," she announced from the edge of the room.

My brow creased. An unscheduled visit from them was never casual. I sighed and spun around. "You'd best notify Ari. He's in his office—working, as usual."

"Yes, Miss Teddy." She scuttled off toward his study.

"Thank you, Rosa," I added belatedly—not that she heard.

I rose, smoothed the front of my floral maxi dress, and made my way downstairs to the lower ground floor, greeting Audrina and Jaxson in the entryway.

"Audrina, Jaxson—what a pleasure." I smiled, embracing them each in turn. "Not that we mind the unexpected visit, but don't you usually entertain the Bradfords on a Sunday after church?"

Jaxson's dark blue pinstriped suit was far too formal for a casual Sunday visit. So was the black briefcase clutched in his hand.

"We've been to church," Audrina mentioned with a faint smile as we dawdled back upstairs, "but we're having dinner with them instead. We have an issue that takes higher precedence." She, too, was overdressed—black-and-white striped dress, elbow-length sleeves, a thin belt cinching her small waist.

Sensing their unease, I ushered them into the living room. Ari joined us moments later, kissing his mother's cheek and shaking his father's hand.

"Mother. Dad. What's going on?"

"Maybe we should sit first," Jaxson suggested, gesturing to the vintage tan sofas. "And perhaps a bottle of wine, please, Ari?"

"Better make that two," Audrina added glumly.

Ari raised a brow. "Okay..."

Eager for answers, I retrieved two bottles of Shiraz and uncorked one. Ari gathered four glasses by their stems, the bowls clinking against his thigh as he crossed the room.

"All right, spill. I'll pour, you talk," he commanded, setting the wine glasses on the coffee table.

As he poured, Jaxson exchanged a troubled glance with Audrina—an exchange neither of us missed. Ari's brow furrowed as he handed me my glass. I thanked him quietly and took a bracing gulp.

In heavy silence, Jaxson lifted the black briefcase, removed notepads and folders, passed them to Audrina, then snapped the case shut. He leaned forward, elbows on knees, steepled fingers pressed to his lips.

I'd had enough.

"Whatever you need to ask, Jaxson, just bloody ask me."

Unfazed, he lowered his hands and sighed. "Teddy, our visit is about your case. It concerns the child your mother made you give up."

My stomach dropped. "What about my child?" I refilled my glass, ignoring Ari's sharply raised brow.

Jaxson shifted, retrieving a pen and placing a legal pad on his lap. "I spoke to my brother, Garrett, about taking on your case. He agreed. Unfortunately, he's hit a snag in his research."

"What kind of snag?"

His expression turned grim. "We need to obtain the child's DNA... as proof."

17

Upon hearing the words DNA and proof, something inside me collapsed. I lost all sense of self, sinking into a cavernous despair. I barely registered the glass slipping from my fingers or the red wine bleeding into the Aubusson rug beneath my feet. A guttural cry tore from my chest, drowning out the rising voices around me.

Then warmth — familiar, steady, anchoring — wrapped around me as strong arms closed over my upper body. I turned instinctively, burying myself in Ari's chest, hiding my face from his parents as I clung to his shirt, trembling.

"Shh, you're all right," he murmured, cradling my head as he rocked me gently. His tone sharpened as he lifted his gaze. "You do realise Teddy's child died, don't you, Dad?"

Jaxson cleared his throat, the sound tight and uncomfortable. "It's a fact I'm well aware of, Ari."

Ari's chest expanded with indignation. "Then how in the devil are you meant to obtain this DNA? She might've been cremated for all we know. Anything's possible where bloody Therese is concerned!"

"Ari, please don't swear at your father," Audrina interjected with cool precision. "He's doing his utmost best, given the lack of evidence we have. As it stands, Teddy," she continued gently, "obtaining this DNA would establish the timeline — proving beyond reasonable doubt that Emmett committed statutory rape, knowing you were only fifteen."

Ari glanced down at my blotched, tear-streaked face, his fingers tracing slow, soothing lines along my spine. "Sweetheart, can you sit up and give us any more details?" he coaxed softly.

Reluctantly — and only because it was him — I lifted my head, though every part of me longed to remain cocooned in his arms, hidden from the wreckage I had created.

"I don't see what can be achieved by this," I whispered, voice raw. "And as Ari said, she might have been cremated. Surely there are other avenues?"

Jaxson's expression softened into something almost paternal. "We could attempt prosecution without the DNA, but as Audrina mentioned, having it strengthens the case considerably. Without it, the judge may deem the allegations hearsay and acquit Emmett."

I stiffened. "Meaning that animal will walk free?" Their cautious nods ignited a violent surge of fury. I clamped a hand over my mouth, swallowing the scream clawing its way up my throat. "Well, what a futile exercise this has been then!"

My eyes flashed at my stunned future in-laws as I pushed off the sofa and stormed through the open doors onto the balcony. I gripped the glass railing, fighting the storm inside me.

Audrina hurried after me, her heels clicking sharply across the boards. "Teddy! All is not lost," she insisted, breathless with concern.

"Yes. It. Is!" I hurled back, but when she drew me into her arms, I sagged against her, my head falling to her shoulder as my tears broke into full-bodied sobs.

"Oh, Teddy, my darling," she murmured, stroking my back with a tender, rhythmic hand. "We shall find another way, won't we, Jaxson?"

Her tone was soft, but the strain beneath it betrayed the truth — this wasn't a suggestion. It was a velvet-lined directive, delivered with the poised certainty of a woman long accustomed to being obeyed.

Jaxson's jaw flexed, the faintest sign of resistance before he recalibrated himself around her expectation. "Um... yes... sure," he conceded, the reluctant words pulled from him with a deference he didn't bother disguising. He wasn't afraid of his wife — far from it — but he knew when her reasoning had already cemented itself. And once Audrina Jaeger had decided on a course, the rest of the world tended to fall in line.

I bit my lip, suppressing the inappropriate giggle threatening to escape. In all the years I'd known Jaxson Jaeger, I had never once seen him stumble over his words. But Audrina had that effect — a quiet, elegant dominance that could redirect even the most formidable man with nothing more than a tightened breath and a pointed look.

There truly was a first for everything.

"The upside," Jaxson continued, clearing his throat, "is that the statute of limitations doesn't apply. The defence can't contest that, at least — if that's any consolation."

"See, Teddy? That's a start," Audrina encouraged, her composure returning in full. "We'll have our investigator, Bill

Conlan, do some digging. With any luck, something useful will turn up."

I nodded, mumbling, "Okay." Pulling away from her embrace, I wiped my nose with the back of my hand — earning a scandalised look from my future mother-in-law. She promptly produced a handkerchief from her sleeve and thrust it into my palm.

"My son's unpleasant habits appear to be rubbing off on you."

I snorted at the jab.

"And not in that way either!" she added sharply, rolling her eyes.

"The loather of eye-rolling just rolled her eyes," Ari tutted, amused. "The disrespect, Mother, is appalling."

"The wine has clearly blurred your vision," Audrina countered coolly, gliding back into the living room.

Ari chuckled and finished his glass. "Plausible deniability. Isn't that what you call it?"

"Don't know what you're talking about." She flopped onto the sofa and reclaimed her wine with regal indignation. "Now, can we return to our discussion, please."

The bubbling laughter faded as a memory — one I'd shoved deep into the recesses of my mind — resurfaced with startling clarity.

"I don't know if this will be of any help, but I remember staying at a house with a priest and his housekeeper — a Mrs Beatrice Mercer — somewhere in New South Wales."

Audrina leaned forward, her voice soft but urging. "Do you recall the priest's name at all, Teddy?"

"Um... Father Byrnes. He was old. I remember that much. He may have even passed away by now."

My nose crinkled as Ari chuckled. "What? I was sixteen. Anyone older than twenty was deemed old. I was hating on everyone at that time. Don't judge me."

His mouth twisted ruefully. "I wasn't judging."

I tutted. "No, of course you weren't."

"Church records would be a way of finding him," Jaxson observed, his blue eyes sparkling at the banter. "What else do you remember, Teddy?"

Groaning, I drifted back to the piano and slumped onto the stool, letting my fingers tinker aimlessly across the keys as I gloomily opened up. "It was dark when we arrived."

"Who was 'we'?" he interjected, furiously scribbling notes.

"My mother," I shot back, venom lacing my words. "While Father Byrnes showed me to my bedroom, she spoke with Mrs Mercer. I also saw her hand Mrs Mercer a wadded envelope — I suspect it was cash for my upkeep, or that's what she led them to believe. Who knows?"

The bitterness thickened in my throat.

"Once she'd handled the business side of things, she proceeded to lecture me about my schoolwork: *'Don't fall behind, failure isn't an option. But I doubt high marks will be enough to redeem the shame you've brought upon our family name.'*"

I swallowed hard, trying to hide the sadness creeping into my voice.

"Part of my jail time included helping with chores when asked. And just for shits and gigs, she reminded me about my daily exercise routine: *'Pregnancy's no excuse to sloth around, Theodora. The right man won't admire you if you let yourself go. Use that bottle of moisturiser I packed for you religiously; stretch marks are another turn-off.'*"

"I'd love you regardless." Ari's voice softened, warm and earnest — he always knew how to butter me up. I blew him a grateful kiss.

But his softened gaze hardened as he turned back to his father.

"Dad, I require the use of your investigator — with your permission, of course."

Jaxson's eyebrows shot up. "Oh? May I ask whom, or what, you require Bill for?"

Ari rocked on the balls of his bare feet with elbows perched on his knees, hands clasping and unclasping restlessly. "Emily Smith. Teddy's co-worker from Bricks and Mortar."

"And why her in particular, son?"

"There's something about her that just doesn't quite fit," Ari revealed, his tone cooling into something dispassionate and analytical. He stretched across the coffee table, clutching the wine bottle by its neck and topping up his glass. "And if my hunch is right, then we're all in trouble."

As he explained his reasoning — and filled his parents in on my recent scrap with Emily — I felt heat crawl up my neck.

My conduct had been far from appropriate; I accepted that. But I didn't need reminding.

Swivelling away from their lamentable conversation, I positioned my fingers over the keys and began playing Beethoven's Moonlight Sonata. Seven minutes of haunting, sombre melancholy — a piece that suited my mood with unnerving precision. The room fell silent, the chatter dissolving as the first notes unfurled. No one spoke again until the final chord faded into the air.

"Please, carry on," I instructed over my shoulder, aloof and unwilling to meet their eyes.

Audrina cleared her throat and resumed as though they hadn't all paused to witness a side of me I rarely revealed to anyone outside my family or Ari.

"You don't think she's Emmett's daughter, do you?" she ventured, uncertainty clouding her expression as she toyed with the diamond choker at her throat. "Another supposition, yes, but anything's possible where my brother is concerned."

She nibbled her bottom lip before capturing my attention with a disclosure that knocked the breath from my lungs.

"Emmett was married before Bree — to your Aunt Liana, your mother's younger sister. Were you aware of this little fact, Teddy?"

I stiffened, twisting in my seat, my stunned expression answering for me. "No. Unsurprisingly."

Pushing away from the piano, I wandered back to the sofa, plopped down, and refilled my glass as Audrina predictably tutted.

"No, I didn't expect you would," she continued, smoothing her skirt with a delicate hand. "But after recent revelations, I figured... what harm could come from telling you, right?"

Laughing humourlessly, I gulped down the Shiraz and topped up her glass as well. "Bring it on."

Curling into Ari's side, I drew my legs up and tucked one beneath me, peering up to find him watching me with an amused, affectionate expression.

"What'd I do now?"

Propping an elbow on the arm of the sofa, he guided me to swing around and stretch my other leg across his knee. "Absolutely nothing."

I eyed his smirk strangely as I sipped my drink, then turned back to Audrina, bracing myself for more of my family's sordid history — which unfortunately meant more talk of her deplorable brother.

"Emmett emigrated to Australia before we did," she began, her tone tightening with distaste, "and it was only after the fact that we learned the true reason behind his sudden departure. Somehow, he'd slithered his way into an unnamed politician's life, and — cutting a long story short — used their illicit affair as blackmail."

"Let me guess," Ari muttered reproachfully, "this unnamed politician gently persuaded her colleagues in Immigration, both in England and here, to expedite his visa."

I wasn't sure what possessed me — the wine, the talk of Emmett, or both — but I suddenly pressed my fingers to Ari's luscious lips. His tongue darted out, licking them with slow, salacious intent, a move that shot straight to my groin.

Audrina cleared her throat sharply and snapped her fingers, dragging our lust-filled gazes back to her. "Excuse me, but do you two mind with the X-rated behaviour?"

"No, not at all." Ari grinned wolfishly as her face twisted into a scowl. "Carry on, Mother."

Tutting critically, she resumed. "Skipping the rest of the gory details — he met Liana through a mutual friend, and they began dating almost immediately. We had barely landed here ourselves when they announced they were getting married."

"Did they divorce?" I quizzed, dread curling around my spine.

Audrina's expression fell, her slick ponytail slipping over her shoulder as she picked at an imaginary spot on her flounced skirt.

"No. Unfortunately... we believe something sinister happened to her. And regrettably, we've never been able to prove otherwise."

My glass paused mid-air.

"Are you sure Liana didn't just run and hide from the deranged prick?"

Audrina lifted her head, her pooling gaze locking with mine. "No. We're quite sure she didn't." Her voice thinned with remembered pain. "The only reason I've drawn such a conclusion is because of the abuse she suffered at his hands. Eve and I both saw the bruises — but more than that, we witnessed the changes in her. For someone once so charismatic, bubbly, and full of life, Liana became a person we barely recognised. A shadow, if you will."

She exhaled shakily.

"Then, out of the blue, Emmett informed us she'd simply upped and left — taking only a small suitcase with a few belongings and a wad of cash from the safe."

Jaxson stroked his wife's hand with a tenderness that contrasted starkly with the story. "That same day, he ordered us to remove everything — family portraits, small photographs, anything that proved she existed. It raised our suspicions immediately. And within two years, he'd remarried."

"Wouldn't he have to prove she'd disappeared before remarrying, Jaxson?" I enquired, sliding my feet to the floor and topping up my glass with the fresh bottle Ari had thoughtfully fetched earlier. The alcohol softened the blow of each new revelation. Tomorrow's consequences could wait.

"He seemed to have every basis covered," Jaxson replied gravely. "He produced divorce papers within twelve months of Liana's supposed departure. I've always suspected they were pre-dated."

I snuggled against Ari, curling my feet beneath me as the wine loosened my tongue.

"I suspect he's abusing Bree too. When she and Emmett came for their appointment at Bricks, he was terrifyingly controlling — forceful with every decision. The impression I got from their interaction was undeniable. She's frightened of him."

"I thought as much," Audrina murmured, her voice weighted with quiet grief. "I sincerely hope Bree comes to her senses soon, before she suffers the same fate as Liana. Eve and I tried warning her off him, but she refused to listen. She brushed us off, insisting we had our brother all wrong."

By the sound of it, Audrina had resigned herself long ago to the truth: her brother was a sociopath.

"With any luck," I ventured, "if we accrue enough evidence, maybe she'll realise you were right all along."

Ari gripped my jawline and tilted my chin, pressing his lips to mine. My stomach flipped at the searing expression in his eyes as we parted.

"Even drunk, you're quite the optimist."

I shrugged nonchalantly. "Eh, alcohol skews life's views. I'll deal with the reality tomorrow."

He tapped my nose. "Not to mention the horrendous hangover."

I was in hell.

As Ari predicted, the hangover was horrendous. And my head — oh wowsers — it pounded at my temples like a jackhammer on heat. Judging by the infernal snoring beside me, Ari wasn't in any better condition after he and his father got stuck into the bourbon over several rounds of snooker, consequently cancelling their dinner with the Bradfords.

The person I truly felt sorry for was Rosa, surprisingly. She'd no doubt begun cursing us all the second she stepped foot downstairs and in the upstairs living room. First for the mess. Then for the stain I'd left on the rug.

Crap. Red wine was a bitch to remove.

Through my self-inflicted lamenting, the memories — along with the reason behind Audrina and Jaxson's unexpected visit — came flooding back. My stomach roiled.

No, wait. That was the excessive alcohol.

I groaned and rolled my head, burying my face beneath the pillow, desperate to hide the pathetic noise I croaked out.

"Ow, do you mind?" Ari grumbled beside me. The overstuffed pillow clearly wasn't enough to drown out my misery.

Lifting my aching head, I winced and peered across the large bed.

"Soz, bro."

Ari cracked one eye open, still half-dead from the hangover, but the moment he looked at me — hair a mess, pillow-creased cheek, oversized T-shirt slipping off one shoulder — something in his expression shifted.

That slow, wicked smile. The one that always spelled trouble. "Reality hit you?"

I grimaced. "Yeah. Like a brick. And the after-effects aren't pleasant either."

"I'm happy to show you something a little more pleasant if you'd like." He chuckled, rolling over the top of me with that lazy, hungover confidence only Ari could pull off.

"Let me shower first. I feel gross. And don't get me started on my teeth — I think they grew fur overnight."

Ari let out a low, pained laugh that immediately turned into a wince. "Ugh... don't make me laugh. My brain's rattling."

"Your brain?" I croaked. "Mine's trying to claw its way out through my eyeballs."

He flopped onto his back with a dramatic groan. "We're a disgrace."

"Speak for yourself," I muttered, dragging myself upright. "I'm a hungover goddess."

"Mm-hmm," he rasped, eyes still closed. "A goddess with furry teeth."

"Shut up."

I swung my legs over the edge of the bed, fully intending to drag my sorry carcass to the shower — but Ari's hand shot out, fingers curling around my wrist.

Not forceful. Just certain.

"Teddy..."

I paused, glancing back.

He tugged me gently, guiding me until I toppled back onto the mattress beside him. His eyes were half-lidded, still foggy with sleep and bourbon, but the look he gave me was unmistakable — warm, hungry, and threaded with that quiet, velvety affection that always undid me.

"You don't need a shower," he murmured, voice rough and intimate. "You're perfect like this."

"Ari..." My protest was embarrassingly weak.

He shifted, sliding a hand along my thigh, his touch slow and deliberate — not rushed, not demanding, just... sure.

The kind of touch that made my pulse trip over itself.

"Come here," he whispered.

And when I leaned in, he met me halfway — a soft, warm kiss that tasted like sleep and regret and something far sweeter.

The hangover didn't vanish, but it blurred at the edges, softened by the way he held my waist, the way he breathed against my mouth, the way he pulled me closer as though the morning, the mess, the world outside the bed didn't exist.

The sheets rustled.

His fingers tightened.

My resolve dissolved the moment Ari's expression darkened with intent. In one swift movement, he shoved my T-shirt up and over my head, trapping my arms until the fabric bunched at my wrists. His hand closed around them — steady, unyielding — holding my bound wrists together as he lowered his head.

I moaned in pure ecstasy as his mouth skimmed over my breast, sucking on my stiffened nipples. And his fingers teasingly traced my inner thighs, skating over my cleft. He slid a finger inside me, stroking, teasing, my hips bucking as his thumb brushed my clit. Ari's mouth trailed over my ribs and along my midriff – he paused and peered up at me.

Maddened with desire and need, I growled, "Don't fucking stop!"

Ari smirked and rolled me onto my stomach, my wrists still trapped in the bunched fabric above my head. Even though he'd released his hold, the unspoken command for them to remain in place hung thick in the air. His palm landed sharply on each cheek — a stinging reprimand drawing a helpless whimper.

He yanked at my hips and jerked my thighs apart before slamming balls deep inside me with force so great, it ripped the oxygen from my lungs.

I groaned loudly, fumbling as I reached for the top of the headboard. I clung on tightly as each powerful thrust plunged, pushing me farther up the bed.

Everything about his brutish lovemaking I relished – the

roughness, the searing pain from his fingertips as they dug into my hips. But just when I thought he couldn't get any deeper, he did, triggering a resounding yelp.

He hammered into me, and snaking his arm around my torso, our sweat-slathered bodies collided as Ari pulled me upright. My insides tightened, painfully, around his engorged cock.

"Dammit, Teddy, stop squeezing the fuck outta my cock," he grunted, breathing harshly, "and just fucking come!" Relief washed through us both as I shuddered against his sweat laden torso. Our fulfilled cries soaking the air as Ari swiftly pulled out and fisted his cock, covering my back with his semen in hot, lengthy spurts.

We collapsed together, laying breathlessly close to one another as Ari ran a hand through the dampened strands of his thick hair and chuckled. "Damn, talk about getting down and dirty."

"I can't move. You fucked me good and proper, Jaeger."

"Such a potty mouth, Ms McGovern," he playfully tutted, slapping my backside.

"Ow!"

He quickly rose off the bed, chuckling. "Let's shower; we have things to do today."

I turned my head on the pillow and peered up at him. "Like what? Don't you still have work?"

Ari tapped his nose. "No, all done. Now, come."

I snorted. "I did already."

"All right, Miss Smart Mouth, shower, tic toc, time's a-wasting."

As I watched his delicious behind saunter into the bathroom, I smiled surreptitiously. He's so dominating, oh yes, he is.

18

“Where are you driving us to now?” I quizzed, my head swivelling as we wound our way up Beach Road, the ocean glittering beside us and the bayside suburbs drifting past in a lazy, sun-washed blur. My relaxed gaze eventually landed on a jubilant Ari. His good mood practically radiated through the car, carried along by the warm breeze teasing the tips of his tousled hair as it drifted in through the open sunroof.

And dressed casually in white chino shorts, a mint-green polo with the collar popped, white canvas shoes, and dark sunglasses hiding those gorgeous eyes... he looked rather delectable too. As always.

Ari grinned. “You’ll see.”

For a man who’d drunk more than his fair share the night before, he was irritatingly chirpy — not a hint of a hangover anywhere. He had the constitution of an ox.

Me, on the other hand? My head ached horribly.

I eyed him suspiciously as his fingers tapped in time with the mellow revival of a classic drifting through the speakers. “Aha, we’re playing that game, are we?”

His sharp eyebrows wiggled above an equally mischievous expression.

“No, but I will say this — you’ll like my surprise. In fact, you’ll love it.”

“As long as it doesn’t involve getting naked, I’m sure I will,” I muttered, peering out at the last flash of brilliantly blue water before the coastline slipped away and Ari turned inland toward Port Melbourne, merging onto the CityLink ramp.

A hearty laugh rumbled out of him. “No, no getting naked. And since when do you complain?”

“Since you pushed my vagina out of my mouth this morning.”

Another full-bodied laugh erupted. “I’m sorry.”

My lips twitched, failing miserably to suppress my own laughter. “Yeah, you sound it. But believe you me, I never thought I’d be the one saying don’t touch me for at least a week.”

Ari gaped, genuinely flabbergasted.

“What, are you shocked? The great Ari Jaeger is speechless. Quick, call the press!” I mocked, lifting my phone to my ear.

His hand slid to my knee and squeezed — delicious shivers curling through my sex-weary body. “Your vagina might be sore, but there’s always option number two… or three.”

“True. But seriously, the love machine needs a rest. A well-earned one, wouldn’t you agree?”

His head cocked. “Love machine? Hmm. Yes, I suppose a little break wouldn’t hurt. If you recall, you blatantly vetoed my thoughtless and disgraceful suggestion only yesterday.”

I scrunched my nose. “Yeah, yeah… no need to rub it in.”

A devilish smile flickered over his lips. “Pun intended?”

“Of course.”

He placed his hand firmly on my thigh, refusing to lift his caressing fingers unless he needed to change gears. The flex of muscle in his forearm and biceps, the power in his thigh as he pressed the clutch — it was a sight I thoroughly enjoyed.

We swept past the low sprawl of South Wharf's outlet stores hugging the edge of the Yarra, the river flashing silver beneath the late-morning sun. Moments later, the road lifted beneath us, and as we rose onto the Bolte Bridge, the twin silver towers cut clean lines against the bright midday sky. The skyline slid past on our right, crisp and sharp in the clear light, as the car hummed along the elevated span.

The city fell away behind us as Ari joined the freeway, the suburbs blurring past in a warm, shimmering haze, each kilometre carrying us farther from the coast and deeper into Melbourne's northern fringe.

Eventually, he slowed, weaving sedately along Mountainview Lane until reaching our makeshift driveway. My jaw dropped, eyes widening as he drove through the wide entrance. The cleared block stretched before us, and Ari's grin grew as he parked.

His brows shot up. "Surprise."

I stepped out of the car slowly, shaking my head in wry amusement before walking straight into his smug arms. "I should've known. And I don't know why I'm asking this, but how on earth did you manage to gain approval so quickly?"

"Let's just say I offered an incentive toward one of the council's latest projects. They're looking for a builder to renovate their offices, so I put my company forward at a reduced rate. They were... very receptive."

I tutted, feigning disapproval, especially when so many others were forced to wait months. "Of course you did. It's a small price to pay, I suppose... and well worth it if our house gets built sooner." Regardless, excitement bubbled through me, and I threw my arms around his shoulders.

Pleased, Ari sifted his fingers through my billowing hair and held me fast. His lips slanted over mine in a salaciously hot kiss. I melted into him, hands roaming, taking full advantage of the closeness.

"I knew you'd see things my way," he cooed, rising for air.

"You can be rather persuasive at times," I murmured against his mouth through soft, chaste kisses. "Particularly when it comes to pleading your case — a tact learnt from your parents, no doubt?"

He traced his thumb over my bottom lip. "Of course. It's a tact that often comes in handy."

He often used the power of persuasion with me — and rarely did it fail.

"I'm sure," I replied dryly as a shit-eating grin spread across his face.

"I had Rosa fix us a picnic lunch. Want to have it here on the grass beneath the oak trees?"

I nodded. "Sure."

While he strolled back to the car to grab the picnic basket, I wandered across the block, trying to imagine where our house would sit, how it would look once completed. My gaze drifted along the row of well-established English oaks — thankfully spared at Ari's instruction. Their broad canopies offered abundant shade in summer, though they were in dire need of a trim.

"What are you thinking?" Ari called, spinning me back to him.

I trekked across the temporary gravel driveway and stood in his line of sight as he flicked open a green tartan blanket and spread it across the grass. "I was thinking of a tree-lined driveway, using the established trees already here."

His head bobbed in agreement. "Sounds good. We may need to plant a few more, considering you want the house set back quite a distance from the road. Along the front fence line might be nice too. What style of fencing would you prefer?"

"Preferably one high enough to keep unwanted visitors out," I muttered, earning an eye roll.

"Besides the obvious, what's your preferred look? Metal? Stone? Or here's a thought — security fencing with electrified razor wire and monitored by armoured prison guards?"

I let out a small laugh. "The thought had crossed my mind. But seriously, I'd be happy with stone and wrought iron, no taller than eight feet."

"Sounds reasonable enough," he mused, arranging the small containers of salad and other goodies across the blanket.

"Drink?" he asked, holding up the apple cider.

I sagged with relief. Oh, thank God — no alcohol.

Ari chuckled. "I thought an alcohol-free day wouldn't hurt either of us."

I gave a thumbs-up before piling chicken Caesar salad onto our plates. "Damn straight. My liver will cry if I abuse it any more."

"Sounds like your vagina, too."

I threw a crouton at him. "Gross."

The day had started idyllically.

With my head in Ari's lap, we spent most of the afternoon discussing our plans for the house — inside and out. Suitable materials, the layout, the furnishings to fill the enormous space.

We even agreed on my preferred landscaper to oversee the gardens. Then we moved on to our bedroom.

All was going smoothly until I suggested we install a playroom.

That derailed everything.

Ari flipped. One moment he was relaxed and sun-drenched, the next he was gathering everything in sight — tossing containers into the basket, reefing the rug off the ground, storming toward the car with a fury that made my stomach twist.

"I told you, I'm not a Dominant — in any sense of the word!" he snapped, carelessly throwing everything into the boot. "I don't mind adding toys or other aspects, but I utterly refuse to entertain that lifestyle on a permanent basis or take our sex life beyond what it is now!"

He raked both hands through his hair, frantic and frustrated. "When you called me sir, I freaked out — so did my dick! It's a title reserved for me out of respect from my employees, not for the fucking bedroom!"

I leaned against the side of the car, flexing my fidgeting fingers. "Yet you were considering it only yesterday. Why the sudden change of heart?"

Ari's jaw tightened. "You and I both agreed we'd speak with Doctor Montgomery and my colleagues first—"

"I'm aware of this," I cut in sharply, "but I don't understand the problem with adding a room that would service our needs without us ever having to leave the house. I've been nothing but transparent about my needs and the relief I gain from BDSM, so why are you refusing me?"

His livid gaze snapped to mine as he slammed the boot closed. He pointed a long, accusing finger at me. "As I said, I'll entertain added extras when and if the mood arises — but never, under any circumstances, will I allow that fucking room to be added to our family home. You hear me, Teddy? Ever."

"That's not an answer. And I'm the architect — I say it's going in. End of story."

Ari stalked toward me, exasperation radiating off him. "What about when we have children, hmm? Children are curious creatures — have you bothered to entertain the possibility of their little discovery? Or the deriving consequences?" His tone was glacial, clipped, and unmistakably indignant. "How would you explain to *our children, Teddy*, why we own a room designed for debauchery and debasement?"

I dug my heels in. "Simple. It would always remain locked behind a hidden door."

He folded his arms across his puffing chest. "You've always got an answer for everything, haven't you? Well, here's some transparency for you — I'm saying no. To the room and to this BDSM lifestyle you think you crave."

"You know nothing about it!" I screamed.

"If you go behind my back and do it anyway, I'll be pissed — more than I am now!" he shot back, thundering around the car and ripping the door open. He flung himself into the driver's seat, buckled up, and turned the key, revving the engine with deliberate aggression.

I rolled my eyes and slid into the passenger seat, buckling up just in time as he tore down the driveway, gravel spitting behind us.

"Out of anyone, I never thought you would act so closed-minded," I snapped.

Ari slammed the brake, jolting us forward. He twisted towards me, a dark scowl cutting across his face.

My stomach dropped.

"Have you not heard a word I've spoken? Have you not been in the same room as me when we've acted out our own form of kink and debauchery? Have I not pleasured you enough to fulfil your needs?" His voice dropped to a dangerous growl. "Judging by this incessant need of yours, I'd say not."

I opened my mouth, but Ari raised a finger — silencing me instantly.

"Don't."

The sternness in his voice, the ticking jaw — it was a warning. One I wisely heeded. I'd already pushed him too far.

The rest of the drive was suffocatingly silent. I turned away, gripping the door handle as Ari weaved through traffic, cursing at anyone who dared slow him down.

"Get out of the fucking way!" he barked, honking.

"If this is your mood, I want no part of it!" I shrieked. "Take me home. Now."

"As you wish."

He flung the car across two lanes and shot up the nearest ramp toward North Melbourne. The trip took half the usual time — I wouldn't be surprised if several speeding fines arrived in the mail. They'd be well deserved.

The BMW screeched to a halt at the kerb outside my house.

Silence. Awkward, aching silence.

I waited — tearfully, stupidly — hoping he'd say, *"I'm sorry. Please come home with me."*

But Ari stared straight ahead, jaw locked, refusing to look at me. No goodbye. No softening. No kiss.

Nothing.

I unbuckled, opened the door, and hesitated — one last chance for him to stop me.

Still nothing.

Every movement felt robotic as I climbed out and shut the door. Ari sped away without a backward glance.

Heartbroken and in tears, I ran up the footpath and inside.

∞

Emmett

I stroked my chin.

Well, well... that was interesting. A lover's tiff, perhaps — or had they broken up? One could remain hopeful. The shortest engagement in history, if so.

Teddy looked dreadfully unhappy, and who better than me to remedy the situation? Ari, on the other hand, drove off like a man profoundly pissed off.

Moments later, out of my peripheral vision, a black town car with heavily tinted windows pulled into the driveway. Well, well... what did we have here? The view that followed was even more intriguing: a decadently made-up Teddy rushing out the front door — and without her engagement ring.

A roguish smile curled across my lips. Perhaps I was right. Perhaps Ari wasn't meeting her needs after all.

Delightful.

"But why the short overcoat in this stifling heat, Teddy?" I murmured, craning my neck over the dash as she slid onto the backseat. The answer revealed itself the moment the coat shifted — and I licked my lips, hungry for the sight parading before me.

Ah. That explained that. And who doesn't appreciate a perfect set of pins wrapped in black, lacy thigh-highs?

My interest thoroughly piqued, I speculated where the delightful Ms Teddy might be heading. And if my instincts were correct — and they usually were — I knew exactly where. I was sure to follow.

Keeping a respectful distance, I tailed the town car for ten minutes until it slowed and turned down a narrow road I recognised instantly. The vintage, windowless, red-brick warehouse with its blackened door was familiar too. The very same club I'd followed her to several times before.

A low chuckle escaped me.

Was Ari incapable of meeting your needs, sweetheart?

My gaze remained glued to the car — and to Teddy — as she stepped out in killer heels onto the footpath. Concern marred her beautiful face as she scanned her surroundings, ensuring lover boy hadn't followed... or that no one saw her. Then the driver handed her a mask, which she donned quickly.

An opportunity I refused to miss.

I snapped a few more photos.

Leverage. Perfect.

She disappeared through the darkened doors past a hulking bouncer.

I slipped on my own mask and shadowed her inside.

19

Ari

Purgatory had landed. Two days. Two nights.

Neither with so much as a peep from Teddy.

With only Asher and a few bottles of bourbon for company, I'd spent both days drowning my sorrows. Today was just another blurry repeat with another sore head.

Not helping my cause was my mother's infernal nagging and raised voice. Come to think of it... why was she even here?

Mum had apparently come over for a casual catch-up — poor woman had no idea she was walking into the aftermath of my personal apocalypse.

"Ari Jaeger! Get out of that bed now!"

I groaned, peering out from beneath my pillow, my fuzzy gaze squinting at her as she buzzed around the bedroom, picking up the slovenly trail of clothes littering the floor.

"And for goodness' sake, get into the shower — you smell like death!" she declared, gingerly lifting a pair of my boxer briefs between two fingers. She scrunched her nose. "A bit like this room! Ugh!"

"Please, Mother, just waltz in as if you own the place," I muttered dryly, rolling over and flopping my arms across the rumpled sheets.

She shot me a reproachful glare. "Don't start with that smart mouth now, son."

I mock-saluted. She underappreciated my humour.

"Get up!" she barked. I winced. "What on earth transpired here, Ari, for your room to look this... appalling?" She held up a hand. "Actually, don't bother answering."

My eyes rolled. "Then why ask?"

She wordlessly delivered a deathly glare and pointed a long finger towards the bathroom.

"All right... I'm going!" With an exaggerated huff, I flicked the sheet back and rolled off the mattress — prompting my mother to hastily shield her eyes.

"A warning next time, please, Ari!" she admonished as I staggered past.

I smirked. "Sorry, Mother. Love you."

"Yeah, yeah."

Stepping beneath the welcoming shower spray, the chill of the water cooled my aching head, sobering me up somewhat. Didn't mean my skull had quit its relentless thumping. I reached for the vanilla and almond-scented shampoo Teddy favoured, pouring liberally into my hand. I began scrubbing my hair whilst my foggy mind retreated to our inane dispute two days ago.

Christ, I loved her, but at times, her attitude was just vexing. Lately especially. Blame I placed squarely on Teddy's high sex drive along with her ruthless quest for this damned playroom. This outlandish need seemed to be producing chasm sized cracks in a once flourishing relationship. Added to my frustration were the two days of silence, simply because she refused to accept my opinion. That alone left me less inclined to contact her or to see her in person for that matter. However, as the Bricks and Mortar Christmas party was that evening, and unless she alternately decided, I was accompanying her. Our unresolved issues weren't the only issue concerning me about the night's dinner.

My head tilted back, I rinsed off and started my usual regime of facial scrub and body wash; an intimate act that Teddy loved, mostly the body washing for obvious reasons, raising a small smile. But it quickly evaporated as Emily entered my thoughts.

Although Emily had stated otherwise, I sincerely hoped she'd had the sense to change her mind about attending, as a catfight would not bode well for the company. I snorted. Logan had better accompany us then, more as a precautionary measure. Likewise, Saturday, at my parent's yearly Christmas party, expressly after speaking with my mother. With the knowledge that Emmett's ever annoying presence shall be skulking about, erring on the side of caution lately had become the new normal.

Speaking of my mother. Her knuckles suddenly and impatiently rapped on the bathroom door, dragging me out of my reverie. "Ari, are you drowning in there?"

I wished. "Unfortunately, no," I droned. "I'll be out in a minute."

"Okay."

I heard the bedroom door open and close, taking that as my cue to exit the shower. I shut the water down and grabbed a towel off the rail, wrapping it around my waist upon strolling into the bedroom. I paused, absorbing the neatened state she had kindly left behind with my weary gaze. A freshly made bed with clean sheets, and a duvet cover, she had indeed gone to town. Also opened, was the sliding door to the balcony, possibly to blow out the deathly stench I had seemingly caused. Goosebumps rose as the refreshing breeze grazed my dampened skin whilst breathing in the blended fragrance of the artfully arranged white floral arrangement of lilies and roses inside the crystal vase lovingly placed on Teddy's bedside table.

Her side. My side. Our side.

What difference did it make when we shared the king-sized bed?

A bed that always ended up a shambles by the time we'd finished making love. Our sated bodies typically tangled as we collapsed against the mattress and dropped off to sleep. Everywhere I looked, Teddy's presence lingered, eclipsing my aching heart. Her clothes, the scent of her perfume, even the pale blue diamond tufted bench seat placed at the foot of our bed, along with the numerous cushions piled against the pillows I had unwittingly acquired at Teddy's insistence. The bedroom needed a woman's touch, apparently. In other words, to her taste, not the decorator's I'd initially hired upon purchasing the house.

Feeling woeful, I slumped onto the padded seat and sighed, running the flat of my palm over the soft linen fabric. I missed Teddy terribly: her wicked laughter, the merciful teasing, her touch, and the warmth of her body beside mine.

Was I that consumed by our relationship, she'd clouded my judgement, changing me into a man I no longer recognised? No, surely not? Recent circumstances had affected us, yes, but we always worked our way back to each other without fail.

Always.

I leaned forward, pitifully perching my elbows on my knees to nurse my thumping head between my hands. Presently though, we appeared to be at an impasse as neither of us seemed to be willing to make the first move. A shaky breath exhaled as I thrust a hand through my wet hair. Well, someone had to, and I guess that someone had to be me.

What greeted me first upon entering Teddy's house was an uncharacteristic silence.

In a home occupied by four rambunctious women who treated each other like family, noise was the norm. Without the echoing laughter or the streamed music drowning out the over-the-top nattering between our sisters and Poppy, the quiet felt... wrong.

But as soon as I thought it, the silence shattered.

An upbeat song burst through the speakers — Boom by Anjulie, if I wasn't mistaken.

I smiled. Music was Teddy's go-to in tough times.

I ventured closer to the kitchen, listening to her sprightly sing-along — and my smile faded as I registered the meaning behind the song. It was the kind of track people played when they were wrestling with themselves, not the world. A knot tightened low in my stomach.

She twisted at the waist and glanced over her shoulder, offering me a small, conflicted smile — the kind she used when she'd been caught thinking something she didn't want to admit.

"Ari — impeccable timing as always."

The wry tone told me she'd heard me come in. And honestly, I didn't appreciate the attitude — mostly because it meant she was hiding something from me again.

"Would you like a smoothie?" she asked, turning back to the fruit on the chopping board.

Leaning a shoulder against the narrow wall, I nodded. "Please."

She worked in silence, slicing fruit with that calm, methodical focus she always slipped into when she didn't want to think too hard. Her loose curls swayed across the back of her forest-green babydoll dress as she pressed the lid down and hit the button. The dull drone drowned out the music — and any chance of a civil conversation — until the blending stopped.

She grabbed two highball glasses and set them beside the blender. Pushing the off button, she lifted the jug, removed the lid, and poured equal measures into each glass.

I refused to waste the opportunity.

I stepped behind her and snaked my arms around her narrow waist, caging her between the island bench and my torso. Burying my nose in the luscious tresses cascading down her back, I breathed in the scent I'd craved for days. I gathered her hair in my hand, twisting it over her right shoulder, ready to press my lips to the creamy skin of her nape—

Teddy abruptly squirmed out of my grasp, sidestepping away. "Ari, no!" she objected firmly. "We can't just fix this... us, I mean... with sex. We need to talk."

My arms dropped uselessly to my sides. "I was merely holding you and kissing your neck." A bitter laugh escaped me at the sceptical look she shot back. "But of course you'd interpret my affection as a conciliatory fuck."

"No!" She let out an exasperated sigh, tilting her chin up and folding her arms across her chest. "That's not what I meant..."

"Then what did you mean exactly?"

I mirrored her defensive stance, leaning back against the opposite bench. Her dithering tested my already frayed patience. "I'm waiting, Teddy."

"I know we don't use sex to fix our problems… anymore, but I thought that's what you were trying to do," she murmured defensively.

Unbelievable. No — that's you, not me, a thought I wisely swallowed.

"No. I've missed you. And this—" I gestured to the gulf between us, "—has killed me. Not being with you."

Teddy gaped incredulously. "Well, whose fault is that? It certainly wasn't mine!"

My jaw clenched. "You demanded I drop you home simply because my mood was intolerable, apparently."

"You wouldn't see reason…" she muttered.

"Of course I'm not going to see reason over your bloody existential crisis!" Choking on my anger, I curled my fingers tightly around the benchtops square edging. "What caused our argument in the first place was this incessant need of yours to put a fucking sex dungeon in our house! Our fresh start, Teddy! For our future children — and for us!"

Despite my effort to contain my fury, my breath quivered. "You get off on debasement, is that it?"

"I do." Her gaze hardened. "But it's not for the reason you think it is — and nor is it an existential crisis."

"Well, enlighten me then…"

She moved around the island with deliberate calm, fingers raking through her hair as she perched on a barstool. "I need this debasement to free me from Emmett — what he did and what he took. Control. And what he still tries to take. By controlling my environment and the actions within it, I can prevent certain triggers."

"You'll feel safer, is that it?" I queried, dubious but listening.

She nodded tentatively. "Essentially, yes. But above all, I want to stop feeling like a slave to everyone else's demands — and to this deep-seated fear that you'll trigger a memory. Like... moments where something catches me off guard." Her voice wavered under my scrutiny. "It's the only way I feel I can explain myself to you."

My brows rose. "Moments like what?"

Perplexed, her brows pinched. "I thought we'd put that behind us."

"You're the one who brought it back into the conversation," I shot back. "And if you'd trusted me with your past earlier, then what happened in the bathroom that day wouldn't have blindsided you. I would've bloody well avoided it if I'd known."

The anger in my voice made her flinch.

"I'm sorry... I know I should've prewarned you. But explaining everything wasn't easy, and neither were the implications once you knew."

"Yet you still expected aggressive sex — and still do! No wonder I'm bloody confused!"

"You don't need to be, not if we venture down this road."

Fidgeting with her fingers, she timidly peered up at me. "Doctor Montgomery agreed with me — that practising BDSM is the best course of action, as long as we follow the rules and play sensibly."

Her guilty expression spoke volumes.

My entire body tensed. Disappointment washed over me. My head dropped as my fingers flexed over the marble countertop, fighting off the anger boiling inside. She damn well knew speaking with Doctor Montgomery as a couple was the agreement.

Indignant, I flicked my hand in a sharp, dismissive arc. “Oh, the good doctor did, did he? And when did this... conversation without me take place?”

Teddy stiffened at the gesture, her shoulders drawing in as if bracing for impact. She lifted her glass with trembling fingers, taking several sips of the pale pink smoothie before finally meeting my hardened expression.

“Well?”

“Yes... yester... day.”

My jaw cramped from the tension. “Huh. You didn’t think to inform me of this appointment? Or were there things discussed I wasn’t privy to?” The disdain in my voice was impossible to hide.

“I’m sorry, but I didn’t think you would want to come.”

I scoffed — right before I exploded. “You didn’t think I would come? You didn’t even try to ask, Teddy! A simple phone call — even a fucking text — would’ve sufficed. But no, you couldn’t even extend me that simple courtesy.”

I surged towards the island, my palms slamming against the countertop. “I thought we were in this together. If we were, you’d at least have the decency to include me in decisions regarding what is supposed to be *us*,” I ground out through clenched teeth. “For the past few months, all I’ve done is live and breathe us — for the damned future we planned. Together. If I didn’t care, I would’ve left the second you opened up about your past, and I most certainly would not have fucking proposed!”

Silence dropped between us – heavy, punishing.

Tears pricked as my temper erupted again, fuelled by slow-burning frustration. "Dammit, Teddy, I love you like nobody ever has. Christ, I've cried for you. I've even sacrificed my own sanity just so you can have yours!"

Teddy's tearful gaze tore away from mine. "I'm aware of the interest and the time you've vested in me, Ari, and I love you so, so much for it. But this is the one need I refuse to give up."

"Even if it means destroying what we have?"

"That's not what I want either. I'd prefer to explore this alternative lifestyle *with you* — but you refuse to even meet me halfway."

I scoffed, disbelief scraping my throat raw. "I only recently expressed — twice — that I'd prefer to discuss this possible scenario with Davina and Seth, and the good doctor first. I've relented by adding spanking, bondage, and a few toys, haven't I? If that's not meeting you halfway, then what is?"

Teddy's gaze flickered — evasive, guilty — making my head shake.

"You haven't given me a chance to process what BDSM means, or what it truly entails. I haven't wanted to delve further sexually for that reason. And you only just said you were worried about me triggering you." My voice tore through the room, harsher than I intended, but my frustration had boiled over and any grip I had on my temper slipped. "I'm struggling to understand what it is you want from me."

Teddy's throat bobbed. "I want... I want something that keeps me safe."

"Safe?" The word scraped out of me. "From what, Teddy? From me?"

"No," she whispered, shaking her head. "From myself. From my reactions. From the things I can't control."

I froze.

She swallowed hard, her voice barely holding together. "When I don't have structure, things happen. I react before I can think. I hate it. I hate feeling like my own mind is waiting to jump me."

The shower incident. The terror in her eyes. The way she'd run from me like I was the threat.

It hit me all at once.

"You weren't scared of me that day," I murmured. "You were scared of being blindsided."

Her breath stuttered — a tiny, broken sound.

"This isn't about sex for you," I went on, the truth settling heavily in my chest. "It's about making sure you're never ambushed by your own trauma again."

Her eyes glistened and her shoulders curled inward. "I just... I need to know what's coming. I need rules. I need structure. Because when I don't have that, things happen. And I can't go back to feeling like that again."

"So... the structure isn't about kink," I breathed. "It's about safety."

Her expression tightened, a tangle of defensiveness, shame, and reluctant relief. "Don't make it sound pathetic."

"It's not pathetic." My voice softened despite everything. "It's the first thing you've said that actually makes sense."

The truth of Teddy's confession sank in, slow and unavoidable.

Although I'd spoken briefly with the Coopers about BDSM, they never divulged specifics. They were vague about the finer details, evasive even, and I'd never pushed. I understood they derived intense pleasure from their experiences — as did I with Teddy, using the added tools they'd suggested — but I would never enjoy intimacy at the expense of humiliating someone. That was the line I couldn't cross. The idea of taking pleasure in deliberately inflicting severe pain simply wasn't ingrained in me, and Teddy needed to understand that aspect.

But as steely determination stared up at me, I realised that might take some convincing — especially as she folded her arms across her chest.

"We started incorporating aspects of BDSM before you even knew about my past, and it didn't bother you then, *did it*?"

Her words hit harder than I wanted to admit.

Defeated, I thrust both hands through my hair. "No, I suppose it didn't," I gruffly capitulated. "Only to a small degree, though."

"Okay, but if you really want to get semantic about details..." Teddy's eyebrow arched pointedly, her tone calm but unyielding. "You've happily participated, regardless of your knowledge of my past."

My head sagged into my hands over the island. There was truth to Teddy's words; not one ounce of our debauchery had bothered me. At all. So, what was I afraid of, and why was I making excuses? A part of me relished in our antics – in and out of the bedroom. In the end, what difference would it make if we incorporated more, without the need for sadism? Maybe if I stipulated the rules regarding the infliction of severe pain, limiting our play to pleasure, I could manage it? As long as it remained contained to the bedroom, I shouldn't have an issue with expanding our repertoire. A dedicated playroom, however, was entirely out of the question, regardless of Teddy's *need* for one.

I made my suggestions, advising her of my additional terms as she silently considered my offer.

"Introducing you to Davina and Seth and speaking with Doctor Montgomery, is pertinent before I even consider this arrangement further. That, I won't compromise on."

Her lips curved into a victorious smile. "All right. That's a start."

"You don't have to act so damned smug about it, you know?" I smirked, sliding my hand over the smooth marble as I stalked around the island in a slow, predatory arc.

Teddy swivelled sharply on the barstool, catching me off guard as she wrapped her legs around my waist. Her ballerina flats fell to the floor with a dull thud while she locked her ankles behind me, holding me fast in a vice-like grip. "That's your perception..."

A spark flared between us — familiar, dangerous, impossible to ignore. The way she seized me so suddenly — all heat and intention — obliterated what was left of my irritation. And I hated how easily I yielded to it, how quickly I let her steer us back into the one language we never failed at. She knew it. I knew it. And still, I stepped into it because losing her terrified me more than being handled by her ever could.

The suddenness of her confidence, the way she pulled me into her orbit, melted the last of my resistance. My hand slid instinctively into her hair, and the moment I fisted the soft strands, her breath hitched. I claimed her mouth with mine, the kiss deepening almost instantly, turning ravenous as days of tension and longing collided.

Her fingers threaded through my hair, tugging just enough to make my pulse spike. The argument, the tension, the fear – all of it blurred beneath the heat of her mouth and the certainty of her touch. She always knew exactly how to pull me back to her, how to turn the sharp edges between us into something molten.

My free hand swept along the silken skin of her thigh, pushing the flared skirt of her dress higher as she arched into me. She moaned softly, but when my hand drifted higher, she caught my wrist, stopping me.

"Why not?" I breathed against her lips, kissing her in short, hungry bursts.

"I'm still far too sore after our recent escapades," she confessed, just as breathlessly, as my lips traced the line of her throat.

I lifted my head with a shrug. "Fair enough. Doesn't mean we can't kiss. Or that I can't touch those delicious—"

"No," she cut in with a wry twist of her mouth. "They're tender too." Sensing my dismay, she pressed a palm to my chest and fluttered her lashes up at me. "Doesn't mean we can't kiss. Or... improvise." Her hand slid down my torso, her touch deliberate, teasing, suggestive — and the look she gave me was nothing short of incendiary. "Or...how about I suck you off? Would that please, sir?"

"Would that please you, sir?" she murmured, the title laced with mischief rather than submission. I ignored the flicker of the tugging displeasure at the word, because the heat in her eyes was impossible to resist.

"Mmm," I murmured, my voice low. "The possibilities."

She tugged me closer, her movements slow, deliberate, and wickedly confident as her tongue swept over the swollen head of my cock — and the rest blurred into sensation, into heat, into the kind of intimate haze where thought dissolved and only the two of us existed.

20

The relaxation coursing through my body was nothing short of miraculous. The resolution of our issues had played a considerable part as well, and as long as a particular individual didn't rub me up the wrong way, maintaining my calm throughout the evening shouldn't have been a problem.

Too late.

It was as if the devil himself had conjured Emily purely to spite me. The sight of her slinking past, attempting to enter The Skyline inconspicuously, was enough to send my spine ramrod straight. My darkened gaze slid to Logan, who nodded knowingly. Yes — he'd spotted her too.

The arm wrapped around Teddy's waist tightened, silently reinforcing that I intended to keep her close until the night was over. But first, the bar — and a top-shelf bourbon — beckoned.

Steering Teddy towards the bar, I'd barely gotten close enough to taste the burn of bourbon on my tongue when fate intervened.

"Ari! So glad to see you made it, mate!"

I warmly gripped a slightly inebriated Spencer's firm hand and chuckled. "Spencer, mate, had a few already, my old friend?"

"Aw, just a few..." He sheepishly grinned, enveloping Teddy in one of his bear hugs. "Ah, the delightful Teddy. You look gorgeous."

She yelped affectionately as he yanked her against his chest. Having sparred with him on several occasions, I knew hitting his chest was like hitting a brick wall — and I usually wore the tell-tale signs for days afterward.

She giggled. "Good to see you too." Rising onto her toes, she pressed her lips to his clean-shaven cheek. "Oh — whoops, I've stained your face with pink lipstick."

"Eh, don't worry about it." Spencer waved a hand as she tried to wipe the mark away with the handkerchief she'd swiftly stolen from my breast pocket. "Besides, it's a kiss I'll treasure." His eyes sparkled under The Skyline's intimate lighting.

I hauled Teddy back to my side. "Hey, enough of that, you old flirt. Teddy's mine — officially now," I added proudly, clasping her left hand and lifting it high enough for the glittering diamonds to catch Spencer's widened gaze. Was that a tear in the big guy's eyes?

"Oh, wow!" he gushed, laying a hand over his heart. "Congratulations to you both. However, Ari," he announced with a dramatic sigh, placing his oversized hand on my shoulder, "I have to say I'm a little disappointed..."

I cocked my head. "Oh? Do I dare ask why?"

"I expected a rock much bigger than this one."

"It's not about the size, Spencer." I chortled. "Well — not in the stone department anyway."

Teddy's eyes rolled mockingly. "You two have sunk to a new low. If this is where the conversation is headed, I'm going to need a glass of champagne."

I cheekily pressed a kiss to her cheek. "I'll have my usual poison, please, love."

∞

Teddy

I felt Ari's arm tighten around my waist before I even registered why. One moment he was warm beside me, relaxed in that rare, unguarded way whenever it's just us — and the next, every muscle in his body locked beneath my palm. His breath stilled. His posture sharpened. The shift was so abrupt it sent a ripple through my own spine.

I followed the line of his stare. Emily.

She slipped through the entrance like she was trying to fold herself into the wallpaper — head down, shoulders drawn in, the picture of someone hoping not to be seen. But Ari saw her. Of course he did. And the moment he did, the air around us changed.

So that was it.

He didn't speak, but he didn't need to. The tension radiating off him was enough. His jaw clenched, that familiar muscle ticking — a silent warning I'd learned not to ignore. I slid my hand over his forearm — not to soothe him, he'd never accept that — but to anchor him. To remind him I was here. That whatever storm Emily brought with her, he didn't have to weather it alone.

He guided me towards the bar with a determination that bordered on territorial. I let him. I'd learned that giving Ari the illusion of control was often the surest way to keep him from spiralling.

We didn't make it far before Spencer barrelled into us, all warmth and bourbon-tinged enthusiasm. His bear hug nearly lifted me off my feet, and I couldn't help but laugh as he squeezed the air out of my lungs. Ari's tension eased by a fraction — Spencer had that effect on people — but I still felt the tautness in his grip, the way he kept me close, as if Emily might materialise behind us at any moment.

When Spencer congratulated us and Ari lifted my hand to show off the ring, something inside me softened. The way he said officially now — proud, certain, claiming me without hesitation — sent a quiet warmth through my chest. Spencer's dramatic sigh and mock disappointment over the size of the stone made me roll my eyes, but the truth was, I loved the ring. Loved what it symbolised. Even if a quiet ache lingered beneath that love, reminding me of the secrets I carried.

But beneath the laughter, beneath the champagne jokes and Spencer's theatrics, Ari's pulse thumped too fast beneath my palm. Emily hadn't even spoken to him yet, and already she'd unsettled him.

And that... that worried me more than I wanted to admit.

The tension in him hadn't eased — if anything, it had coiled tighter beneath my touch. The last thing he needed was more fuel on that fire, so I slipped from his side, brushing my fingers along his wrist in a silent promise that I'd be right back.

"A glass of champagne and a bourbon, straight up, please," I asked the bartender, offering him a bright, polite smile. He was mildly handsome in that middle-aged, well-kept way — the kind of man who'd once been a heart-throb and hadn't entirely lost the polish. My gaze followed his efficient movements as he worked, the jazz band's sultry vocalist rasping her way through Tainted Love.

Of course it would be that song.

"Ironic, isn't it, Theodora?"

My smile vanished before I even turned. Emily's voice scraped across the air like nails on glass, sharp enough to sour milk. She stood behind me, her arms folded, and lifting her chin in a way that tried — and failed — to look confident.

"The song, I mean," she added, her tone dripping with false innocence. "Tainted Love. Isn't that what you and the great Ari Jaeger have?"

Not missing the sarcasm, I scoffed. "Emily... I'd say what a pleasant surprise," I drawled, letting a slow, fiendish smile unfurl as I pivoted on the deadly spikes of my six-inch heels to face her. "But lying is a pointless exercise."

"You're right about that." A brittle laugh scraped out of her as her gaze dropped to my left hand.

"I guess I wasn't too far wrong about the engagement, was I?"

"No, I guess you weren't." I lifted my hand, admiring the sparkler Ari had slipped onto my finger. My smile sharpened. "You're very intuitive, aren't you?"

Her dark, apathetic eyes flicked up to meet mine — and there it was, the first crack in her composure.

"It's a joke, Emily. Learn to take one occasionally; it might ease the tension you drag around with you." I let my gaze drift past her, deliberately bored. "By the way, where's your date? Or couldn't you find one?"

I knew the answer. But provoking her was too much fun. Usually the fishing was good — except tonight, she wasn't biting.

Fine. I'd poke harder.

"Ma'am, your drinks."

The bartender's lilting voice drew my attention. I twisted at the waist and accepted the gold-rimmed flute with a soft thank you. I swivelled back to Emily, watching her over the rim as I took a delicate sip.

Time to unleash my inner bitch.

"Envy can make you bitter," I purred, twirling the flute between my fingers. "And at a guess, Ems, I'd say you've been that way for a long time."

My gaze travelled over her petite frame — and I begrudgingly admitted the strapless navy-blue dress with its layered tulle skirt was stunning on her. Annoying, but true.

"But what intrigues me more," I continued, letting my tone soften into something almost conversational, "is why you applied to Bricks. I'm presuming your angle was to be close to me, solely to report back to Emmett?"

A flicker — brief, but unmistakable — crossed her pitch-black eyes.

There it was. The tell.

I scoffed lightly. "That prick is completely unhinged and incapable of understanding boundaries, isn't he?" Her silence was answer enough. "Glad we cleared that up. I dislike obscurity immensely."

"Anyway — at first, Ari and I wondered what your connection to him was. Quite the puzzle." I tilted my head, studying her with a kind of detached curiosity. "But once we fitted the pieces together, the discovery was... startling. I'm sure you're dying to know what it was."

"I'm sure you'll take pleasure in telling me," she muttered.

"Oh, you're right about that." A small laugh escaped me — soft, amused, lethal. "Ari's astute. If something feels off, he follows his instincts. And he was very glad he did once he realised who you were."

Her face reddened. Good. I'd struck something raw.

"What gave me away?" she whispered.

"Surely you've noticed the family resemblance." I leaned in, lowering my voice to a dangerous whisper — a move I'd learned from my fiancé. "Ari tried to convince himself it was coincidence, but mannerisms speak volumes."

I let the pause stretch, watching her unravel.

"Once our investigator revealed you're, in fact, cousins, he actually shuddered."

Her fists clenched.

Mine nearly did too — but for entirely different reasons.

"Don't deny it," I snapped, letting the steel slip into my tone. "You're the result of an affair Emmett had with your ailing mother while he was married to my aunt."

Her mouth dropped open, a strangled sound escaping.

"Emily Smith isn't even your real name. It's Amelia — after Emmett's mother." I shook my head slowly, almost pityingly. "And Smith? Really? It's so... generic." A humourless laugh slipped out as I shook my head at her. "You're also younger than I am, by what — three years? Spencer will be fuming when he finds out you've pulled the wool over his eyes. I'm pretty sure fraud's a federal offence with a maximum of ten years imprisonment. I'd add a few more years just for your complicity in aiding and abetting a child molester, too, if I were you..."

I took another sip, watching the broken wheels turn and fall off their axles — the exact moment she started to believe me. I was bluffing, of course — I knew as much about federal sentencing as I did about astrophysics — but she'd swallowed it whole.

"Sounds horrifying, doesn't it?" I mused. "Serving time for someone else's dirty work. It would certainly make me think twice about helping them again."

Logan's fast-paced steps approached. Time was up.

I grabbed Ari's drink from the bar and turned back to Emily, softening my voice into something almost pleading — the final twist of the knife.

"Help me lock him away, and I'll make sure the Public Prosecutor goes easy on you." I shrugged coolly. "Your choice."

"Ms McGovern," Logan said, tone clipped, "Mr Jaeger requests you by his side — immediately."

I sighed, as if inconvenienced. "Okay, I'm coming. I just had to deal with the shit stuck beneath my shoe — and what a pest it was to remove."

Logan peeled away the moment I stepped past him, but the damage was done — Ari had already turned, already found me in the crowd. His eyes locked onto mine with that unnervingly accurate read he has, the one that makes me feel both exposed and understood in the same breath.

He didn't move at first. He just watched me approach.

And that was somehow worse.

I crossed the room with Ari's bourbon in hand, my heels clicking a steady rhythm that didn't match the pulse hammering beneath my skin. The confrontation with Emily still buzzed through my veins — the satisfaction, the irritation, the faint tremor of adrenaline I refused to acknowledge.

Ari saw all of it. He always does.

By the time I reached him, his jaw had tightened again, but not with the same tension Emily had triggered earlier. This was different. Sharper. Protective. His gaze swept over my face, cataloguing every micro-expression I hadn't meant to reveal.

"Teddy." Just my name — but the way he uttered it made my breath catch.

I handed him the bourbon, my fingers brushing his. "Your drink."

He didn't take it immediately. Instead, he wrapped his hand around mine, steadying the glass and me in the same motion. His thumb pressed lightly against my knuckles — a silent question, a silent demand, a silent *tell me*.

"I'm fine," I murmured, though the words felt flimsy even to me.

His eyes narrowed, not in anger, but in that quiet, surgical way he has when he's cutting through my defences. "You're lying."

It wasn't an accusation. It was an observation.

I exhaled slowly, forcing my shoulders to relax. "She approached me at the bar. I handled it."

Ari's jaw flexed. "Handled it how?"

"With grace," I replied sweetly. He didn't buy it for a second.

His hand slid to the small of my back, pulling me subtly closer — not possessive, but grounding. Protective. His body curved around mine like a shield, even though Emily was nowhere in sight.

"Teddy," he murmured again, softer this time, "what did she say?"

I met his gaze, letting him see just enough of the truth to satisfy him — but not enough to worry him. "Nothing I couldn't deal with."

His eyes darkened, but he nodded once, accepting the boundary even if he didn't like it. That was the thing about Ari — he'd push, but he'd never force.

"Stay with me," he breathed.

"I wasn't planning on going anywhere."

His expression eased, just barely. He lifted his bourbon, finally taking the drink from my hand, and brushed his fingers along my wrist in a gesture that mirrored the one I'd given him earlier.

A quiet, private exchange. A promise. A tether.

And just like that, the room settled around us again — but the current between us had sharpened into something electric.

The remainder of the evening unfolded without a hitch. Once the formalities wrapped up and guests abandoned their chairs, the atmosphere loosened enough for us to mingle freely. It also gave our wary gazes the chance to sweep the room with precision. When we finally realised Emily had vanished, Ari and I relaxed just enough to enjoy ourselves.

Our only other dampener was the Travers — specifically Elise, who had practically salivated over my fiancé all night.

Not ever going to happen. Not while I still lived and breathed.

With Logan typically hot on my heels, I exited the bathroom after powdering my nose and strolled across the floor, appreciating Ari in my approach. The expensively tailored black slim-fit three-piece suit displayed his perfectly toned physique to devastating effect. No wonder half the women in the room were champing at the bit just to speak to him.

As I edged closer, my gaze caught the slow, methodical way his long fingers stroked the matching baby-blue tie that complemented my fitted backless satin dress. I bit down on my lip as a wicked thought rose. That might be useful later — after we'd gone home. Possibly beforehand. We'd see.

Relief washed over Ari's bored expression the moment he spotted me. He may have been happy to see me, but my presence clearly wasn't enough to deter Patrick Travers' desperate attempt to broker a business deal with him.

I had to save him.

"Hey, handsome, would you do me the honour of accompanying your fiancée to the dancefloor?"

Petty? Absolutely. But Elise Travers had pissed me off too many times to count this past year. I'd run out of fingers first.

A giggle threatened to bubble as her mouth dropped open. I slid my left hand over Ari's broad shoulder, leaning in just enough to twist the knife. "Close your mouth, dear — you look like a codfish." I reached out and gently nudged her jaw shut with the tip of my forefinger.

Ari arched a brow, smirking at my theatrics. He stayed silent, except to extricate himself with impeccable politeness. "Excuse me, Patrick, Elise — it appears my fiancée requires me for a dance." In his typically British manner, he offered a stiff nod before whisking me away to the dancefloor.

And just like that, we were back in our bubble, swaying to a soulful rendition of The Way You Look Tonight under the watchful eye of Logan, whose steely gaze swept the room with relentless precision. The rest of the evening blurred into warm light and soft music, Ari's arms steady at my waist while Logan hovered at the perimeter — a distant reminder of everything beyond our little world. But for now, I let myself breathe.

21

"Oh, here you are... I've searched the entire house looking for you. I require your talented eye for my attire this evening," Ari murmured, his lilted, chipper rasp filling the quiet of the formal dining room.

"Come to join me in my moment of self-pity, have you?" I replied gloomily, propping my elbows on the table as his quiet footfalls crossed the timber boards. He stopped behind me, his presence folding around me like a shield. Even his familiar citrus scent — usually enough to lift me — couldn't pull me from my spiralling thoughts. Nor could the gentle nuzzle of his cheek against my neck, a gesture that normally melted me instantly.

"Why so glum, my love?" he asked, concern threading through his voice. "You should be over the moon with your grandparents joining us for dinner. And it smells delightful in here."

I snorted. "You're a bottomless pit."

"And it's a habit that'll never change, I hate to tell you," he teased, pressing a soft kiss to the crown of my head.

I wrinkled my nose, a reluctant smile tugging at my lips. "Oh, I know it won't."

He moved around me and pulled out the chair beside mine. "Now that we've addressed my insatiable appetite, let's discuss what's eating you."

I exhaled a heavy, aching sigh. "I'm worried about my grandparents' reactions — both sets. Telling them about my rape is a huge step, and it's tying my stomach in knots. But the part I'm dreading most is revealing my mother's involvement. Nan and Pop will be devastated." My voice cracked as I dropped my head into my hands. "Please tell me I'm doing the right thing..."

Ari responded in his typically clear-cut manner. "Your mother's betrayal will have a resounding impact; I don't doubt that," he replied gently, leaning forward to take my hands. The soft sweep of his thumb over my knuckles loosened the tension in my shoulders. "But don't underestimate the strength of your family — especially your grandparents. I'm certain they'll handle your truth with more grace than you expect."

I leaned across the table, meeting him halfway, and brushed my lips against his. "As always," I whispered, tracing the line of his jaw, "my gorgeous man, you came through for me. Thank you."

Ari's grin widened, bright and boyish. "You're most welcome. Excellent job on the table, by the way." His gaze drifted over the white linens, polished silver, fresh white flowers, and sprigs of pine arranged between crystal candelabras. "It looks stunning."

Typical of me, I brushed it off. "Eh, it's just something I threw together."

In truth, it had taken nearly an hour. It had to be perfect. The preparation was the only thing keeping my nerves from swallowing me whole. I'd told my family it was just a simple pre-Christmas dinner. Abel declined, of course — work, as always. Nothing ever changed. But at least I'd tried.

"Well, however you did it, it looks gorgeous." Ari's tone shifted, warm and mischievous. "So... how about you join me for a shower?" Ari flipping a switch and eyeing me indecently very swiftly dragged me out of my ornery mood.

I eyed him suspiciously. "Just a shower?"

His expression gave him away instantly — that wicked, barely contained smile he could never quite hide from me. I rose from my chair and settled into his lap, sliding my hands up his arms and over his shoulders.

"That usually leads to trouble," I murmured.

"Oh, I'm fully aware," he breathed, brushing his lips against mine, his hands settling at my waist with familiar certainty. His tongue tasted the inside of my mouth as his hands wandered beneath my singlet. "No bra. Nice." Cupping my breasts in his palms, he tweaked my puckered nipples between his fingertips, a pleasure that shot straight to my aching sex.

"Aha," I moaned against his lips.

Panting with want, I tugged an eager Ari towards the bedroom. And eventually, the shower.

∞

Ari

"Oh, Teddy, the house looks exquisite — far better than any Christmas display I've ever seen in a store window," Vivienne gushed, clapping her hands together with unrestrained delight. "All this silver and white gives the appearance of a winter wonderland in England."

At a guess, I'd say Vivienne was homesick.

Delighted by the praise, Teddy offered her grandmother a beatific smile. "I thought we'd share in the joy of a white Christmas with Poppy, even if it is thirty degrees difference."

"What about you, Ari?" Vivienne's cheerful, twinkling gaze followed me as I popped the cork on a champagne bottle. "What do you think of Teddy's decoration skills?"

"I believe Teddy truly outdid herself." Pouring several flutes, I winked devilishly at my blushing fiancée. "Although, I would rather peer through her windows — they'd be somewhat more pleasurable."

Teddy's face flamed, which only made me chuckle.

"I always knew there was a perfectly good reason behind my granddaughter's happiness!" Vivienne hooted, accepting one of the long-stemmed flutes I offered. "That's all the confirmation I needed, Ari!"

"Anytime." I winked again, laughter erupting as Teddy's eyes widened in horror.

"Oh my God! Just stop! Both of you!"

Grabbing another champagne flute, I passed it to her. "Are you not amused, love?" I ventured, slinging an arm over her bare shoulders and grazing the soft skin along the elasticated edge of her strapless dress with my fingertips. She met my tickled gaze with something far less entertained.

"Don't encourage my grandmother; she's filthy enough."

"Vivienne's a woman after my own heart."

Glaring, Teddy briskly removed my arm from her shoulders and let it fall to my side. "I am now going to do something less mortifying by checking in on dinner."

Unimpressed, she spun away and marched into the kitchen where the catering staff were busily preparing the evening meal, leaving Vivienne's hysterical laughter ringing behind her.

"So, Teddy, when are you and Ari planning on announcing your engagement to the rest of the family?" Violet quizzed cheerily as we waited for our final course — mini pineapple upside-down cakes with rum caramel sauce, crafted with me in mind.

Teddy shrugged, noncommittal. "We haven't given it much thought, really, Gran. Possibly after the New Year... but it all depends on—"

"Depends on what exactly?" Violet's thinning brows drew together. "Teddy? Ari? What's going on?"

A ripple of awkwardness swept the table, unmistakable and heavy.

"There's something we need to tell you..." Teddy drew a deep, quivering breath, set her wine glass down, and reached for my hand. "But I need you to hear me out, without interruption, please."

Once everyone nodded their agreement, she began revealing her long-kept secret, her voice trembling as the truth spilled into the room and dragged the atmosphere into a sombre hush.

With each word that left her lips, my heart tore further. Their pain, their sorrow — I recognised it intimately. By the time she finished, both Vivienne and Violet were sobbing into their linen napkins. And though the men remained stoic, their tightened jaws and clenched hands betrayed their distress. My fiancée wasn't faring any better.

"I am so sorry — to every one of you — for not having the guts to tell you sooner," she wept. "I just didn't know how to tell you, or where to even begin."

"Oh no, dear, don't apologise," Barrett implored. "The fault lies elsewhere — with the perpetrator and your mother. Besides, none of us were ever made aware of your situation. Not by anyone."

He cast a reproachful look down the table at his son before pushing his chair back and striding to Teddy's side. Gently lifting his sobbing granddaughter from her seat, he folded her into his arms. "The perpetrator, Ari — what of him? Have any legal steps commenced to apprehend him?"

"Yes and no," I replied grimly, stretching across the table for the bourbon decanter. As I removed the lid, I glanced up at him before lowering my gaze to pour. "My father and Uncle Garrett are currently building a case against him."

"Surely Teddy's testimony is enough to have the bastard arrested and thrown into prison where he belongs?"

I set the decanter down and met his bewildered stare. "It's a little more complicated than you realise."

Barrett's jaw ticked violently. "What's so complicated about protecting my granddaughter? Or does Teddy not know her attacker?"

"Calm down, Barrett," Vivienne reprimanded sharply, waving a hand as she turned in her seat. She regarded her granddaughter with grave tenderness. "Darling... do you — and dare I ask this — know the man who raped you?"

Teddy's head moved stiffly against Barrett's chest. "Yes... yes, I do. Ari, c-can you please tell them? I c-can't... but they need to know," she stammered through her heart-splintering sobs.

"It was..." I tossed back the entire tumbler, the burn searing down my throat as I forced the words out. "...Emmett who raped Teddy."

A deathly silence fell over the room. Shock rippled across every face as the gravity of the revelation settled like lead.

Violet, voice trembling, was the first to speak. "Oh... now I understand the complicated part. And I also understand the need for the DNA from the baby you bore."

Relief washed through me. Thank God someone had the sense to remain pragmatic before Teddy's grandfathers each took a turn attempting to detach my head from my neck with a steak knife.

"Without it," Teddy murmured sadly, "it may end up as a case of he-said-she-said, regardless of the fact I was only fifteen at the time. If it helps strengthen the case against him, I'll do whatever I can to get it."

"Wouldn't the child's birth certificate provide proof?" Violet asked. "Surely either that or the death certificate?"

My brows furrowed. "That was an avenue that hadn't even crossed our minds, actually. Thank you for the suggestion, Violet. I'll call my father tomorrow — hopefully he can track one or both down."

Inwardly, I prayed copies existed. Unless Therese had found a way to circumvent their lodgement — a very real possibility.

"What about your mother?" Benjamin ventured, his voice thick with sorrow as he reached for his wife's hand. "Where does she fit into all this? And will my daughter go to jail?"

"I'm not sure," Teddy whispered. "Garrett hasn't reached that part yet. I can only presume the outcome would be similar to Emmett's — time served in jail. She needs to be held accountable for her actions."

Her grandparents looked shattered.

Teddy hesitated, then turned to Vivienne. "Nan... there's something else I need to ask you, but I don't know how."

Vivienne rose and wrapped her arms around Teddy's shoulders. I watched the tension melt from my fiancée's frame — a testament to how deeply she trusted her grandmother.

"You're going to ask me about Liana, aren't you?"

Her intuitive, misty green eyes met Teddy's with a tenderness that struck me. "It's fine, dear child. Ask away. Your grandfather and I have nothing to hide."

Teddy sniffled. "You're very perceptive."

"I may be getting on in age, but my brain is still as sharp as ever, my girl." Vivienne's face brightened with a soft laugh. "Not only was our Liana beautiful, but she was high-spirited and loved to laugh. Oh, did she ever. She made everyone laugh — including your mother."

She held Teddy at arm's length, chuckling at the surprise on her face. "Oh yes, even your mother. They were extremely close, just like you and Scarlett are now. She was also incredibly talented."

"By any chance, did Liana play the piano? And the only reason I ask is that I recently found a photo after I went snooping through the photo boxes hidden on the shelf in the wardrobe at Phillip Island," Teddy coyly admitted. "Sorry, Dad."

"All good, sweetheart." Evan's amused expression made her blush.

"At first, I thought it was my mother, but then I remembered she never played, so I simply assumed it was you, Nan."

Vivienne nodded, elegantly lowering herself onto the sofa. "Come, sit." She patted the cushion beside her, her voice cracking as she struggled to contain her emotions. "Liana was a natural when it came to learning — a musical ear, I suppose. She'd hear a compilation and pick up the notes just like that," she murmured proudly, clicking her fingers. "The Rose was the first piece she ever perfected, and that's why it's always remained my favourite. Always will be until the day I leave this earth. You too play it just as flawlessly..."

"Now I understand why you cry every time you hear it," Teddy comforted, wiping away Vivienne's flowing tears with the floral handkerchief she handed her.

"If anyone would, it would be you."

"Liana had dreams of becoming a music and drama teacher," a just-as-proud Benjamin added, his saddened expression softening into a lopsided smile. "She spent years studying the arts at university — excelled at it too." His smile soured into a scowl. "During which time she began dating Emmett. Unfortunately."

"Did Liana ever graduate university?" I enquired.

"She did, surprisingly. Those were her terms, which Emmett willingly accepted. On the surface, anyway. By professing his undying love for her, he charmed her irrevocably. At the time, nothing we said would convince her otherwise." Benjamin's scowl deepened. "I always remained on the fence with the smarmy bastard. He seemed—"

"Too good to be true?" I remarked, finishing the thought for him. "Well, that's because he was — and nothing's changed there either, I'm afraid."

"I don't doubt it for a second." Benjamin scoffed. "I just wish I'd followed my gut and swayed Liana out of marrying the mongrel, but she was in love."

Regret clouded his ageing face as tears spilled freely. "He turned into a monster the moment that ring was on her finger. He controlled everything. Sometimes we didn't see her for months — not even a phone call. And the few times he allowed us to visit, her appearance had changed so drastically I barely recognised my little girl..." His emotional tribute rippled through the room, stirring memories in others as Evan exhaled heavily.

"I know exactly what you mean, Benji," Evan murmured. "Emmett refused everyone — even her own sister. Therese despised him for keeping them apart, not to mention the mind games he played."

Baffled, I frowned. "If Therese supposedly disliked Emmett, then why was she socialising with him — especially that night?"

"The only conclusion I've drawn is that she was keeping up appearances. My wife doesn't have the best record when it comes to honesty — with anyone," he spat bitterly. "So who knows what her reasoning was behind that ludicrous decision."

His evasiveness was obvious. I wasn't surprised. Withholding damaging truths seemed to be a McGovern family speciality. I swallowed the last of my bourbon, irritation simmering.

"Liana wanted nothing more than to share in the joy of our children," Evan continued, his hostility toward Therese momentarily set aside. "She doted on you and Abel — spoiled you both rotten. She'd often say to you, Teddy, *'Miss Teddy, you are trouble.'* She must have recognised that rebellious streak and seen herself in you, even as an infant."

Vivienne slapped her knee and laughed heartily. "Ain't that the truth! You are the image of our beloved Liana, Teddy. It's as if her soul — wherever it may be — is in you," she whispered, sadness enveloping her.

I straightened in my chair. "So you have no clue as to Liana's whereabouts? At all?"

Vivienne shook her head, her voice dropping to a mournful whisper. "No. And the likelihood of ever finding out is slim. Our intuition told us something sinister must have occurred when Therese came to our home, frantically demanding we remove photos or any evidence of our daughter. She insisted it would be easier for us to move on, that we were better off not knowing what happened. Her behaviour made me suspect she was too afraid to tell us the truth. Whatever happened to Liana... it changed everything about her from that moment on."

My brow creased. Oddly enough, my mother had spoken those exact words, stirring a wave of troubling speculation.

"Not for the better either," Evan added. "She changed dramatically. She never paid attention to Teddy anyway, and she cried when we had Scarlett. Not in joy, either. Sorry, Scars."

"It's all good, Dad; I'm used to it by now."

Her casual response made me chuckle.

"Abel was always the light of her life anyway, Evan," Violet muttered with a grimace. "But I never understood her attitude towards you, Teddy. Unfortunately for you, it was a dislike that began the day you were born. I sometimes wondered if Post-Natal Depression was to blame."

Regrettably, I knew that wasn't the case. Yet I still couldn't shake the conversation I'd had with Therese — not fear, because she'd never shown any, but that warped logic of hers had settled indelibly in my mind. And with my uncle already disproving her nonsense about girls being worse than boys, the whole thing resurfaced like a bruise I couldn't ignore. Rather than enter the debate, I poured myself another drink and pushed the memory back into the dark corner where both she and Emmett belonged.

"You know as well as I do, Mother, that Therese never believed in PND — let alone acknowledged its existence," Evan countered sharply. "Even the suggestion of it was enough to ignite that temper of hers."

"True," Vivienne murmured, brows knitting, "but I wonder if Emmett did or said something to her, and it shook her up." She paused, thinking. "Although I do remember Therese desperately trying to talk her sister out of marrying that lunatic — her words, not mine," she added defensively, lifting her hands.

"We'll never know, because it's something else she'd never admit to," Evan muttered, his tone emphatic.

"Maybe in time, when all of this comes out, Mum might tell you."

Pragmatic as ever, Teddy clung to hope. "You never know. These things have a way of making people open up."

"Still the optimist, sis!" Scarlett chirped. "Now where is this scrumptious dessert I've been patiently waiting on?"

"Now, that wasn't so bad, was it?" I murmured to Teddy as I unclasped the silver Armani smartwatch from my wrist, sliding it free and placing it on the bedside table.

It was late by the time dinner ended, and even later as our guests lingered in the entryway. Only after the final round of goodnight hugs and kisses tapered off were we able to close the front door and retreat to the bedroom. Where I had thoughts of lovemaking, Teddy had other ideas — unconsciously replaying the evening I considered a success.

Her unrelenting chatter followed her even as I unzipped the back of her strapless dress and eased it down her svelte frame, coaxing her to step out of it with all the patience I could muster. Her lingerie followed with the same quiet efficiency

"My poor grandparents. Their despair was what made me cry — not reliving my torrid past, believe it or not."

"I figured as much." Guiding her backwards toward the bed, I eased her down onto the mattress before kneeling to slip off her heels one at a time, placing them neatly beside my feet. "You've come a long way, and I believe it's due to the consistency of your therapy sessions."

I stripped off quickly — uncharacteristically leaving my clothes where they fell — because Teddy needed a distraction, something to pull her out of her spiralling thoughts. Preferably one of a more intimate nature.

But her nattering didn't falter, not even as I drew her gently onto her back, my hands gliding over her shoulders, my lips tracing a slow path along warm skin.

None of it had the desired effect.

"I'll make a concerted effort to call in on them tomorrow, just to make sure they're okay," she continued, utterly oblivious to my attempts. “I might even take my grandparents out for lunch. What do you think, Ari?”

But as I blew on a nipple and clasped its elongated length between my teeth, tugging relentlessly, her attention finally swivelled in our direction. Her back bowing off the bed, she gasped, “Ari…what…ever …happened…to talking?”

Slithering a finger between soft, fleshy folds, I lifted my head slightly. “Talking’s overrated.”

22

Teddy

Hanging above the several pairs of heels lining the timber floor was a white lace halter-neck dress I intended to wear to Audrina's annual Christmas party — the same dress I'd been indecisively eyeing from the safety of my chair. Ari's earlier suggestion about wearing a hessian sack was, by far, starting to look like the better option. Anything to keep Emmett's perverted gaze off me.

I snorted. When that ghastly man wanted something, nothing ever stood in his way.

Dread brewed low in my stomach, thick and nauseating. Exchanging pleasantries with a man I despised wasn't my idea of an evening well spent. Yet I had to go. If I didn't show my face, Emmett might grow suspicious and start asking questions neither Audrina nor Jaxson were prepared to answer.

Another person I wasn't thrilled about encountering was Carys. Unless her mother had given her a stern talking-to, she'd likely avoid me altogether. In all likelihood, it'd be the latter — making the entire concern moot.

"There you are. I was beginning to think you'd disappeared to Narnia."

Ari's cheerful chortle drifted into the walk-in robe as he sauntered inside.

"Don't be daft," I demurred, rising from the chair. "The only place I seem to have gotten lost in is my shoes."

Scooping up a pair of white laser-cut six-inch heels with thin laces and red soles, I held them against the dress. Cute. They might just work.

"Wasn't your outfit sorted?" he enquired, nuzzling his nose through my tumbling hair as his hands began to roam over my half-naked torso. "Teddy, did you hear me?"

"Ari, STOP!"

The word tore out of me as I abandoned his grasp and shrank back against the island in the centre of the wardrobe. He froze immediately, respecting the boundary without hesitation.

Concern creased his brow as my breaths quickened. "Does this have something to do with Mother's party tonight — and the knowledge Emmett shall be present?"

Bile surged up my throat. I forced it down and nodded tentatively. "What if he tries something? What if..."

Ari paused, choosing his approach with care. His hand lifted slowly, tucking a loose tendril behind my ear with a gentleness that nearly undid me. "Stop worrying about the what-ifs. I've already spoken with my mother about tonight, and she's taken the necessary precautions to ensure he won't have a chance in hell of getting anywhere near you."

"How are you going to manage that among a crowd of what — fifty or more people?" I stared at him incredulously. "You know that won't stop him from trying."

"Due diligence, my love. Someone will always be by your side," he promised through a crooked smile. "Even when you go to the bathroom..."

But as his dark eyes lit up like the Christmas tree in the living room, I folded my arms over my chest and tutted.

"That doesn't mean you can get kinky and watch me pee, you know."

He pouted. "You truly know how to spoil my fun."

∞

Ari

As in her customary manner, my mother had outdone herself. Erected in the middle of the lawn was a translucent silk-voile marquee draped in brightly lit fairy lights, complete with all the usual trimmings — except for one notable difference. Instead of her traditional red-and-green theme, she'd opted for an English winter wonderland, an idea she'd cheekily borrowed from Teddy. Not that Teddy minded; it had given her the chance to work alongside my mother, strengthening their bond in a way that still surprised me.

I paused at one of the round tables to admire their handiwork and smiled. Admittedly, the ladies had done a sterling job. Each table was lavishly decorated with pillar candles in varying shades of white and blue, sprigs of pine sprayed silver, and what appeared to be a million snowflakes scattered across the pristine white cloths. Overkill, if you asked me — but I'd learned not to argue. My mother certainly hadn't appreciated my critique of the tables or the Christmas tree beside the faux fireplace.

According to her, I was clueless and needed to leave decorating to the experts.

She knew how to wound a man's pride.

But as usual, she was right. My expertise lay in handling Teddy — especially as she knocked back her third glass of champagne and was about to down her fourth until I intervened.

Swiping the flute from her hand, I set it on the wooden bar table beside me. "Perhaps you ought to consider eating a few canapés?" I murmured, sliding an arm around her waist and drawing her close enough to whisper firmly in her ear. "Or slow down on the champagne. Drinking more than your fill won't help you — particularly if you run into Emmett. You might end up doing or saying something you'll regret."

"I don't care," she snapped, her tone sharp enough to cut. "What more can that deranged prick do to me that he hasn't done already?"

I understood she was lashing out — but I refused to become her verbal punching bag.

She turned to storm off, but I flicked an arm out and caught her slender wrist. Her glazed expression met mine as I tugged her gently back and stroked her cheek with the tip of my forefinger.

My voice remained controlled, firm. "Are you deliberately trying to force my hand?"

She understood instantly, her gaze dropping. "Please don't ever speak in such a despairing manner again. Are we clear, Teddy? Look at me."

She lifted her eyes from beneath a fan of thick lashes, her glossy lips parting, cheeks flushing. "Yes, sir."

Considering I'd never wanted my future wife to address me that way — given my initial reluctance — I now found it unexpectedly arousing. I'd adapted quickly to our new dynamic, especially because Teddy was thriving. She'd abided by every rule we'd agreed upon. One was my need to converse with the Coopers for guidance during scenes to avoid any mishaps — something that should never occur if both Master and submissive paid attention and exercised care. I'd undertaken a small amount of research myself, but avoiding regression remained my highest priority. That was where the good doctor's advice mattered most. Teddy understood the importance and agreed to keep play confined to the bedroom — and to a minimum.

Meaning I was flying by the seat of my pants until further notice.

Not an easy task for a novice.

"Thank you for listening. Now go and grab something to eat — and a glass of water." I released her wrist with a gruff command.

"Okay, Mr Bossy, I'm going," she murmured cheekily, trailing a hand down my arm as she turned away. Our fingers grazed, and I hauled her back, pulling her flush against me.

"How am I meant to get my water or food if you won't let me?" she giggled, bouncing lightly off my chest.

"The thought of smacking your cheeky arse crossed my mind, but your plush mouth was simply too enticing," I purred, brushing a kiss over her parted lips — just enough to leave her breathless.

"Maybe later..."

The whisper of promise lingered between us. She always found a way to top from the bottom — another term I'd learned during my research.

My brows shot up as I took a sip from the fresh flute of champagne in my hand. "Are those shoes all you'll be wearing later, if that's the case?"

"Perhaps."

I smiled broadly as Teddy swung away from me, deliberately shaking that delectable arse as she sauntered toward the buffet, fully aware of the effect it had on me. She'd certainly know about it later — that much was guaranteed.

My amusement faded the moment I caught Emmett's leering gaze slicing through the crowd to follow her across the lawn. The smirk he wore sent an icy chill down my spine, stiffening it to iron. Thank God for Logan's ever-hovering presence; he'd sniffed out my perverse uncle long before we had. His unblinking stare tracked Emmett's every step, a silent warning in motion.

I watched Emmett lick his lips — and it wasn't due to the balmy air lingering from the day's heat. My fists curled, the temptation to take him out rising like a tide.

But under sufferance — and my mother's stern finger-wagging — I'd sworn to both my parents and Teddy that I'd table my feelings and bury my volatile temper. For now.

All bets were off if he provoked me.

My parents intercepted him before he could swoop in on Teddy, and I chuckled darkly at the displeasure etched across his face. With his petite wife Bree and their two adult children, Aayden and Liana, glued to his side, he was swamped. He couldn't have looked more disgruntled if he tried.

My laughter died abruptly as something unsettling struck me:

Why was my cousin named after Emmett's allegedly dead ex-wife?

The thought sickened me, sending another shiver down my spine. I highly doubted Liana knew the disgusting reason behind her beautiful name. Personally, I'd be monumentally pissed. And the antipathy of it — the salt rubbed into an open wound — was a cruelty I couldn't fathom. What possessed a human being to inflict such long-lasting pain on two of the most loving people I knew?

A sociopathic bastard like Emmett, that's who.

The sooner he was brought to justice, the better. Only then would any of us sleep more soundly.

My brows furrowed as he suddenly disappeared from my line of sight.

"What's got you frowning ever so seriously?"

And that would be why.

I sighed at the droning of my uncle's voice and reluctantly pivoted to face his smug expression. "So, you found me, my dear Uncle Emmett," I deadpanned.

A fiendish smile curled beneath his cold, beady eyes. "No need for the contemptuous attitude now, nephew; I only come in peace."

I snorted loudly — an outright lie if ever I'd heard one. "Oh, of course you do."

I swapped the champagne for a bourbon, plucking a tumbler from a passing waiter's tray.

"You and Teddy, huh?" He cocked his smarmy head, suspicion dripping from every syllable as he treaded on dangerous ground. "Who would've thought?"

"Oh, just about everybody who matters." I smirked, slipping my curling fist into the pocket of my black dress pants. "I'm certain my parents told you — in fact, I know they did. Didn't Bree mention something when you both visited Bricks and Mortar for a consult with Teddy?"

He choked on his champagne and blanched.

Unable to help myself, I smacked his back harder than necessary, provoking a delighted chuckle as he lurched forward. "Can't have you choking now, can we?"

Not when I wanted the pleasure of strangling him myself.

"Mother might consider it rude if you snuffed it at her Christmas party."

That's where we differed. I'd happily celebrate the mongrel's death and piss on his grave afterward. It was on my wish list, after all.

He tugged at the bright red tie around his neck, loosening the Windsor knot as though it were strangling him. A move I'd witnessed too many times in the boardroom. Clearly, he was uncomfortable with the knowledge that I knew his crimes.

A narcissistic sociopath at his finest — being caught with a finger in the pie never sat well.

The arrogant bastard composed himself quickly, carrying on as if nothing had transpired. "Bree and I wanted Teddy to redesign our house; she is an architect after all. Although, according to her boss, Spencer, her plate was already full — too full, apparently. As was Bricks and Mortar's."

His distrustful gaze skimmed over the rim of his crystal flute. "I wonder why that would be, nephew?"

Uncommitted, I shrugged and turned back to the table. "I haven't the faintest."

Evidently, Emmett was unaware I'd had a hand in Spencer's refusal to take him on as a client. After witnessing — and suffering — the fallout of his heinous behaviour during Teddy's last encounter with him, I intended to ensure that distance remained permanent. Business or not.

Not even Teddy knew it was my doing, and she'd be furious if she found out I'd meddled. As far as she was concerned, Spencer had told him exactly what Emmett recited: Bricks and Mortar had a full plate.

"Well, aren't you and Spencer so-called mates who ride together?"

My spine stiffened. My head swivelled slowly, meeting eyes that mirrored mine.

How the hell did he know about my extracurricular activities?

Not even my parents knew.

Hostility surged, sharp and immediate. Why on earth had I agreed to behave?

I remained impassive. "Yeah, so? Doesn't mean we discuss business. Downtime is important when one's busily and successfully running a company. Oh, that's right — you aren't familiar with such a task. You're merely a little minion who works for a successful company."

The haughty smile dropped.

Not that he quit prying.

"Teddy rides with you both, doesn't she?"

His knowledge of our private life confirmed my suspicions — he had been stalking us.

I bristled. "Teddy enjoys riding, so what?"

"I bet she does," he purred, the nauseating tone making my skin crawl. "From what else I've observed about your precious Teddy, she's inordinately close to Spencer. Close enough to disappear into his office and close the door. I believe they were in there for quite some time, too. With the door locked."

He enunciated each word with deliberate malice, baiting me.

I refused to bite — not with my teeth, anyway. “They were conferring on a project. A major one Teddy informed me.”

A lie, but one rooted in truth — I knew exactly why she’d locked herself in Spencer’s office.

“Ah yes, confidentiality. You aren’t privy, of course. You’re the opposition after all.”

He leaned in, voice dripping poison. “Perhaps Teddy’s a spy for him, taking projects away from you?”

My fist curled around my glass. My lips tightened. “Teddy’s integrity wouldn’t allow her to betray me in such a despicable manner. And do you know why?”

Waving a hand, he smirked. “Enlighten me.”

“Unlike you, our relationship is built on honesty and trust. Does your wife realise what — and whom — she’s married to?”

His smile vanished.

Oh, hell.

My eyes slid closed as I exhaled heavily at the stupidity spilling from my mouth.

I blamed the alcohol. Plausible deniability worked for my mother — why not me?

The slimy bastard snorted. “You’re losing it, Ari. Is the stress of commitment getting to you? Maybe take a break from one another. Sounds like you need to.”

His hand clamped onto my shoulder — and for all the weight I’d carried lately, it might as well have been a slab of lead.

My temper detonated.

Teddy’s past, her pain, her fear — it all erupted at once.

“Fuck you, you piece of shit!”

I wasn't myself anymore. I became a voyeur in my own body, watching from the outside as my fists flew. Emmett stumbled backwards, shocked.

"Ari! Stop!" he shouted, flailing to block me.

But I couldn't.

I kept swinging, taking savage satisfaction in pummelling his face.

He eventually retaliated — a pathetic swing that barely jerked my head as his fist connected with my cheek.

"What have I done, nephew?" he spluttered through blood.

"You raped Teddy when she was only fifteen!"

"I have no idea what you're talking about!"

His denial poured petrol on the fire.

"You're — a — sick — mother — fucker!"

I roared each word, marching toward him and hammering his battered face until he crashed to the ground. I straddled his chest, pinning him beneath my weight, unleashing strike after strike as he tried to shield himself.

"Ari! Stop!"

Frantic women screamed. Men tried to haul me off him, but when one was fuelled by homicidal rage, not even a former SAS soldier's strength could hold me back.

A hardened fist blindsided me, cracking across my jaw and sending me sprawling onto the soft lawn. Blood filled my mouth as my seething gaze lifted — first to the white heel tapping beside me, then to the blazing eyes above it, framed by my mother's reproachful glare.

My jaw dropped. "It was you? What the fuck, Teddy?"

"No, Ari — what the fuck did you do?"

Bree's voice cut through the chaos as she fussed over her idiotic husband. Their daughter, Liana, passed him an ice-filled napkin.

"Thank you, sweetheart."

I rolled my eyes and flung an arm. "The moron fucking deserved it!"

"Ari Colton Jaeger! Get off the ground and march that moronic arse into my office, NOW!"

My father's bellow cracked through the marquee as my mother stormed off, ushering the stunned crowd toward the tables for dinner. Ever the perfect hostess.

"Coming, Father."

Groaning, I hauled myself upright and dusted off my suit.

Emmett's family helped him to his feet, and within seconds he made a beeline for Teddy, making my hackles rise.

"Teddy, I just want to—"

"Don't you dare fucking touch her!"

I lunged between them, gripping him by the scruff of his shirt as pleas echoed around us.

"Go ahead, nephew. I dare you."

He leaned in, whispering venom.

"Alienate Teddy. Push her into a real man's arms. She never truly belonged to you. She never has."

Each sickened word tightened the fist clinging to his shirt.

"You are truly deranged..."

"Sir, please." Logan's voice cut through the chaos as he forced himself between us, his unwavering gaze locking onto mine. "Let him go... he's not worth it."

"You should listen to your bodyguard," Emmett niggled, slapping Logan's shoulder — a move Logan clearly didn't appreciate.

"I suggest you shut the fuck up, Mr Stark, and let me handle this," Logan growled, "or I'll punch you myself — and this time you'll need an ambulance to cart you out of here."

For once in his miserable life, Emmett heeded someone else's advice.

"Sir," Logan pressed, "remove yourself from this situation. You're upsetting your family."

For once, I listened.

But the moment I released my grip, Emmett smirked and sidled past me. His slimy voice curled through the night air as he addressed my fuming fiancée — and my rage reignited instantly.

"I suggest you move, Logan. Now."

My bodyguard didn't budge. "No."

Fury flared at his blatant disobedience. I stepped closer, jaw ticking, fists curling. "Excuse me?"

Steeling himself, Logan held firm. "I said no. And as you can see, Mr Jaeger, Ms McGovern already has the cocksure idiot handled."

My hostile gaze shifted around Logan's shoulder just in time to see Teddy's knee drive hard into Emmett's groin. I winced as he gasped and crumpled to his knees like the sack of filth he was.

"Stay the fuck away from me, you perverse fuck!" she snapped. "Or I'll have you charged with stalking. And don't thank me for hitting my fiancé — I didn't gain any pleasure from it!"

"No, it's the other way around, isn't it, Theodora?" he grunted, clutching himself.

She froze. Paled.

My brows creased.

What the hell was he insinuating now?

Had he peered through our windows too?

Was he the one who'd left footprints in the garden bed months ago?

"Come, Ari," she ordered brusquely, grabbing my elbow and dragging me with her. "We need to move before your father comes back and drags you inside by your ear."

As we crossed the lawn, Grandma Amelia's trembling voice drifted through the dark, tearfully admonishing her son for his abhorrent behaviour. My steps faltered as Emmett reacted by verbally threatening her.

By some mercy, my grandfather Colton stepped in — his Scottish lilt booming as he comforted his distraught wife and hurled profanities at his wayward son, reminding Emmett exactly what a disappointment he was to the Stark name.

A proud smile tugged at my lips.

Let the bastard have it, Grandpa.

Teddy blocked my view sharply. "Ari! Move it! You've already caused enough damage tonight!"

My darkened gaze snapped to her, bewildered. I gestured angrily toward Emmett. "Well, Emmett shouldn't have antagonised me!"

Arms folded, she glowered. "You had one job tonight — one bloody job — and you couldn't help yourself, could you? Again, making this about yourself and your feelings. What about mine? Or your family's, Ari? You turned the entire night into a bloody three-ring circus because you couldn't — or wouldn't — control that damned temper!"

Her misting eyes blazed.

"Now God knows what Emmett will do to retaliate. As if our lives weren't complicated enough. Well, thank you very fucking much for making it worse!"

Disheartened by her dressing-down, I watched her march ahead and disappear through the French doors without me. I trudged after her, lost in the echo of her words.

What if she was right?

What if my thoughtless actions became the catalyst for revenge?

I paused at the bottom of the steps.

Emmett hadn't proven himself a formidable opponent — surely he wouldn't be that stupid.

Would he?

My father appeared in the doorway, voice booming. "Ari! Quit your dilly-dallying. Now!"

I exhaled heavily. "Coming, Father."

∞

Teddy

"What in the devil were you thinking, Ari?" Jaxson's voice ricocheted off the walls, sharp enough to make my temples throb. He paced the length of his study like a man trying to outrun his own fury. "Because of your recklessness, Emmett shall now be aware we're onto him and his proclivities!"

"No, he won't," Ari scoffed, arrogance masking the tremor in his voice.

"Don't be so obtuse, son. Of course, he knows!" Jaxson's glare could have cut glass. "You called him a rapist to his face!"

"That's the truth, though, isn't it?"

"Regardless, you promised your mother – and Teddy – that you would contain that foul temper of yours!" He swung toward him, face reddened, his finger jabbing the air. "Or was cooperating with your mother and me for just one fucking night too much a menial task for you? Well, was it, Ari?"

"I apologise – but his atrocity wasn't the only reason I belted him. He also insinuated that Teddy and Spencer were in cahoots to steal clients and –" A humourless, drunken escaped him. "Apparently they're having an affair."

Jaxson's scowl deepened. "This is no laughing matter! Your actions may have direct consequences on the case we're trying to build."

I wasn't laughing, either.

And Ari knew it.

He slumped into the chair, shoulders caving inward, his head hanging sorrowfully between battered hands. He flicked a shame-filled glance towards me, mouthing a quiet apology, "Sorry."

I folded my arms, my spine rigid. "Don't. I'm still mad at you."

"Your father's right, Ari," Garrett interjected, settling on the edge of the desk. "The defence will want to paint you as the jealous boyfriend – claim your jealousy drove you to lash out."

Ari twisted at the waist, incredulous. "Well, that's a tad far-fetched."

"We're aware of that," Garrett countered, "but Emmett's attorney shall say whatever it takes to have his client acquitted."

Their voices blurred into a low, heated drone as my gaze drifted over Ari's dishevelled state — the bruised knuckles, the blood spattered across his once-pristine shirt, the swelling along his jaw.

My doing.

Not my proudest moment.

But my mind kept circling back to Emmett's final words before his family dragged him out.

He couldn't possibly know my secret.

No one knew.

I'd been careful — obsessively careful.

Ari assumed I'd frozen because Emmett used my full name. That was the explanation he offered, and I'd let him believe it. But something in Emmett's tone… something in the way he looked at me…

He'd left something out.

I could feel it like a cold hand closing around my throat.

A headache pulsed behind my eyes. I was starving, and thanks to Ari's spectacular lack of self-control, we hadn't eaten a thing. The room felt too small, too loud, too full of male voices arguing over my life like I wasn't standing right there.

I needed air.

I needed space.

I needed to get out before the cracks showed.

"Excuse me, gentlemen — I need to get something to eat."

They stood at once, instinctively polite. Ari seized the moment to wrap his arms around me.

He pressed a soft kiss to my lips, remorse threaded through his voice. "I'm sorry for the trouble I've caused."

"I'm sorry too."

One of his dark brows arched.

"For hitting you."

"Ah, yes. How's your hand?"

He lifted my injured hand gently, brushing tender kisses over each bruised knuckle — a gesture so gentle it nearly undid me.

"I'll survive," I murmured, eyeing the damage.

"Emmett's dignity, on the other hand, may not."

Ari chuckled. "His pride will be bruised for weeks. Poor fellow."

The corner of my mouth twitched. "Do I detect pity?"

"Not even remotely. Though I admit, I winced when you made contact. Bree may have to help him recover — I'm fairly certain his Adam's apple is now the size of a baseball."

A reluctant laugh escaped me. "All right, I'm off to eat. You — behave."

Ari pressed a hand to his heart, feigning injury. "Always, my love."

But as I stepped out of the study, the laughter died in my throat.

The headache sharpened.

The room tilted slightly.

And Emmett's voice — that final, smug, poisonous whisper — replayed in my mind like a curse I couldn't shake.

He knew something.

Something he shouldn't.

Something I'd buried so deep I'd almost convinced myself it never happened.

And for the first time in a long while...

I wasn't sure I could keep myself from cracking.

"Teddy!"

I had barely stepped onto the rear stairs when my name rang out — sharp, urgent, disembodied. I spun, scanning the dark corners of the garden, pulse ticking in my throat.

"Who's there?"

"It's me. Carys."

Of course.

Because tonight clearly wasn't finished with me.

I exhaled, weary. "Where are you?"

"Over here. Beneath the oak tree."

Following the clipped, posh lilt of her voice, I descended the remaining steps and found her sitting alone on the bench beneath the sprawling branches. One look at her blotched, crumpled face and my heart clenched.

"Oh, Carys..."

I sat beside her immediately, pulling her into my arms.

"I'm... sorry... Teddy... that I wouldn't... speak to you." Her words broke apart between sobs. "What Emmett did... I denied it by refusing to believe you — I couldn't, because it meant..."

Her voice dissolved.

My stomach dropped.

"What are you saying, Carys?"

The question scraped out of me, thin and tight.

She drew a shuddering breath. "I couldn't believe you because it meant facing him for his crimes."

Tears streaked down her cheeks, dragging her makeup with them. I reached into my bra, retrieved my handkerchief, and pressed it into her hand.

A small, watery smile flickered. "Thanks. I probably look atrocious."

"No, you're still beautiful. If you're worried, we can sneak inside and fix your makeup."

She shook her head, wiping her eyes. “No. Michael’s used to seeing me like this after a long day — only a little more horrifying.”

Her laugh was fragile, but it tugged one from me too.

Then her expression softened, grief pulling at the corners. She took my hand, squeezing tightly. “From the bottom of my heart, Teddy... I’m so sorry for how I treated you. My behaviour was abysmal.”

“I’m sorry too,” I murmured. “I never wanted discord in your family. I just wanted peace — and justice.”

“Acceptance of the truth matters too,” she whispered. “I understand better than you realise. That’s all any of us want.”

A cold prickle crawled up my spine.

Her tone.

Her phrasing.

The way she couldn’t quite meet my eyes.

“Carys...” My voice barely held steady. “Emmett didn’t... Did he?”

She looked away.

And that was answer enough.

I gasped. “He molested you?”

She nodded, shame and anguish twisting her features. “Not to the same extent. But still... touching someone like that — inside your own family — it isn’t right. It isn’t normal.”

Shock hollowed me out. I slumped back against the metal bench, trying to swallow the enormity of her confession. “Do your parents know? Or Michael?”

Her head shook violently. “No. Unlike you, I haven’t had the guts. I was terrified of their reaction — Ari’s especially. But after tonight… seeing how fiercely he loves and protects you… and how my parents didn't turn away…"

Her voice wavered. "It made me feel braver."

"I'll support you however you need," I promised. "Even if it means handcuffing Ari to a table while we tell them."

I didn't mention I'd brought a set for… other reasons.

Her lips curved, affection warming her expression. "He's extremely protective, isn't he?"

A snort burst out of me, making her laugh. "That's an understatement. Sometimes he's a little too protective and needs to learn to back off."

I squeezed her hand. "But that aside — we're in this together."

Carys looked toward the glowing marquee, her bottom lip trembling before she steadied it into a determined smile. Her mother's loud, cheerful voice carried across the lawn, grounding her.

"Yes," she whispered. "I can do this."

"Yes, you can," I murmured. "We can — together."

23

Come the following morning, a none-the-wiser yet palpably tense Jaeger clan drifted through their usual Sunday routine — showering, descending the stairs, offering bright good mornings that fooled no one — before settling around the large oak kitchen table. I perched beside Ari, quietly surveying the room, trying to gauge the emotional temperature. They were already sombre from the previous night's chaos, and I knew that once Carys shared her secret, the atmosphere would shift again — violently.

Somewhere between the third round of strong coffee and the serving of eggs, she began to speak. What followed was heartbreaking — a slow unravelling of every emotion imaginable.

Jaxson was first. His expression swung between deep-seated rage and tragic despair as he mourned the loss of his eldest daughter's innocence. At least he expressed something. Audrina's silence, however, was alarming. She had folded inward, the same way she had when I told her about my own assault. Except this time, the wound was her daughter's — and the grief was a different creature entirely.

My rape she had processed — barely — once she learned her brother was responsible. She surged forward to support me, to help me seek justice. But this... this was her child. And the grief that tore through her was unlike anything I'd ever witnessed. When a mournful howl ripped free — raw, unrestrained — none of us recoiled. It was the kind of sorrow that silenced rooms, swallowed air, and settled deep, turning the world colder, more fragile.

Her other children cried openly beside her. Yet in true Jaeger fashion, they wiped their tears, straightened their shoulders, and pushed their grief aside to support the one who needed it most. It was a strength I both admired and envied.

Though in this case, the pain was their sister's — making the task infinitely harder.

What surprised me the most was Ari. Amidst everyone else's tears, he remained unusually quiet — calm, at least on the outside. But his demeanour told the truth his voice didn't; the tension in his jaw, the rigid set of his shoulders, the restless flex of his bruised hands — all of it making his state unmistakable. He was furious, he was hurting, and he was silently unravelling for his sister while trying to appear composed.

At present, though, it was his father — Mister by the law books — who looked ready to commit cold-blooded murder. Oh, how the tide had turned.

Michael, Carys's fiancé, had fled the table entirely. Through the window, I watched him pacing the garden, wearing a trail into the neatly cut grass beside the koi pond. His hands raked through his hair, pausing only to wipe away the tears streaming down his face. His struggle mirrored Ari's — raw, helpless, furious.

Unlike someone else, though, he had the sense not to punch a fence. Not that he wasn't tempted. But as a highly skilled heart surgeon, he knew better than to risk the hands that saved lives.

Beside me, Ari watched him too, chin resting on his clasped, bruised hands. After several minutes, he dropped them onto the table with a dull thud and pushed his chair back, heightening my concern.

I placed a hand over his twitching bicep. "Where are you going?"

"My loathing for that animal needs to take a backseat," he murmured. "Michael and Carys need my support, not my anger."

His gaze flicked from Michael to me, the fury in his eyes softening into something steadier. "That was a mistake I made with you — and it's not one I intend to repeat. Besides, my mother may not appreciate me breaking another priceless artefact after my last little temper tantrum."

"There's nothing little about your temper," I reminded him, warmth threading through my voice despite everything.

Ari's mouth curved into a modest smile — the first hint of light in a morning thick with grief.

"No, I suppose there isn't," he murmured, intertwining his fingers with mine in a gesture so gentle it softened the entire room. "But having lived through this with you... I feel like I'm the only one here who truly understands Michael's fragility and torment. He needs to know he's not alone in this."

The conviction in his voice made my heart skip. Pride warmed my chest — a quiet, steady glow — because this was the same man who once struggled to even hear my truth, let alone hold it. And now he was stepping forward for someone else.

I tilted my head, smiling up at him as he rose to his feet.

"Have I told you how much I love you today?"

"No, you haven't."

Warmth flickered through his dark eyes as he leaned down, gently catching my chin between his thumb and forefinger. He pressed a slow, toe-curling kiss to my parted lips before pulling back with a soft smile. "Slacker."

He was about to walk away when Carys caught his arm, her wide, tear-filled eyes pleading. "Ari, please—"

He didn't let her finish. He already knew. "It's fine, Carys. I'm going to speak with him now."

"Thank you..."

In another tender gesture, Ari bent and pressed a kiss to her forehead. "Everything will be fine. You'll see."

She nodded silently, her gaze glued to him as he moved.

From the graceful way he rounded the table and slipped through the French doors, to the quickening of his steps as he crossed the patio, to the widening of his stride as he marched across the lawn toward Michael — she watched every second.

And when Ari called out to her fiancé, his voice tight with emotion, Carys's hand flew to her mouth, stifling a sob. I gripped her other hand, holding my breath as I watched two mirrors collide — Michael collapsing openly into Ari's arms.

Two men, both broken in different ways by the betrayal of someone they once admired. Two men carrying wounds inflicted by the same source. Two men trying to hold themselves together for the women they loved.

As I sat back in my chair, observing the Jaeger family from the sidelines, the weight of the morning settled over me. Their idyllic world was cracking apart, and I was caught between two conflicting truths.

One part of me drowned in guilt.

If I hadn't opened Pandora's Box, they might have remained blissfully unaware. Carys's secret might have stayed buried. Their family might have been spared this devastation.

But the other part of me — the part that had carried my own truth alone for far too long — felt something close to catharsis. I had unburdened myself. And in doing so, I had unknowingly given Carys the courage to unburden herself too. Yet as she sobbed beside me, voicing her fears about the repercussions — for herself, for Michael, for their future — the guilt surged again.

I recognised that fear instantly — mine hadn't gone anywhere. It still sat under my skin, influencing every decision I made, even the ones Ari knew nothing about.

I knew how paralysing it could be, how it twisted the future into something uncertain and sharp-edged.

I squeezed her hand gently. "The emotions you're feeling right now are foreign — not just for you, but for Michael and the rest of the family. But none of this is your fault. Emmett made choices without caring who he hurt. He's responsible for the pain your family is feeling. Not me. And certainly not you."

"That's comforting... I think," she whispered, wiping her nose for what felt like the hundredth time. I couldn't fault her for struggling to feel hopeful. I had once sat exactly where she sat now — and it was a place no one should ever have to occupy.

But I stood firm in my belief: Emmett was the cause of this suffering. He always had been.

Through countless conversations with Audrina, one detail about the Stark family had remained constant: their reputation. They were respectable, disciplined, principled. Colton Stark had led his family with stern, military precision, but never with cruelty. Love and affection came from Amelia, warm and unwavering.

But Emmett...

Emmett had always lived by his own rules.

And he always would.

He proved that to be the case by fighting against everything Colton and Amelia attempted over the years. Whether it was specialised treatments, implemented rules, or carefully set boundaries, he disregarded them all. Their despondent efforts were met with defiance every time, until eventually, the relationship with their only son simply ceased to exist.

The soft click of the dining room door recaptured my attention.

With a small smile resting on his luscious lips, Ari stepped over the threshold, closing the door behind him just as a summer shower began to fall. He moved around the table with quiet purpose and paused beside Carys, crouching to murmur something meant only for her. Whatever he said broke her open; tears streamed anew, her head bobbing frantically before she rushed outside to her lost love's side. They collided in the rain, clinging to each other with a desperation that clenched at my heart — a cliché, perhaps, but a tender one, painfully reminiscent of the moments Ari and I had weathered together during our darkest storms.

"Everything all right, Ari?" I asked, watching him settle into the chair beside me. He leaned across the table, lifting the stainless-steel jug from its iron trivet to refill his empty coffee cup. A satisfied smile curved his handsome mouth as he set it back down.

He nodded. “Once I explained everything. It was like a switch,” he murmured, clicking his fingers before raising the cup to his lips for a careful sip. “Michael realised the anguish he felt was nothing compared to what Carys has endured. It’s made him more determined than ever.”

Curiosity tugged at me. “Oh? How so?”

A coy smile formed. “He’s telling my stubborn sister they’re getting married within the next few weeks — as we speak. Once he’s made the necessary arrangements, of course. He was adamant: no more holding off, and absolutely no more excuses.”

My jaw dropped, excitement widening my eyes. “Really? That’s marvellous news!”

Happy tears pooled. “It just shows that when life gives you lemons...”

“...you make lemonade?”

“Precisely.” I snaked my arm through Ari’s, curling my hand around his as I rested my head on his shoulder. He pressed a lingering kiss to my forehead and curled a warm hand over my thigh — bliss.

With Ari’s grandparents off on their pre-booked cruises, the entire family gathered for Christmas. We planned to stay until our New Year’s mini-break in Sydney — without our ever-watchful bodyguard. Thankfully, and with a little persuasion on my part, Ari granted Logan a much-needed break, much to the delight of both me and my sister. Scarlett, on the other hand, was practically buzzing, glowing with the triumph of convincing Logan to spend Christmas and New Year’s in Fiji with her. She’d talked about nothing else for weeks — beachside sunsets, cocktails, the freedom of having him all to herself. It was, as she put it, the perfect escape.

"Ari, wake up! It's Christmas Day!" I shouted, shaking his shoulder with far more enthusiasm than he appreciated.

He didn't budge. "Go back to sleep," he mumbled, rolling from his stomach onto his back with a groan.

The movement revealed a sight that made my breath hitch — all long limbs, tousled hair, and the kind of effortless morning disarray that tested every ounce of my self-control. The luxurious Egyptian cotton sheet clung to his hips, and for a moment, I regretted every rule we'd agreed upon. Especially as I hungrily eyed Ari's protruding erection.

He had been clear: if we were going to explore anything within the realm of dominance and submission, it had to be on his terms. A boundary partly shaped by Doctor Montgomery's guidance — a way to help me manage my impulses, to find steadiness rather than acting on every flicker of emotion. Sensible, measured, healthy.

But on the odd occasion, I still found myself tempted to push, to coax, to top from the bottom in the only ways I knew how.

Like now, as I eased the sheet down inch by inch, testing the boundary between mischief and restraint. Ari noticed the shift immediately — of course he did — the subtle drag of fabric, the shift of weight as I crawled over his thighs to straddle him. Even half-asleep, his body reacted before his mind caught up, a low sound escaping him as he stirred. His neck arched, his back lifted from the mattress, every line of him responding to the slow, deliberate glide of my movements as I lowered myself over his hardened length.

That was as far as I got. A firm grip closed around my hips, halting me mid-movement, stopping the slow roll of my body before it could become anything more. Heat shot through me at the contact. I lifted my gaze tentatively, meeting the sleepy but unmistakably heated look staring up at me — a look that sent a sharp thrill through my chest, because I knew exactly what it meant.

I quivered, and my insides tightened around Ari's cock. He grunted before rearing up and swiftly flipping us over, pulling out of me amidst ordering me to flip me back onto all fours.

I smirked salaciously.

"I saw that," he growled, his voice rough with sleep and something darker. His hand came down in sequential strikes across my rear – a sharp, decisive reprimand, making me yelp and my backside sting. Heat bloomed across my skin. The message was clear. So was the warning.

"Sorry, sir."

"Much better." His tone softened but didn't lose its edge. "Now lay your head down so I can still see your beautiful face. And grip the pillow."

There was no mistaking the trust threaded through his voice — trust we had built carefully, deliberately, with more honesty than either of us had ever offered another person. It was the same trust that had carried us through long conversations, research, and more than one heated debate in Doctor Montgomery's office.

We had even discussed visiting a reputable club in the city — only as observers, at the doctor's suggestion. Ari had shocked me by agreeing. I'd made my disappointment known, loudly, which led to a spectacular argument in front of Doctor

Montgomery. He eventually coaxed us into a compromise: if we ever participated, it would be strictly instructional, with a vetted Dominant or Domme guiding us, and only with each other. After that, everything would remain private, at home, where temptation could be managed — mostly on my part.

"Yes, sir." I moaned as his tongue rimmed my entrance whilst firmly gripping my inner thighs. I suspected it was to hold me in place.

"You're so wet already," he murmured, kneeling at my raised behind and gliding his fingers back and forth through the soft flesh of my aching folds.

I gasped as he stroked a crooked finger against my inner wall. I quivered. "Ari..."

Two smacks to my rear. "Excuse me?"

"Sir," I gulped, "please let me come."

Ari abruptly removed the stroking finger, leaving me trembling – and without an orgasm. "You can wait now, thanks to your lack of manners."

"Sorry, sir." Out of my peripheral, I saw his mouth quirk up into quite the satisfied smile.

"Much better. Now, where were we?"

∞

Ari

The sharp sting across her skin jolted me awake faster than any alarm ever could. One second I was drifting in that warm, heavy fog between sleep and consciousness, and the next I had Teddy straddling me, mischief radiating off her like heat.

Of course she'd try something the moment she thought I was too far gone to stop her.

Her smirk told me everything I needed to know — she'd been testing boundaries again. Pushing. Teasing. Seeing how far she could get before I caught her.

I tightened my grip on her hips, anchoring her in place. "I saw that," I growled, my voice still rough from sleep.

The way she yelped — the way her breath hitched — nearly undid me. She had no idea how close she came to getting exactly what she wanted. Or maybe she did. With Teddy, it was always hard to tell where impulse ended and intention began.

"Sorry, sir," she murmured, and the apology was genuine enough, but the glint in her eyes was anything but repentant.

"Much better," I said, though my pulse was still thundering. "Now lay your head down so I can still see your beautiful face. And grip the pillow."

Her obedience wasn't submission — not really. It was trust. Hard-won, fragile, and something I didn't take lightly. Especially after everything we'd worked through with Montgomery. Especially after the arguments, the compromises, the nights spent talking instead of touching.

We'd agreed on boundaries. We'd agreed on structure. We'd agreed on terms that kept her impulses from running the show — and kept me from losing myself in the parts of this dynamic I still didn't fully understand.

And yet... here she was. Testing me before sunrise on Christmas morning.

Typical.

I exhaled slowly, grounding myself. The club, the research, the compromises — all of it had been for moments like this.

Moments where I needed to stay steady even when she was anything but.

She lowered herself just as I asked, her cheek brushing the pillow, her eyes locked on mine. And despite everything — the rules, the restraint, the work we'd done — I felt that familiar pull in my chest.

God help me, she was going to be the death of me.

"Merry Christmas, my love," I whispered, handing her the first gift from the comfort of my thoroughly ruined bed — the top sheet discarded somewhere on the floor thanks to her earlier antics. "This one is for my eyes only."

Suspicion narrowed her hazel eyes as she sat up, the covers pooling around her waist. "Why? Is it something naughty?"

I caught her chin between my fingers and tugged her closer, pressing a firm, chaste kiss to her swollen lips. "Just open it."

I watched her with a slow stroke of my thumb along my jaw, taking in every flicker of excitement as she tore at the broad red ribbon and tossed it aside. The lid followed, landing somewhere near the foot of the bed. Her enthusiasm faltered only when she peeled back the store's signature black tissue paper.

She bit her lip — hard — as she lifted the black lace half-cup bra with the red ribbon detail. A girlish giggle escaped her, bright and unguarded.

"Now I see what you mean. There's definitely not much fabric to this."

"No. That's the point." My mouth twitched, especially when she held up the matching panties with a pointed look.

"Neither do these."

"But you'll wear them for me?" I asked, unable to hide the hope in my voice.

A blush rose beautifully across her skin as she nodded. "With lace-topped thigh-highs."

My girl knew me well.

"Your black patent leather Louboutins?"

"You're very particular," she muttered, rolling her eyes — a move that nearly earned her a different kind of Christmas morning entirely. "But yes."

"Mmm." I let the sound linger, low and appreciative. "I truly look forward to seeing you in them."

And I did. More than she realised.

"About time you two finally came down."

The pun wasn't subtle. Teddy caught it. So did I.

"He heard us," I muttered, cuffing the back of Bryson's thick skull. Teddy snorted.

"Obviously."

"The whole house bloody heard you!" Dominique piped up as my brother yelped — music to my ears.

"Ari Colton Jaeger, I saw that!"

Twice in as many days I'd been reprimanded by my full name. A new personal record. Perhaps a hat trick was worth the inevitable scolding.

"Sorry, Mother."

"Sorry, Mother," Bryson squeaked in a pathetic imitation.

I tapped my fingers against my lips. "Did Olivia suck out your manhood overnight, brother?"

He scoffed. "No, she didn't, much to my disgust."

I barked a laugh. "You really know how to dig yourself a hole."

"After that particular comment, you'll be lucky if it ever happens again," Olivia replied dryly, not missing a beat, teasing him with the croissant in her hand before he grabbed her wrist and took a dramatic bite out of it.

I checked my watch. "Is it five o'clock yet? Because after hearing that, I need a drink. Preferably something stiff to wash away the ghastly image of my brother's boring sex life."

"Not a bad idea," my father agreed, joining me at the wet bar in the corner.

Under my mother's caustic stare, I filled two tumblers with bourbon.

"Gentlemen, spare me, please! We haven't even opened gifts yet!"

My father waved her off. "Audrina, it's Christmas Day — a blessed day spent with our children and their partners. Rules don't apply. Besides," he added, eyes twinkling, "we're still waiting for Michael and Carys. So until they join us, let us have a drink."

I smirked. Judging by the grunts and honeyed moans we'd heard passing their bedroom, we might be waiting a while.

Mother's expression softened. "Fine. But I'm choosing what we drink."

She crossed the room, pausing to gaze up at my father with that look she reserved only for him. Their lips met in a tender kiss.

"Merry Christmas, my love."

"Pop the champagne, darling."

I clicked my fingers at them. "Hey, you two — enough. Your children are present."

Mother twisted at the waist and shot me a glare. "Says you, Mr PDA."

The cork popped, champagne bubbled over the lip of the bottle, and my father poured each of us a flute. We followed their lead, raising our glasses.

"Merry Christmas, my darlings!"

"Merry Christmas!" we shouted in unison.

24

Loud and positively messy, we celebrated Christmas Day in true Jaeger style – mother's freshly polished boards, and steam cleaned rugs swiftly disappearing beneath a kaleidoscope of wrapping paper, ribbon, and boxes. Overshadowing the jovial chaos, however, were current events and uncomfortable admissions. Both cast a faint but undeniable tension amidst the gift exchange; hence the two bottles of champagne consumed before midday. Not that we'd discussed the last few days – or the last few months – either. *That* topic we avoided like the plague.

I snorted. Forgetting was something one could only dare dream about. Leaning back in my poolside chair, I watched my family in their blissful ignorance. They joked, splashed, teased, lounged in the spa with endless drinks in hand — unaware of the hell waiting just beyond the horizon. Or perhaps it was just my sluggish, alcohol-soaked brain overthinking again. Maybe they were doing exactly what I should be doing: living.

But believing our private lives wouldn't draw scrutiny once the New Year rolled in? That was naïve.

Emmett's arrest alone would unleash hell — the devil himself and his spawn of lawyers and reporters.

Both would pry relentlessly. One to plaster our once-private lives across the tabloids. The other to twist the truth into something unrecognisable for court.

Christ. Why was I thinking about this miserable shit now? Another drink should be enough to drown the thoughts clawing at me. I exhaled sharply and dragged a hand through my now-dry hair.

"Do you want another drink, my love?" I slurred, my hungry gaze travelling along Teddy's svelte sun-kissed figure.

She pushed her new sunglasses down her nose, giving me a glassy-eyed grin as she lifted her empty flute. "Is the Pope Catholic?"

I slid off the chair with a grimace. Dammit. How did she always know when my thoughts turned dark? Perhaps I really did need to attend church more often — if only to silence my mother's persistent nagging.

Since Teddy's and my engagement, she reminded me often that my attendance was essential. A conversation she was once again raised over brunch, vexing the hell out of me.

"To whom?" I had argued.

"To the Reverend, of course! If you are to be married there, especially." Her indignant and swift reply irked me further.

I let out a disgruntled sigh. "We haven't even set a date yet, and as it stands, neither Teddy nor I have the inclination to do so, thanks to recent events."

My curt response was highly uncalled for, apparently, nor should we allow these 'recent' events to consume our lives.

Teddy had thankfully concurred with me, thoroughly disappointing my mother. Asked if she was happy with a long engagement, Teddy informed her that she refused to be railroaded into marriage, nor would she allow Emmett to cast his despairing shadow over our special day. And until he was locked up, no such wedding plans would take place, putting that argument to rest, for now.

"I'll get you another champagne then," I grumbled, plucking the flute resting between the tips of her fingers in her outstretched hand.

"What's eating you?" Teddy quizzed, springing from her chair and following me to the bar. She pushed her sunglasses onto hr head and crossed her arms over her tiny bikini – a bikini that covered, well... barely anything. She watched me pour our drinks with a raised brow. "You're rather grumpy all of a sudden."

"Nothing's wrong. I'm drunk, it's stifling hot, and I'm horny – again. It's that damned bikini. You might as well be naked in that thing." Not a complete lie. Just an omission of the thoughts gnawing at me.

She stepped closer until I smelt the sweet scent of her perfume and felt the firmness of her breasts against my chest. Her nipples tightened beneath the flimsy fabric, and she tilted her head with a knowing smile. "What do you want to do about it then? Does sir need servicing?"

I curved a hand around her nape and kissed her – hot, hungry, claiming – whilst my other hand skimmed down her bare back.

I cupped her backside, squeezing potently. She moaned against my mouth. “Meet me inside in five minutes; be naked and readily waiting on your knees for me.”

Her gaze intuitively dropped. “Yes, sir.”

Our lips met in another ravenous kiss. “Good girl.”

The afterglow was silently blissful for both of us.

Or so I thought.

Teddy’s soft laughter still lingered in the air when she finally collapsed against my chest, her breath warm and steadying. For a moment, the world outside our bedroom didn’t exist — no reporters, no court cases, no looming New Year ready to drag us through the mud. Just her. Just us.

She traced idle patterns across my sternum, feather-light and soothing. “You’re thinking again,” she murmured, not accusing, just observant in that way she always was when my mind drifted somewhere darker.

I rolled my head on the pillow and met her glinting eyes.

“How’d you know?” I asked dryly. “Hmm?”

She sighed, shifting her leg before rolling onto her stomach and propping her chin on her linked hands, feet swinging lazily behind her. “You’ve worn that torturous expression all afternoon. It’s the same look you get every time you’re worrying — and lately, it’s happened often.”

The corner of my mouth lifted. “You’re perceptive. Too much for your own good sometimes.”

“No, I don’t think so. It’s a trait I’ve learned — had to, really — thanks to my wonderful upbringing and... well, you know who.”

“Yeah, I know,” I muttered, dragging a hand over my face before gruffly urging her closer. “Come here. I need to hold you.”

She rolled her eyes but shuffled back across the bed, weaving her limbs around mine. “Better?”

“Much.”

She rested her cheek over my heart, listening to its uneven rhythm. “Now,” she whispered, “what were you thinking about?”

I tapped the end of her nose. “Persistent, aren’t you?”

Her shoulders lifted in a playful shrug.

“All right,” I conceded, “I’ll tell you if it stops your nagging.”

She smacked my chest lightly, and the humour softened the edge of what I said next.

“Everything. Nothing. The year ahead. The mess we’re walking into.”

She lifted her head, her expression gentling. “We’ll handle it. Together.”

I huffed a quiet laugh. “You make it sound simple.”

“It’s not simple,” she countered, brushing her thumb along my jaw. “But it’s doable. And you’re not doing it alone anymore.”

That landed harder than she probably intended. My throat tightened. “I know.”

“You’ve carried too much for too long, Ari. Let someone else shoulder some of it.”

“I’m trying,” I admitted, surprising even myself.

“I know you are.” She pressed a kiss to my chest. “And that’s enough.”

For a long moment, I simply held her, letting the weight of her words settle. She always had a way of grounding me — not by dismissing my fears, but by reminding me I wasn’t facing them alone.

Outside, the muffled sounds of my family drifted through the open balcony doors — laughter, splashing, the clink of glasses.

Life continuing, blissfully unaware of the storm gathering on the horizon.

Teddy shifted again, curling closer. “You're allowed to enjoy this, you know,” she whispered. “Today. Right now. Me.”

A faint smile tugged at my lips. “I am enjoying you.”

She nudged me with her nose. “Good. Because I'm not done with you yet.”

I arched a brow. “Oh?”

Her grin turned wicked. “Not even close.”

She traced a slow line down my torso, her touch warm and teasing. “But before I distract you again... may I make a suggestion?”

I nodded.

“Why don't you have Thomas write statements as needed? He's worked in HR, and he's helped you and Asher before.” She shrugged lightly. “Rather than waste his talent, use it. Makes sense, don't you think?”

My arm tightened around her in an affectionate squeeze. “Yes, it does. He's extremely good at what he does. Which reminds me — I need to give Thomas a pay rise once work resumes. He's worth his weight in gold.”

Hazel eyes glinted mischievously. “I know what else is worth its weight in gold.” Her fingers skimmed along my torso and stopped at my cock, grasping, and fisting the growing length lying in the palm of her hand.

“Oh, you do, do you?”

She hummed, pleased with herself. “It's the gold at the end of a rainbow. My rainbow.”

“Well,” I murmured, rolling us over, “we'd better make sure it pays dividends then.” We made love until dinner time.

As a surprise for Teddy, I'd hired us a private jet to fly us to Sydney with the roomy Gulfstream offering us the privacy and comfort we desperately needed, without the annoyance of strangers gawking at us. Plus a few other benefits Teddy was plotting to explore.

"Do you think we could join the mile-high club?" She twisted in her seat, eyeing me optimistically.

I let her down gently. "Sorry, love. The plane's not big enough for a bedroom." Her pout was adorable. I promised to make amends elsewhere. "Besides, the flight's only an hour and a half, and I'm sure even you, Little Miss Horny, can manage to abstain for that long."

I honestly knew that wouldn't be the case for either of us.

"I'll try," she huffed, turning away dramatically.

My laughter only added to her discontent.

"Mocking me now, are you? Keep that up and there'll be no sex for you for the entire trip!"

"You and I both know you can barely last a day without wanting to climb my cock!" I spluttered, amused.

"You're hardly a poster boy for restraint either!" she countered.

"True." I leaned in, trailing my lips over her exposed neck as she pretended to ignore me. "How about a compromise?"

"I'm listening..."

"If I promise to guarantee you a splendid time later... by fucking you until you cry..." I paused; I was about to say uncle but thought better of it. "Until you decide no more. Shall that quench your thirst for now?" Her silence was answer enough.

Subsequently, we joined the mile-high club — much to my fiancée's unrestrained glee — as Teddy set about seducing me with a determination that made the word no vanish from my vocabulary altogether. Her skillset knew no bounds, nor did her ability to shock me.

It wasn't until her fitted dress skimmed tantalisingly up her lean figure, sliding past her waist, that I realised she'd boarded the plane without underwear. The discovery was... positively delightful. And with the abundance of space at our disposal, I couldn't resist taking full advantage.

The Gulfstream was immaculate – four supple grey-leather seats lining either side of the aisle, another pair of singles towards the back, and a matching sofa running perpendicular to the cabin. Retractable walnut tables sat between the chairs, polished to a shine – and conveniently stable. The small lavatory was tucked behind a glossy walnut panel, more decorative than practical we quickly discovered. The challenge to try was a barrel of laughs, nonetheless.

Amidst our enthusiasm, we overlooked the feelings of our poor stewardess, Emma. She emerged from the galley at precisely the wrong moment, no doubt expecting to offer us cold beverages. Her startled, "Oh my god's," echoed through the cabin at the optimum moment as Teddy and I climaxed loudly. Emma swiftly fled back to the galley, the door slamming behind her.

From that point onwards, until we landed at the private terminal in Sydney, we barely saw her unless it was absolutely necessary. And even then, she couldn't look us without turning crimson. When we disembarked and thanked her for her hospitality, she managed a strangled goodbye without meeting our eyes.

The sight of Teddy's breasts bouncing whilst riding me like there was no tomorrow was a vision she'd never forget. That I was sure of.

Regardless, the experience gave us quite a laugh.

"God, we're shameless," I mused as Teddy's tireless seduction flowed seamlessly from the jet to the back seat of the town car on our way to my penthouse in Lavender Bay. Fortunately, I wasn't the one driving.

With a sly little smirk, she reached forward and pressed the button to raise the privacy screen hidden behind the front seats. The soft hum of the mechanism filled the space.

I chuckled. "Don't want an audience this time?"

"Uh-huh," she rumbled, shaking her head fractionally whilst unbuttoning my jeans. Sliding the zipper down, she shovelled her hand inside my boxer briefs and grasped my rising cock, gently tugging it free – the entire length rapidly engulfed as she lowered her head. Whilst I relished in the feel of her warm mouth and her skill, she hummed appreciatively, triggering a pleasant tingle that gradually wound its way around my cock. My eyes slid closed and my head flopped against the backrest, lapping up the attention. Her head bobbed whilst her tongue swirled around the girth, tasting every inch, including my balls, which led to quite an explosive orgasm.

Not that her appetite diminished.

As persistent as ever, she kept up the tireless seduction until finally rolled away from me on the floor of the master bedroom, limbs sprawled, chest rising and falling in ragged breaths.

Stiff and exhausted, she groaned, "Oh, God... I don't think I can move."

I groaned along with her. "I'm fairly certain I used muscles I forgot I had."

She hot me an impish smile, sassing me with effortless insolence. "Is Austin not working you hard enough?"

With a grunt, I managed to roll onto my front and drag my squealing, slippery lover back towards me by the waist. “Have I not been the one to screw you into the middle of next week, or was it some other bloke?”

Lust-filled eyes glittered upwards as long fingers threaded through my sweat-damp hair. “Oh, it was most definitely you.”

I brushed a stray strand from her forehead, my thumb tracing the warm, damp skin at her temple. “How about a bath to soothe our weary bodies? I couldn’t raise another erection even if I tried.”

“Bath,” she agreed breathlessly, “then dinner at a fancy restaurant somewhere in the city.” A copper brow raised with hopeful mischief. “Can we go clubbing, too? Please?”

How could I say no?

“Sure, why not?” I groaned, pushing upright with exhausting effort. “Let’s use and abuse the rest of our muscles.”

25

Dinner was at Agave, a five-star restaurant in Circular Quay. The meal was exquisite, as was the view of the harbour glittering beneath the night sky. But neither compared to the enticing woman beside me on the beige linen bench seat. Dressed in a short black chiffon dress with sequinned trim and strappy silver heels, Teddy sat quietly, savouring the triple-chocolate mousse cake in front of her.

Little did I realise, as I sipped on a glass of bubbling champagne, Teddy's quiet demeanour was simply a ruse.

Initially, I paid no mind to her long fingers curving over my upper thigh. But as her palm gradually drifted higher, her ulterior motive became abundantly clear. My brow lifted as she obscenely licked a smear of mousse from her spoon – a gesture far too deliberate to be innocent. Particularly upon hearing the distinct sound of the zip in my dress pants lowering. At that point, as her hand shovelled inside my boxer briefs and our impassive gazes locked, I found myself profoundly grateful for the draping tablecloth. Another blessing was the dreamy voice of my favourite jazz songstress crooning overhead, drowning out my unsuppressed moans as Teddy's deft fingers curled around the shaft of my cock. A smug smile slowly graced my lips as the little daredevils swirling movements trailed south.

Oh yes, things were indeed looking up.

My satisfied moans smothered by the flute at my lips as the tips of her French manicured nails found that sensitive spot beneath my sac, I relaxed against the tall back of the bench seat. Merely had I begun to relish in Teddy's boldness when my inebriating pleasure came to an abrupt halt. Irritated, I flicked my gaze sideways – only to find a composed Teddy lifting a mouthful of dessert to her plush mouth.

I cleared my throat pointedly.

Her head turned slowly, eyes glinting with wicked amusement. She tipped her chin towards my lap and murmured, "Don't forget to do up your pants..."

"How remiss of me to forget?" I muttered tightly, zipping my fly beneath the pristine white tablecloth.

Then, in a move as gutsy as it was calculated, she leaned in, whispering her yearning to play. "...Sir."

Well, she asked, so she shall receive.

Glowering, I threw back the last of my champagne and set the empty flute down with a decisive thud. "Then you'd best hurry and finish that dessert."

She placed the spoon beside the half-finished mousse without a word.

"Good." I nodded curtly and signalled the waiter for our bill, my hand gliding along the small of her back. "Things really are looking up — for me, anyway," I hissed, my fingers curling possessively into her waist.

Deliberately taking my time, I spoke with our driver outside the car, requesting a long, slow drive to Amo Bailar – a Latin nightclub in Elizabeth Street – with a few scenic detours along the way. Davina had recommended the club on my last visit to Sydney, insisting it was *the* place to be if you fancied something sensual and intoxicating with your partner.

I had every intention of teasing Teddy in the same manner she'd tormented me at dinner. She was getting her just desserts the moment we slid into the back seat.

I pressed the button for the privacy screen. "The driver doesn't need a show. Now, come here," I directed, pointing to my lap.

Teddy obeyed instantly, sliding her long torso over my thighs.

"I also don't believe the spanking I'm about to give you needs an explanation, do you?" I asked calmly, lifting the light fabric of her dress up to her waist and massaging each cheek over the top of her sheer black lace panties.

"No, sir." Hr breath hitched as I gently curled my fingertips over the elasticated edge and slowly eased the delicate fabric down, leaving two peach-soft cheeks exposed to my heated gaze.

"Ten times should be sufficient for your misdeeds." I tilted my head, studying her. "Do you agree with me?"

"Yes, sir."

"Grab the door handle...," I firmly purred, skimming a finger along the parting of her cheeks as she reached out and gripped the chrome handle. "...and don't move."

A perceptive smile tugged at my lips. Knowing Teddy, she'd usually flinch on purpose just to earn more. But in a first, she surprised me – not a single movement. Even as my palm connected at the junction between her thighs and dripping cleft. There was nothing more than the combined sounds of her soft moans and slapping flesh pervading the confined space. As beautiful as she sounded, our play had left me inflicted with an unbearably hard erection straining against the zipper inside my black dress pants. I gently skated my fingers through her soaked folds, making her mewl in protest as I teased her engorged nub.

"That little stunt you pulled inside Agave has cost you an orgasm," I chastised, covering her bottom with her panties before lifting her off my lap. She moved automatically, silently kneeling beside me on the seat – perfectly poised, as always. I tucked a stray strand of hair behind her ear and tipped her chin upward, guiding her gaze to mine.

"You left me with a full sac and a hard-on from hell, but that doesn't mean you can't finish the job you started. Hop to it." A smile danced on my lips as she began to release my cock from its confines. "Strap yourself in first though...just in case the driver has a sudden urge to brake."

"Yes, sir." Beneath her contrition, a flicker of a satisfied smile appeared – one that made my own lips curve in response.

As soon as Teddy eased her tender backside onto the seat and buckled herself in, I tapped the privacy window, signalling our driver to take his time and wind slowly through the city.

I smirked whilst she worked me over, in the same delectable manner she had dished out earlier before swallowing the load that swiftly followed.

As she quietly uncurled and straightened, I reached into my jacket pocket and flicked open my handkerchief, letting it dangle between my fingers.

"To wipe the corners of your mouth," I eloquently expressed.

Teddy took it at once, murmuring her thanks. The delicate was she dabbed at her lips stirred something deep and possessive in me.

I tapped a finger against my lips. "I've decided to up the ante. Remove your panties and give them to me."

She didn't hesitate. Silently, she lifted her beautiful backside and lid the sheer lace don her legs. When she dropped them into my open palm, I tucked them into my jacket pocket without breaking eye contact.

"Good girl. Now, lift your dress higher and part your knees."

Again, she obeyed without question.

"But keep your hands behind your back." Starting at her knee, I let my fingertips drift slowly along the inside of her thigh. Each light pass made her body shift, her breath catching in anticipation. I considered ordering her to stay still, but the sight of her writhing – restrained only by obedience – was far too exquisite to interrupt.

When I encouraged her to spread wider, she di so shamelessly, drawing her knees upward and positioning her endlessly long legs on either side of her body, her feet braced on the seat's edge. Her flexibility was something I indulged in often, and this moment was no exception. The enticing sight of her dripping sex highly exposed took all the restraint I could muster not to take her, here and now on the backseat.

At the sight of her gaping mouth and the sound of her breathless pants, my mouth quirked smugly. "Annoying when someone toys with you, isn't it? Then they audaciously leave you right on the cusp..." I deliberately slid a single finger into Teddy's snug heat before inserting another, triggering a tightly controlled fluttering of muscles.

or someone who had supposedly only read about BDSM, she had miraculous control over her climax. Control like that didn't come from curiosity alone — it came from training, from experience. The thought should have raised questions, but I brushed them aside as quickly as they surfaced. I was far too enamoured with her to look too closely at anything that might disrupt what we had.

And truth be told, I took pleasure in exerting my dominance over her — as much as she took pleasure in yielding to it. Especially when I reminded her of the rules, my voice low and deliberate: "Don't come. Not until I say so."

She'd been right about one thing, though. There was a satisfaction threaded through each session that I hadn't expected. It made me feel free, easing the day's stress and quieting the noise in my head in a way nothing else ever had. Likewise emphasised, as my fingers circled inside her, and my delighted gaze skirted over Teddy's quivering body as she fought against the will to orgasm.

A lazy smile formed as I abruptly withdrew my fingers, generating an exasperated scream from Teddy as she bared her clenched teeth at me.

"No, please, sir...I need to come."

I sucked on my fingers, relishing in her sweet flavour. "Soon, very soon, my love," I crooned, my eyes twinkling in amusement. She, of course, found it less so and threw herself back into the seat. About to cross her legs, my hand swiftly landed on her upper thigh. "Did I give you permission to cross your legs?"

"No, sir, you did not." She resisted the urge to bite back, but the misting eyes told me the struggle was real.

I offered her a compromise. "You may draw them back together if you like."

"How kind of you...sir..." she muttered, her tone edged with irritation. Indeed, my girl had teeth and enjoyed testing boundaries – but I was nowhere near ready to dish out a severe punishment. She'd simply have to wait until I had appropriately mastered the craft.

She huffed, dropping one leg beside the other, eyeing my hand with a mixture of longing and annoyance as it remained firmly on her thigh until we were parked kerbside in front of the club.

I opened my door and stepped out, offering my hand as she swung her legs from the SUV. Its height ample enough in helping her maintain her dignity as she took my hand and exited the car gracefully.

"Thank you, sir," she uttered tightly. Her mood hadn't simmered enough to warrant giving her the orgasm she urgently craved.

I clasped her waist and tugged her close enough, leaning in to murmur words she understood all too well. "Table your emotions, or you'll force me to make you wait even longer."

Teddy exhaled a cleansing breath and waited for my cue to walk the short distance from the kerb to the door.

"Better now, my love?"

"Much."

"Let's go in then, shall we?"

The hulking bouncer unhooked the thick red rope from its brass counterpart, and stepped aside, paving the way for us to enter through a single glass door.

The muffled pulse of Latin rhythm seeped through the hallway walls, and the air between us shifted – anticipation sharpening into exhilaration. As we stepped onto the main floor, our gazes swept over the half-dressed figures swaying erotically across the dancefloor. It was easy to see why Davina had recommended Amo Bailar; it was a lover's paradise.

Teddy and I blended in effortlessly, moving with a shared hunger that matched the room around us.

The music wrapped around us the moment we stepped onto the main floor, warm and pulsing, coaxing even the most guarded bodies into movement. Teddy's fingers tightened around mine, her earlier frustration dissolving as the atmosphere swallowed us whole.

Then her gaze drifted across the room.

Just a casual sweep — nothing more.

But something caught her.

Someone.

Her breath hitched, so softly it could have been mistaken for the rhythm catching her off-guard. A flicker of recognition passed through her eyes, quick and sharp, before she smoothed it away with practiced ease.

If I hadn't been watching her so closely, I might have missed it entirely.

But she recovered almost instantly, lifting her chin, letting the music pull her back into the present. Whatever — or whoever — she'd seen, she tucked it away with quiet precision, as though it belonged to a part of her life she had no intention of bringing into mine.

She stepped closer, her hand sliding up my arm in a gesture that felt both grounding and deliberate.

"Dance with me," she murmured.

And because tonight was meant to be ours — uncomplicated, unburdened — I didn't question it. I simply drew her into the rhythm, my hand firm at her waist, guiding her into the music as though nothing at all had shifted.

But something had.

Not enough to disturb the night.

Just enough to whisper that Teddy's world was larger — and more layered — than she let on. A dangerous calm settled over me, the kind that always surfaced when she pushed me this close to the edge. Once we were home, I would finish our dance properly — and she'd feel every moment of what she'd stirred in me.

"Ah, fuck...Ari...I c...can't!" Her stuttered protest was fruitless. Teddy's orgasm hit hard as our sweat lathered skin hit the bed after a long-drawn-out session of unfettered sex – on my terms. Her body writhed while her head thrashed against the mattress as I furiously ate at her swollen and throbbing cleft.

With her bond wrists high above her head, she screamed, clawing at the badly crumpled sheets. Her strong thighs tightened around my shoulders as another orgasm hit, washing over her like a tidal wave.

Again, I barely gave her time to recover and flipped her over sinking balls deep inside her, slapping our dampened flesh together with each punishing thrust. I gripped her hips, my fingers sliding over her slick skin as my thrusting became unrelenting. In the end, I snaked an arm around her waist and held on, fucking manically until my climax erupted just as violently.

Ultimately spent, I rolled off Teddy and onto the mattress beside her, releasing her wrists from their bonds. She stiffly climbed off the bed and staggered into the bathroom for a shower.

I tiredly followed.

26

Finally recovered from what Teddy gleefully dubbed our sexpedition, we decided it was time to venture out and explore the city. The frenetic energy of Sydney's CBD swept us along as we wandered through sights I'd never bothered with during business trips. I usually flew in, handled what needed handling, and flew straight home. Running a company didn't leave much room for sightseeing.

Dodging the bustling crowds, I sighed and hauled a cheery Teddy to my side. She shivered in delight as I slung an arm around her waist, my fingers brushing the bare skin revealed beneath the hem of her frilled off-the-shoulder top.

"Keep that up, and we'll end up in an alleyway somewhere."

My nose scrunched at the suggestion — distasteful, reckless, and blatantly illegal. "How dirty. And who knows who's loitering around — like the police, for example. They'd arrest us for indecent behaviour. Something you reminded me of not too long ago, if I recall."

"It's my prerogative to change my mind."

I elicited a low growl, sharing my displeasure. "Be grateful we're in public, because right now I have no qualms about spanking your arse for the mere suggestion." Not that my threat dissuaded her either.

"Take a risk for god's sake and stop acting so damned safe!" she jeered, rolling her eyes.

Our aggrieved footsteps faltered in the middle of the footpath as our determined gazes met, forcing the tide of pedestrians to detour around us with muttered curses. Ignoring them, I brusquely yanked her forward and held her firmly against me.

"Unless you want a blazing row in the middle of the CBD, then quit pushing the issue." I gripped her chin, lightly stroking her plump bottom lip as I chastised her. "And quite frankly, I need a break! All we've done is fuck, and the point of this trip was to rebuild our relationship – reconnect in other ways. You were aware of this little fact before we left Melbourne of my intentions, were you not?"

Teddy's chin tilted defiantly.

Annoyance flared. I dropped my arms and crossed them over my chest. "Did I not make my intentions clear enough?"

"*Yes, Ari, you did,*" she replied with infuriating sarcasm.

"Quit with this petulant behaviour!"

"I'm not a child!"

"Then stop acting like one!"

She stomped her canvas-clad foot, twisted on her heel and stormed off.

"Teddy, wait!" I pushed through the irritated pedestrians I'd bumped into along the way, my patience fraying with every step. My continual pleas were futile until I finally caught up — and irritation tightened my jaw as I found her perched on a low concrete fence bordering the cathedral lawn, a serene backdrop that clashed spectacularly with her infuriatingly carefree demeanour.

"Jesus Christ, Teddy, what in the devil are you playing at?"

The corners of her mouth quirked, her chin jerking toward the century-old limestone building behind her. "Blasphemy, Ari. You're outside a church, if you hadn't realised."

My lips flattened into a hard line. "This is not the time nor the place for your sassy attitude, Teddy. And what in the hell was that little tantrum about?"

She shrugged — wordless, insolent.

A visceral growl tore from my chest. "Dammit, Teddy, at least have the decency to give me a defined answer."

And then it dawned on me. "You're deliberately going out of your way to provoke me... You want me to punish you severely, is that it?"

"What if I am..." she gloated, unable to hide the small smile tugging at her lips.

Teddy seemingly needed reminding that our arrangement wouldn't work if she kept flouting the rules and boundaries I'd put in place.

I grasped her hand — firm, not rough — and pulled her to her feet. "No. Absolutely not," I said, marching her up the narrow-pebbled path and into the church, away from prying eyes and ears. "And this is most definitely not the time or the place for that," I added in a low whisper, pushing my sunglasses onto my head. Teddy wisely did the same, her gaze dropping to the smooth limestone floor when she caught my expression.

I exhaled and sank onto the nearest pew, gesturing to the space beside me. “Sit down. Please.” For the sake of the conversation, I allowed her to keep her submissive posture.

Leaning forward, my forearms braced on my thighs, I rubbed my hands together, trying to steady the frustration simmering beneath my skin. “This expectation you have of me — to wield dominance over you — you’re pushing me to do more than I’m capable of right now. Don’t misunderstand me; I’m enjoying the added intensity between us far more than I ever anticipated. But I’m still a novice. I have a lot to learn before we go any deeper.”

I raked a hand through my hair. “I’ve arranged dinner with Seth and Davina later this evening at their place. Can you at least wait until I’ve discussed everything with them first, please?”

Awaiting Teddy’s response, my attention drifted towards a creaking side door. My wary gaze followed a stooped elderly priest as he exited the room he’d been occupying. Aided by a wooden walking stick clasped in a hand twisted by rheumatoid arthritis, he shuffled closer — and a perceptible gasp escaped him as his ageing eyesight homed in on Teddy.

“Teddy, lass? Is that you?”

If ever there was a moment for her to set her needs aside, it was now. Thankfully, curiosity overtook her defiance. “I’m sorry, but... how do you know me?” She pushed off her hands and rose, her approach guarded as she took a few tentative steps toward him.

The priest came to a gentle stop before her, balancing his ailing frame with the stick. “I never forgot you, Teddy McGovern. From the moment you turned up here one rainy day with your mother, I knew you were special.”

Still unconvinced by the vague explanation, she eyed him warily and stepped back, preparing to run. "That still doesn't tell me anything. Or who you are."

"You don't remember?" His brows creased. "At all?"

"I'm sorry, Father, but the days leading up to my arrival at Father Byrnes' house are nothing more than a blur."

Miffed, he blew out a despondent sigh and glanced at the floor before lifting his gaze again. "You had both better follow me, then." With a shaky sweep of his hand, he motioned toward an identical door at the back of the church and began plodding toward it at a snail's pace.

Expecting Teddy to follow, I moved after him — only to halt beside her. "It would be impolite to keep Father Callaghan waiting," I pressed, gesturing impatiently. "So why aren't you moving?"

"Should we, though? I… I don't know him."

Frustration flared. "What have you got to lose by not?"

She chewed the corner of her bottom lip, glancing toward the open door. A heavy sigh escaped her. "Nothing, I suppose."

"Shall we, then?" I placed a hand at the small of her back.

She nodded curtly and allowed me to guide her into a small but cosy room. Our heads tilted upward in unison as we took in the towering bookcase dominating the wall beside Father Callaghan's antique desk — an extraordinary collection of dusty, leather-bound volumes.

Noticing our darting gazes, he smiled and pointed to the highest shelf. "Some of the oldest scriptures remain up there for a reason. One dates back as far as the sixteenth century."

I gaped. "My mother would be in her element. She loves history."

He regarded me curiously. "Is your mother a historian, Mr...?"

It dawned on me that he had no idea who I was or why I was here. Remembering my manners — ironically instilled by the very woman we were discussing — I extended my hand. "Ari Jaeger, Teddy's fiancé."

A warm smile spread across his face as he shook my hand. "Congratulations."

"Thank you. And to answer your question, my mother's a corporate lawyer. Though she's been contemplating a career change lately."

His faded denim eyes twinkled. "A great researcher, then?"

I nodded. "She's too inquisitive for her own good."

"Perhaps she could come work for me," he chuckled.

I scoffed. "As much as I adore my mother, Father, she'd drive you mad within ten minutes."

"Point taken." Father Callaghan shuffled behind his desk and gestured for us to sit. "I wondered when this day would come."

"How do you know Teddy, Father?" I quizzed, sidestepping across the front of his desk and settling into one of the occasional chairs beside him.

Father Callaghan slowly rotated the traditionally upholstered chair around and eased himself into the worn leather, the movement deliberate and careful, befitting a man in his eighties. His attention shifted directly to Teddy. "I'll do my best to fill in the blanks, sweet girl."

Beside me, still in shock, she nodded wordlessly, her gaze fixed on his trembling hands as he turned a key in a locked drawer. Her worry deepened as he produced a bound document folder and set it before him.

He rested a hand atop the ochre leather, his voice softening. "Our primary goal here at Saint Andrew's is to aid families in desperate need. With the number of cases we see, losing track isn't uncommon... but yours stayed with me." His warm expression dimmed as he continued. "When your mother, Therese, first contacted me, she appeared the epitome of grace, despite her concern for your situation. But her refusal to let you speak for yourself — and the way she held herself around you — raised my suspicions." Over the rim of his small, round-brimmed glasses, his gaze settled on Teddy with quiet sympathy. "My instinct told me something was dreadfully wrong with the picture she painted. And as it turned out, I was right."

My interest sharpened. I leaned forward and gestured toward the unopened folder. "May I, Father?"

"Of course." He slid the folder across the desk, and both he and Teddy watched intently as I unravelled the thinning string and drew out several documents — a crinkled birth certificate among them — along with a handful of photographs.

While I examined each page, he continued, revealing to an increasingly emotional Teddy everything he remembered.

"I was deeply concerned for your wellbeing. Your mother's story didn't add up."

A scoff escaped me. "Nothing ever does." His finger lifted to his lips — a polite but firm request for silence. I cleared my throat and relented. "Apologies. Please continue."

His lips twitched with restrained amusement before he pressed on. "Therese claimed you were a drug addict. At first, I believed it — your unsteady gait, slurred speech, and inability to focus all pointed that way. Once we placed you in Father Byrnes' care, we asked our resident doctor to investigate. Again, my hunch proved correct. It appears your mother had taken it upon herself to administer a significant dose of sleeping pills." His tongue clicked in disapproval. "I was surprised you were still standing. Or alive."

A hand flew to Teddy's mouth, stifling the cry threatening to break free. "Is that why my baby died?"

Horror widened his eyes. "Who told you such a despicable lie?"

"Therese. And the doctor…" I clarified, curling my hand around Teddy's trembling fingers as I pushed aside the documents.

"Well, it certainly wasn't our doctor," he countered, indignation colouring his tone. "Two weeks before you were due, Therese arrived unexpectedly with a Doctor Richard Garner. Naturally, I questioned why she'd brought in another obstetrician when the hospital was fully equipped. But because your child was to be adopted, she insisted on 'the best.' No room for mistakes, she told me. Garner also demanded complete privacy to examine you — that request alone concerned me more than anything."

"I don't remember that part either," Teddy whispered.

"That's understandable," he murmured. "During those final weeks, you grew subdued and withdrew from everyone until you went into labour."

"When you're woken abruptly by the worst pain imaginable, it's not something you forget easily, Father…" she uttered, swiping away tears with the back of her hand. "Everything after that became a blur. It's a part of my life I wish never existed. It's too painful."

As I held her wringing hand and watched their exchange, the moment became unexpectedly humbling. Both she and Father Callaghan had suffered under Therese's self-serving choices — unsuspecting victims of her manipulation.

His cracking voice pulled me from my thoughts. “Ari, would you hand me the section clipped together, please?”

“Why those specifically?” I scanned the documents until I found the bundle he meant and passed it over.

His piercing gaze lifted to mine as he folded each page back until he reached the one he sought. “I want to clarify that we shared no part in your mother’s... ideologies.” The disdain in his voice was barely contained. “We conducted further tests after you delivered. Again, I was suspicious. And as you’ll see, the results speak for themselves.” He returned the papers to me.

I wished he hadn’t.

As my eyes widened over each revolting detail, the pulse in my neck hammered against my skin. And yet, beneath the rising fury, I could almost feel the phantom slap to the back of my head from my mother — a reminder to remember where I was. On the basis of avoiding Audrina Jaeger’s wrath, I kept my customary cursing inward.

I swallowed tightly and dragged a shaking hand through my hair, fighting to remain gentlemanly. “I’m... I’m lost for words,” I stuttered, struggling to contain the demonic rage clawing up my spine. “This is downright mortifying. They gave you something to induce labour — and during the delivery of the placenta, they sedated you as well.”

Teddy tore the page from my hand, her gaze pooling as she skimmed the damning evidence that her mother had orchestrated everything. “How could she? How could my mother do this to me?” Fury ignited, and she flung the pages across the desk. “How could she decide when my baby was born? I thought I went into labour naturally.” She scrubbed at her screwed-up face and shot to her feet, only to collapse to the floor in heart-wrenching sobs. “The doctor told me my body couldn’t grow any further — that’s why I went into labour early. He lied. HE LIED!”

I rushed to her and crouched, desperate to comfort her, but Teddy recoiled violently.

“Don’t touch me!”

I tried to reason with her. “Teddy, please… let’s go back to the apartment. We can call my dad—”

Her glare cut through me. “What can Jaxson do? Tell me, Ari — what the hell can your dad do?” She pushed herself upright, her body trembling as she staggered backwards. She was about to run — and the thought made my heart slam against my ribs.

I rose quickly and reached out. “Teddy—”

Her hand snapped up, halting me. “No. I need to get out of here — and do not follow me.”

Dejected, I could only watch helplessly as she bolted, disappearing through the doorway and into God knows where. My legs gave out beneath me, and I slumped into the nearest chair, sagging under the weight of it all.

A moment later, Father Callaghan’s trembling hand settled gently on my shoulder.

“Give the wee lass some space, son. I’m sure she’ll find her way back to you.”

27

Hours later, I returned to the apartment empty-handed and worried out of my mind. I was seconds away from calling the police when a raucous in the doorway behind me snapped my attention.

"What in the devil –"

I spun around just as Teddy toppled onto the textured grey timber-look tiles, giggling as she sprawled across the floor. I loomed over her, glaring at her glazed, dilated pupils smirking up at me.

"You don't look ver...very hap...py to see me..." The stench of alcohol spewed from her pores as she attempted to string two words together. Whatever else she had taken was anyone's guess, which appeared to be a non-issue for her.

Regardless of her inebriated state, the willpower not to rant and rave about the hours I had spent combing the streets for her or calling upon several favours in my fruitless search took a boatload of strength to hold in. Teddy, of course, expected that rage — expected a punishment — and pouted when I didn't immediately oblige.

"Why not? I've been a bad, bad, girl and sir should punish me."

I inhaled sharply. "Right. That's it!"

She clapped her hands, delighted, utterly delusional. "Yay! Are you going to spank me?"

"If I were you, I wouldn't get too excited!" I hauled her upright by the armpits, slung her over my shoulder, and marched us both into the master bedroom. Confusion flickered across her face as I strode past the bed and into the ensuite.

"Why'd you come in here?" Her curiosity bubbled as I stepped into the spacious shower stall and set her on her feet. "Are we having sex in here? I thought you were going to –" Her incessant rambling switched to screaming blue murder as I flicked the chrome tap and pushed her fully dressed figure beneath the cascade of icy water pouring from the ceiling rose. "That's freezing! Let me out!"

I cocked my head, meeting her glare as she fought against my hold. "I'm just exercising my right as your Dom to punish you. It's what you wanted, is it not?"

Teddy had the audacity to snare, "Fuck you!"

"Disillusioned are we, love?" I snorted, wrestling with the row of metal buttons at the crotch of her soaked jeans. "A side effect of illicit drugs, I'm told. Frying one's brains cells in such a manner isn't exactly my cup of tea, but who am I to judge one's preferred choices – distasteful as they are." I ignored the evil eye she shot me and tugged her jeans down to her ankles. "A little help here, please?"

Coaxing Teddy into cooperating with me was quite the ordeal, especially as copper lashes fluttered and her fingers tangled in my drenched hair. “I lurve your hair, Ari... it's sooo sexy.”

“Seducing me won’t earn you any points. Step out of your jeans.”

“If it pleases, sir, I will.”

Hearing her address me as such made me cringe – but I also realised I had little choice but to go with the flow if I wanted to get her sober. “It would please me immensely. So please, do as sir requested.”

A drunken giggle burst from her as she lost her balance and crashed onto the polished marble bench behind her. She winced. “Ow. That hurt my butt.”

Incensed, I growled. “Your arse ....” but the awareness of where this could lead stopped me cold. She reached for my belt buckle, proving my point.

“My arse what – sir?” she purred.

I swatted her hand away and stepped back, leaning my soaked backside against the tiled half wall. Beyond frustrated, I barked, “Finish stripping – NOW!”

“Okay, I’m stripping. Calm your farm.” “Okay, I’m stripping. Calm your farm.” She yanked at her peasant top, only to get tangled in the sleeves. “I’m stuck,” she whined, peering at me through the gap between the fabric and her forearms.

I rolled my eyes and blew out an exasperated sigh. “Can you at least stand for me?”

“I ‘spose so,” she grumbled, heaving herself upright. In the process she overbalanced, spun in a full one-eighty and toppled backwards. I caught her in the nick of time and pushed her back onto her feet. "Whoops, sorry about that." Her laughter merely added to my growing irritation.

"For goodness' sake, Teddy..." The words trailed off, prompting her to peer at me.

"Ari? Are you going to help me?"

My arms dropped to my sides as my hapless gaze locked onto the welts marring her beautiful skin. I didn't want to look – but I couldn't stop myself. My eyes travelled down her back, to her buttocks and to her thighs – a horrifying sight that compelled me to bite down on my knuckles, masking the anguish clawing through my chest. She had betrayed me. Knowingly. Deliberately. She had visited the one place I had explicitly forbidden – and she had let someone else do this to her.

"Ari, can you please help me!" she shouted, snapping me back into the room, back into the pain she'd caused by shattering our trust — and, most alarmingly, our love.

Stuck in my own head, I forced myself to untangle the mess of fabric trapping her arms. Once she was free, I dragged my lead-filled legs into the walk-in wardrobe, stripped out of my drenched clothes, and redressed with mechanical detachment.

Afterwards, I numbly dried her off and guided her into bed. She passed out instantly, unaware of anything — including my absence.

I stormed into the kitchen and cancelled our dinner plans with the Coopers. Facing anyone in my current state was impossible. My stomach churned, my anger roiled, and the thought of sitting across from friends discussing BDSM over a glass of wine felt absurd.

As it stood, Teddy couldn't entertain anyone. She wasn't even conscious enough to realise I'd left the room.

The remainder of my night was spent sprawled across the black leather modular, drinking far less bourbon than I expected while I simmered over Teddy's reckless behaviour.

First and foremost — what in God's name had she been thinking, mixing alcohol and illicit drugs with her antidepressants? I didn't dare dwell on the possible consequences. Shaking my head in disbelief, I knew there was only one way to handle this disastrous turn of events: I had to sit Teddy down and talk to her about her reprehensible behaviour. Or at least attempt to, even if it killed me.

Ridiculously, it was the conversation I feared most. I wasn't worried about how she'd receive my concern — it was the responses that might follow. I wasn't sure I was prepared to hear her excuses. And if there was even the slightest chance her mother had been right... I needed to know. More to the point, I needed to prove that woman wrong — prove that Teddy wouldn't intentionally break my heart.

I scrubbed at my face and rolled off the cushions, my bare feet hitting the cool tiles before I pushed myself upright. Not forgetting my glass or the bottle of bourbon, I wandered out to the balcony and set both on the wide timber railing. Leaning my elbows beside them, I stared out over the crowded harbour with a bitterness I couldn't swallow.

My resentment extended to the moored boats and their high-spirited guests, all enjoying their hosts' hospitality in the balmy night air. Across the water, restaurants and clubs buzzed with life; like Melbourne, Sydney never slept, encouraging stragglers to stay out until sunrise. Once upon a time, that had been me. Now I was just another person choosing to "party" from the safety of home. The only difference: I was a party of one — an injured party of one at that.

I lifted my half-filled tumbler and sipped gingerly, contemplating the mess my life had become. How was I meant to handle our relationship now? Since the moment we became a couple, I had devoted every waking second to Teddy — the woman I'd loved for years and had just asked to marry me. Love, trust, honesty… three virtues I now found myself questioning. And ironically enough, they were the same virtues I'd thrown at Emmett not long ago. Imagining the smug prick rubbing every last one of them back in my face made me feel nothing short of foolish.

Downing the last of my bourbon, I stalked back across the tiles into the kitchen, rinsed my glass under the tap, and left it in the sink. I headed toward the bedroom, only to stop with my hand on the door handle.

Teddy's duplicity had left a bitter taste in my mouth — and a gaping hole in my chest — making the decision for me. I turned away and detoured to one of the spare bedrooms, choosing the one furthest away from her.

Bacon, eggs, and coffee were usually an arousing combination to wake up to — not this morning. The familiar ache returned the moment the scent hit me. Cooking smells and blaring bass meant Teddy was up. A bit early for music that loud, I thought, glancing at the bedside clock. I had to look twice. Nine o'clock. I had never slept that late in my life.

I rolled off the mattress sluggishly, scrubbing a hand through my unruly hair before pushing to my feet and heading for the ensuite. I showered quietly, half expecting Teddy to burst in and join me as she usually did. To my relief, she didn't. Nor did she appear while I dressed. Maybe she'd thought better of it after last night's disaster. Or maybe she was in denial. Or she simply didn't remember. Considering her state, anything was possible.

Again, it all came back to the conversation ahead.

Slipping on a pair of canvas loafers, I blew out a shuddering sigh and opened the bedroom door, making my way toward the kitchen. The closer I got, the less appealing the inevitable felt.

Teddy was whistling along to Halsey's Bad at Love while buoyantly flipping eggs onto a plate and pouring my usual coffee at the island bench. "I hope you're hungry — breakfast is ready."

My stomach revolted. I swallowed hard as bile crept dangerously close to the surface. How could she act so buoyant? So damned flippant? Wordlessly, I slid a barstool out from beneath the white quartz breakfast bar and perched on the upholstered seat. My sullen gaze tracked her as she bounced between the cooktop and the island with eggs for herself.

My nerves were too shot to eat. Between the loud music and the whistling, something inside me snapped. My cup shattered as I hurled it at the fridge. Hot coffee streaked down the stainless steel, pooling darkly across the grey tiles.

Startled, Teddy screamed, "What the hell, Ari!"

The stool crashed behind me as I shot to my feet. "I ought to be asking you the same fucking thing," I snarled, snatching up her iPhone and flicking the music off.

Heat crept into her cheeks. She set the frying pan down, switched off the gas burner, and walked tentatively to the sofa, lowering herself slowly.

I scoffed as she wrapped her arms around her waist. "Your demeanour tells me you know exactly what I'm talking about.

Where did you go yesterday, Teddy?" Silence. "Answer me, dammit."

"What do you want me to say, Ari?" She at least met my eyes. "That I went out to a BDSM club and did the unspeakable?"

"What. Club. Did. You. Go. To?" Fury laced every clipped word.

Her guilt-ridden eyes lifted heavenward. "Does it matter which one..."

"Don't be fucking evasive. WHAT club?"

She flinched. "Forbidden. I went to Club Forbidden. Are you happy now?"

I inhaled sharply. The irony was almost laughable. How that place was still operating was beyond me. "No, I'm not happy. Firstly, because you went behind my back — cheating on me — and secondly, why in God's name would you go there? One of the worst clubs with the worst reputation?"

Teddy half-shrugged. "It was the first one that came up in the search engine, and it wasn't that bad."

Infuriated by her barefaced attitude, my gaze hardened. "How would you know? You were too off your fucking head to know the difference. And don't bother asking how I know — you already know the answer."

"Seth and Davina," she muttered, defiant.

Her composure was eerily still. She knew I was furious, yet she sat there calm, fearless, as if everything in her world was perfectly fine. I frowned. Where had the beautiful woman I loved disappeared to?

I pressed on. "You're aware Forbidden is a club specifically for hardcore participants, aren't you?"

"Yeah, so what?"

I stared, incredulous, my brain evaporating under the heat of her carelessness. “How could you betray me like this? How could you go to a club renowned for breaking rules? A club so unsafe even Seth and Davina refuse to scene there. Surely that’s reason enough. Perhaps that’s what you want, Teddy. Would being abused make you feel something again? Is my love not enough to reach you anymore? Because right now, that’s the message I’m receiving — loud and fucking clear.”

“Like you, I needed a release. You use the gym. I use BDSM.”

Astounded, my jaw dropped. “That’s not remotely comparable.”

“You get a workout either way, don’t you?”

“Jesus Christ, Teddy. I can’t deal with this — with us — anymore.” My arms flung outward, motioning between us. “We’ll attend Jason and Tim’s party tonight, but when we come home, I’m going back to my place, and you can go to yours. I need a break.”

I stalked toward the foyer and yanked the front door open, slamming it behind me.

So much for our trip becoming one of reconnection.

28

Teddy

The front door rattled in its frame long after Ari disappeared behind it. The echo vibrated through my skull, sharp enough to slice through the last remnants of the hangover I'd been pretending I didn't have.

For a moment, I just stood there in the kitchen, staring at the splatter of coffee streaking down the fridge, the shattered ceramic glittering across the tiles like tiny accusations. My ears still rang from the music I'd blasted far too loud — a pathetic attempt to drown out the parts of last night I didn't want to remember.

But the silence Ari left behind was louder.

My legs buckled before I realised I was moving, and I sank onto the sofa, arms wrapped around myself as if I could hold my insides together. The eggs on the bench were already cooling, the toast curling at the edges. I'd made breakfast like everything was normal. Like I hadn't detonated our relationship less than twelve hours ago.

I pressed my palms to my eyes, trying to force the memories into order.

The club. The lights. The hands. The drugs.

The numbness I'd chased so desperately I didn't care who I hurt in the process.

Ari's face when he saw the marks on my skin.

That was the image that gutted me.

Not the yelling.

Not the swearing.

Not the cup smashing against the fridge.

It was the look — the devastation — like I'd taken something sacred between us and ground it into the floor.

I curled forward, breath hitching. "What have I done..."

The truth was, I didn't know why I'd gone to Forbidden. Not really. I could pretend it was curiosity, or rebellion, or needing a release — but none of those excuses held up under the weight of Ari's heartbreak.

I'd gone because I was spiralling.

Because I didn't know how to sit with my own pain.

Because I didn't know how to ask for help without feeling weak.

Because part of me still believed I didn't deserve him.

And now he wanted a break.

The word lodged in my throat like a shard of glass.

A break.

I dragged my fingers through my hair, wincing as my scalp throbbed. My head pounded, my stomach churned, and my skin still felt cold from the shower he'd shoved me under — a punishment I'd begged for without understanding what I was really asking.

I looked toward the door he'd slammed, half expecting him to walk back in.

He didn't.

Of course he didn't.

For the first time since we'd become a couple, Ari wasn't here to catch me.

And I had no one to blame but myself.

Attending our first New Year's Eve party as a couple was supposed to be exciting — a milestone, something to look forward to. Instead, the day had unravelled from the moment Ari exploded over breakfast. Then he stormed out, leaving me foolish enough to believe that was the end of it. That he'd said his piece. That the worst was over.

I couldn't have been more wrong.

Hours later, I'd barely poured myself a glass of wine when the front door crashed open and Ari stumbled inside, drunk enough that the door rebounded and smacked him in the face. He didn't even flinch.

And everything that followed — the accusations, the confessions, the screaming, the police — only confirmed what I already knew.

I'd broken us. And I didn't know how to fix it. Only just though.

Hours later, I'd barely poured myself a glass of wine when the front door crashed open. Ari stumbled inside, drunk enough that the door rebounded and smacked him in the face. He didn't even flinch.

"You eventually found your way home, I see," I murmured, sliding the Sauvignon Blanc back into the fridge, my voice far steadier than I felt.

He ignored the jab. He slammed the door, lurched toward the kitchen, and jabbed a shaking finger at me. “You went to Forbidden and had sex with another man, didn’t you?” His voice was a vicious snarl, his eyes sharp despite the alcohol. “And don’t you dare try to deny it.”

There was no point denying it. Denial would only make everything worse.

“Yes, Ari, I did.” My throat tightened. “Are you satisfied now?”

His sneer was a knife. “Obviously, you aren’t. I knew I wasn’t enough.” He staggered sideways into the waterfall edge of the island bench, caught himself, then glared at me with a darkness that made my stomach twist. “I bet you’ve done this before, haven’t you?”

“No, Ari. I haven’t. Honestly.”

He stroked his stubbled chin, eyes narrowing. “Mmm. I don’t know whether to believe you. Especially after one particularly sex-crazed morning… you looked a little too experienced for a supposed novice submissive.”

Heat crawled up my neck. Shame, humiliation, and the sting of being dissected under his gaze.

I forced myself to hold his stare. “No, I haven’t,” I repeated, quieter but firmer. “Last night was the first time. Ever.”

His expression didn’t soften. “If you say so. But just so we’re clear — we aren’t doing anything until you’ve had yourself thoroughly checked out. God knows what those sycophant fucks were carrying.”

“I listed bareback as a hard limit—”

“How does that make what you did behind my back any less fucking worse?” he roared, making me flinch.

From there, everything detonated. Our argument spiralled into one of the worst fights we'd ever had — screaming, accusations, tears, venom — until frantic knocking rattled the front door.

The police.

A complaint had been made "on my behalf," according to the handsome Senior Constable. When I asked who made it, he refused to say. He didn't need to. I already knew.

Clementine Conrad — our snobby, eavesdropping neighbour — who stupidly gave herself away by peering through the crack of her slightly ajar door. Ari caught her, and glaring at her only made things worse.

"Keep your sticky nose out of our business!" he snapped, forcing both officers into defensive stances as they braced for the possibility of restraining my drunken fiancé. They ordered Clementine to close her door. For once, she listened.

I stepped in front of Ari. "Trust me, I'm okay. There's no need to arrest or charge anyone," I insisted, darting a look at the officers. Sick of arguing, I yanked off my cardigan and lifted my hair. "See? No bruises. No marks. Anywhere."

They didn't budge.

"Miss, it's our job to make sure you're safe," the Senior Constable replied.

"Do you want me to strip completely to prove he's not a monster?" I snapped, popping the buttons on my blouse before Ari grabbed my hand.

"You shouldn't have to!"

I shot him a glare over my shoulder, mouthing, "You're not helping."

The young female Constable shrugged. “Regardless, we’re required by law to advise you to call triple zero if you feel threatened by Mr Jaeger.”

“I’m fine,” I refuted sharply. “And I’m not under any threat.” Their scepticism was infuriating. I crossed my arms. “If you weren’t aware, Ari’s the CEO of Jaeger Property Development. He’d be a fool to jeopardise everything he’s worked for. His father and uncle are highly respected criminal lawyers. And he despises abusers. So your concern is completely unfounded.”

They exchanged a look — disbelief mixed with resignation — before the Senior Constable relented. “Fine. But here’s my card.” He made a point of staring at Ari as he handed it to me. “Just in case.”

I shoved it into the pocket of my pink linen shorts. “As I said, Ari would never hurt me. Whether you believe me or not is on you.”

I stepped back, gripping the doorframe, silently urging them to leave. Thankfully, they did. I lingered in the doorway until the lift dinged and the stainless-steel doors slid shut — the Senior Constable’s bright blue eyes locked on me the entire time.

Knowing full well Clementine was watching through her peephole, I yelled, “In future, Mrs Conrad, mind your own goddamned business — and get a goddamned life while you’re at it!”

Her scandalised gasp echoed through the hall. “Well, I never!”

Satisfied she’d heard me, I spun on my heel and slammed the door theatrically behind me.

My smirk faded instantly. Ari was gone.

And this time, he hadn’t just stepped out to cool off.

He’d disappeared.

As I stepped past the foyer and further into the apartment, I found him in the living room with a bottle of bourbon in one hand and another full glass in the other. His gorgeous body swayed drunkenly as he danced around the sofas toward the balcony, singing along to the rock ballad blaring from the overhead speakers — The Arctic Monkeys' R U Mine.

He paused in the wide-open doorway when he spotted me, taking in my disgusted expression. "Do you like my choice of song? Quite fitting, wouldn't you agree?"

My lips tightened. "Charming, Ari. Really charming. Why don't you just get it all out of your system and yell at me some more if that's how you truly feel."

He waved the bottle at me impatiently. "No. I'm over yelling... it's exhausting..."

I scoffed. "So you'd rather use music as your way of showing how much you resent me instead?"

He laughed — hysterically, cruelly — before jolting to a stop and slamming the bottle onto the small glass table beside the bi-fold doors. My heart raced as he inched toward me in slow, wobbling steps. He stabbed a finger at his chest, his voice gravelly and fraying at the edges. "Unlike you — I at least have the decency to behave in a transparent manner."

Tears stung the backs of my eyes. His words hit harder than any shouting ever could. And his feelings didn't stop there. The song switched to Bishop Briggs' River, and the lyrics he sang along with felt like a verdict — a confirmation of everything he thought of me now. Of us. Of what I'd destroyed.

What if I was wrong? What if I was just overthinking, like always?

But as my tears spilled freely, I knew Ari meant every word, even if saying them hurt him. He'd never minced his words in all the years I'd known him. I wasn't an exception.

I had no one to blame but myself for going to Forbidden — the one place named after the one instruction Ari had explicitly given me.

"In no uncertain terms was I to visit or participate in a BDSM club without him. Ever. And performing sex with strangers was totally out of the question. Period."

I'd broken that rule. I'd broken him. And the issue had clearly festered in his mind all day while he obliterated himself with alcohol, widening the gulf between us.

So now, as I dressed — an intimate ritual we usually shared — I was alone. The absence of his compliments, his hands, his warmth... it was a physical ache. I bent to slip my feet into my heels, dragging my fingertips over the rough texture. A small, sad smile tugged at my lips. Ari loved me in heels — mostly because they accentuated the length of my legs, as he'd told me more than once.

"It has nothing to do with my legs," I'd teased. "You have a foot fetish, plain and simple."

He'd disputed it, of course. "Not at all. I simply like the look of your legs in those overpriced heels with their ridiculously high stilettos."

It was because of that obsession that I'd secretly packed the heels — and *the dress* from my twenty-first — to surprise him tonight. But since he'd decided to start the party early at the bar downstairs, I wouldn't be getting the reaction I'd hoped for.

I lifted the pointed toes off the floor and sighed. What a waste of a perfectly good outfit for a party I didn't even want to attend.

But we were expected. Playing the role of the happy couple wouldn't be easy — not in a crowd of people who knew him so well.

What I really wanted was to curl up on the sofa with a bottle of wine and cry myself into oblivion. Mrs Conrad would love that. But that would make me a hypocrite, considering Ari's current state.

He was hurting. I understood that. But drowning his sorrows wasn't the answer. It only fed the anger, blurring the rational part of him. And I'd worn the brunt of that all day.

Again — my own stupid fault.

I needed to move, or he'd start banging on the door again. He'd already bellowed at me twice in the last hour, crudely telling me to hurry up. His impatience, paired with the constant cussing, had stomped on my last nerve.

Blowing out a shaky breath, I rose from the velvet stool and twirled in front of the full-length mirror. I winced at the red welts across my back. Maybe wearing a dress with a deep V was a bad idea. Too late now. Time to face the music.

As I opened the bedroom door and stepped into the living room, the rim of Ari's half-filled tumbler paused at his mouth. His darkened gaze raked over my attire. For a moment — a single, fragile second — time stilled. I thought maybe, just maybe, something in him softened.

I was wrong.

Not a flicker of adoration. Not a nod of approval. Nothing but open contempt.

My heart sank into the chasm already carved wide open inside me.

I swallowed hard and attempted a small, hopeful smile. Ari rejected it instantly, snorting before tossing back the rest of his bourbon in one gulp.

My brows furrowed. I didn't realise it would hurt this much — but it did. It hurt in a way that hollowed me out completely, dragging me back into the dark I'd fought so hard to escape.

Back into the place where the future I'd imagined with Ari Jaeger no longer felt certain.

∞

Ari

About to throw my umpteenth bourbon back, I paused at the sharp clicking of Teddy's heels. My hazy gaze lifted over the rim of my glass, and for a moment — a fleeting, treacherous moment — I simply stared.

She looked beautiful. Of course she did.

The short white sequinned dress.

The glittering heels.

The familiar silhouette.

It took my fogged brain a second to place it, and then it hit me.

Her twenty-first. That night. That dress.

I should've felt something close to joy. Instead, irritation flared. She thought — in whatever deluded corner of her mind — that wearing that would soften me. That nostalgia would make me benevolent.

It didn't.

It vexed me further.

She smiled coquettishly, that beautiful, flirtatious smile she'd always reserved for me. For a heartbeat, she gave me a glimpse of the woman I'd loved my entire life — even when her choices were questionable. Especially her latest escapades.

The thought alone made an irreverent snort burst from me as I tossed back the bourbon. My reaction visibly upset her; her brows furrowed, her expression tightening.

But Teddy recovered quickly. A mask slid over her features — impassive, self-assured — as she strode behind me. My head turned stiffly, following the measured click of her heels to the fridge. She noticed, of course, as she bent to retrieve the bottle of Dom Pérignon I'd bought for tonight.

"Spit out whatever else is on your chest burdening you, Ari."

I had every intention of doing exactly that. But as I swivelled and opened my mouth, I choked on the last dribble of bourbon. "Shouldn't you cover up that abhorrent state on your back, Teddy?" I spluttered, wiping my mouth with the back of my hand before gesturing angrily at the deep V of her dress. I slammed the tumbler onto the bench. "Or would you rather people judge and assume the worst of me?"

She rolled her eyes as she poured champagne. "No one would ever dare assume the worst of you. Even me, believe it or not. You're the great, perfect, do-no-wrong Ari Jaeger. Words I used to describe you to the police earlier, remember?"

"But did you actually mean them?"

Her lashes flicked up sharply as she glowered. "Who knows after today..."

"Well, haven't you sunk to a new low? Who knew you were so bloody capable! Maybe the apple doesn't fall far from the tree after all!"

Pools of hurt replaced her anger. Her eyes misted. "If that's how you feel, then perhaps we ought to call off the engagement. God forbid you're forced to marry my mother."

My nostrils flared. "At least I'd know exactly where I stood."

She slammed the champagne flute onto the bench and yanked my handkerchief from my jacket pocket. Delicately, she dabbed at her tears, careful not to ruin her makeup. "I understand that you're hurt, Ari, but sinking that low is even beneath you."

Her perfume drifted toward me — that soft, floral scent I'd always loved. I closed my eyes, breathing it in, clinging desperately to the reasons I'd fallen in love with her. But the alcohol blurred everything. When I opened my eyes again, they travelled down her lean figure — a body I'd cherished, believing it would remain untouched by another man for the rest of our lives.

How wrong I'd been.

I spun back to the bench and shakily refilled my glass. Then I turned, holding it up in a mocking salute. "Well, we're perfect for each other then," I growled, just as the door buzzer sounded. "That'll be our driver."

I set the empty glass in the sink. "Shall we go and at least pretend for the evening that we're happy and madly in love?" It wasn't entirely a lie. I still loved her — deeply, madly — and I wasn't ready to give up. Not yet.

A humourless laugh escaped her. "Sure. Why not."

She curled one arm through mine, clutching her silver purse with the other. We plastered tight smiles onto our faces and walked toward the door. I twisted the handle and stepped aside.

"After you."

My face was going to ache by the end of the night.

29

Jason flung open the door with the enthusiasm of a man greeting royalty — until he actually saw me.

"Ari! You're—"

His smile collapsed.

"Oh, darling... you're drunker than a sailor on shore leave."

I chuckled, earning a synchronised eye-roll from both Jason and Teddy.

"This is not amusing, Ari Jaeger," Jason scolded, hands on hips. "What am I supposed to do with you? And what would your dear mother say about this behaviour?"

I scoffed. "Who do you think taught me to drink?"

Jason gasped as if I'd insulted the Pope.

"Do not drag Audrina Jaeger into your bourbon-soaked downfall. That woman is a saint, and I will defend her with my life."

Before I could respond, he looped an arm through mine and hauled me inside with surprising strength.

"You need food," he declared, waving a pair of tongs like a conductor's baton. "And not the liquid kind you've been inhaling."

He piled a gold-rimmed plate with pastries and fruit, then thrust it onto the table.

"My love, you're two bourbons away from interpretive dancing, and nobody deserves that. Sit. Stay. Eat."

I bristled.

"If you start scratching behind my ears, I'm leaving."

Jason didn't miss a beat.

"Darling, if I scratch anything on you tonight, it'll be your dignity back into place."

I glowered but obeyed, shoving a pastizzi into my mouth like a sulking child.

"I'm not a bloody dog."

Jason ignored me entirely.

"Now that we've dealt with the reprobate," he announced, turning to Teddy with a dazzling smile, "I'm Jason Kline — Ari's business partner, COO of JPD Sydney, and tonight's designated babysitter."

Teddy extended a hand, cheeks warming as Jason lifted it to his lips.

"Teddy McGovern, the reprobate's fiancée."

"I can still hear you," I muttered around a mouthful of salmon vol-au-vent.

Jason waved a dismissive hand.

"We know, sweetheart. We're ignoring you until you stop speaking in italics."

Teddy snorted. I scowled.

Jason slid an arm around her waist.

"You, girlfriend, are simply gorgeous. Ari undersold you terribly."

"Lucky you're gay then," I grumbled.

Jason didn't even look at me.

"Nobody asked for your opinion, angel."

He guided Teddy toward the living room.

"Come, my dear. I must introduce you to my husband, Tim. He will absolutely adore you."

Left at the buffet like a misbehaving toddler, I crossed my legs and watched from a distance as Teddy charmed both Jason and Tim with ease.

Then — because the universe clearly hated me — Ricky Martin's voice blasted through the speakers, crooning about beautiful women in leather and lace.

Perfect.

Just what I needed.

A song about seduction and temptation while my fiancée mingled with half the room looking like a goddess.

I growled under my breath, resisting the urge to bribe the DJ to change it. Jason was already cross enough with me.

"So where is the charming and delicious Ari Jaeger?" Tim asked, scanning the room.

Jason didn't hesitate.

"We left him by the buffet, sobering up. He was halfway cooked when he arrived."

I rolled my eyes so hard I nearly saw my brain.

If Jason tried to spank me for being disrespectful, I'd probably let him — purely for the irony.

Apart from their equal height, I'd never truly noticed just how opposite Jason and Tim were in appearance. Jason's chestnut waves were styled to perfection, every strand obeying him like a well-trained soldier, while Tim's blond hair was wild and unruly — much like mine. Jason preferred tailored suits and polished shoes; Tim lived in tight muscle tees and jeans. Yet despite their contrasting styles, they fit together seamlessly. A perfect balance.

They also had an adopted daughter, Tia — my goddaughter.

At nine years old, she was elegant, astute, and frighteningly talented, mastering the piano before her eighth birthday. With long mahogany curls, warm olive skin, and deep brown eyes that saw only kindness, she was breathtaking. Which, frankly, posed a problem for her future. I pitied any poor lad who dared date her in adolescence. Between Jason, Tim, and myself, she'd never stand a chance of slipping past our overprotective tendencies. Then again, that was typical of me with anyone I loved profoundly.

Teddy was no exception.

From my seat at the buffet, I watched her shine among total strangers, slipping into conversation with effortless grace. She never missed a beat. Neither did my heart. I propped an elbow on the table, clasped my hands, and crossed my ankle over my knee, my gaze glued to her wherever she moved.

Her lithe body swayed as she walked toward me — until a fair-haired woman dressed head-to-toe in silver lightly touched her arm. Their interaction seemed innocent enough, until the woman gestured for Teddy to twirl. I stiffened. As expected, the woman's curiosity sharpened when she caught sight of the red welts across Teddy's back.

My stomach dropped.

I prayed Teddy would offer a plausible explanation.

She did — effortlessly.

She told the woman I'd applied her sunscreen poorly and she'd sunbathed too long in the scorching heat. The lie rolled off her tongue with such ease it almost startled me.

Relief washed through me.

I lifted my coffee just as Teddy approached. My gaze drifted down to her heels, then slowly up the length of her legs, her torso, until I met her brightened eyes.

Despite our blazing row, despite the anger simmering beneath my skin, my body betrayed me. Ignoring her was impossible — not in those heels, not in that dress, not when she looked like every dream I'd ever had.

Teddy broke the silence first.

"Dance with me, please? If we're going to keep up this charade, we need to look the part."

Her eyes — apologetic, shimmering beneath smoky shadow — pleaded with me as Kelly Clarkson's Slow Dance drifted through the speakers.

"How could I forget?" I murmured bitterly, taking her hand and leading her to the centre of the makeshift dancefloor.

One arm circled her waist; the other slid over the bare skin of her back, tracing the soft curve of her spine. I drew her hips flush against mine. Her breath hitched, her hazel eyes darkening as a soft gasp escaped her parted lips.

Instinctively, our lips brushed — a delicate, tentative connection that deepened with each passing second. Our hearts pounded in unison, the kiss slow and aching, reminding me that despite everything, the depth of our feelings hadn't changed.

Not really. Not at all.

Barely four months together, and we'd already weathered more heartbreak than most couples faced in a lifetime. Yet somehow, by some miracle, we were still standing. Barely — but standing.

A mournful sound escaped Teddy as she buried her face in the crook of my neck, tears slipping onto my skin. She hid from the prying eyes around us, but I felt every tremor.

"I'm sorry," she whispered. "For hurting you. It was unforgivable."

I closed my eyes and drew her closer, resting my cheek against her forehead. I inhaled the sweet jasmine scent I craved more often than I cared to admit. We swayed in place, feet unmoving, song after song passing as we held each other.

We nursed our wounds the only way we knew how — quietly, intimately, clinging to the fragile thread that still bound us together.

Eventually, we parted — a separation that left us both feeling bereft and empty. But Teddy had needs, and as she sauntered off toward one of the many opulent bathrooms in Jason and Tim's house, I ventured to the bar and requested my usual choice of poison.

Jason's voice rose behind me, dripping with theatrical disapproval. "I hope you're taking it easy, Jaeger. We don't need a sequel to your earlier performance, Mister."

I clutched the tumbler and chuckled. "I don't plan on it, trust me. And look — ice. That's practically sobriety."

Jason narrowed his eyes, unimpressed. "Darling, adding ice doesn't make it water. It just makes you delusional."

I tossed a cashew into my mouth with a shrug. "And yet here you are, supervising me like a disappointed nanny."

Jason sniffed, lifting his champagne. “Someone has to. You’re a full-time job when you’re vertical.”

My tickled gaze flickered comically. “I don’t doubt it for a second.”

Jason pointedly nodded in Teddy’s direction. Upon her return from the bathroom, she had hit up Tim, dragging him back to the dancefloor. A twerking Tim was an image forever ingrained as they kicked up a storm to the DJ’s upbeat music selection.

“Your gorgeous lady has enchanted us all with her charms. Congrats on finally snagging the girl of your dreams, even though it appeared to take a millennium.”

“A slight exaggeration,” I simpered, “but I would’ve waited longer if I had to.”

A fib my perceptive friend saw through.

“Whose leg are you trying to pull?”

I snorted. “Not yours, that’s for sure.”

“Pity. You’re such a handsome devil, too, Ari Jaeger.”

My brows shot up. “Are you hitting on me?”

Jason waved a dismissive hand, mocking me. “Don’t flatter yourself.”

“Oh, you wound me.” I chuckled, feigning hurt. Then I steered the conversation toward a subject much lighter, and far more pleasant. “How’s my gorgeous goddaughter?”

Pride washed over Jason’s expressive face. “Growing like a weed, and even more beautiful with each passing day, if that’s possible. Perhaps I’m just biased.”

“In all the years we’ve known each other,” I ventured, “I’ve never bothered to ask how Tia came to be yours.”

Not that it mattered — she was adored by one of the most loving couples I’d ever known, besides my parents, of course.

Jason sipped his champagne before replying. “We’ve never discussed it openly because it never felt important. All that mattered was that she completed our little family.”

“Was a surrogate used?”

“No — adoption. At the time we wanted a child, surrogacy unfortunately wasn’t even an option thanks to our backward country.”

I placed my glass on the bar and indicated to the bartender for a top-up. “Oh. I always assumed Tim’s sister had carried her. Apart from the dark eyes, Tia looks incredibly like you.”

“Aw, thank you. I always thought so too,” he gushed, smiling widely.

“Agency or private adoption?”

Jason’s head cocked. “Why the Spanish Inquisition, Ari? Are you and Teddy unable to have children?”

“She’s rather fertile, believe me. I’m just curious, is all.” Leaning a forearm on the bar, I picked up my refilled tumbler and took a tentative sip. “My mother had four children naturally, so I wondered what it was like for people who couldn’t.”

“Fair enough. My darling sister Camille never had any issues conceiving either. She only had to drop her pants and poof — pregnant. Five children later, the last one a wonderful surprise, of course.” He paused, leaning closer to whisper, “But between you, me, and the lamp post, I think my nephew inherited the gay gene.”

A hearty laugh rumbled out of me. “Well, if that’s the case, your nephew has two wonderful uncles who’ll be there to offer some much-needed guidance.”

“Or lead him astray up the garden path.”

"Or that too. Where is my precocious little petal tonight anyway?" I smiled fondly, thinking of my precious goddaughter. "I was looking forward to seeing Tia."

Jason blew out a disheartened sigh. "The little petal wanted a sleepover with her cousins. Can you believe she chose to sleep under the stars over the party of the year?"

Another hearty laugh erupted. "Without a doubt, my worrywart friend, Tia's undoubtedly scoffing her face with crap food and having a marvellous time. Don't become one of those helicopter parents, for God's sake, or you'll suffocate her."

He scoffed. "That will be you, not me."

Jason had me pegged; that would indeed be me.

I chuckled affectionately. "True. So tell me, where on earth did Tia inherit such a precious gift for the piano? Because she certainly didn't get it from you."

"Now I'm the one who's mortally wounded." Jason laid a hand over his heart. "Honestly? I don't know. Maybe her mother or father played? It was a silly notion I swiftly put to bed."

"Oh? How so?"

"How could a drug-addicted parent own such a talent?"

Without making eye contact, Jason held out his glass, and the bartender intuitively topped it up.

"How did you know the birth mother was a drug addict?"

"Doctor Garner — he informed us before the birth out of courtesy."

The name hit me like a slap. My pulse spiked.

"A Doctor Richard Garner?"

Jason's brows creased. "Yes, the same one. Do you know him?"

I shook my head far too quickly. "No. I've just heard the name in passing, that's all — one of the best OBGYNs around. You know me, only the best where Teddy's concerned when the time arises."

The biggest cockamamie lie ever to roll off my tongue, yet Jason accepted it without hesitation.

"Of course. You can never be too careful when it comes to the safe delivery of our loved ones."

"Of course." I forced a tight smile and kept digging. "So... did this Doctor Garner's courtesy extend to helping you and Tim finalise the adoption?"

"Yes, as a matter of fact, it did. He also delivered Tia and brought her to us the night she was born. She arrived two weeks early — did I ever mention that?"

He downed the rest of his champagne and had his glass refilled before I could blink.

My gut twisted. If my instincts were right, there was a very real chance Tia was Teddy's supposedly dead child.

"No, you never did. But do tell me more — this is rather interesting." I waved a hand, encouraging him to continue, masking the tremor in my fingers.

Deep dimples flashed as Jason warmed to the topic, singing like a canary. My grip tightened around my glass with every detail. Then he dropped a name that made my spine snap straight.

"Sorry — I believe I misheard you. Did you say you met the grandmother?"

Jason nodded. "Yes. The night Tia was handed over to us, she was present. Stunning woman — bright red hair, classy too. If only I could remember her name."

Rage surged, hot and blinding. I downed my drink in one swallow and signalled sharply for another.

"Oh! I remember now." Jason flapped excitedly. "Therese — the grandmother's name was Therese Burgoyne."

The glass slipped from my hand.

30

Whilst a waiter promptly swept up the remnants of shattered glass around our feet, my mind spun violently with the weight of what I'd just uncovered. I needed space — and answers — before I lost the ability to mask the storm brewing inside me.

I cleared my throat. "My apologies, Jace, but I ought to call my parents before they're far too inebriated to recognise my voice."

Jason's dry scorn cut through the noise.

"The way you're throwing those drinks down, you'll be speaking a garbled mess along with them, my friend."

I chuckled, forcing ease I didn't feel. "True. Do you mind terribly if I borrow your office to call them? Less noisy in there."

His mockery flipped instantly into exuberance. "Ooh, you can see the latest photo of Tia while you're in there!"

His grin, bright with paternal pride, was infectious. He practically danced across the tiled floors, leading me down a short hallway before flinging open a set of double doors with theatrical flair.

He stepped aside, gesturing grandly toward the back wall. "Ta-da!"

I looked up.

Mounted above a sleek glass desk hung an enormous canvas — at least three feet by five. Jason, Tim, and Tia lay on sunlit grass, dressed in matching white shirts and denim, bare feet kicked up behind them. The mid-morning light haloed Tia's glossy mahogany curls, illuminating her cheeky grin.

But it was her expression — that scrunched little nose, that impish smile — that punched the air from my lungs.

Teddy wore that same look as a child. Exactly that look.

Jason slapped my shoulder, jolting me. "Your silence says it all, my friend."

I forced a scoff. "I have no idea what you're talking about."

Thankfully, he was too intoxicated to notice the real reason behind my stunned stare.

He chuckled, his glassy gaze drifting back to the canvas. "Tia's beauty — I feel precisely the same way whenever I see her." He steepled his hands, eyes softening. "I'm going to have kittens the day she brings home her first boyfriend. Or girlfriend. Whatever floats her boat."

A shaky breath escaped me, rattling through my chest. "Yeah... I'm not looking forward to that part either."

"Stress less, my friend. It'll be a few years before that happens with your precious goddaughter."

I ran a hand through my hair, chuckling weakly. "Of course."

Jason clinked his glass against mine. "On that crazy note, I'll leave you to call your parents. And don't forget to send my love."

Leaning casually against the edge of his desk, I tugged my mobile from my jacket pocket. “You do realise they’ll forget by morning that I even made an effort to call.”

Jason laughed loudly as he backed toward the door. “That I do believe is true.”

He spun on the heel of his atrocious loafers, waltzing out with a wink and a pointed finger. “Good luck.”

I snorted. “Thanks. I’m going to need it.”

If only he understood the true meaning behind my jest.

The moment he disappeared, I rushed across the room and clicked the lock — more for my nerves than any real security. It didn’t help. My hands shook as I turned to the custom lateral filing system lining the wall.

Never in my life had I stooped to something so dishonest. But there was a first time for everything.

Jason’s meticulous organisation made the search insultingly easy. Well. That was convenient.

A small victory — short-lived.

I sank into his outrageously opulent velvet office chair and flicked open the manila folder clutched in my hand. My gaze widened, my mouth dried, and my pulse thundered as I scanned Tia’s birth certificate.

I blinked. Reread the date. Swallowed hard. Oh, surely not.

Fuck. Fuck. And double fuck.

Perhaps I misread?

No — the numbers were clear.

Coincidence? People shared birthdays all the time.

Or a typo? Government staff made mistakes.

Yes. A typo. I clung to that.

But as I turned to the adoption papers, flicking through each page with increasing desperation, denial became impossible. The scrawled signature in the bottom left corner sealed it.

I tutted bitterly, laying each page out in front of me like evidence in a trial.

"You truly do lack a conscience, Therese McGovern," I murmured, lifting my mobile to scan copies for Garrett.

Time had slipped through my fingers by the time I finished reconciling the truth: Tia was indeed Teddy and Emmett's daughter. An unsettling realisation — but what could I do about it? Nothing. Not yet.

I gathered everything into a neat pile, intending to return it before Jason or Teddy came looking for me. But as I slid the documents back into the folder, a small photograph fluttered out and landed face-up on my lap.

An infant Tia.

I could only assume Doctor Garner had given it to them.

Leaning back in the chair, I held the photo between my fingertips. Despite everything, I couldn't help but smile. As a newborn, she was adorable — still was. Perhaps I was biased. Her button nose, rosy cupid's bow mouth, that mop of dark hair so similar to mine... her features were perfect in every way.

But the dark eyes? Emmett's. Without question.

Fortunately for us, Tia didn't view the world as he did.

My gaze drifted to the oddly shaped freckle on the arm of the person holding her — a freckle I knew too well. The confirmation hit me like a blow to the chest. The implications followed swiftly, each one heavier than the last.

My stomach lurched. I clamped a hand over my mouth, swallowing hard against the rising bile. How did one even begin to navigate something like this? How did I confront the people I loved with a truth that would shatter them?

Teddy would be overjoyed at first — that much was inevitable. But once the joy faded, the hurt would come. Then the anger. And that terrified me. She was already showing signs of regression, and the thought of her mother's betrayal... I couldn't bear to imagine the fallout.

Then there was Jason and Tim. How would they cope? They had fought so hard to become parents, weathered so much adversity, and Tia was their world. If she were taken from them, they'd be destroyed.

But above all else, Tia would suffer the most.

Why should an innocent little girl pay the price for someone else's selfishness? I would never allow that. Not while I still drew breath.

I shoved a hand through my hair and blew out a shuddering breath, taking one last look at the photo before slipping it back between the birth certificate and adoption papers. But as I returned the folder to its place in the filing cabinet, frustration clawed at me.

Hiding the truth from Teddy — and from Jason and Tim — felt like swallowing glass. I knew it would come back to bite me eventually. But for now, it was the only option. The only way to protect them all until the time was right.

Whenever that would be.

I slammed the drawer shut, the sound echoing through the office, and realised I didn't have an answer.

Not even close.

The party was in full swing by the time I reappeared, grabbing a bourbon from a passing waiter's tray. Over the thumping bass of an R&B artist I didn't recognise, Teddy's boisterous laughter drifted from the outside deck, ringing through the warm night air.

Breathless, she pressed a hand to her chest.

"Oh my God, Jason, you're so crude!"

I raised a brow. That was news?

Drawn to her instantly, everything else faded into instinct. My arm slipped around her narrow waist from behind, my lips brushing the base of her nape as my fingers grazed the curve of her spine. She shivered beneath my touch.

"I was certain I warned you before meeting him, Teddy?" I droned, joining the conversation midway. My jest earned a playful slap to my shoulder from my faux-offended friend.

Jason scoffed. "Oh, that's the pot calling the kettle black, Jaeger. I'll have you know I had an innocent mouth until I met you."

My lips twisted in amusement. "Have you been comparing notes with Bryson? Because he once spoke those precise words, if I recall..."

Teddy giggled. "Before you drowned him in the pool." She paused, then added quickly, "Figuratively speaking," as dread washed over Jason's mortified face.

"Please don't throw me in the pool," he begged, gesturing frantically to his outfit. "This suit cost me a small fortune!"

I laughed heartily. "Don't worry, old friend. I'll wait until you're in those bloody horrible budgie smugglers."

He inched closer, lifting a perfectly shaped eyebrow. "You may mock my swimsuit, Ari Jaeger, but I'll have you know they're what scored me the hottest man in history."

With a dramatic flick of his wrist and a click of his fingers, Jason pirouetted on the heel of his loafer and marched off into the crowd, leaving us behind.

"Still a drama queen, I see," I murmured, spinning Teddy around and drawing her closer.

She melted into me instantly. Nuzzling her neck, I trailed my lips over her softly scented skin. She moaned softly, head tipping back to grant me better access.

"Are you ready to get out of here?"

Her answer came in the form of a firm, hungry press of her lips against mine.

She was more than ready.

Despite my drunken reaction to Teddy's betrayal — and my firm declaration that nothing intimate would happen between us until after testing — every shred of resolve I'd clung to dissolved the instant we stepped back into the apartment.

It wasn't rational. It wasn't wise. It certainly wasn't what I'd promised myself.

But the moment the door clicked shut behind us, the weight of the night crashed over me — the secrets, the discoveries, the fear of what lay ahead — and all I wanted, all I needed, was her. The familiar warmth of her presence. The reassurance of her touch. The reminder that, despite everything, we were still tethered to each other in ways neither of us fully understood.

Teddy turned toward me, eyes soft and searching, and whatever fragile boundary I'd tried to erect between us crumbled like ash.

I went against every word I'd spoken. Every rule I'd set. Every line I'd drawn.

Because loving her — even when it hurt — was instinct. And resisting her was impossible.

More importantly, I wanted to savour us — to hold onto whatever fragile peace we still had — regardless of the fact we were due at the airport before dawn. The night had unravelled in ways I hadn't anticipated, and the truth I'd uncovered sat like a stone in my chest, but none of it mattered once we crossed the threshold of the apartment.

We were still making love as the sun crept through the windows, blanketing the city in yet another stifling summer's day.

It wasn't planned. It wasn't sensible.

It certainly wasn't what I'd vowed only hours earlier.

But the moment her hands found me, the moment her breath mingled with mine, every boundary I'd tried to erect collapsed. I needed her — not out of desire alone, but out of something deeper, something raw and terrified and human. I needed the reassurance of her warmth, the familiarity of her body curled against mine, the reminder that despite the chaos, despite the secrets, despite the hurt, we were still tethered.

And she needed me just as fiercely.

Together, we collapsed onto the dishevelled bed, holding each other close.

Our lips softly grazing, I brushed the damp hair from Teddy's brow and swallowed hard.

"I love you..."

Teary hazel eyes searched my face. "But?"

My resolute gaze held hers. "We must remain pragmatic about our future — finding our way back to each other by rebuilding trust... You hurt me deeply."

A deep, shuddering breath escaped her as tears spilled freely. "I know... and I'll do anything to gain that back."

"Actions speak louder than words, Teddy. Isn't that what you once told your father?"

She nodded stiffly.

"I need your absolute promise that it won't ever happen again."

Her head bobbed with earnest conviction. "I promise."

Doubt lingered — stubborn, unwelcome — even as I rolled and pulled her tightly against my chest. Somehow, I had to find it within me to lay those doubts to rest and trust she wouldn't jeopardise our relationship any further.

So I let the night take us.

Let the dawn find us tangled together.

Let the world wait.

Because for those few stolen hours, nothing existed beyond the two of us — not the lies, not the fear, not the truth I now carried like a live wire beneath my skin.

Just us.

Just the fragile, desperate love we were still trying to hold together.

Teddy fell asleep almost the moment we levelled out above the clouds. For once, she didn't reach for me, didn't tease, didn't whisper anything suggestive about revisiting the mile-high club. She was simply too exhausted — emotionally, physically, utterly spent.

Her head rested against my shoulder, her breath warm and steady against my neck, and I sat there motionless, afraid that even the slightest shift might disturb her. She deserved the rest. God knew she needed it.

I reached for the porcelain cup on the tray table — elegant, weighty, the kind used on aircraft designed for people who expected refinement at thirty thousand feet. The coffee inside was strong and freshly brewed, its warmth seeping through the china and into my palms. It grounded me in a way bourbon never could. I needed clarity, not oblivion. Not today.

But even the coffee couldn't quiet the truth gnawing at me.

I turned my head slightly, studying Teddy's face in the muted cabin light. She looked younger when she slept — softer, unguarded, almost fragile. The faint shadows beneath her eyes told the story of the last few days: the arguments, the tears, the guilt, the desperate attempts to hold us together.

And now this.

This secret.

This impossible truth lodged beneath my ribs like shrapnel.

Tia.

Her daughter. Alive. Thriving.

Loved by people who had no idea the child in their arms had been stolen from the woman sleeping against me.

My chest tightened painfully.

I brushed a stray curl from Teddy's cheek, careful not to wake her. She murmured something unintelligible and burrowed closer, trusting me completely — the very thing that made my stomach twist.

How was I supposed to tell her?

How was I supposed to shatter her world again when she'd only just begun piecing herself back together?

And Jason… Tim…

The thought of their faces — their devastation — made my throat constrict.

But above all else, it was Tia I kept seeing.

Her smile. Her innocence.

Her entire life built on a lie she never asked for.

I took another sip of coffee, though it tasted like nothing now.

Teddy shifted in her sleep, her fingers curling weakly around my forearm as though she sensed the distance growing inside me. The gesture nearly undid me.

I lowered my head, pressing a soft kiss to her hairline.

"I'm here," I whispered, though she couldn't hear me.

And even if she could, I wasn't sure it was true.

Because the truth was eating me alive.

And sooner or later, it would devour everything we'd fought so hard to rebuild.

31

Our soon-to-be home. Five hundred square metres of brick and mortar to be exact, top to bottom. Preparations for the underground cellar and the pad had already been laid while we were away, putting us slightly ahead of schedule — a win, according to my foreman, Wes Beaumont. He'd assured me that as long as he didn't encounter any unforeseen issues, the handover of keys should still fall within the arranged eighteen-month timeframe. But with Melbourne's unpredictable weather patterns, setbacks were always a probability. Whatever will be, will be.

While I waited for Dad to arrive, I let my gaze drift over the skeletal beginnings of what would one day be our home. Even in its raw, unfinished state — steel bones jutting from the concrete pad, the faint outline of rooms only just taking shape — I could already see Teddy's vision breathing through it.

French-inspired, she'd called it.

Elegant without being ostentatious.

Romantic without being fragile.

The façade would eventually be rendered in a soft, warm stone that caught the afternoon light, giving the whole structure a gentle, timeless glow. Tall, narrow windows with delicate mullions would frame the front, and a steep slate-coloured roofline would crown it all, punctuated by dormer windows that made the house feel as though it had always belonged here.

Inside, she'd designed wide hallways and high ceilings — airy, open spaces that flowed into one another with that effortless French sense of proportion. French doors would open onto a terrace overlooking the back paddock, where a state-of-the-art stable was planned for Bear. Teddy had insisted the stable blend seamlessly with the main house: limestone accents, arched timber doors, and a roofline that echoed the same elegant pitch. Even Bear, apparently, was getting a touch of French luxury.

A curved staircase would greet you the moment you stepped through the front door, its wrought-iron balustrade something she'd sketched a dozen times until it felt right. And the cellar — my contribution — had been softened by her touch too, with arched niches and warm lighting that made it feel carved from the earth rather than poured from concrete.

It was us, in architectural form.

Her softness. My structure. Our future.

A future I was suddenly terrified might not survive the truth I carried.

A horn beeped excitedly, snapping me from my thoughts. Dad's shiny black BMW sedan zoomed toward me before coming to a grinding halt. He opened the door slowly, swinging one leg out at a time. A wry smile tugged at my lips as he pushed to his feet with a groan.

"Do I dare enquire as to why you're exiting the car like an arthritic old man?"

"Your mother and her crazy ideas."

I raised a brow, shaking his proffered hand and patting his back.

"Let me guess — you finally conceded to Mother's nagging about attending Zumba classes with her?"

He grimaced over the top of his sunglasses.

"No, worse — a damned triathlon."

"Oh, that's not so bad. But don't fret, Dad, I'll be sure to be there encouraging you from the sidelines."

"More like mocking my suffering." He scoffed, clearly unimpressed by both the triathlon and my amusement. "You won't be laughing when I'm calling on you to take care of me because I can't walk, or worse can't—"

I held up a hand.

"Please don't elaborate. I get the nauseating picture. But I know a decent massage therapist who can work out the kinks as a preventative measure; she has magical hands," I teased, waggling my brows.

Dad's eyes lit up.

"Do those magical hands happen to give happy endings too?"

"Never bothered to ask. Never felt inclined to either. Besides, Mother would kick our arses for even making such a dastardly suggestion."

"I agree. Her arsenal is well-stocked as it is, and we don't need to give her a reason to use it — on us expressly."

He jerked his chin toward the steel framework.

"The new pad?"

I smiled proudly.

"Yeah. Teddy's design."

"The perfect home for the perfect couple, then?"

My smile slipped, sadness tightening my chest.

If only that were true.

"Our home will be one of a kind, that's for sure."

Dad's brows rose.

"Trouble in paradise, son?"

Perceptive. That was Jaxson Jaeger all over.

I folded my arms, leaning against the side of my car, clutching the precious cargo against my chest.

"It's nothing I can't handle."

He let out a low chuckle, nodding while hiding discerning eyes behind his sunglasses.

"You know where I am if you ever feel the need to talk."

"Ta." I nodded stiffly, then quickly changed the subject, handing him what I considered the golden goose.

"Here's the reason I wanted to meet you away from prying eyes and ears."

He rested the plastic folder in the crook of his elbow and flicked the cover open. His eyes widened as he read the birth certificate.

"What the...? Is this for real? Teddy's daughter — alive?"

If it weren't for the muscles keeping my head attached, it would've fallen off from all the nodding.

"I can't believe it. How did you come across this magical piece of information?" His mouth tightened. "Or daren't I ask?"

"Read the adoption papers. You'll see where."

Dad shoved his sunglasses to the top of his head and dropped beside me, eagerly flicking through the pages. His jaw fell open as he scanned the adoption documents.

"You're kidding me? Jason and Tim inadvertently adopted Teddy's daughter? I can't believe Therese signed the papers..." His voice darkened, scandalised.

"Surprise."

He swiped the back of his hand over his mouth.

"Talk about complicated."

My brows creased.

"How's it complicated? Teddy's supposedly 'dead' child is alive and well, and Therese perjured herself. End of story."

Dad's brows lifted over a suddenly worried gaze.

"Unfortunately, Ari, it's not that cut and dry. Unless we find a way around how you stumbled upon these papers," he said, shaking them at me, "they'll be deemed inadmissible."

So much for being prepared.

I let out an exasperated sigh.

"Why?"

"For a smart man, you astound me," he scolded.

"You acquired confidential information illegally. No judge in their right mind would accept these. And irrespective of the facts, the defence would have a field day. These would be thrown out before they even hit the bench."

I deflated, shoulders sagging.

"Oh. I didn't think of that. Sorry."

A beat.

"Well... what now?"

"Unless I mitigate..."

Dad pressed a finger to his lips, pacing, kicking up clouds of dust with each frantic step.

"If I plant the suggestion that Bill got ahold of the information," he proposed, abruptly stopping and swivelling to face me, "that might be enough to cover our arses."

It was painfully clear what was required to rectify my mistake — even if it meant bending the law further. Anything, if it meant locking those two low-lives up for the rest of their natural, miserable lives.

"Would Bill be up for it, though?"

"You'd be surprised," he murmured.

"Leave it with me."

"All right."

I nodded stiffly, tucking my hands into the pockets of my chino shorts.

"Can we keep this on the down-low for now? I haven't told Teddy yet."

Dad's mouth thinned into a hard line.

"Why not? She's entitled to know."

Under his stern gaze, I shifted uncomfortably.

"Because I didn't want to get her hopes up... in case I was wrong."

"What harm could come from Teddy knowing? She needs to know, Ari — especially if it gives her the closure she needs to move on."

Anger surged, boiling over before I could stop it.

"I don't want Emmett's devil spawn as part of our future!"

Without warning, Dad grabbed me and shoved me firmly against my car. His bright blue eyes turned glacial, jaw ticking with fury.

"First and foremost, I raised you better. Secondly, Tia is your goddaughter — or had you forgotten that?"

He jabbed a finger at my chest.

"She did not ask to be born, nor does she know the circumstances of her conception. And irrespective of who her low-life father is, she is still Teddy's flesh and blood."

I shoved at his chest, snarling,

"Get off me!"

He stepped back, but his disappointment cut deeper than his grip.

"You surprise me, son. I never imagined you could be so cold toward an innocent child. A child you've known since birth. A child with two loving parents who entrusted you with the honour of becoming her godparent if anything ever happened to them."

His finger wagged angrily in my face.

"If I had my way, I'd be advising Jason and Tim to change their will. Immediately. God forbid the day comes when you're left with no choice but to parent a child you claim to despise."

I dragged a hand through my hair, glaring darkly.

"I don't despise Tia."

"You could've fooled me."

I sagged, breath shaking out of me.

"Look... what I said was wrong, okay? The reality of the situation scares me. I worry about Teddy's reaction—"

"That she'll spiral again?"

"Yes. She's fragile. Still."

Dad's expression softened. He stepped forward and pulled me into a firm embrace.

"I know, son. I know."

He stepped back, giving my shoulder a final squeeze before glancing at his watch.

"I'd better get going. Your mother will have my hide if I'm late."

I huffed a weak laugh, and he offered me one last steady, reassuring look before heading toward his car. The engine faded down the long drive, leaving only the rustle of leaves and the distant hum of machinery from the building site.

Under the protected shade of the old oaks, their full-leafed canopy shielding me from the afternoon sun, the adrenaline of our argument ebbed, replaced by a heavy, aching quiet. And there, in that pocket of stillness, everything I'd been holding back finally spilled over.

Dad had listened — really listened — as I purged the mess of our near-disastrous trip away. My fears. My doubts. The truth I'd uncovered and the truth I was terrified to share. He hadn't interrupted. He hadn't judged. He hadn't pushed for decisions I wasn't ready to make.

He simply listened.

Offered support — quiet, steady, unconditional.

For that alone, I was grateful.

When he left for his standing lunch date with Mum, I stayed behind, staring out at the rising skeleton of the house and the life Teddy and I were supposed to be building. Contemplating. Deciding. Another bad habit I'd fallen into lately.

Teddy was one of those decisions — the biggest one — and it was a subject I'd raised during my recent session with Doctor Montgomery.

∞

"Describe the difference between your business and your relationship with Teddy," he'd said.

"How do my business and my relationship correlate? You're not making any sense." I'd baulked. But once he explained the why, the logic clicked.

"Compared to my relationship with Teddy, running a million-dollar business is a piece of cake."

The good doctor had blinked, stunned.

"Go on."

"Each day is predictable. I wake, I work out — not always at the gym either."

He'd blushed; I'd smirked.

"I shower, eat breakfast, then drive along that headache of a freeway to sit behind my desk and bark orders at my minions."

"Minions?" he'd echoed, amused.

"I'll explain later."

He'd nodded, signalling for me to continue.

"Life is routine. Nothing changes. Problems arise, I handle them. Simple. Whereas with Teddy..."

I'd inhaled sharply.

"Our relationship is — and still feels like — an anomaly."

His brow had lifted.

"It's not your typical run-of-the-mill relationship, is it?"

"No. Unfortunately, it isn't."

He'd leaned back, observing me with that unnervingly perceptive gaze.

"And the existing issues — you struggle to handle them because they feel out of your control? Out of your depth?"

"Admittedly, yes. And that's putting it mildly."

I'd stood, pressing my palms to the warm timber windowsill, staring out at the traffic below as I fought the urge to spill every emotion I'd been holding back.

"Solutions come easily to me... usually. But now?"

A heavy sigh.

"I'm struggling. Terribly. Overcoming any issue that arises with her — or for her. We're trying to reach that middle ground we're supposed to find, but every time we do, life throws another curveball. And we're right back to arguing."

∞

Standing beneath the oaks now, Dad's words and Doctor Montgomery's insight collided inside me.

Fear. Control. Love. Uncertainty.

All tangled together.

And somewhere in the middle of it all... Teddy.

Inadvertently, my gaze dropped to the tungsten steel band I anxiously twirled around my finger, and a humourless scoff escaped me. Infinity represented forever, yet unnervingly, forever was beginning to look less certain. Or had I simply adopted one of Teddy's irritatingly bad habits by overthinking myself into a corner? It didn't stop the irrational questions from circling.

Had we jumped too far ahead too soon?

Rule number one of any relationship was to build solid foundations first — and we'd shattered that rule spectacularly. We'd let the rush of finally being together consume us. The intensity. The sex. The fantasy of us. In the process, we'd failed each other. My forgiving her so quickly for her indiscretion was just one example. Her erratic moods were another — and they were beginning to gnaw at me. I intended to get to the bottom of them sooner rather than later.

A relentless buzzing in my pocket cut through my spiralling thoughts. I tugged out my phone, checking the caller ID before answering.

"Teddy, I'm coming now—"

Her hysterical screams tore through the speaker, making it nearly impossible to understand her.

"Teddy, slow down! What's wrong?"

Fear surged, cold and immediate.

I hung up and bolted for my BMW, the engine roaring as I sped off. I didn't care how many laws I broke — only that I reached her. My tyres screeched as I slammed to a halt at the kerb.

My stomach dropped.

There was a trail along the footpath — not something I could ignore — leading straight to her front door, which hung wide open. My pulse thundered as I sprinted inside.

"Teddy!"

Nothing.

I ran toward the kitchen.

"Teddy!"

"Ari!"

Hope flared as her voice echoed down the stairs, followed by frantic footsteps. A shuddering breath escaped me as she collided with my chest, shaking violently. I wrapped my arms around her, holding her as tightly as I dared, the distant wail of approaching sirens growing louder.

Her hands clutched at me, trembling.

"Teddy, why are you—" I caught her wrists, pulling back enough to look at her properly. Her shirt was stained, her face pale, her eyes wild. "Teddy, please. Tell me. Whose blood is it?"

Her red-rimmed eyes widened, her lips trembling as she tried to speak.

"S... Sc—"

Before I could piece it together, heavy footsteps thundered through the front door. Paramedics rushed past us, followed by police, their voices sharp and urgent as they called instructions to one another.

A towering paramedic halted in front of us.

“Ma’am, where do we need to go?”

“Upstairs — the... first bedroom... on the left! Please hurry!” Teddy sobbed, pointing upward.

I reached out instinctively, catching her arm as she moved to follow.

“We need to stay out of the way so they can help whoever’s up there.”

My earlier question still hung between us, unanswered and suffocating.

“Teddy... what happened?”

Her face crumpled, tears streaming as her voice broke apart.

“Sc... Scar... Scarlett. Em... Emmett killed Scarlett!”

Her anguished scream pierced the air just as I hauled her back into my arms, holding her as tightly as I could while the world tilted beneath us.

A deep, shuddering sob tore from my chest.

No.

No, no, no.

32

Poor Scarlett. Wrong place. Wrong time. A case of mistaken identity — that was the police's initial assumption until I corrected them, making them aware of Emmett's previous threats. Threats we should've taken more seriously, considering the carnage he'd left behind. The irrational prick had clearly felt cornered and acted out of desperation — a conclusion I'd drawn after speaking with Logan.

We found Logan upstairs in the bathroom, severely injured from a gunshot wound to the shoulder. Even through the haze of painkillers, he managed to recount what happened. His bloodied hand reached out, grasping my arm as the paramedics prepared to move him.

"Ari..." he spluttered, "...Emmett was here."

Every muscle in my body tensed at the confirmation.

"I managed to shoot the bastard... twice."

He let out a mirthless laugh before wincing and passing out. My faint smile faded instantly. The reality of losing Scarlett wouldn't hit him until the drugs wore off — and when it did, it would destroy him.

"Sir, we need to rush Mr Ayres to the hospital immediately."

The barrel-chested paramedic's grey eyes regarded me impatiently.

I frowned. "Which hospital?"

"The Austin."

I nodded curtly, making a mental note to call Logan's family later — once I'd taken care of everyone else first.

Minutes passed in a despairing blur as a deathly silence settled over the house. Close friends, family, and the authorities whispered amongst themselves while my least favourite cretins camped outside, clogging the road and verge, shoving cameras and microphones into everyone's faces. Thankfully, they were ordered to leave — along with us — once the police declared Teddy's house a crime scene. Not that it stopped them. They followed us all the way to my parents' house in Toorak, each reporter desperate for an exclusive. They weren't getting one. Not if I had anything to say about it.

The police questioned everyone before leaving, including me. My patience thinned rapidly as they badgered a catatonic Teddy until I snapped and told them to back off. Evan, on the other hand, became fearless and unrestrained, lashing out at anyone who tried to calm him. His attempt to run upstairs to Scarlett's bedroom — where his daughter lay — ended with him being physically restrained. He punched a young constable in the face in the process. The sympathetic officer refused to press charges, thankfully, chalking it up to grief.

Now, surveying the sombre living room, I watched my mother remain quietly stoic, making pot after pot of tea, shuttling between the kitchen and the lounge, delivering cups to Scarlett's heartbroken grandparents. Frances, my parents' long-time chef, assisted her, ensuring everyone had something to eat. My father and Uncle Garrett had sequestered themselves in Dad's study with the lead detectives, discussing legalities. Judging by the bellowing, the conversation wasn't going well.

The only person not present was Therese.

I frowned at the oddity. But then again, why would she be here? Everyone knew she held nothing but contempt for her daughters. Abel, at least, had the decency to show up. It didn't mean I'd forgiven him for his treatment of his sisters — or his father — but he was here, holding a softly whimpering Teddy in his arms, gently stroking her hair.

I crouched beside the sofa and whispered,

"Abel, has anyone contacted your mother?"

His hazel eyes — so much like Teddy's — lifted to mine, etched with anxiety.

"I tried. Several times on the way over. She didn't answer the house phone or her mobile."

As much as I despised Therese, a knot of worry tightened in my gut — something Abel noticed immediately.

"You don't think something's happened to her... do you?"

Uncommitted, I shrugged.

"Let's get the police to check..."

I held up a hand as Abel's chest began to rise and fall too quickly.

"...Just in case."

His misting eyes pleaded with me.

"Please, Ari. I know Mother hasn't been the easiest person to get along with, but she's—"

"Your mother. I get it."

I rested a hand on his shoulder, softening my tone.

"Let's not mention our suspicions to your grandparents just yet. They're distraught enough as it is."

"Understood."

Pushing to my feet, I made my way to the study.

Father stood as I entered, politely addressing the two detectives with him. One — tall, dirty-blonde, disarming blue eyes, scars on both cheeks — regarded me with thinly veiled suspicion. His colleague, a tall Indigenous man, watched me with a gentler curiosity as Dad introduced us.

"Detective Burns, Detective Tait, this is my son, Ari Jaeger."

I shook their hands firmly, meeting their gazes without flinching.

"Gentlemen. Before you start questioning me, I have a request."

Brows lifted around the room, but Detective Burns was the first to speak.

"What is it?"

I perched on the edge of my father's desk, arms crossed.

"Abel's been trying to reach his mother, Therese, without success. House phone, mobile — nothing. Given the current situation, I'd appreciate it if someone could check on her."

Garrett and Dad exchanged an odd look. I shrugged.

"It's the right thing to do. After the tragic events at his sister's home, Abel's naturally concerned about his mother and her safety."

Detective Tait offered his notepad. “Write the address down. We’ll send a couple of uniformed officers to Mrs McGovern’s immediately.”

“Much obliged.”

I scribbled the address and handed the notepad back. As I rose to leave, Detective Burns cut in sharply.

“I take it you aren’t a fan of your fiancée’s mother?”

The accusatory tone snapped my patience. I scowled. “What exactly are you implying, Detective?”

“Don’t deflect, Mr Jaeger. Just answer the question. Do you not like Mrs McGovern?”

Before I could respond, my father interjected.

“Don’t answer that, Ari. When you gentlemen have factual information, you may return. Until then, we’re done.”

Detective Burns’ face hardened.

“Fine. Since you and your brother are lawyers, you understand how this works: don’t leave the city, and don’t enter Ms McGovern’s premises until forensics have swept the entire place.”

“Understood. Now, leave,” my father said curtly — polite only in tone.

A smirk tugged at my lips. “Don’t let the door hit you on the way out.”

“Ari, enough!” Garrett snapped. “Smart-arse remarks won’t help.”

“I don’t trust that smarmy-looking Detective Burns.”

“Regardless,” Garrett warned, “we need to keep our emotions in check and not aggravate an already volatile situation.”

"Fine. I need to attend to my distressed fiancée anyway. Let me know if — and when — you have any news regarding Therese's whereabouts."

Wordlessly, Garrett nodded and returned to the notes in his hand. The police had shared what little they knew about Emmett's possible location. Since committing his heinous crime, he'd vanished without a trace.

Hopefully, he was dying in a ditch somewhere, suffering a long and painful death.

One might hope so anyway.

A few hours later, the detectives once again graced us with their presence — only to deliver more bad news.

"Unfortunately, we found Mrs McGovern badly beaten and close to death on her bedroom floor," Detective Burns informed us, his tone dispassionate. "I can't disclose any details at this time as to the weapon used — if there was one."

I surmised Emmett had gotten to her too.

"Sounds just like my uncle's MO. Getting violent with women isn't beneath him; trust me, I know firsthand."

Detective Burns glowered.

"Can you be certain it was your uncle, Mr Jaeger? What about you? Where were you this morning between the hours of nine and twelve?"

My father intervened before I could respond — or embarrass him, though I suspected the latter.

"My son was with me, looking over the progress of his and Ms McGovern's build in Mountainview Lane, Mickleham."

Burns spun on the heel of his polished chocolate-brown lace-ups and attempted to stare my father down. He severely underestimated Dad's ability to remain impassive.

"Can anyone verify your presence — besides you two, Mr Jaeger junior?"

"My foreman was there if you're seeking clarification," I replied brusquely, noting the flicker of disappointment across Burns' face.

Detective Tait stepped in, far more sensible.

"Does this builder have a name?"

"Wes Beaumont. I'll even give you his number. Then you can check for yourself whether my father and I are both liars. Which, of course, we aren't."

Tait gave me a curious glance — thoughtful, not accusatory — before scribbling the number into his notebook.

"Very well, then."

Grief settled over the McGovern and Burgoyne families like a suffocating fog. One member gone without warning, another fighting for her life. The crushing strain finally took hold of Vivienne, and we could only watch in horror as her grief-stricken frame sagged in her frantic husband's arms.

"Vivi! No, I can't lose you too!"

Benjamin lowered her to the floor, attempting CPR, but he was far too distraught to manage the lifesaving rhythm. His fingers tangled in his hair as he cried out, "Someone, help me, please!"

I immediately called triple zero, pleading with them to hurry, while my mother took over, applying compressions with steady, practiced hands. We tag-teamed until the paramedics arrived and took over with their well-trained efficiency. They praised our efforts for keeping her alive before swiftly transporting her to the hospital, Benjamin pale and trembling at her side, praying he wasn't about to lose his beloved wife as well.

He wasn't the only one.

Having already suffered the brutal loss of her sister, the commotion triggered a fresh wave of anguish in Teddy. The prospect of losing her grandmother tipped her over the precipice, and she unravelled completely. No amount of comfort helped. Every attempt was met with a raw, anguished command to leave her alone.

Out of ideas and drowning in despair, I called Doctor Montgomery — a decision I made without shame. He rushed over immediately and, through sheer persistence and calm authority, managed to settle her, eventually sedating her.

Now she slept peacefully upstairs in my old bedroom, a nurse stationed beside her as a precaution — one I fully supported, given her fragile state.

Amidst the lamentation, I found a rare moment of quiet and took the opportunity to pour myself a tumbler of bourbon. Nursing the glass, I sat in the corner of the living room, surveying those who remained. Death had a peculiar way of bringing people together. Evan and Abel were proof of that. The warring pair had finally set aside their differences, grief outweighing old resentments. Watching Abel gently care for his devastated father and help him into the car before the ambulance left was unexpectedly heart-warming. Seeing them united gave me a sliver of hope that old wounds could be healed, especially in times like these.

Still, there was nothing more anyone could do tonight. Not until Emmett was caught and thrown in jail. What a waste of taxpayers' money. And why had the death penalty ever been abolished?

"Ari... perhaps you and Teddy should stay at your house for now?"

Dom's unusually quiet voice pulled me from my thoughts.

"Or you could stay here. Mum won't mind."

Lifting my head felt like lifting a boulder. I'd been running on fumes all day, and now even that thin thread was fraying.

"Not a bad idea — either of them. But the place for us is my house," I agreed wearily. "We aren't authorised to return to Teddy's anyway. And even if we were... who in their right mind would want to?"

"Yeah... I agree. I don't think I'll ever go back..."

Her voice broke, and she dissolved into heart-wrenching sobs for her lost friend.

"Completely understandable, sis," I murmured, pulling her into a warm embrace. "In time, this nightmare will be over."

"Why... why did Emmett have to murder my best friend, Ari? Why did he feel the need to?"

I fought my tears and lost, resting my cheek against the mop of raven hair covering her head.

"Revenge, mostly... for Teddy and me being together."

A shuddering sob escaped me.

"I have a feeling I set the entire wheel of disaster in motion at Mum and Dad's Christmas party by lashing out at Emmett — even after promising them I wouldn't. So if it's anyone's fault Scarlett's lying on a slab in the morgue... it's mine."

Dominique jerked back, shaking her head vehemently, anger flaring through her grief.

"Ari, no! It's not your fault Scarlett's dead!"

Her head snapped up, blazing blue eyes locking onto my sorrowful expression.

"It's nobody's fault but fucking Emmett's! He chose this path — this obsession with Teddy — and he's nothing more than a wicked man who gets off on playing wicked games with people's lives. So don't you ever blame yourself, please? You're nothing like our uncle; you're honourable, at least."

Dom cupped my cheek with a tenderness that nearly undid me.

I laid my hand over hers, offering the faintest smile.

"Thank you for that intransigent opinion, Dom. You're the best sister a brother could ask for."

Her face brightened, giving me a glimpse of the old Dom — the one untouched by today's horrors.

"And don't you forget it."

I snorted.

"You leave me little choice. Ever thought about changing careers and becoming a lawyer?"

Dominique scrunched her nose.

"No way! I love my job as a hairdresser — it's less stressful and far more satisfying."

Her eyes narrowed.

"Why do you ask?"

"Because you sound just like our mother when you argue," I teased, earning a punch to the upper bicep.

"Ow."

A brief, fragile peace settled between us, a quiet reprieve from the day's brutality.

Then, softly, she said,

"After this is all over, I'll be doubling my efforts to ensure you never forget me."

She tugged my arm across her shoulders and nestled into my side.

"After this is all over, Dom, I'll be doubling my efforts where the family's concerned in general. If this tragedy has taught me anything, it's never to take your loved ones for granted."

Dominique sighed, wiping her face and nose in a decidedly unladylike manner, making me chuckle.

I held out my handkerchief by the tips of my fingers.

"Here. Use this before Mother catches you and scolds you for your disgraceful behaviour."

She giggled and made full use of it.

"I don't think Mother will care about my manners today. She's just as consumed by everything as we are."

She wasn't wrong.

Across the room, my usually boisterous mother sat beside her distraught parents, tending to them with quiet devotion. Colton and Amelia, despite their grief, still managed to object to her fussing.

"Quit your fussing over us," Grandpa had protested sternly.

"You've lost today too, not just us. Look after yourself. We're fine."

In typical fashion, Mum argued the point until Dad stepped in and gently asked her to heed their advice. I chuckled, remembering his old claim that he was the only one who could placate her — and today, he proved it.

Turning back to Dom, I stroked her upper arm.

"On a side note, you and Teddy are about the same size, aren't you?"

"Pretty much. I'm shorter, so pants might be a tad small on her. Why?"

"Teddy wasn't allowed to grab any clothes. She'll need a couple of outfits to get her through until we can safely go shopping."

"Sure. I might even have a black dress she can borrow."

I nodded stiffly as tears welled.

"For Scarlett's funeral, of course."

I pressed a kiss to her forehead, silently thanking her, and we both headed upstairs to her bedroom.

One look at the black dress Dominique handed me made the enormity of Scarlett's death horridly real. The thread I'd been clinging to finally snapped. My composure crumbled, and anguished sobs tore free as my mother gathered me into her arms on the floor of Dom's walk-in wardrobe.

She held me long after the sobs subsided, her fingers combing gently through my hair as my head rested in her lap — quietly ensuring I was steady before allowing me to leave my sister's room.

Without the constant flow of undying love and devotion from my parents, I'd be lost — left sitting in the dark, wondering how I was meant to deal with the overwhelming angst and hurt life had unexpectedly laid at our feet. Their compassion knew no bounds. They took the initiative to contact Poppy themselves. Informing her over the phone wasn't ideal, but there was no other way unless I flew to England — which, under the circumstances, was impossible. Talk about a rock and a hard place.

Naturally, I made my illogical objections known as I argued with them in the privacy of Dad's study.

"Isn't informing someone of another's death over the phone a tad distasteful? Not to mention disrespectful to our dearly departed Scarlett?"

Mother, sensibly, countered with a point I couldn't refute.

"It's the only way, son. Or would you rather Poppy hear about it on some ghastly news report?"

Naturally, I was wrong, and my mother was right.

Poppy's immense gratitude — that we'd taken the time to consider her feelings despite the chaos — proved that beyond a shadow of a doubt. Her first thought, of course, was Teddy.

"I'm coming home. Teddy will need me," she breathed through her tears.

Her instinct to put others first, even in crisis, never ceased to amaze me. Despite Mum's objections, I immediately jumped online and booked her a first-class ticket on the earliest flight from Cambridge back to Australia.

"I'll pay you back every penny, Ari. Thank you."

"Don't be ridiculous. Besides me, you're Teddy's closest confidante. Buying a ticket was the least I could do if it means having you home sooner rather than later. I'll send someone to pick you up from the airport as well," I insisted, leaving no room for debate.

"No arguments."

And for once, she offered none.

The house had finally fallen into a fragile hush — the kind that follows catastrophe, where every breath feels borrowed and every footstep sounds too loud. With Poppy's flight booked and my mother's arms still lingering like a phantom around my shoulders, I made my way upstairs, each step heavier than the last.

My old bedroom door stood slightly ajar, a sliver of warm lamplight spilling into the hallway. I pushed it open quietly.

Teddy lay curled beneath the soft throw my mother had draped over her, her breathing slow and even, her lashes resting like faint shadows against her cheeks. Sedation had smoothed the anguish from her features, but it hadn't erased the pallor or the faint tremor in her fingers. Even unconscious, she looked heartbreakingly fragile.

The nurse — a calm, middle-aged woman with kind eyes — rose from the chair beside the bed as I entered.

"A good sign," she murmured softly, nodding toward Teddy's steady breathing. "She's resting deeply. The sedative will hold for a few more hours."

I nodded, my voice caught somewhere between exhaustion and gratitude.

"Thank you... for staying with her."

"It's no trouble. Doctor Montgomery thought it best she not be left alone for now."

Her tone was gentle, but firm — the voice of someone who had seen too many nights like this.

I stepped closer to the bed, brushing a stray curl from Teddy's forehead. The simple act nearly undid me.

"She's been through hell today," I whispered, more to myself than to the nurse.

"She has," the nurse agreed quietly. "But she's safe here. And she's not alone."

I swallowed hard, the truth of that hitting deeper than I expected.

The nurse gathered her things with quiet efficiency.

"I'll be downstairs if you need me. But she's stable. You can sit with her as long as you like."

“Thank you,” I murmured again, though the words felt too small.

When the door clicked softly shut behind her, the room settled into a stillness that felt almost sacred. I lowered myself into the chair beside the bed, elbows on my knees, hands clasped loosely as I watched Teddy sleep.

The rise and fall of her chest.

The faint crease between her brows.

The way her fingers twitched, as though reaching for something she couldn’t quite grasp.

My heart clenched.

“I’m here, sweetheart,” I whispered, leaning forward, letting my forehead rest against the back of her hand. “I’m right here.”

The day’s horrors pressed in — Scarlett, Vivienne, Therese, Logan, Emmett’s shadow stretching over all of us — but here, in this quiet room, everything narrowed to one truth:

Teddy was alive. And I wasn’t leaving her side. Not tonight. Not ever.

A soft knock sounded behind me, and I lifted my head from Teddy’s hand as the nurse re-entered the room. Her expression was gentle but purposeful — the look of someone who knew the night was far from over.

“I’ve spoken with Doctor Montgomery,” she murmured, keeping her voice low. “He’s comfortable with her being moved, provided she remains supported and warm. If she stirs, speak calmly and don’t let her sit up too quickly. Her blood pressure may dip.”

I rose slowly, careful not to jostle Teddy. “Anything else we need to watch for?”

"Only if she becomes distressed or disoriented. If that happens, call Doctor Montgomery immediately. He'll be on standby for the next few hours."

She placed a small card on the bedside table. "My number as well, in case you need guidance on the way."

Her professionalism was unobtrusive, almost tender.

"Thank you," I murmured, and for once the words didn't feel inadequate. "For everything."

She offered a soft smile. "She's lucky to have you. And she'll be safer away from here tonight."

With that, she gathered her bag and slipped quietly from the room, her footsteps fading down the hallway until the house swallowed the sound entirely.

I turned back to Teddy, brushing my thumb along her cheek.

"We're going home, sweetheart," I whispered. "Somewhere safe."

I pressed a final kiss to her temple before lifting her carefully into my arms. She didn't stir — only breathed, slow and steady, her head resting against my shoulder as though she'd been waiting for me to carry her.

It was late as we eventually threw the packed bags between two vehicles and carried an oblivious Teddy to the car, laying her across the back seat and stretching the seatbelt over her limp body.

Quietly closing the door, I leisurely spun around and questioned my sister, "Are you able to drive your car from here, Dom? If not, you're more than welcome to travel with me."

"No, I'll drive myself over as I'll need my car to get around."

I gazed intently. "Emmett's still out there..."

She threw her arms around my shoulders, hugging me affectionately. “Thanks for caring, Ari, but I’ll be fine, I promise.”

My hand rubbed over her back. “As long as you’re sure?”

“Yeah, positive,” she assured, giving one last smile before sidestepping towards her zippy little Volkswagen Golf.

“We’ll follow you both, okay, Ari, Dom?” Mother added, worry etched in her voice. “Jaxson, is the house secure?”

“As secure as it can be.”

“Let’s get on the road then.”

As each car pulled away from the kerb, my gaze flicked instinctively to the rear-view mirror. Another vehicle had slipped into formation behind us — too close, too deliberate. A cold prickle crawled up my spine.

I tapped the hands-free.

“I believe a black Mercedes has joined our convoy, and they’re sitting awfully close to your bumper, Dad.”

Dad’s voice crackled through the speakers.

“Are you sure it’s not the media, Ari?”

A humourless snort escaped me.

“The car and its lone occupant were camped across the road the entire evening. The moment we drove away, it did a massive U-turn and has been glued to us ever since. Check the number plate — you’ll see I’m right.”

Shuffling. Silence. Then my mother’s shaky voice.

“You were right… it is Emmett’s car.”

A growl rumbled low in my chest.

“Logan obviously didn’t aim high enough. How in the hell is he driving if he’s wounded?”

Dad exhaled sharply.

"My brother's resourceful, son. Just keep driving as if he's not there. I'll call the lead detective — he should advise us on decisive action."

"I'll stay on the line," I murmured, gripping the wheel so tightly my knuckles blanched. Through the speakers, I could hear my mother arguing with Detective Burns — her voice taut, controlled, but fraying at the edges.

A heavy sigh followed.

"Detective Burns advised we remain calm and continue acting as though we haven't seen him."

I let out a low, incredulous growl.

"That's bloody helpful, isn't it? Please don't alert Dom — she'll panic. The last thing we need is her having an accident."

"Agreed," my father replied. "Although... let's turn at the next set of lights to see if he follows. I want to be sure."

"All right," I conceded reluctantly. "I hope you know what you're doing, Dad."

As predicted, Emmett followed — never missing a beat, shadowing every turn, every light, every lane change with unnerving precision.

By the time I hit the button on my dash for the garage door, my pulse was a steady roar in my ears. I drove straight in, Dom pulling up beside me, blissfully unaware of the extra weight we'd carried home. Dad flew in behind us. For the first time, I closed the electric gate, locking Emmett out.

Mother climbed from the SUV, frowning as she fished her buzzing phone from her jacket pocket.

"Audrina Jaeger speaking," she answered professionally — but the sudden paling of her skin and the terror in her eyes told me it was neither the police nor a client.

Her throat bobbed.

"Emmett," she enunciated cautiously. "What can I do for you?"

She immediately put the phone on loudspeaker.

"Hello, my dear sister. Nice night for a drive, isn't it? Where's that scrumptious Teddy? You can't hide her away from me forever!" he spat, venom dripping from every syllable.

Mother's voice remained steady, but I could hear the tremor beneath it.

"I haven't the slightest clue what you're talking about, brother."

"Don't lie to me!" Emmett snarled. "Ari has never locked the gate. Believe me when I say eight-foot metal won't keep me out!"

A cold shiver stilled my spine.

"How do you know I never shut the gate, Emmett?"

His laugh was a low, vile rasp.

"Nephew, I'd say what a pleasure, but I'd be lying. You're my nephew — how wouldn't I know?"

And there it was — the confirmation of what I'd long suspected since Mother's annual Christmas party.

He'd been watching us.

33

"Good luck climbing over the spikes," I haughtily challenged. "Perhaps the Gods will do us all a favour and impale you."

Emmett elicited a disapproving tut.

"Now come on, nephew, there's no need to be spiteful. Besides, I haven't the slightest clue what you're talking about."

Smug bastard — turning Mother's words back on us.

"Teddy wanted me, not the other way around. She wants what you can't give her..."

A faint, involuntary wince crackled through the line — pain he couldn't quite mask.

Good.

Let him suffer.

"I'm presuming you aren't aware of Teddy's little secret and the double life she leads?"

I refused to play into his sick fantasies. Silence was my only defence.

"Our stunning beauty is into something more alternative... more erotic..."

He enunciated each word slowly, deliberately, twisting the knife.

"Shut up. Shut the fuck up before I come out there and sort you out."

"The truth hurts, eh? Your precious Teddy isn't so perfect after all, is she?"

A distraught Dominique dug her fingernails into my forearm, sharp enough to make me wince.

"Ari, ignore him," she implored, her voice cracking. "He's playing with your emotions — getting into your head and planting seeds of doubt. He wants you and Teddy to break up. Can't you see that?"

"Dom's right, son," my father added, steady but strained.

Both my mother and sister couldn't be wrong... surely?

Confusion snapped my brows together.

Did he follow us to Sydney?

Or was he privy to something I wasn't?

Highly likely — the bastard always slithered into places he didn't belong.

I retaliated the only way I knew how.

"Fuck off home to your wife and leave us alone!"

Before he had the chance to react, I snatched the phone from my mother's hand and ended the call, shutting the device off entirely.

"There. He can't call anymore."

"That won't stop him," Dom retorted bluntly. "Emmett can still leave messages."

I growled.

"Good. Let the loser leave his bloody messages — hopefully the idiot incriminates himself."

Anxiety bloomed, thick and suffocating. What increased my angst tenfold was the knowledge that Emmett remained outside my house — dictating every move within these walls from the other side of my fence.

Firstly, my parents. They refused to leave, driven by concern not only for my wellbeing but for their own. Considering the atrocities Emmett had committed in a single day — possibly two — who knew what he was capable of?

Secondly, Teddy. Keeping a vigilant eye on her became an undertaking my mother took to heart. She informed us, quite firmly, that checking on Teddy was her burden to bear and hers alone.

I questioned her gently.

"Why is it wholly and solely your responsibility, Mother? Especially when we're here to help?"

I swept my hand around the dining table, motioning to Dad and Dominique.

"I have an obligation to Teddy..." she stressed, her forlorn gaze flitting between us.

"We wouldn't be in this position if it weren't for my brother's psychopathic tendencies."

The guilt that had been gnawing at her finally surfaced.

"...So as his sister, I feel it's my duty to keep her safe from any further harm."

But as the hours passed, her suffering began to show.

The brisk trips up the stairs slowed to a tortoise-like crawl.

Her regal posture slumped as she flopped into a chair or onto the sofa.

Her bright, twinkling eyes dulled, heavy lids drooping only to snap open again as she fought the exhaustion clawing at her.

We echoed our concerns, but Mother stubbornly resisted our support.

"It's imperative I remain busy," she contended, attempting to tie her voluminous hair back. She gave up halfway, letting her raven locks tumble messily around her shoulders.

"Or I'll crack otherwise."

By ignoring her grief, she ignored the inevitable — something we all saw coming even if she didn't. The pressure she placed on herself was nothing more than a ruse, masking a torment eating away at her. Dealing with her brother's crimes inwardly took its toll, and eventually she gave in to her emotions, collapsing at the bottom of the stairs, crying inconsolably.

Never in my life had I witnessed my mother so broken.

Her distress was so severe that my father tenderly carried her up the stairs, quietly reassuring her that the dark clouds would eventually lift, allowing the sun to shine again over our lives.

I took it upon myself to usher Dominique upstairs not far behind them, her fatigue mirroring our mother's. She protested at first, but once I tucked her into bed and her head hit the pillow, she was out cold. I closed her door softly and wandered to my own bedroom to check on Teddy. Thanks to the sedation Doctor Montgomery had administered earlier, she remained deeply asleep.

Heading back downstairs, Dad joined me. Too wired for sleep, we retreated to the study, each grabbing a bourbon and a cigar, lighting them just outside the open French doors. I considered downing my drink and pouring another, but complacency never crossed my mind. I couldn't afford to be — not with that maniac parked outside on the opposite side of my fence.

I wandered back inside to check the live feed on my computer from the security cameras I'd installed the moment I discovered my uncle was Teddy's rapist. And as sure as day was light and night was dark, the leech hadn't moved.

Eventually, having had enough of his lingering presence, I vented my frustrations.

"Dad, it's time to call in a favour and use one of your connections to have that prick outside removed. The conspicuous bastard has kept us prisoner for hours — watching, waiting. He's obviously biding his time!"

I gestured furiously toward the road, pacing across the engineered timber boards. In what was ordinarily a light, spacious room, I felt caged in and claustrophobic.

"Why aren't the police doing anything? I don't understand!"

Dad remained maddeningly calm.

"The police are doing something, son. They're stationed up the street — both ends — in unmarked cars, biding their time as well. We simply need to be patient, a serious flaw you need to learn to exercise."

I scoffed at the pointed remark.

"Besides," he continued, "if he's wounded, how in the devil can he scale a blasted fence? Emmett's bluffing — trying to put the wind up us, that's all."

My jaw dropped.

"I can't believe what I'm hearing. Unbelievable."

Dad's bloodshot gaze peered over the top of his nose, disapproving but steady.

"The cars out there are one of the many favours I took the liberty of organising the minute that deranged prick made us aware of his presence," he stated matter-of-factly.

"The alarm's set, isn't it?"

Thrusting a hand through my unruly hair, I nodded tautly.

"It is. I set it as soon as we closed the door."

Groaning, Dad pushed to his feet.

"Go to bed, son. Everyone else has, and I've decided I'm following suit."

His hand squeezed my tense shoulder, warm and sympathetic.

"Go to bed. You need your rest. Sitting here waiting for that slimeball — who's clearly biding his time — isn't healthy for either of us."

He was right. We were powerless to do a damned thing.

"All right. I'll finish locking up and checking the house, then I'll go to bed."

He patted my cheek affectionately before pulling me into a tight hug.

"Goodnight, Ari."

"Yeah... night."

Emotion swelled as I watched his fatigued figure head upstairs. I scrubbed at my eyes, fighting the inescapable lethargy myself. I was terrified that the moment we let our guard down, Emmett would try something.

Maybe that was the key to getting him locked up after all.

One last check of the security cameras revealed he was still parked outside, his sinister face staring directly into the lens. I glanced toward the stairs, breath trembling with relief that Teddy hadn't stirred once. Given the day's horrific events and the emotional upheaval, I'd expected nightmares or restlessness —

but if the next few days were anything like what we'd just endured, getting a decent night's sleep would be the least of our problems.

34

True to my word, the next day had worsened.

The day began unceremoniously well before sunrise, the shrilling alarm jolting the entire household awake. I flew out of bed and tore down the stairs, only to discover my worst nightmare in the family room — or so I thought.

Not far behind me, my father's fast-paced footsteps skidded to a halt.

"What in the devil happened here?"

"I have a sneaking suspicion..." My thoughts lagged as my furrowed gaze swept the room, seething at the deadly constellation of glass shards scattered across the timber boards.

"Let me call the police and get them here first. You need to go and check on Teddy."

The tone in his voice hit me like a blow. I'd overlooked her presence in our bedroom. Panic surged violently as I sprinted toward the stairs, taking them two at a time. I barged through the open doorway of my room, my frantic gaze scouring the empty bed. I rushed into the ensuite, then the walk-in robe.

Nothing.

My jaw clenched as my fingers gripped my hair.

I yelled out to my parents and Dominique, alerting them to my whereabouts.

"Teddy's missing! We need to search every inch of the house!"

Silently, they nodded and scattered, chanting Teddy's name as they checked every room — upstairs, downstairs, cupboards, corners, anywhere she could have wandered.

Nothing.

Not a sign of her anywhere.

Warm blood suddenly ran cold. The walls shrank around me in a suffocating bubble.

"Where. In. The. Fuck. Is. Teddy?"

Dad's jaw trembled, his voice thick as he spoke cautiously.

"Think about it, son… smashed windows…"

"Em… Em… Emmett took… took her?" I hoarsely whispered, stumbling over the words.

Desolate, my father nodded.

Without hesitation, I bolted out the front door — only to halt in the driveway as my horrified gaze landed on the wide-open gate. A guttural cry tore from my chest, dropping me to the concrete as a deluge of grief engulfed me.

My weeping mother sank beside me, enveloping me in her warm embrace.

"The police are on their way. Hopefully they'll be able to tell us what happened."

My head shook vehemently.

"No, they won't!" I argued, forcing myself to my feet.

"The cameras will tell us more than they can."

I stormed toward the study — then froze mid-stride as a chilling thought sliced through the panic.

Two unmarked police cars.

One at each end of the street.

Stationed there all night.

My breath hitched.

"How... how did they not see him?" I whispered, more to myself than anyone else.

"Dad, those cars were meant to be watching the street. How didn't they notice Emmett getting out of his car? Or walking up to the house? Or carrying Teddy away?"

The question hung in the air like a curse — unanswered, unanswerable — and the silence that followed only deepened the dread.

Dad's face paled, but he said nothing.

Mother's hand flew to her mouth.

Dominique stared at me, wide-eyed, as though the thought had only just occurred to her too.

A sickening weight settled in my gut. Either the officers had been asleep... or distracted... or Emmett had found a way to slip past them entirely.

None of the possibilities made me feel any better.

Resolved, I rushed into the study and slipped into the chair, furiously tapping at the keyboard. Images slowly appeared, paralysing me as I watched Teddy's abduction unfold before my watering eyes.

At some point during the night, a perceptibly disoriented Teddy had woken and wandered downstairs, her footsteps faltering as she attempted to navigate the darkened house. She made her way into the kitchen, retrieved the juice from the fridge, and — in her groggy state — poured most of it over the bench. Barely enough remained for a sip, not that she realised as she lifted the glass to her lips. From there, she drifted into the living room and curled up on one of the large sofas, falling asleep again instantly.

Unbeknownst to her, a noticeably limping Emmett prowled outside under the cover of darkness. He bypassed the electronic gate, gaining unfettered access to my property. Following the path alongside the house, he entered the backyard through the smaller timber gate, collecting rocks from the garden beds along the way. Then, less subtly, he lifted his right arm and smiled up at the camera as he threw the first rock, hitting the double-paned glass with a thud.

Hell-bent on getting in, he persisted, hurling rock after rock until the glass shattered, giving him enough room to enter the house unlawfully — and without triggering the alarm.

How?

My fists clenched under the knowledge he'd been inside my home and gotten away with it.

Purposefully, he wandered through the kitchen and hallways, again smiling triumphantly at the cameras when he found his prize strewn across the sofa. Lifting Teddy and throwing her over his shoulder in a fireman's hold, he walked out the victor, carting my unconscious fiancée off into the night.

The worst part — the part that hollowed me out — was that she never stirred.

My anger swelled as I slumped into the chair behind my desk.

"How in the fuck did Emmett bypass my gate? Or switch off my alarm? Worse still, how in the fuck did I not realise Teddy had left our bed and come downstairs? How..."

I motioned helplessly to the screens.

"How, Mother? How? I failed Teddy! I swore I'd protect her... from... from that animal!"

I huddled against her warm, comforting embrace.

Mother stroked my back, her voice trembling but resolute.

"Emmett's an intelligent man with an IT degree. He's capable of hacking any computer. Without a doubt, that's how he opened the gate."

"If he's so damned smart, why didn't he just hack my computer and shut down the cameras?"

"He wanted you to see... that he'd gotten the better of you. That he'd won."

Her voice wavered, but her resolve held.

"We won't let him. We'll find Teddy and bring her home, okay?"

But as I listened to her words, I felt no reassurance.

Emmett had Teddy — a calculated move guaranteed to leave her more traumatised than she already was. The promising future we'd planned was slipping through our fingers.

Whether or not we'd recover what we once had remained to be seen.

Detective Tait and Detective Burns arrived on my doorstep wearing grim, remorseful expressions — as they damn well should have. I wasn't in the mood for their grovelling. They needed to do their job for a change.

"About bloody time," I growled, reefing the door wide open.

They blanched at the icy wall they'd walked into.

"Mr Jaeger," they chimed in unison as they stepped over the threshold. I slammed the door behind them.

"We sincerely apologise for our lapse in judgement."

"Oh, cry me a fucking river, will you! At this point in time, I don't give two flying fucks about your apologies!" I snapped, glaring at them with every ounce of fury I possessed. "Thanks to your oversight, my fiancée is missing — God knows where! So you two—"

My finger stabbed the air between them. "—had better start praying to whatever God you bloody well pray to and bring Teddy back home to me. Alive."

Throats gulped. Adam's apples bounced.

Detective Tait's whiskey-brown eyes dropped, shame flickering across his features.

"Of course, Mr Jaeger. May we please proceed to your office and check the camera feed for ourselves?"

Detective Burns, naturally, was less intimidated. His steely blue gaze met mine directly. "Lead the way."

"By all means," I gestured sharply. "Follow me."

I left my mother to hover and supervise forensics while my father joined us in the study.

Before I even touched the keyboard, another thought — one that had been gnawing at me since dawn — surged to the surface.

I turned on them, voice low and laced with venomous sarcasm. "Before we look at anything, answer me this — where were the two unmarked cars my father arranged to sit at each end of the street? You know, the ones you lot didn't bother organising yourselves?"

Tait blinked, startled. Burns didn't flinch.

"They were patrolling," Burns replied with a shrug that made my blood boil. "It's possible they were called away briefly. Happens sometimes."

Tait's head snapped toward him, a frown carving deep into his brow.

"Called away? We weren't notified of any redeployment," he murmured, more to himself than to us.

Burns shot him a warning look — subtle, but unmistakable.

I stepped closer, fury simmering. "So let me get this straight. Two cars assigned to watch my street — to watch my house — just conveniently vanished at the exact moment Emmett broke in, abducted Teddy, and walked out with her over his shoulder?"

Burns cleared his throat. "As I said, Mr Jaeger, patrol units get redirected. It's not unusual."

Tait's discomfort deepened. "That's... not standard procedure," he admitted quietly.

A cold, sickening weight settled in my gut. Something was wrong. Very wrong.

But Burns was already gesturing stiffly toward the desk. "Let's review the footage."

I forced myself into the chair, though every instinct screamed that something wasn't adding up.

You'd think watching the video feed for the second time would be easier. Truth be told, it was worse. Much worse. Harder still was reading the ominous note Emmett had kindly left attached to one of the rocks he'd hurled through my window.

Both my hands and my voice shook as I read it aloud: *"I warned Teddy once. I don't ask twice. Don't expect her back. Ever."*

If I'd had my way, I would've torn the succinct message to shreds and burned it to ash in the fireplace. But the police deemed it evidence, so it now sat sealed inside one of their plastic bags, preserving Emmett's fingerprints and preventing me from destroying the vile thing.

Thrusting the poisonous letter into Tait's hand, I roared, "I'm placing the blame for Teddy's disappearance squarely on your shoulders, Detectives! If only you pair had listened to me in the first place — if you'd spent less time playing the blame game over Scarlett's death — then we wouldn't be here! Because at least my psychotic uncle would've been locked up by now!"

"We will do everything we can to return Ms McGovern, Mr Jaeger," Burns uttered, his tone clipped.

I stared at him darkly, my voice dropping to a lethal register. "You had better hope so. Or there'll be hell to pay

∞

Teddy

I stirred as a sheet of tin clattered violently in the howling wind, the sound ricocheting around me like a warning shot. A shiver rippled through my body as a cold draft threaded across my skin, raising goosebumps. For a moment, I couldn't tell if I was dreaming or drifting somewhere between sleep and consciousness — the tranquiliser Doctor Montgomery had given me still clung to my veins, heavy and numbing.

My eyelids felt glued shut. My thoughts lagged behind themselves.

Nothing made sense.

I tried to shift, to roll onto my side, but something tugged sharply at my arms — metal clanking above my head.

A confused frown creased my forehead.

I tried again. The same resistance. The same cold bite of metal. And then the ache hit me.

A deep, throbbing burn radiated from my shoulders down to my elbows, the kind of pain that only came from being held in one position far too long. My hands tingled with pins and needles, the blood flow sluggish and wrong. My muscles trembled under their own weight, exhausted from supporting me while I'd been unconscious.

My breath hitched. Why couldn't I move? Why were my arms suspended? Why was everything... wrong?

I forced my eyes open — or tried to. Darkness pressed against them, thick and impenetrable. A blindfold. Panic fluttered in my chest.

"Hello?" My voice cracked, thin and unsure. "Is... is someone there?"

My ears pricked up as the sound of hard, uneven footfalls scraped across bare concrete — slow, dragging, deliberate. Each step echoed through the cavernous space, bouncing off unseen walls and tightening the knot of dread in my stomach.

"Let me go," I called out, my voice trembling despite my best efforts to steady it. "Please... I want to go home!"

Silence.

A silence so thick it pressed against my skin.

Frustration and fear tangled in my throat. "Answer me, damn you!"

A low chuckle slithered through the darkness. "Now that I've finally spirited you away from Ari and have you all to myself, you won't be going anywhere in a hurry, my darling Teddy."

That voice.

Recognition hit like a blow to the chest.

"Emmett..." I whispered, horror hollowing me out.

He clapped slowly, mockingly, each strike of his palms echoing like a taunt. "Bravo. It's just you, me, and the sea, sweetheart. Oh — and a few seagulls."

Somewhere beyond the walls, waves crashed against something — rocks, timber, metal — I couldn't tell. The wind howled through unseen gaps, rattling loose sheets of tin overhead. The whole place felt unstable, exposed, wrong.

His presence closed in, the reek of stale cigarettes and whiskey hitting me like a wall. My stomach lurched violently. But it wasn't just the smell. It was the sound. A rough shuffle. A dragging scrape.

A rhythm that was wrong — uneven, off-balance.

My breath caught. I knew that gait.

A fractured memory flickered through the fog of sedation: Logan's gun raised, the deafening crack, Emmett collapsing with a howl of pain. The image was hazy, disjointed, but the limp... the limp was unmistakable.

He was injured. He was here. And he'd come for me anyway.

A cold wave of dread washed over me as the footsteps drew closer, each uneven step confirming what my mind desperately wished wasn't true. Even without sight, I could feel him invading my space, hovering over me with a familiarity that made my skin crawl.

I flinched, despair knotting in my stomach as Emmett's hands roamed. A cold rush of horror swept through me as I became acutely aware of how truly exposed I was – he'd stripped me naked. I was completely vulnerable and utterly stripped of control. Horrified, my breath hitched, a strangled sound escaping before I could stop it. Shame burned hot beneath the fear, twisting deep in my chest. Whatever dignity I'd had left felt ripped away, leaving me raw and trembling.

"No good recoiling, you're unable to run away, my love."

"Get the fuck away from me!" I snarled, the words ripping out of me before I could think. I spat in his direction, desperate to put even the smallest barrier between us.

For a heartbeat, there was nothing.

Then a sudden, violent jolt snapped my head to the side — a burst of pain blooming across my cheek, sharp enough to steal my breath. My teeth clamped down hard, the metallic tang of blood rising instantly on my tongue. The shock of his slap — the speed, the force, the humiliation — sent a tremor through my entire body.

"Watch your fucking mouth!" Cold hands roughly cupped both breasts as his fingers painfully tweaked each puckered nipple. A cry tore from my throat, raw and involuntary. "Now, you're going to be a good girl and be subservient. You're going to do everything I tell you to do."

I choked on my anger. “Don’t fucking touch me!” Studded leather connected sharply with the fronts of my thighs. My scream echoed as warmth dripped down both legs.

Emmett’s fingertips clamped around my face, forcing my head still. His grip was cold, possessive, and far too tight, making my skin prickle with dread.

“Every time you disobey me,” he murmured, his voice low and poisonous, “there will be consequences. You’ll address me properly – as your Master. Understand?”

A tremor ran through me — fear, fury, humiliation — but I refused to let him see me break. I gathered what little strength I had left and spat in his direction again, the only act of defiance I could still claim as mine.

He retaliated without hesitation, the movement so fast I barely registered it before my head jolted violently to the side. A fresh sting bloomed across my other cheek, sharp enough to make my eyes water. Heat flared beneath my skin, the burn spreading in a hot, humiliating rush. My pulse hammered in my ears, a frantic, uneven rhythm that made it hard to think, hard to breathe, hard to do anything but tremble. Another crack resounded across the backs of my thighs, then my behind, with each vicious hit making me scream, beg, anything to make him stop. Blood seeped, and unbidden tears relentlessly dripped.

He’d left me with little choice but to comply, cornering me so completely that even breathing felt like a negotiation. My stomach rolled, bile rising as humiliation and terror tangled in my throat. I forced the words out between sobs, each syllable scraping painfully against my pride.

“Yes… Master.”

A pleased hum vibrated from him, low and satisfied.

"Now there's a good girl. Let's get started then, shall we?"

The shift in his tone — that grotesque blend of triumph and anticipation — made my stomach churn violently. A moment later, rough fingers tore the mask from my face, and a harsh flood of light assaulted my eyes.

I blinked rapidly, vision swimming, shapes blurring and reforming until the world finally snapped into focus.

Emmett stood directly in front of me. Naked.

And he was high.

Visibly, unmistakably high.

His pupils were blown wide, dark and glassy, darting over me with a feverish intensity that made my skin crawl. He looked unhinged — wired, jittery, intoxicated by whatever cocktail he'd taken and by the twisted power he believed he held over me. His crazed gaze travelled up and down, taking sickening pleasure in admiring my forced nakedness.

I tore my gaze away from him, desperate to anchor myself to anything else. But the room offered no comfort — only horror.

My eyes widened as I took in the surroundings.

The ropes. The chains. The metal fixtures bolted into concrete. The crude, makeshift structures arranged with disturbing deliberation.

An abandoned warehouse... transformed into something far darker. A perverse imitation of a "BDSM sanctuary," built for one purpose — his purpose.

Dread clawed up my throat. "You've got to be kidding me..." I whispered, the words barely audible.

"Aw, don't sound so disappointed, Teddy. I thought erotic was your flavour?" he murmured, the condescension dripping from every syllable as he unfastened the restraints around my wrists.

The sudden release sent a rush of blood flooding back into my arms, leaving them tingling and weak. Relief flickered — brief, fragile — before dread swallowed it whole.

Because the moment he reached toward me, instinct took over.

I shrank back from his outstretched hand, curling inward, desperate to shield myself. My arms moved on their own, trying to cover what little I could, trying to reclaim even a shred of dignity.

I barely managed to cross my arms over my breasts before he slapped my hands sharply back to my sides. The sting shot up my forearms, making me wince.

"Don't even think about it," he growled, the sound low and possessive. "Keep them there. And don't move."

His gaze dragged over me with a slow, sickening satisfaction, as though he were savouring the moment, savouring my fear.

"I want to finish bathing in this beautifully delicious sight before I have my way with you." His beady eyes fixated, he divested himself of his clothes before grabbing his flaccid penis and stroking until he had an erection.

A violent shudder tore through me at the implication, dread coiling tight in my stomach.

He dragged me across the cold concrete with a sudden, brutal urgency, my feet scrambling uselessly beneath me. Before I could catch my breath, he forced me face down against the solid, unforgiving surface of a whipping bench — the impact knocking the air from my lungs. Metal clamped around my wrists, then my ankles, each lock clicking shut with a finality that made my entire body tremble.

I lay there, pinned and helpless, my pulse thundering in my ears as fear surged through me in a sickening wave. Every instinct screamed at me to fight, to run, to do anything — but the restraints held firm, and my body shook uncontrollably with the terror of what he intended.

I swallowed hard, forcing down the rising panic, the rising nausea, the rising certainty that I was running out of time.

Please, dear God...

Please let Ari find me before it's far too late.

Bonus Section from Clouded Judgement,

Chapter 14

Teddy

To any unsuspecting passer-by, the old nineteen-twenties building — all ageing red brick and narrow-street anonymity — looked no different from the dozens tucked away across Melbourne's back lanes. If only they knew the truth hidden behind the matte onyx metal door facing the road. Beyond it lay an entirely different world, a secret world, one built to indulge the unspoken desires of those who sought a discreet life behind the walls of Club Freedom.

Goosebumps prickled every inch of my skin as I pushed the door and stepped inside the spacious foyer. From the black wallpaper with its swirling velvety texture to the dark-stained timber floors, everything about the interior radiated a dark, seductive energy – likewise, Max, the half-naked security guard stationed beside the frosted glass doors. His dark gaze gleamed, appraising me from head to toe through the narrow slits of his pentagon-shaped Venetian mask as he took my club ID from my outstretched hand.

"Ms M, looking fine as always." A smile tugged at his sculpted lips as I blatantly swept my gaze over his robust frame, unable to ignore the glistening expanse of his chest. Club rules forbade mentioning members' names for privacy reasons, as was the use of contraband. But Max, like me, was a rulebreaker. He swept a forefinger beneath his nostrils, a discreet signal checking whether I needed anything. One of our many secret codes. Safer for both of us that way.

I paused deliberately before offering him a knowing smile. "You really ought to look into taking some antihistamine for that hay fever of yours, Max."

"I'll be sure to take your advice, Ms M." He chuckled, sliding my ID back into my palm – with my little package tucked neatly beneath it.

Eager for my fix, I slipped both into my bejewelled clutch and headed towards the powder room just inside the wide hallway off the foyer. As I rounded the corner, I glanced up the narrow steel staircase leading to private offices on the first level, envy prickling at the thought of the second floor above it. A dedicated level reserved exclusively for the club's most private members – those who required absolute anonymity for their unfettered play. If I played my cards right, I might earn the privilege of using one those rooms with another Dom... someone other than my favourite, Master Noel.

A small smile graced my lips as I pushed open the bathroom door and slipped inside, locking it behind me. I dropped the toilet lid and sat, diving into my clutch for the tiny zip lock bag. Tugging it open, I shook a small dose of its powdery contents along the top edge of my thumb, I snorted. My veins thrummed instantly, anxiety loosening its grip – a result of the days tension.

Max's broad smile greeted me as I strolled from the bathroom. "You have yourself an enjoyable evening, Ms M."

Feeling as though I were walking on air, I sauntered past him, flicking my curls over my right shoulder. "Oh, I plan on it."

The prospect of a Master or a Mistress dominating me had my body buzzing – more so because I was up for anything tonight. I felt needy, restless, and a night of debauchery was exactly the therapy I needed to loosen the tension coiled tight through my limbs.

As I strolled down the dimly lit hallway toward the rear of the building, a thought tugged at me — the possibility of visible welts or marks left behind for Ari to find. Undoubtedly, he would question me about them. But I was perfectly capable of crafting a plausible explanation; I'd had to before, whenever the occasion called for it.

The end of the hallway opened into a vast communal room, each section carved out by clusters of furniture that created pockets of semi-privacy. Couples and groups had already gathered, their movements fluid and unapologetically bold. Their sexual prowess and skill were openly — almost proudly — on display for anyone to witness. If you were lucky, a Master or Mistress might beckon another submissive to join their scene, a rare invitation I'd accepted more than once. Threesomes were fun, admittedly intoxicating in their own way, but tonight needed to be about my needs alone.

At least, that had been the plan.

Because as I drifted toward a leather sofa positioned at the room's centre, my resolve wavered. The scene unfolding before me was impossible to ignore — magnetic, enticing, a slow pull I felt deep in my bones. I could already feel myself slipping into that familiar headspace, the one where being both voyeur and participant felt not only natural but necessary.

If asked, I'd be more than satisfied to join.

I stood riveted, my breath caught somewhere between my ribs and my throat, as the highly experienced Dominant secured his submissive — a willowy brunette — to the Saint Andrew's cross. He worked with practised precision, fastening her wrists and ankles one by one until she was fully splayed, her body held in a perfect, deliberate tension.

Only when he was satisfied with her positioning did he reach for the delicately patterned black lace blindfold draped over his wrist. With a slow, intentional movement, he slid it over her downcast eyes, the gesture both tender and commanding in equal measure.

Ensured it was to his satisfaction, he began skating his splayed fingers over her small, rounded breasts and tweaking a raspberry-coloured nipple. The submissive let out a feverish moan, thanking her Dom for the pleasure. My excitement spiked sharply as the Dominant reached down and selected his chosen implement — a buffalo-hide flogger resting at his feet. He lifted it with a practised ease, letting the leather strands cascade over his hand before sweeping them delicately across her skin.

The way she arched her body into the touch; the way he controlled every inch of the moment, sent a warm rush through me. I couldn't tear my eyes away.

Watching the submissive's head loll and her lean body writhe was a pleasure in itself, a shared current of bliss that seemed to ripple between them. The warmth flooding through her was unmistakable, and it stirred something deep within me, awakening my own simmering desires. They intensified as the Dominant shifted from his warm-up, flicking his wrist with practiced precision as he struck her harder. Everywhere. Her moans grew louder with each impact — across her torso, front and back, her pert behind, her shapely thighs — until her petite body glistened with sweat. She fought desperately to obey his earlier command not to climax, but as I watched her curvaceous back bow and her long, slender legs tense and shake, I knew she'd failed.

As expected, the Dominant's movements halted abruptly. The flogger hit the floor with a resonant thud, echoing through the room. I frowned as he sternly informed his submissive of her forthcoming punishment. Perhaps she was new to the scene — that might explain her inability to hold back.

But the moment he turned his back to select another implement, a small, triumphant grin flickered across her lips.

The cheeky minx. She'd played her Master.

Well, well... that submissive is a girl after my own heart.

My breath hitched as I watched her frisson — that intoxicating blend of fear and anticipation I knew all too well — while the Dominant bent to whisper in her ear, no doubt instructing her to count.

Her voice, a hoarse whisper, trembled with a perfected blend of obedience and excitement. "Yes, sir."

Having straightened his muscular frame to its full height, the Dom circled her with a slow, predatory grace, the silicone hurra cane swinging lightly from his hand. Then, without warning, his arm lifted and came down in a sharp arc, striking the left cheek of her backside and forcing a sharp inhale from her lips.

Her failure to follow his instruction compelled him to raise his voice. "I said, count!"

She responded without delay, her voice clear and loud enough for everyone watching to hear.

"One, sir!"

Unsurprisingly, the harsh punishment sent a bolt of heat through me, my nipples tightening as warmth pooled between my thighs.

"Like what you see, Ms M?"

The voice — one I knew intimately — curled around me, husky and controlled, carrying the same authoritative tone as the Dominant before us.

I dropped my gaze to the floor, remaining silent, earning exactly the reward I sought.

"Good girl. You may answer me."

He brushed my long curls over my right shoulder, his warm, scotch-laced breath ghosting over the side of my bare neck. I quivered at the light touch.

"It's highly stimulating, sir."

I tried to steady my breathing by focusing on the provocative music drifting from the overhead speakers, but it did nothing to calm me. Master Noel could read me far too easily.

He leaned in, inhaling deeply. "I bet if I slipped my hand between your superb legs, you'd be incredibly wet, wouldn't you? Answer me."

"Extremely so, sir."

"May I feel for myself?"

My breaths quickened. "You may, sir."

"Keep watching that spectacular view whilst I check."

"Yes, sir."

A coolness — likely his tumbler of scotch — settled beside the arch of my foot on the floor, followed by a stern warning as he straightened with effortless grace.

“Keep still… or knocking my drink over will most certainly earn you a punishment.”

Clutching the hem of my short dress and rolling it up to my waist, leaving my naked derrière exposed for everyone to view, he hummed appreciatively.

“Good to see you weren’t wearing any underwear: time-wasters as far as I’m concerned.”

Funnily enough, Ari held the same sentiment.

Master’s long finger leisurely slid through the aperture of my behind, pausing to part my cheeks. “I think I may take this tonight….” he clearly asserted, circling my quivering rosebud. “What do you think?”

“Whatever pleases you, Master,” I hastily replied, relaxing against Master Noel’s lean, naked torso as he tugged at my hips. I mewled as he slipped a finger inside me while the other hand glided between my slick folds and palmed my clitoris.

“Don’t come, or you’ll receive the exact punishment like the other sub,” he sternly advised, his chin jerking towards the couple still playing in front of us. I bit down on my bottom lip and moaned. “Well, that’s settled then. Except, not here; I want you all to myself tonight.” Sliding his fingers out of me, he urged me forward. “Our usual room should do nicely. You know where to go. Once in there, strip completely for me; I want the whole show.”

“Yes, sir.”

A hard slap met one of my bare buttocks. “I didn’t tell you to speak, sub. Strip here, now, and be quick about it. Then you’ll receive your punishment in the room. Hop to it. And don’t worry about your dress; someone else can grab that.”

Shit. I quickly removed my dress and tossed it aside.

“Shoes too.”

I removed them in a rush before preceding Master to a small room with a two-way mirror, making our session visible to others without us seeing them. He tapped the floor with the sole of his barefoot. “Kneel here and spread your thighs nice and wide for our guests on the other side of the mirror. Keep your hands on your knees, too....”

I descended into the requested position with obedient elegance.

“Wider.” Bloody hell. Rather than complain, I shuffled my legs across, spreading them until I was well and truly exposed. “Wait here; I’ll return in a minute.” He slid out of the room, leaving me alone with the realisation that the night ahead was going to be an awfully long one.

AUTHOR NOTE

Teddy and Ari will be back in the final installment of The Masquerade Trilogy, Unmasked...

The fallout continues until the very last breath.....

www.ingramcontent.com/pod-product-compliance
Lightning Source LLC
LaVergne TN
LVHW020518100826
845148LV00010B/1271

* 9 7 8 1 7 6 3 8 3 2 8 1 7 *